Love Comes in Many Colors

By

Virginia Merritt Pesnicak

Copyright © 2009 by Virginia Merritt Pesnicak

Love Comes in Many Colors
by Virginia Merritt Pesnicak

Printed in the United States of America

ISBN 978-1-60791-671-0

All rights reserved solely by the author. The author guarantees all contents are original and do not infringe upon the legal rights of any other person or work. No part of this book may be reproduced in any form without the permission of the author. The views expressed in this book are not necessarily those of the publisher.

All scripture verses are taken from The King James Bible.

Notice – "Love Comes in Many Colors"

Virginia Merritt Pesnicak is not my legal name.
All business between us must be addressed to
Virginia E. Pesnicak
Same address.

www.xulonpress.com

ACKNOWLEDGEMENTS

First I would give thanks to the Lord
who gave me the idea to write this book,
plus the ability and strength to complete it.
To Him goes all the honor and glory.
I also wish to thank all those who helped or
encouraged me while writing this book, especially
my daughter Laurie, my friends
Nadine, Sandra, and Leslie, and all my family.
Special appreciation to Darla,
and in memory of Eve.

BOOKLETS

The Silver City Book. Vol. 1 "Wild and Woolly Days" Published by Silver Star publications, 1978

"Echoes of the Bugle" by Professor Dale F. Giese, Department of History. Western New Mexico University, Silver City, New Mexico.

Information used from these booklets
was moved about in time to enhance this story.
All names used are fictional.

IRISH BLESSING

May the road rise to meet you,
May the wind be always at your back,
May the sunshine warm upon your face,
And the rain fall soft upon your fields,
And until we meet again,
May God hold you in the hollow of his hand.

LOVE COMES IN
MANY COLORS

The wagon train circled quickly after their scout, Link Morgan, returned; warning the travelers of the danger of Indians. He pulled up beside Sam Johnson, the wagon master, his horse hot and sweaty.

"Sam, there are fresh signs that a large party of Indians, probably young braves, have just passed west of the hills ahead; we'd best take time to protect ourselves. They are headed north, but you never know whether they had a look-out who might have spotted us."

Under Sam Johnson's direction, everyone moved swiftly pulling the wagons into a circle. The area inside the wagons fortunately was full of bushes, rocks, and tall grasses, giving cover for the woman and children.

Sam warned the women, "There might be snakes in the area. Be careful where you step and hide, one can lose their life if the snake is the Western Rattlesnake." His remark frightened the women, all fearing snakes. Each woman and their children walked carefully in the area, hopefully hiding in a safe spot.

Everyone moved quickly, with the men positioning themselves under or behind the wagons; some laying flat on the ground, making it harder to be hit by arrows or rifles.

As they waited in the hot sun, many prayers for their safety were said. During the long wait the heat became fierce, Kathleen's hair and body began perspiring; the long skirt and sleeves of her dress were getting wetter by the minute, let alone her hair.

The woman held her five year old daughter, Molly close; encouraging her to stay quiet, the girl's eyes wide with fright. Several hours went by, and finally Link rode out to check the area. When he returned with an "all clear", everyone was very relieved.

It was still several hours before sundown, and Sam gathered the men together. "We could go further today, but both Link and I agree that we would be taking a needless chance, therefore, we've decided it would be best to stay here tonight. I realize there's no water nearby, but we have plenty for now. It would also be best if we had no fires tonight, smoke can travel long distances on the wind, and we do not want anyone smelling our fires."

"We especially do not want the Indians to know we are here, so have your ladies prepare a cold supper tonight." Some people were grumbling about Sam's decision, but they did as they were told.

During the night the men took turns keeping watch. By morning a cold wind had begun blowing, and everyone was cold; all yearning for a cup of coffee, but Sam said, "No fires this morning, folks. Eat something quick and we will be on our way.

There's a stream up ahead, and we should be able to reach it by evening; by then we will be far enough away that we can have our fires."

Even though a few complained, most of them followed Sam's orders, and soon they were on there way moving west.

Many months ago, and what seemed like a world away, Kathleen's husband, Patrick McGinnis, Paddy to his friends, had sold their farm in Ohio. He was taking her and their three youngsters from their home to follow his dream of having his own cattle ranch out west. He had heard tales from men going both east and west that one could make a good profit, raising cattle. They told of the endless lands to the west, ready for cattle; with plenty of good water, and meadows available only for the taking.

Kathleen had resisted his urge to raise cattle out west. She felt he knew little about the cattle business, being a farmer by trade. She had tried to dissuade him saying, "We don't know much about raising cattle", but he had not listened. So they sold their farm, bought a wagon and oxen, took their two horses and headed west.

Michael, the youngest son, was looking forward to their arrival in Santa Fe. As with most boys of fourteen, Michael's imagination had been fired up by stories they'd been told by the soldiers at the different forts, and people in the towns along the way; all filling the boys' head full of tales about Indians, mountain men, trappers, prospectors, gunfighters, and gamblers, as well as silver, copper, and gold you could almost pick up on top of the ground. Michael could hardly wait to see it all for himself.

The boy had become very capable at guiding the oxen that pulled their wagon, while traveling west. When going through the Kansas prairies, shortly before turning off onto the Santa Fe Trail, the wagon train had come upon several old, broken, and whitened wagons. They looked so abandoned and lost, out on the wide open land; nearby were several weathered crosses. When Kathleen saw them, she felt a shiver run down her spine, she couldn't help but think about the poor souls who traded their dreams for a grave, and she thought of the many families that never completed their long journey west.

A silence came over everyone; for they'd all heard about the cruelty of the Indians in the west, and each wondered if that had been the fate of the people buried in this lonely place.

When they did turn south onto the Santa Fe Trail, everyone felt somewhat relieved knowing they were getting closer to Santa Fe, their destination. Although they did know they would probably have to face the Kiowa Indians, a very fierce tribe that lived in the area they were now traveling.

The land was beautiful, the skies were the brightest blue, and the colors on the mountains changed according to the time of day. The sunsets were magnificent, the colors changing from flaming reds and pinks, to the more subtle colors as the sun set in the west.

Only a few days after turning south, the wagon train began to be plagued by torrential rains, making travel especially difficult. There was one good thing that came out of the heavy rains; the wet days seemed to keep the Indians away.

The oxen struggled, pulling the wagons through the sticky mud; as well as the overflowing creeks and streams. Often the water rushed south, causing the wagons to stop, and wait until the water slowed down, as it rushed southward.

It was a difficult journey, many times the women and children, had to walk; which made it easier for the oxen pulling the wagons. More than once, the wagon train needed to stop, giving the animals a chance to rest.

It had been a long and difficult journey. As they drew closer to Santa Fe, the weather turned colder. They had passed Fort Union, and smaller forts, and villages along the trail.

Michael, the family's second son, whose strength and endurance had grown from the rigors of the long journey; was often allowed to drive the oxen pulling the family's wagon. On this particular day, he sat directing the animals for several hours; he was growing tired, though he liked the feeling of being in charge.

Michael could hardly wait to be a man, though most fourteen year olds could do the work of a man. If Michael could have seen himself, he would have realized how much he had already changed since leaving Ohio.

The morning had dawned with a cold sun rising in the sky, and a heavy layer of glistening frost covered everything. Their was a crispness in the air which grew colder as the day progressed.

Now the sky was filling with dark and menacing clouds. As the winds began howling through the area they were traveling in, Michael hunkered down; pulling down the brim of his hat, the sharp winds cutting through his coat, and feeling chilled. He remembered this kind of cold on the farm, and knew snow would soon start to fall.

Michael felt chilled to the bone, and trying to keep warm, he ducked his head down hoping the cold would go away. Soon, small snowflakes began falling; the wind sweeping them into Michael's face, making it hard to see where the wagon was going. He had to trust the oxen, struggling as they followed the wagon ahead of them. He would do the best he could, for his father had put his trust in him.

Michael turned, looking inside the wagon to check on his mother and sister. "Are you two alright ma? It's getting cold out here", he shouted above the winds. Kathleen assured him she and his sister were fine. He saw they were wrapped in warm blankets, so he turned back to the job at hand.

It wasn't long before Paddy McGinnis turned his horse, and rode back toward their wagon. He tied the horse to the back of the wagon, and jumped up on the seat beside his son, quickly checking on his darlin' Kathleen and wee Molly.

"Here laddie, let me be doing that", and he took the reins from his son. Michael was relieved; he had been worried the oxen might get off the trail, and he knew it would be easy to get lost in the storm.

Timothy, Michael's older brother joined the family, tying his horse beside his fathers, and then quickly climbing inside the wagon, hoping to get warm; all the while his teeth chattering. "It's getting really cold," he told his ma. Meanwhile the small flakes grew very large, flying into the faces of the father and son; making visibility very difficult, and it became harder and harder to see.

Everyone was more than tired; they had left Independence, Missouri so long ago. The days had stretched into weeks, and the weeks into months. Everyone had had enough of the scorching heat, torrential rains, hot days and cold winds, and now they were facing winter.

Sam Johnson had informed everyone that when they arrived in Santa Fe there would be living quarters to winter over in, all built by the army men stationed in the area. The women could hardly wait to move out of the wagons, and have some sense of normalcy again. Everyone was exhausted, cold, and weary from living without the comforts they were used to.

Michael, having been relieved of his job, was free to let his mind wander back to the summers on their farm. He missed their home, everyday had been full of work, but he had not minded. He and his brother had their free time after working long hours; they could swim in the creek that ran alongside their farm during the hot Summers; the boy missed the greenness of those summers; all he had seen for so long now were dry, brown prairies; there were many trees scattered around their farmland, and in the spring, many wildflowers bloomed in the area, one of his favorite times on the farm, the fields were always so colorful.

Another favorite memory was the fragrant yellow climbing rose that grew up a post holding the roof over the porch. It had crawled across the roof, and he remembered its rich fragrance filling the air; especially on warm summer nights as he lay in bed before sleep came. It seemed he could almost recall the sweetness of those roses.

He missed his grandmother who died two years ago, and thought of her often.

He remembered her sitting in her rocking chair, talking about Ireland, he listening to her every word.

"Me fither cud dance 'n Irish jig betr'n anyone else in Cork County. Prowd of 'im I was."

She described to him the stone cottage where she was born and raised, the narrow, dusty roads and the stone walls that stretched along those roads. He could still see them in his minds eye. She talked about the wild roses that crept over those same walls, and grew out in the bright green meadows. As a child, she had walked along the streams, the water chuckling down over the rocky stream bed. It was still vivid in his mind as she told him that every year as the air grew warmer. She searched for the sweet smelling, delicate purple violets that hid among the rocks alongside the streams and around rocks out in the fields. When she had a bouquet large enough, she'd always take them to her mother. Someday, perhaps, he might be able to go and see the land of his ancestors.

Grandma also had a wonderful sense of humor that always made him laugh. He thought his ma was very much like her. Michael especially missed hearing his grandma, with her Irish brogue, read from her bible, explaining what she read so he could understand it. He knew without a doubt, he believed in God because of her and his ma.

His reverie took him back to the days on the farm, when he and Tim had their chores to do. Often, if their pa was out of sight, Tim would slip away, leaving Michael to finish the work alone. If he complained, he would be scolded for tattling, pa always taking Tim's side. It hurt, but he learned not to say anything, to avoid his pa's anger.

Many times Michael had talked to his mother. She understood, but she had always encouraged him to forgive both his father and brother, and not to hold a grudge. He did find out that was one of the hardest things he ever tried to do.

The bitter winds and blowing snow brought back the many snowy days and nights on the farm, the warmth of the fireplace with his pa often singing Irish tunes before bed time; the whole family joining in. His pa had a wonderful tenor voice, which made everything seem right, even when the day had been difficult. His parents would often dance around the room, his mother laughing as they whirled around and around. He missed everything from those nights, and wondered if they would ever have times like that again.

Each family traveling with the wagon train had different plans. Some, like his pa, planned to start a cattle ranch, while others wanted to raise horses, look for gold, or just wanted to get a place with water on it, and have a small farm where they owned a few head of cattle, a cow, and some chickens; a place where they could raise their own food. At first it had all sounded exciting to Michael, but now, after seeing the rough land, and traveling this long trip west, Michael wasn't so sure about his pa's plans. He wondered if the money his pa had gotten from the sale of their farm would be enough to start a cattle ranch. After all, what did his pa know about cattle, he was a farmer! Further more, he had seen some pretty bad characters on the trip; only time would tell.

The winds were howling loudly, and the bitter cold went right through Michaels' clothing, not even the gloves he was wearing kept it out. His face and hands felt like they were freezing, and he started to slap his arms around to his back hoping the action would help. When that didn't help, he pulled his hat further down on his head, and wrapped his scarf more tightly around his neck; wishing the freezing winds would stop.

Through the howling wind, he began to hear shouting up ahead. He truly hoped they were coming into Santa Fe. Sam rode back along the wagons telling everyone they were, indeed about to enter the small city of Santa Fe. Everyone was jubilant and their shouts could be heard above the winds.

Kathleen, Michael's mother, said a prayer of thanksgiving to the Lord, so grateful for getting them to Santa Fe. Their arrival here meant they could finally be out of the dirty and dusty wagons, and sleep within walls where they would be warm and safe.

As the wagons entered the town they had traveled so far to reach, everyone was able to look the town over. The storm had eased and they saw a long adobe building, apparently some kind of governmental building, plus other flat top homes and businesses.

Everyone traveling had heard the story of Don Juan de Onate, a Spaniard who arrived in the area from Spain in the year 1598, long before the Pilgrims landed on the Plymouth Rock in 1620. It was hard to believe another country had laid claim to this area so many years ago, though now it was a territory.

They soon came to a walled compound, and were directed in through a wide opening. Once inside they saw a large "U" shaped building with a smaller square building in the middle, there were corrals off to one side, partially covered, and surrounded to protect the animals from the weather; adjoining a small area where the horses could be out when the weather permitted.

As the wagons stopped, all the men jumped down and gathered around the two leaders. Sam began assigning the living quarters to the families, as the men huddled together against the cold, all talking at once. Tempers flared when Joe Templeton complained loudly that the rooms he was given were too small for his wife and five children.

Sam told him, "Joe, I'm sorry, but every unit is the same size, wish I could help you, but that's the way it is." Others began grumbling when they should have been glad, they no longer had to live in the wagons.

Paddy, seeing the problem, began singing a light hearted Irish song, and soon the men began to settle down, though not everyone complained. They all liked Paddy, he had not always carried his load on the trip, but his sharp wit, and happy ways, along with his extra-ordinary tenor voice helped them through the long, tiring days and nights when discouragement so easily crept over them.

It wasn't long before everyone had been assigned a place of their own. Kathleen could hardly contain herself as they stepped into the two adjoining rooms they were given. "It will need to have a good Irish cleaning," she thought, but after that it will be a wonderful place for her and her family to spend the winter. Being on one corner of the building, they had three windows. One of the rooms could be divided into sleeping quarters by canvas or blankets, and the other room had a wood stove along with two of the three windows. There were shelves to store pans and food, a table with benches, and enough room for all of them to sit. There was room to put Kathleen's mother's rocking chair in a warm spot. The wood stove had an oven, which meant she would be able to make bread again. Kathleen saw it would be a warm, homey place where they could live out the rest of the winter comfortably. Here they could be happy just being a family again. She was such an optimist that she could see curtains at the windows. How fortunate there were such places for travelers she thought. "God surely has taken care of us."

Kathleen loved to cook and sew; she was exceptional at both, and people had always loved eating with them. She was well known as the best cook in the valley where they had lived. She had been sewing since she was a young girl, as many had, but she had a real flare with the needle and thread, keeping her family well clothed.

Kathleen was thrilled to find out that her best friend, Jeannie, and her husband, Lawrence, were assigned to the rooms to the left of them. Around the corner on the right, however, were old man Vester and his wife Thelma. Julian Vester was an angry, disagreeable man that she had tried to avoid throughout the long months on the trail. Whenever he looked at Kathleen, she felt as though his eyes were looking right through her clothes, which made her feel extremely uncomfortable; she did not like him at all. He was very cruel to his wife, and couldn't seem to get along with anyone.

His wife, Thelma was in charge of the "gossip trail". Kathleen avoided both of them as much as she could. She hoped that living so close to them would not bring problems into their lives. She had always prayed for them, and she would continue to do so.

The morning sun woke Kathleen, and for just a moment, she wondered where she was. The events of the day before slowly came to mind. She quietly stepped out of bed; she dressed and went into the larger family room. A warm fire was soon burning in the stove. She wrapped a shawl around her, and for a while she sat and rocked in her mother's chair. Her mind wandered back to the days before her mother's death. After her father's death, Paddy and his brother, Aaron had added on an extra room to their small house, and her mother had moved in with them. She and her mother had been so close, and especially so since they had lost her father in the war. It all brought back memories of Aaron, Paddy's brother. Before she and Paddy had married, Kathleen thought he was not only a tall, handsome young man, but more importantly, he was kind with a quiet and gentle way about him. She had loved his wavy, dark reddish hair, and deep blue eyes. She had dreamed that one day Aaron would like her as much as she liked him, but he had not said a word to her. When she was sixteen, she decided that he must not like her as much as she liked him, and when Paddy asked her to marry him, she'd said yes.

It wasn't long after their marriage that Aaron decided to leave home. He had ended up fighting in the Civil War like her daddy had. Later, after the war, they received a short note from him; the note was from Texas, but after that, they had heard nothing.

Kathleen began to hear people waking up, so she quickly made the coffee and started breakfast. After they had all eaten, everyone pitched in to clean up their new home, and bring the rest of their supplies in. Before they knew it, it was time for lunch.

Molly ate a small amount, but she was so tired from running around that Kathleen took her into the sleeping quarters and put her down for a nap. She had nearly outgrown naps, but there had been way too much excitement that morning. "Here darlin", her mother said, "You take a small nap, sleep well my wee one", and with Molly's eyes already closing, she slipped quietly out of the room.

Everyone was glad Molly was asleep, she had run in and around them all morning long; making the whole time much more chaotic.

During the morning, Tim had wanted to leave and join his friend, Johnnie. They had spent a good deal of time together on the trip; both had been trying to avoid anymore work than they could. The boys made plans to go exploring today, but Tim's pa kept him busy all day long.

The horses and oxen had to be fed and brushed down, which Tim hated doing, but having his father right beside him, he could see no way of leaving. Before they knew it, the first day had come and gone. The sun had already lowered in the sky when Kathleen called them to supper.

Michael had spent the day scrubbing floors and cleaning the walls, he was as glad as Tim, that the day was over. Everyone was tired, but Kathleen was delighted to have it all done.

At supper that night, a short prayer was said thanking their Heavenly Father for a good and productive day, plus Kathleen added to Paddy's prayer, her gratefulness for having arrived safely in Santa Fe after their long and arduous journey from Ohio.

Paddy was in a good humor, and after supper he began to sing an old Irish tune his mother had taught him. His beautiful tenor voice floated on the air, and soon they had all joined in. After Kathleen snuggled into bed, she thanked God for the special time they had together as a family; it was almost like being back home again.

Chapter 2

Their arms were full of supplies as they wandered up the street, each looking in a different direction. They had to step carefully, for there was mud everywhere. The mud stuck to their shoes, causing them to scrape it off each time they crossed the street, or walked from one set of buildings to the next.

Kathleen's eyes spied some material in a store she really liked, while Paddy saw excitement everywhere he looked. There were mountain men, prospectors, gamblers, beautifully dressed women, accompanied by finely dressed men. He saw cowboys, soldiers, and Indians. It excited him to see this western city; he'd never been in a western saloon, and thought they looked really intriguing.

His wife broke into his thoughts. "Oh Paddy, do you see that blue material in the store window? Can I get some to make curtains for our windows? It would brighten up our place so much." "Of course darlin', if it would make you happy, then go ahead", he told her. "While you're in the shop, Tim and I will take the supplies we've gotten so far back to our place,

I'll leave Michael here with you and Molly, so he can help carry whatever you buy." Giving her some money, he and Tim left.

With a squeal of delight, she grabbed Molly's hand, picked up her skirt to avoid the mud on the sidewalk, and with her son following, ducked into the little shop. A sweet middle aged woman helped her choose the amount of material she might need. Kathleen thought this soft blue cloth would really brighten up their place. She also bought extra material to cover the cushion for her mother's chair.

Hurrying out of the store, with Molly in hand, and Michael right behind her; carrying the package, she bumped into a very tall, handsome man, dressed in fine clothes. "Oh my! Please forgive me," Kathleen said. "I nearly knocked you down, I am so sorry." The man smiled, making him even more handsome; he bowed slightly, doffing his hat, and said,"Lovely lady, it's my pleasure." She flushed from his reply, pulled Molly close, and rushed away so fast she nearly stumbled down the steps. The man reached out to steady her, and Kathleen's face turned a bright red; embarrassed, she flew down the street, Molly in hand, and Michael trying to keep up with his ma.

They arrived home just before noon; Michael began the task of cleaning the mud from all their shoes. After showing her husband what she had bought, she quickly fixed some lunch. She had no intention of telling her husband about the incident with the man, she knew how jealous he could get; she was just glad to know Jeannie lived next door to them. Kathleen and Jeannie had become close friends on this trip, and Kathleen knew she could confide in her, and the story would go no farther.

While Kathleen was busy sewing that week, the men able to do hard work went to the forest to cut wood to replenish the wood supply. The soldiers had gathered enough wood for the first few days, but the travelers were informed they would have to cut enough for the rest of the winter. They were told where a lot of dead trees were so the wood would burn easily.

Tim and Michael, with the other boys from the families, were given the job of gathering up the wood as the men cut it. The boys placed the wood on the platform that had been built, and then the horses would pull the wooden structure back to the compound at the end of the day. The brothers worked side by side, Michael enjoyed the work, and the chance to be out away from town. At one point he looked around to find Tim was nowhere in sight, "Oh well, he thought, he wasn't that much help anyway." He kind of liked working alone, this way there would be no arguments.

In the distance he could hear his pa singing, he always enjoyed hearing him sing, but it was far more beautiful here in this small wooded valley; on and off the rest of the afternoon he could hear his father's voice as he sang.

While the McGinnis's were eating their supper that night, Michael began talking about the man his mother had bumped into the day before as they were leaving the store. "I've never seen ma so embarrassed," he said. "You should have seen her face turn red, the man was good looking too." Michael's father turned two shades of red, and his eyes blazed with anger. The boy had seen that look before, whenever another man had paid attention to his ma, yet he knew his ma had never encouraged any man, ever.

Paddy was really angry now, and when he got like that the whole family was afraid of him. His anger was directed at his wife, and all she could do was deny that she felt any attraction to the stranger from town. She was devastated that her husband would not believe her. Yelling all kinds of accusations at her, he grabbed his coat, and burst out the door; slamming it with a loud bang! All the joy of their first few days in Santa Fe was washed away by his anger and jealousy. Michael really regretted saying anything about the episode.

After Paddy walked a short way towards town, his anger began to wane, and he wished he had not lost his temper, but as he drew nearer to the center of town, boisterous noises came spilling out of the 'Longhorn Saloon'. His curiosity aroused, he opened the door and stepped into the middle of a large smoke-filled room. It was full of all kinds of men, ranging from cowboys to gamblers. There were beautiful, buxom woman scantily dressed; sitting on men's laps, drinking and laughing while music blared from the tin-pany piano. After ordering a drink at the bar, he spotted a table in the corner where there were several men playing poker; something he had never been involved with. This was a whole new experience for Paddy, he had spent his days on the farm that his parents started, after coming to America from Ireland. They were quiet, God-fearing folk, and spent their days with family and friends in the area. Ohio seemed a long, long way from this moment though as he watched all the different things going on with great interest.

He was going to order another drink, when he realized he'd been gone from home for several hours as he had watched the men play cards. What would Kathleen think of him, being gone for so long? He knew his wife loved him, how could he ever think otherwise?

By the time Paddy reached home, everyone was asleep. He climbed into bed quietly, trying not to wake his wife. She did not stir, but Michael had heard his pa come home, and he asked God to *please* make life easier for his ma. He had heard her crying in the family room after he went to bed, and felt like it was his fault that pa had become so angry; he silently asked God to forgive him. Michael wondered why his pa lost his temper so easily. He had seen it happen from time to time for most of his life.

Morning burst into the bedroom as the sun rose above the horizon, bringing with it warmth and a feeling of new life and new beginnings. As usual, Paddy woke up in a happy, playful mood, showing Kathleen he had not really meant what he had said the night before. Coming up to her while she was cooking breakfast, he took the spoon out of her hand, and with a light-hearted kiss he began to sing and spin her around the room. Soon they were both laughing, and all was forgotten from the night before – at least in Paddy's mind. For Kathleen, however, there was a real sense of apprehension as he rambled on during breakfast about the night, and all he had been introduced to. His anger was not mentioned, but it was the foremost thing on Kathleen's mind all the time Paddy was rambling on about his adventuresome night.

Tim was coming into manhood; at sixteen, he had decided that he no longer had to listen to his parents or be obedient. He was tired of being told what to do and when to do it, not that he had ever been one to really pay attention to such things. Since he was a small boy, he had worked around his pa to get what he wanted or to do what he pleased. Though his pa had never really admitted that this was true, he did feel his eldest son was the "special" son. Kathleen had watched this oldest boy of hers' grow up spoiled, and belligerent, and though she had tried to talk to Paddy, he would hear none of it; now things were really beginning to get out of hand. Tim had found new friends here in Santa Fe, friends that spent their days hanging around outside the saloons, teasing girls and making fun of nearly everyone that walked by looking anything less than perfect. For the first time, Tim thought, "I finally have good friends." It made him feel good to have them pay attention to him and include him in all they did. Often he would not get up till late, grab a bite to eat, and head out the door without saying a word to his ma, or listening to anything she said; she pleaded with him, but to no avail. One afternoon the sheriff came to their door with Tim in tow, it seemed that he and the other boys he spent his time with, had surrounded a young woman and tried to get her to kiss one of them. They became very rowdy, and in the process, she was knocked down. About that time, her father had come out of the store across the street. Seeing what was happening, he tried to break it up and help his daughter. One of the boys pulled out a gun and shot the man, hitting him in the leg. The sheriff had taken the boy who fired the shot to jail, and the rest of the boys were being escorted to their parents. "I didn't do anything", Tim yelled. "Why are you picking on me?" Tim started to squirm out of the sheriffs hands. "You just stand still young fella", the sheriff bellowed. "Ma'am, this boy of yours is running with a pretty rough crowd, if I were you, I'd keep a tight reign on him, or he's liable to get into some really bad trouble; try to keep a close eye on him."

Kathleen was so embarrassed and upset. After the sheriff left, she tried to reason with this unruly son, but to no avail. He ran out the door, shouting that he didn't care what she thought of him; he was a man and would do as he pleased. Kathleen was beside herself with fear; no matter what she said, it seemed to have no effect on him or what he did these days. It wasn't long before Paddy came home to an angry and upset Kathleen. She told him about the sheriff, and what Tim had been involved with. Though her husband listened, he wouldn't take what she said seriously. "I trust Tim. The shooting was probably an accident, and anyway, you know how kids are; I'm sure Tim really wouldn't hurt anyone on purpose. Now don't you worry me sweet one, I'll have a talk with the boy when he comes home," but he never did. Paddy was engrossed in other things. Without his wife knowing, Paddy had begun getting into some of those poker games that were so intriguing to him. He had only done it awhile in the afternoons, and he hadn't won, or lost much money; it was just enough to wet his appetite.

As the days progressed, he was getting home later and later for supper. Kathleen found herself talking more and more to the Lord about her husband and son; it was Jesus she clung to. He was her strength, and would be even more in the days that followed.

It wasn't long before the man was missing supper altogether, he started getting home quite late; many times he would not be home till long after everyone was asleep. Many nights Kathleen would lay awake for hours, hoping to hear his footsteps. Paddy started drinking heavily, and often came home drunk. The life that they once had, was quickly slipping away, and was replaced with a nightmare.

While Kathleen would listen for Paddy to come home at night, her mind would think of better days, when they had been happy. When Paddy was courting her, he was so sweet to her, and so full of fun. He had a wonderful sense of humor, and often made her laugh. She had pictured her life with him so different than it had turned out to be.

Although Aaron, Paddy's younger brother, had left home shortly after she and Paddy had Timothy, she started wondering why he had left; was it because she had married Paddy? Why was she even thinking of him at all she wondered? She loved her husband,

and they *had* been married for eighteen years now; no longer the young girl she was when she first had her eye on Aaron. She was unhappy and confused about what was happening with her marriage.

One night as Kathleen was deep in her thoughts, she heard footsteps outside the door; something hit the door with a loud bang! She knew immediately that her husband was home, and that he had been drinking too much. She jumped to her feet, threw on her robe, and rushed into the family room to quiet Paddy down, so he wouldn't wake the others. She took one look at him, and her heart seemed to stop; Paddy began to stumble toward her in a drunken rage, and as he reached out at her, he fell over a chair. Kathleen tried to help him up off the floor, but Paddy cursed her, and pushed her aside with such force that she almost fell over. Yelling at Kathleen, Paddy said, "What's wrong with you woman? I don't need any help, leave me alone!" He struggled to his feet, and in the process, knocked over the pitcher of water on the table; water went everywhere, and as his wife scurried around cleaning it up, Paddy became even more enraged, and he started yelling at the top of his lungs, swinging his fists at her; hitting her on the side of the face, and knocking her to the floor. Paddy didn't stop, he went after her again as she quickly got to her feet. Tripping again, Paddy fell flat on his face in the middle of the room, and Kathleen ran over to see if he was alright, but he had simply passed out.

At that moment, Kathleen thought of their family. She looked up and saw Michael standing at the opening to the sleeping quarters. Tears began to well up in her eyes, as her son carefully put his pa to bed.

Touching the side of her face, Kathleen realized it was bleeding. Michael then tended to his ma, and got a soft, wet cloth to gently wipe the blood away. As Michael held his ma close to him, Kathleen's sorrow exploded inside her, and she began crying uncontrollably. What would she do now? What would happen to all of them? Her mind was flooded with questions, but the warmth of Michael's arms seemed to calm her, and in time she stopped crying.

After a while, being the strong woman that she was, Kathleen calmed down and finally sunk into bed. As she lay next to her drunken husband, she started thinking about the cause of that night's anger. She knew Paddy had started spending more and more time at the local saloon; he had been taking money with him each day, but never putting any back. He had been playing cards every night lately, and apparently, was very bad at it. He'd lost a great deal of the money they had gotten from the sale of their farm; the money that they planned to invest in their new life! What was going to happen to them if he continued to gamble their future away? The only thing the woman could do was turn to God for comfort; He alone could help her now.

As she spoke to Him, she remembered a verse from Psalms that read; "The Lord will command his loving kindness in the daytime and in the night, his song shall be with me." She began to hear a whispered song of gentleness, and she felt herself fill with God's unconditional love; it was a promise that He was with her, no matter what would happen, and it comforted her.

After a few short hours of sleep, Kathleen slipped out of bed, being very quiet not to disturb her family. Sitting and rocking in her mothers' chair, sipping her first cup of coffee she felt renewed. Having the Lord sing to her during the night, she knew that somehow, someway, things would work out. The Lord would be with them. She need not fear, it was all in His hands.

There was little talking in the McGinnis household that morning. Paddy did not remember what had happened the night before, he just knew he had a terrible headache; the coffee helped. Michael and Molly were quiet, but in Kathleen's heart there was a song. After Paddy left and all the chores were done, she told Michael he could join his friends. She and Molly dressed up in their prettiest dresses and coats, and headed down to the material shop; Kathleen had in mind to make a new dress for Molly. The song stayed in Kathleen's heart. Once inside the store, she went straight to some pretty green material. While she was considering it for Molly's new dress, Mrs. Fern, the owner, came over to see if she could help. She asked the lovely woman who had made her families' clothes. When Kathleen acknowledged she had made them herself, Mrs. Fern was impressed. "You do lovely work, would you consider working for me? I need a seamstress. The woman that worked for me before had to leave when her husband decided to go to California in search of gold; I was sorry to lose her. The orders for dresses are growing, and there is no way I will be able to keep up with them; there's just too many, I really need someone to take her place. Would you consider taking the job?" Kathleen was so excited, but she told Mrs. Fern she had a family to care for. Although she wanted to say yes, she knew she had to ask Paddy before giving the woman an answer. Mrs. Fern assured Kathleen she could do all the work at home. After buying the material she had chosen, she left with a promise to Mrs. Fern that she would let her know as soon as possible.

Excited, and in some way relieved from the terror of the night before; with her purchase in hand, she and Molly made their way home. Kathleen was determined to talk to Paddy about the work. She was ready to stay up all night, waiting for him to return home, if that was what it would take, but to her surprise, Paddy was on time for supper! She didn't have to ask him why he was home so early, just looking at him told her that he didn't feel at all well.

It was hard for Paddy to agree to his wife working for someone; he never thought she would have a job when he did not. He still had not looked for employment for the winter because the gambling and drinking had taken over his life. If he'd known what he had done to his wife the night before, he would have been so ashamed. Kathleen put up a good argument, telling her husband that she would be sewing, and could do it at home. He finally agreed to it, because he figured she probably wouldn't keep such a close eye on him if she was busy.

The next morning after breakfast was over and the place was cleaned up, she got dressed and asked

Michael to watch Molly, and she set out to see Mrs. Fern at the store.

Edna Fern was overjoyed when Kathleen came through the door and accepted the job. She decided to start Kathleen slow by giving her the cloth for one dress. Within an hour, the woman was back home with the sewing materials in hand. A week later, she returned to the store with the dress in hand. Mrs. Fern looked over the dress, and was so delighted with it that she quickly handed over more of the orders along with the cloth for each. Kathleen was ready to get back to her sewing when she returned home; each day was full of joy for her while she created the beautiful clothes. She poured her heart and soul into each stitch, and thanked God for the ability to do what she enjoyed doing the most.

Life went back to normal for Kathleen. Although Paddy was still not around most of the time, her love turned to her family and her sewing. She continued to meet with the many friends she had made while traveling with the wagon train. There were many that got together each Sunday for church; God had become so real to many of them during their long trip across the plains. The minister of the small gathering was Reverend Richard Smith; he was a good man who loved God. His wife, Eve, was a friend to Kathleen, as she was with all the wives. Each woman on the wagon train knew they could find understanding and love from the minister's wife.

Sunday's were full of friends and fun, the women prepared food ahead of time to bring for a lunch held after church. Everyone would talk, sing, and laugh; the children played games and enjoyed each others' company. Paddy used to sing songs at church, Kathleen loved the way he would sing her favorite song, "The Old Rugged Cross", but he really didn't like church very much these days, he usually stayed home and slept off the night before. The only time he showed up was when he wanted something to eat; he knew where the food was, it was where his wife was.

Kathleen felt that she had made the best out of her life. She spent her time with friends worshipping God, and at home sewing. She also spent a lot of hours with Jeannie and Eve, her best friends. Orders for clothes were coming in by the bushel load, and Kathleen was kept really busy. Women in town thought her fashions were the best they had ever seen, which made her dresses very desirable. The money that Kathleen made for her work was split between the house fund, and what she hid; knowing that she would need it later.

Christmas was right around the corner, and Kathleen could hardly wait. In the past, Paddy had always loved Christmas as much as she. He used to take the boys out to cut down the *perfect* Christmas tree. He would also help decorate it, and lead the family in Christmas carols after supper. Every Christmas morning Paddy would surprise each of his children with something special that he had made for them. In all the years since Tim was born, he had a clever way of always giving each child exactly what they wanted. This year, with their father always gone or drunk, and Tim still hanging around with the wrong crowd, all Kathleen could do was leave Christmas in God's hands.

As the holiday got closer, the snow got worse, and by the day before Christmas, the snow was heavier than they had seen so far that winter. Kathleen waited, and waited for Paddy to come home, but the snow was getting worse, so before lunch, she took Michael and Molly out looking for a tree. They hiked up to a hill behind where they lived to find a Christmas tree; Michael dragged the small, nicely shaped tree back to their place, made a stand for it, and stood it up in the corner of the main room. After lunch, Michael and Molly strung popcorn while Kathleen finished making some pretty little ornaments from scraps of cloth. When the tree was decorated, it looked very festive; Michael helped his ma put boughs of pine branches on the window sills and over the door; that made the whole area smell wonderful. It wasn't like back home in Ohio, but it *was* very nice. Later in the afternoon, Molly helped her ma make some sugar cookies and little tarts from her ma's special dried apples. It was such fun; even Michael got in a playful mood and got his ma's face covered with flour. They worked and played, laughing the afternoon away.

It was time to finish making their Christmas Eve supper, and Kathleen had planned a special meal. She knew that Tim should arrive at any time, and her husband had promised he would be home in time for supper. She had spent extra money to get the fixin's for her favorite beef stew; the meat had been cooking all afternoon. She had added carrots, onions, and potatoes when the meat was nearly tender, and made her wonderful biscuits. She planned to have hot chocolate with the cookies and tarts after dinner, a real treat. Michael and Molly could hardly wait for supper. The house looked so Christmassy and the stew, along with the other baked goods made the house smell wonderful. "When are we going to eat ma?" Michael asked. "I'm hungry ma, where are Tim and pa?" asked Molly. Her mother couldn't give her an answer. She decided to keep a smile on her face and serve supper for the three of them. Later, Kathleen put a disappointed Molly to bed. She prayed quietly for her sweet child that Jesus would watch over her soul. Kathleen and Michael sat near the stove. Michael wanted to go looking for his pa and Tim, but it was still snowing, and his ma would not let him. "Go to bed honey, I'm sure they will be home soon." She told him. He finally did go to bed, and so did she, after asking God to keep her husband and first born safe.

Early the next morning, Kathleen woke to find that Paddy had not been home at all that night, nor had Tim. Frantic, she quietly woke up Michael who got dressed. She wanted him to look for his pa after breakfast; it crossed her mind that Paddy could have fallen in the snow. Suddenly, Molly came bursting into the room to see what was under the tree for her. To her joy, she found there were several packages for her! Kathleen had made her a brand new sweater with matching mittens, scarf, and a hat. Michael had made her a whistle; there were new pajamas for all her family. After looking over the rest of the tree, Molly looked up at her ma and asked "Where are my presents from pa and Tim? I want my pa, where is he", the small girl asked. Kathleen's heart sank as she told her daughter that she didn't know where her father or Tim were. Instead of all of them eating Christmas breakfast, opening gifts together, and then singing Christmas carols, the three ate a quick breakfast. Kathleen looked out the window, and was surprised to see that it had been snowing all night, and now, the snow was nearly up to the window sills. Michael climbed out the window, and began shoveling away the snow in front of the doors. When he finished, he brought more wood in for burning, and then grabbed a couple of biscuits. Then he left to look for his pa and brother. "Don't worry ma, I'll find them." He said as he left.

It didn't take Michael long to find his father, he went straight for the saloon, and there he found Paddy, where he had passed out, lying over a table. It wasn't easy for the boy to get his father home, but soon they were at the front door. After putting his pa to bed, Michael drank a cup of coffee to get warm, and took out again in search of his brother. He first looked in at the jail house thinking maybe he had gotten into trouble last night with his friends, but the sheriff hadn't seen him. Next, he tried old man Fletcher's barn, where the boys often hung out. There, in the hayloft, lay Tim. It seemed that one of the boys had stolen two bottles of whiskey from a crate in back of the saloon, and they all had a party. Being annoyed with his brother, Michael just kicked him, and told him to get up. He yelled at him, telling him that he had ruined Christmas, and their mother had been in tears. "You promised her you would be home. Why can't you ever think of others?" He was disgusted with Tim.

After Tim went to bed, Michael tried to make his sister and ma happy. He got them singing Christmas carols, and then he opened the Bible and read the Christmas story to them. Kathleen was amazed at his strength, consideration, and his faith, as he continued saying a prayer for his pa and Tim. He loved his mother, and respected her for her kindness. He knew that as long as he lived, he would always remember the disappointment and sadness in her eyes that day. It was at that moment that Michael vowed to himself, and to God that he would always choose the way of Christ, and keep Him in his life. Without realizing his decision, Kathleen was so proud of him. She saw in him a maturity she had not seen before, in fact, Michael had really become the man of the house in so many ways. He had been taking care of the livestock; he'd gone to town for necessities for his ma, and giving his ma time to sew by watching over Molly from time to time. He never complained, but Kathleen couldn't help but feel that her fifteen year old son should be out with his friends doing whatever boys do.

By afternoon, Paddy woke up, and he was in a foul mood. He had hidden a bottle in his coat pocket when Michael brought him home, which the boy did not discover. The weather was so bad outside; it had begun to snow again, and Paddy had no desire to be out in the cold. To his wife's dismay, Paddy made himself comfortable in her rocking chair, and began to drink the whiskey. Tim woke up mid-afternoon, and forgot it was even Christmas. He had a horrible headache, and just wanted some coffee and a warm blanket to wrap himself in.

Kathleen began to cook supper soon after Tim woke. Michael kept Molly busy with her toy whistle. The sound really unnerved Paddy, so after his cursing, Kathleen asked Michael to amuse Molly in a quieter way. As she cooked supper, she wished for earlier days when Paddy had been a loving, fun-filled husband. Instead, the reality was that her husband was a completely different person, who no longer washed, shaved, or changed his clothes. He was always smelly, but Kathleen knew she dared not say a word; for fear that his retaliation would be fierce. Her life with her husband had turned into a nightmare, for both her and her family. Paddy was always angry at her, and accusing her of all kinds of improprieties. Would the man she thought she had loved, ever come back to her, she wondered? She could live with the disappointment of this Christmas, as long as she wouldn't have to endure another one just like it again. She was afraid for Molly and Michael. She felt trepidation. What would this kind of life do to them?

The day after Christmas, Jeannie came over to visit. When she heard what had happened, she was so sorry and told her friend so. Then, she proceeded to help Kathleen with some sewing. While they sewed, they talked about their faith in their Heavenly Father. Both women relied on Him for everything. Jeannie laughed on the outside, but inside, she prayed that somehow things would get better for her friend, Paddy, and the three children. She knew that God guides us in our lives, and sometimes brings us through tough times. She knew that with God, all things are possible.

Chapter 3

Someone knocked on the McGinnis's door, and when Kathleen opened it, she found Jeannie standing there. "I have to talk to you," her friend told her. Kathleen beckoned her friend in.

Jeannie pushed past Kathleen, and turning, told her friend, "I'm so sorry Kathleen, I tried to stop her, but she kept right on talking." "Who kept talking?" Kathleen asked.

The words started spilling out of Jeannie's lips. "Several women were in the gathering room mending, and I walked in, planning to do some cleaning. Thelma Vestor was talking, telling everyone gathered there, what happened the night Paddy came home so drunk and hit you; she said she heard it all through their bedroom wall."

"I don't see how she could have heard anything. These adobe walls are thick and dense."

Jeannie continued saying, "She added a lot of bad things to her story, saying she heard Paddy hit you, and you hit him back. She also said that there was a lot of loud yelling from Paddy and you cursed back at him." Thelma then suggested they should all stay away from you and your family. The women were all shocked, but since they were Thelma's friends, they were inclined to go along with what she said. They felt it was your fault, and that you must not be as nice as you've pretended to be.

Kathleen considered some of the women her friends, and couldn't imagine them actually believing Thelma, who, as everyone knew, loved to spread gossip. But when she went out the next day, no one spoke to her; they all glared at her, and avoided her as if she had the plague.

That afternoon, Kathleen went to talk to Reverend Smith. Eve, his wife, excused herself, and went into the sleeping quarters so the two could converse in the living area. Kathleen explained about the night in question, going into detail. She told her minister what really happened that night, saying she had not struck her husband, and certainly hadn't sworn or cursed. She told him how she had tried to explain to everyone that what Thelma said was not true, but no one believed her.

As she spoke, she was trying very hard not to cry, but tears formed in her eyes. Reverend Smith listened quietly to Kathleen; she had been a good friend to him and his wife.

The Reverend handed her his handkerchief, while saying, "I believe you Kathleen. I've known your family a long time now, and know what kind of woman you are. You've been a good and gentle wife and mother since we met, and your faith in Christ shows in all your actions. I'm very sorry this has happened, why don't we join in prayer." They both bowed their heads as Reverend Smith prayed. "*Our Beloved Father in heaven, we love you so much. You are more important to us than anything or anyone. We give you our adoration, praise, and devotion. Father, Kathleen and I come before you to ask that this malicious talk about her will stop. You know just what to do in the hearts of the women involved in this gossiping. We are all sinners Father. Help Kathleen and myself not to judge anyone, but rather to trust you to take care of this matter. We also ask you to show Paddy that what seems exciting to him in his new interests is very dangerous behavior. That drinking and gambling can destroy him, and hurt his family. We do know each of us have been given a free will by you, so we put him into your care. Show him, Lord, how much you love him. Holy Spirit, come and touch all our hearts. We ask this in Jesus' name, whom we love. Amen.*"

That evening Kathleen felt better. Not that anything had changed, but she somehow knew the gossip would stop. Deep in her heart she knew things would work out whether her husband changed or not. She spent some time that night reflecting on Eve, and Richard Smith; how grateful the woman was for them.

When Richard Smith, a newly ordained minister, joined the wagon train leaving Independence, he was a bachelor. He felt the Lord wanted him to go west. Richard was not sure why, he just felt that was his destiny. He could have traveled by train, but decided that by going with the wagon train, perhaps he could be of help. Many times, the people going west were families. He knew the trip would be difficult, but also knew that there would be times when he could serve others. That's why he made the decision to travel on horseback with all his supplies strapped behind his saddle.

Eve and William Wilson had left by wagon with the other travelers. They were young newlyweds, having been married shortly before leaving for the west. Everyone could see how much the two were in love; they seemed to be so happy. It was refreshing for everyone to have them traveling along with the wagons. It was a joy for all to see the young newly weds so in love.

Nearly two months later, while William was busy cutting wood for the fires one evening with Daniel Johnson, a terrible thing happened. While cutting the wood with his axe, William stopped, grabbed his chest, sighed and fell forward. By the time Daniel reached his friend, it was too late. William apparently had a sudden heart attack, and he was gone. When Eve heard what happened to her husband, she went into shock. Kathleen and Jeannie hurried to the widow's side immediately, but it did no good; she turned away from everyone.

As William was lowered into the grave on a hill under a tree, surrounded by prairie, Reverend Smith said a few words and a prayer over the grave. Eve stayed at the grave site, not wanting to leave her husband. What would she do? She wondered. "I'm all alone now," she said as she wept, while Reverend Smith stood afar and watched.

When she turned to go back to the wagon, he walked beside her. He'd hoped the simple service would have encouraged her, but when Eve got to the wagon, she climbed inside. Sitting where she and William had been so happy, she said nothing to anyone. Her friends were worried about the young widow, for they heard her weeping in the night. Both Jeannie and Kathleen could not seem to reach her.

Richard Smith tried in the days following to get the young woman to eat, which she refused to do; only drinking water from time to time. She felt so terribly lost, and everyone understood. Everyone watched as the young minister took over driving Eve's wagon during the days, his horse tied to the back. They also watched as he cooked food over the fire at night, trying to get her to eat. They all decided he might do better than they.

After a few days, she began coming out of the wagon after dark. She spoke to no one, not even to Richard, only sitting, and staring into the flames of the fire Richard always built.

Gradually, her weeping and mourning began to cease. The man did all he could to help her recover, all the while remaining a perfect gentleman.

Kathleen noticed after a week; Eve began to eat a small amount of food Richard prepared for her. The two mostly sat in silence, the young minister being very patient. In time, Eve began to come out of her self-imposed shell. Her friends had decided to stand aside, keep watch and let Richard handle the situation. Everyone could see Eve was improving. Soon, the two, sitting by the fire, started talking to each other.

After a few weeks, laughter could be heard from time to time as they sat by the fire. Kathleen had never seen a more patient or kind young man before.

The long tiring days continued, one at a time. Eventually Eve began to be more like herself. Richard went on being Eve's strength, all the while being so very kind. Eve's friends admired the man's loyalty to their friend. He knew there was no one else to take charge of Eve's wagon, so he continued guiding it west, and they all saw everything he did to help their friend.

In time, Eve took over the cooking, and fed the young minister. Kathleen and Jeannie began stopping by their fire in the evenings, and for Eve things began to change.

The long tiring days continued as they wended their way west. Eve was grateful that Richard had taken control of the wagon. Richard continued being there for the young widow; always quiet and never asking for anything in return.

Several of the men, knowing Richard was a minister, went to him asking if he would read a scripture and say a short prayer each Sunday morning before they traveled on.

Richard always chose a scripture of encouragement, and a few words each Sunday before the wagon train started moving west. They all looked forward to the short period of time, and strong relationships began to be formed between the young minister and the members of the wagon train.

Richard's thoughts often turned toward Eve as they traveled each day. He found himself in love with the lovely woman. She often rode up front sitting beside him, and as the months went by, Richard dared to tell Eve his feelings.

One evening as they were sitting by the fire, Richard told her how he felt. "I know it's been a short time since William died, but I have come to care for you deeply. I know once we reach Santa Fe, you will be all alone, and I cannot bear to think of you like that; nor do I want it to happen. Eve, I could not watch you alone, and with no one to take care of you; I want to be there for you. I would always take the best of care of you, you are a wonderful and lovely woman, and your faith in God has helped you through this lonely time."

"Eve, would you consider marrying me?" "I, I know it's maybe too quick, but nothing would make me happier than having you as my wife."

She looked up at the brown haired, strong featured handsome man thinking, he is so kind. She simply said, "Richard, would you give me a few days to think about this? Then I will give you my answer." Richard said he would wait.

The next day, Eve's thoughts went back and forth between William and Richard. In her mind, she had been so in love with William, but somehow she saw kindness, maturity, and strength in Richard that she loved also. Eve tried to weigh all the things involved in his proposal. True, she had no one. How could I make a living out in the west she thought? Eve knew there were many good men there, but she had also heard of the violence in the west; she was a little bit frightened, not knowing what her future would be. Then, she got realistic with herself, she knew she felt much the same way about Richard that he felt about her; she had found what a gentle Christian man he was.

Yes, she decided she would marry Richard Smith! He was someone special, and she had always felt safe with him around.

She told Richard the next day that she would marry him. "I think, without knowing it, I have come to love you too. I'm not sure how that happened. I loved William, but that was another time. Yes, Richard, I would be honored to marry you; you are a wonderful man and friend."

He looked at her and asked, "May I kiss you?" She reached up, putting her two hands on the sides of his face, and lifting her head, kissed him. From that moment on, they saw only each other.

A few days later, they arrived at Fort Union. Richard and Eve were married by the fort chaplain.

That day there was a flurry of activity, their friends all wanted this day to be special for the young couple. Eve was married in a lovely, long pink gown that Kathleen had packed away in a trunk. The wide neckline, perfect for the warm day, had ruffles around the neck, and large puffed sleeves tapering down to the wrist. It fit Eve perfectly, and she was beautiful wearing a large white bow from Jeannie, and tying her long flowing blond hair at the back of her neck. Some of the women gathered dried wildflowers for her to hold.

Richard, beaming, wore his one and only suit. They were a handsome couple, and everyone was delighted for the two. Everyone could see their love, and knew Eve would be cared for. The baker at the fort baked a cake for the occasion; served with coffee. It was a wonderful day, the weather cooperated, and everyone felt very happy for the young couple. Through it all, Eve, Jeannie, and Kathleen became fast friends, a friendship that would last for many years.

Two days after Kathleen's visit to Richard Smith, it was New Years Eve. Nearly everyone wanted to gather together to thank the Lord for His watchfulness over them on the long journey to Santa Fe. As Richard talked lovingly to the congregation, he included some wise words about how gossip hurts friends and loved ones, most of the women responsible for spreading gossip about Kathleen felt much sorrow for how they had treated their friend. After the service, the women got together and went to Kathleen to apologize for their actions.

Soon after the New Year started, Michael began going to school. His ma had tried to talk Tim into going, but he would have none of it. The teacher was Mrs. Mackem, a middle aged woman who was rather plain looking. Michael liked her right away, probably because she was so pleasant, and had a wonderful smile. Her brown eyes shown brightly with a bit of mischievousness, and there was a sparkle that entranced the boy.

Sitting next to him was a boy with bright red hair and freckles that dotted his face. The two boys hit it off right away, soon becoming close friends. There were other students he liked, but Tommy was destined to be his best friend. The boy, when not in class, was a happy kid; always smiling or laughing. He was very bright, and was a good student. That was good for Michael, for he had been taught by his ma since they left Ohio. Michael was very quick to learn also, taking clues from Tommy on how to settle into the classroom well. Because his new friend had been in Santa Fe for a few years, he either knew everyone, or knew who they were.

There was still snow some days, but nothing like it had been at Christmas time. On clear days, the sun almost felt warm as long as there was no wind. On windy days, everyone bundled up to keep the chill out.

Often, after both boys had finished the work they had to do on Saturday morning, they would spend time playing "cut the pie" using their pocket knives, or wandered around town.

As January turned into February, the weather grew a bit warmer. By March, some days seemed spring-like with warmer days. The boys thoroughly enjoyed each others' company. They were both doing well in school, and because they learned quickly, the boys had more time to spend together, though Michael often brought Molly along to give his mother free time to sew. Tommy didn't mind, and of course the little girl loved every minute of her time with the boys.

By mid March, on a warm Saturday morning, the two boys, having finished their work early, went down near Brown's Mercantile. Each boy had worked, and earned a few pennies, so they went into the store to buy a string of licorice.

They met Mrs. Mackem in the store and stopped to talk with her. Each boy liked their teacher. When they went outside, they sat on the steps of the store talking. Suddenly, Tommy got up saying, "Come on", and started running down the street with Michael right behind him, Tommy calling out, "Scotty, Scotty, you're back in town! I thought somethin' had happened to you 'cause you haven't been around for a long time. How's Cleo? Where is she?" A grubby old man with scraggly white hair and the longest white beard Michael had ever seen; turned around and, with a wide toothless grin said, "Why Tommy boy, you knowed we'd show up one o' these days. Don't we always? Ol' Cleo, she's down at O'Neil's stables restin up, and she's not gitten any yunger ya know, neither one of us is. Who's yer yung friend?" Tommy answered, "This is my best friend, Scotty. His name is Michael, and we have a lot of fun together." "Well hullo boy, any friend o' Tommy's is a friend o' mine." The old man said with his almost toothless grin getting wider.

The old prospector and the two boys sat down on the steps near the bank, and the bearded man began to talk about his and Cleo's latest adventures, the boys in rapt attention.

"That ol' bar was ten feet tall, and he cum upon me an' ol' Cleo when we was a-goin' through them mountains jest north o' Silver City. We were a-moseyin' along a-mindin' our own business last summer when this critter cum a-barrelin' out from behind sum bushes. Well, we jest stood thar a-lookin' at each uther, each one a-tryin' to decide what to do.

Thet ol' bar begun to chuckle, he dun put his paws on his hips, an' jest howled. Now I knowd ol' Cleo was a-kinda wore out luken with her chewed up ears an' her saggy belly, but they warn't no reason fer thet ol' bar to laugh at her, so I jest got me mad, an I started to hit thet fella. Well, it didn't take long af'er he knowed jest how mad I was, an' he took off down thet hill with me rite behind'em, me a-shoutin' at'em all the way."

"With his long steps un my short ones, it warn't long af'er I lost 'em, but I cud hear'em a high-tailin' it o're the next hill. Now, when I dun got back to ol' Cleo, she was jest a munchin' on sum grass like nuthin' had happened. That's one ol' bar! I bet I'll ne'er see again."

"It warn't more then a day after thet we dun run into a hole bunch a injims, an' thet ol' bar dun tol'em bout me an ol' Cleo. When they'd see'd us, they dun treated me with down right reespect! I know'd I had sum friends fer life."

By now a whole crowd had gathered around the white-haired man and the two boys. There were all ages, from small children up to men and women. Everyone howled with laughter, knowing the old man had really told a tall tale this time. Enjoying being center stage, he went on to say "When we were a-goin' thru thet hot desert down thet-a-way last summer, I kep' a-seein' a bunch o' them thar lizards a-runnin' roun' with stickes in thar mouths." Michael couldn't contain himself; he had to ask "Why did the lizards have sticks in there mouths?" With a twinkle in his eyes, the old man replied, "Why yung fella, they war a-carrin' them thar sticks in thar mouths cuz when thet thar desert gets to sizzlin', them ugly li'l things hold thar sticks strait up un climb right up to keep thar feet from a-fryin'."

Everyone had a good laugh over that one, but Michael wasn't so sure. He'd been on the hot prairies, and he'd seen lizards, but maybe that desert was a lot hotter. The old prospector talked on for some time, entertaining everyone and enjoying every minute of it. One man spoke up and said, "I've been hearing tales about men making fortunes in silver down Silver City way, did you spend any time there? Are the rumors true?" Well, the wrinkled old man told them how he had found a nugget of gold in the stream running through Pinos Altos, about eight miles away from Silver City. The money that he got from the gold had given him enough to set himself up for the whole time he was in the area. Because he could not find anymore gold, he had decided to go down to Silver City where there were silver mines, one being the "legal tender". He said he thought he might prospect for some silver in the area; "So Cleo and I high-tailed it down to thet thar town. I started a-diggin' not too fer from thet mine, and I done run into some silver ore. I was so excited, I run all the way to the claims office, pullin' ol' Cleo behind, to git me a claim on thet thar piece o' land, only to find someone had jest beat me to it! Well, I was mad as an injun, but thar weren't nuthin' I culd do 'bout it, so I started lookin' ag'in. 'Bout thet time, they dun found anuther vein of silver in the mine, an' when the news dun got a-round, the town filled up with lots of no-account men. Thar was a bunch of killin's, an ol'Cleo and me dun walked away. No sir'ee, I didn't want eny part of thet town!" Because of what Scotty said, rumors started flying around Santa Fe about the fortunes that could be made in the mountains around Silver City. Paddy McGinnis was right in the midst of the rumors, and he began to wonder if it wouldn't be a good idea to head south to make his fortune there instead of going into raising cattle. He had lost a lot of their money while gambling, and unless he could win it back, he wouldn't be able to buy cattle anyway. It would soon be spring, and they would have to be on the trail again.

That night there was going to be a big poker game, Paddy was excited because he was going to sit in on it. He had not been in a high-stakes game before, so when Dutch, the owner and proprietor of the Golden Stakes Saloon, asked him if he would like to sit in on the game, he grabbed the chance. He had no idea that Ted Spencer, a professional gambler, had set up the game. The gambler needed a green horn in the game, and had asked Dutch to get Patrick McGinnis into the game; he had his own reason for choosing Paddy, mostly because of the man's wife. Ted Spencer was interested in her since the day she bumped into him, she was a beauty! Paddy thought, "Now, here's my chance to make good, I'll show everyone, and then they won't be giving me such a bad time. Especially Kathleen! She was always complaining about him being gone so much, plus his drinking and gambling; he was tired of it!

When Paddy didn't show up for supper that night, Kathleen was relieved. She was almost glad when he didn't come home, that meant they wouldn't end up quarreling in front of the family. Actually, he had not been coming home before the middle of the night for many weeks. The following morning, when she woke up, her husband was not in bed. Kathleen began to imagine all kinds of things. She stopped then and there, and she refused to let herself become negative. It was time to change her ways. It was time to put him, and all of their lives, in Gods' hands, and leave everything to Him. Breakfast came and went, Michael headed for school, and soon the morning was gone. She had been busy sewing all morning, so she asked Jeannie if she would take care of Molly. Soon Molly's father would be home, and his wife didn't want her sweet child to be there. When he did come dragging in, to her surprise, he went straight to bed without one word of anger, or explanation.

A couple of hours later, there was a knock on the door. When Kathleen opened it, Ted Spencer, the man she had bumped into months before, was standing there. "I'm sorry to bother you ma'am, but I've come to pick up the livestock and wagon. Your husband said they would be ready to pick up by this afternoon." "What do you mean you've come to pick them up?" she said, "They are not for sale." The man looked at her in a way that made her feel very uncomfortable, and then told her, "Your husband lost them to me in a poker game last night." This man she had thought was handsome suddenly became disgusting to her. "Now if you will show me where they are ma'am, I'll take them and be on my way," the man said.

After the gambler left she was bereft. How could Paddy do such a thing? She thought. Now we have nothing left! When Michael came home and heard what had happened, he became very angry, but was careful not to let his mother know how he felt. She had enough to contend with, and so he told her, "its all right ma, you wait and see. God will help us, I know He will."

Somehow, just hearing Michael's confidence in God reminded her that the Lord knew all about what had happened, and He had a plan for her family, and she knew everything would work out His way; the whole idea calmed her down. Again, she had to put her family and herself into His hands, and as she did so, she also knew that all the money was gone, but that it would all work out somehow. The thing she kept thinking about was the loss of her husband's horse; he was a beautiful steel-dust grey, and a gentle animal. Somehow she'd always had a special relationship with Mr. Grey. The woman had ridden him, and when she talked to him, he always listened, and nearly always would lift one foot and quietly paw the air as if to say how much he liked her too. She had often given him a carrot, her way of responding to the horses' friendship.

The days following their loss were difficult; Kathleen no longer talked to her husband much. She just didn't want to fight or argue with him any more. Paddy began to carry the load of guilt for what he had done.

There was little money, only what Kathleen made with her sewing. She continued putting some money aside. Spring was coming, and it would not be long before everyone would be leaving. What was ahead for her and her family was unknown, but she planned to be ready for anything.

Bit by bit, her husband began to return to his former self, but she could not let herself trust him. Without money Paddy was not free to live as he had been. The whole episode seemed to snap him out of the selfish way he had been living.

One day he sat his wife down, and apologized for all he had done. "I will never do it again, I promise my sweet one." It went through her mind that she couldn't trust him, even if he was being sweet, and had said he was sorry. Paddy broke into her thoughts, "I hear they need a man to help out with incoming supplies at the mercantile. I think I'll go down and apply for the job. If I get the work, I'm not sure how long it will last, or how much money the job will pay, but it will be a start." When her husband got the job, his wife felt a small glimmer of hope; he did just what he had said he would do. He worked hard, came home right after a hard days work, and brought the money home to his wife each week.

Chapter 4

The news was all over Santa Fe! Everyone was upset about the rash of small burglaries that had occurred over the last several weeks, but that very morning, States Bank had been robbed! A gang of young hoodlums had been hanging around town for a couple of months, and the members were the chief suspects; according to the banker, a large amount of money had been stolen.

"I came to the bank early this morning to catch up on the bookwork. I was just about to unlock the front door, when it flew open, almost knocking me down. Five men were involved, and they looked quite young to me, though scarves were covering their faces, and their hats were pulled down. As they were leaving, I rushed inside the bank. The safe was open, and the money sack holding over $10,000.00 was missing. When I ran outside, they were already on their horses, heading out of town fast."

Kathleen was in the crowd outside the bank, when the sheriff came out, and began asking questions. Surely Tim would not have done such a thing, but she felt he might have been involved; whenever she saw Tim lately, he turned away. She knew he did not want to hear her concerns about his lifestyle, or his choice of friends. What she didn't know, was that he couldn't face her, knowing how unhappy he was making her. He did love her, but there was a streak of rebellion in Tim he could not seem to control.

The sheriff broke into her thoughts, "Ma'am, I'm sorry to bother you. I was wondering, do you know where your oldest son is this morning, is he at home? If he is, I would like to talk to him."

She wished she could say yes to both questions, but she couldn't. "I'm sorry sheriff; Tim has not been staying home for a number of weeks; I wish I could tell you where he is, but I honestly don't know." Tears started to form in her eyes, but she fought them back.

The lawman felt sorry for her, he knew how hard it was on loved ones when a family member stepped outside the law. He also knew she was a good woman, and that more than a son gone bad, was wrong in the McGinnis family. He wished there was a way he could help her, but he had a duty to perform. "Well, I'm sorry to say this, Mrs. McGinnis, but I'm pretty sure your son was one of the robbers."

As Kathleen turned away, she prayed "Oh Father, only you can make a difference in Timothy's life. I give him to you; bring him into your kingdom somehow. Do what ever it takes for that to happen."

Wending her way home, thoughts of Tim when he was a darling little boy, filled her mind; he was their firstborn, a beautiful baby. She remembered when she first held him in her arms; he had won her heart at that moment, so many years ago. His curly dark brown hair and blue eyes; his first smile, she recalled with a mother's love. Now he was in trouble, and her heart cried for this willful son. That night she and Paddy talked for hours about Tim, as well as the future for the rest of the family.

Everyone who traveled west together with the wagon train had been informed it was time to continue their journey, but because Paddy and Kathleen no longer had their wagon and livestock, they could not travel with the wagon train, and must decide where to go and what to do. Paddy suggested they go by stagecoach to Silver City, "There be lots of work in the mines there," her husband suggested.

"Paddy, I don't want to go so far away, what if Tim comes back? He would not know where we were", she told her husband, but in her mind she knew they had to do something. Kathleen was concerned that if they went to the mining town, her husband would start gambling and drinking again, and she told him so.

"Oh darlin', I promise ye, I will never be doing that again. I will never go into another saloon again, never. I've learned me lesson, I have, and as far as Tim is concerned, he told me last week he and Johnnie were headin' south. Kathleen, you knew he would never have stolen anything, he's smarter than that". Paddy continued reassuring his wife that he would never go back to drinking and gambling. "We can leave word with Mrs. Fern, and at the mercantile, she can tell Tim where we have gone." She finally agreed to go to Silver City, and was glad she had set money aside.

The next morning, Kathleen told Edna Fern they were leaving, and where they were going. "Oh my dear, what shall I do without you, your sewing is so beautiful! Your work will be missed by my customers, they have all been delighted with your work, and they will be sorry you've gone. I shall write a letter 'To whom it may concern', recommending you as a first class seamstress should you want to sew again. I also want to give you a much-deserved bonus to help you with your move." Kathleen smiled to herself, thanking God.

The two women hugged, and Kathleen thanked her friend for the sewing work she had provided, and for the extra money. They parted with Mrs. Fern assuring her that if Timothy should come back to Santa Fe, she would tell him where to find them.

"God bless you and your family," Mrs. Fern said, then she gave Kathleen a final hug as she handed her the recommendation letter, and the bonus money.

Michael, on one hand, was really excited about going to the town he had heard about; but on the other hand, it meant he would be leaving Tommy. They had become close friends, and he knew he would miss him. Yet he could hear the echoes of Scotty's tales swirling around in his head. He didn't see any danger; he only experienced the feeling of excitement. He wondered if he would ever see the old prospector again, leaving a week before, Scotty said he would be back, and did not mention going to Silver City.

Love Comes in Many Colors

The family was busy the following week. They packed their trunk, and bought two valises. When buying the stagecoach tickets, they learned that for a small price, the trunk could be strapped on top of the coach, and Kathleen's mother's chair tied to the back. Kathleen was glad she could take all their belongings, including her mother's dishes and the chair, both of which meant so much to her.

When they were in the midst of packing and getting ready to leave, Kathleen heard Julian Vester was extremely ill. Dropping everything, she rushed to the Vester's living quarters. When she knocked on the door, a tired and distraught Thelma opened it

"Thelma, I just heard Julian is very ill, can I help?" Thelma started to cry as Kathleen stepped inside and put her arms around the weeping woman.

"I'm so afraid," the woman said. "The doctor was just here and he told me Julian has only a few hours to live. He had a bad cold, and would not be careful of overdoing; and the cold turned into pneumonia, and now he's dying. What shall I do, I'm so afraid! I'm too old to start out on my own. Where will I go? What can I do?" She was becoming hysterical!

With her arms around the woman, Kathleen told her, "You will not be abandoned, we will see you have a place to live; you will be taken care of." Then she asked, "Thelma, may I see Julian? I would like to pray for him, as well as you."

The older woman seemed to want that, so she led Kathleen into the bedroom. The man looked so old and sick, and he appeared to be sleeping. His wife beckoned Kathleen to his bedside, and as she moved nearer, he opened his eyes. Taking hold of Julian's hand, Kathleen bent near to him, smiled and then bowed her head. She began to pray, "Our Heavenly Father, Julian is so ill. He and Thelma need to know how much you love them." She then spoke to the dying man and said, "My friend, I hope you have accepted Jesus Christ as your savior."

With great difficulty Julian shook his head no, so she continued, "Would you like to become a child of God? If so, do you confess that you have sinned, and want God's forgiveness? Do you desire to accept Christ as your personal savior?"

It was obvious Julian was very close to death. He was trying to speak, and the woman leaned closer as he faintly whispered "yes". At the same time, from behind her,

Kathleen heard Thelma, as she echoed her husband's final word, "yes".

Kathleen then prayed, "Oh, Father, you know and love both Julian and Thelma, and we thank you that you have welcomed them into your fold." She tenderly held each of them by the hand and said, "Oh how happy our Heavenly Father is. You now belong to Him, and your sins have all been forgiven; you are His forever. Someday we will all be together in his Kingdom."

Then, this man, who was so unbending in life, smiled gently, closed his eyes, and within a few seconds, his breathing stopped, and he was gone. Thelma whimpered, and Kathleen turned to embrace her. A whole new life was beginning for the widow, for the old was gone, and all things had been made new within her. The young woman said to the grieving woman, "We are here with you and will not leave you alone."

The McGinnis family was to leave for Silver City by stagecoach in three days, but Kathleen was determined to follow through on her promise that Thelma would not be left alone, and that night she stayed with her.

After Julian's funeral the next day, Richard and Eve went to see Thelma about her future. "We would like you to come live with us. Eve did not have a mother growing up, and she really wants to have you with us, and so do I. Won't you accept us as your family? We would be honored to have you as a part of our lives," Richard said.

Their offer touched Thelma deeply, and after spending some time considering it, she answered yes. She was amazed at the changes that had taken place during the past twenty-four hours. She had always been so lonely, and now she was wanted; about to become part of a family. Not only did the circumstances of her life change, but with the decision to turn her life over to God, she became a new person. She felt so peaceful within.

When the rest of the group that worshiped and prayed together heard about the conversions of Thelma and Julian, and that Thelma was going to be with Richard and Eve, they were happy for these friends they had shared their lives with for so long. They all joined together, clapped their hands, and hugged the new family of three. And so that day, Thelma not only became a mother figure for Eve, but would eventually become a grandmother to the Smith family.

Then Richard informed everyone they had decided they would also soon be leaving for Silver City. "Both Eve and I feel that is where the Lord is leading us." Thelma was so thankful to be part of their lives that she would gladly go wherever they went.

The night before they were to leave Santa Fe, the McGinnis family enjoyed supper with their close friends. It was a good evening, but there was also sadness.

Kathleen was happy that the Smith's, with Thelma, would soon join them in Silver City, but she would miss Jeannie, who was like the sister she had never had. The Cobb's had other plans, and would travel south along the Rio Grande. They had heard there was good farming in several areas near the river. Kathleen and Jeannie promised they would keep in touch through frequent letters.

After supper, they all stood in a circle holding hands. Richard began reciting the
Twenty-Third Psalm with the others joining in.

"The Lord is my shepherd, I shall not want. He maketh me to lie down in green pastures: he leadeth me beside still waters. He restoreth my soul: he leadeth me in the paths of righteousness for his names sake."

As the friends stood speaking to the Lord, they were deeply bonded in their friendship through Christ. Only Paddy felt uncomfortable, but he said nothing.

Before falling asleep that night, Kathleen found herself praising and loving God. His astonishing love touched her with so much love. She was His, forever.

The following day the McGinnis family arrived at the stagecoach station early. Molly was excited, and kept bobbing up and down, her long dark red curls doing the same. She was going to ride on the stagecoach that had just arrived in a swirl of dust that filtered down over everyone gathered to say good-bye.

Tommy was there, freckles and all. Both boys had dreaded the day, and it had arrived, much too quickly. They had become the closest of friends during the few months since Michael's arrival in Santa Fe on the wagon train. They had both matured in that short time with their bodies now taller, manhood just around the corner. But today, today they were just two boys, feeling the pain of being separated from a best friend. They planned to write, but each knew in their hearts that the closeness they had shared would never be the same again.

While everyone stood talking, one by one the women hugged their friend Kathleen, all sorry to see her leave. The men stood to one side, talking about their future plans and saying good-bye to Paddy.

The stagecoach driver and the man riding shotgun on the trip came out of the station. Cat Cook, the driver, went over to Molly, and with a grin said, "Well little miss, are you ready to go?"

Molly, a combination of delight and shyness nodded her head. The man lifted her into the stage as her father winked at her. Now that he was no longer drinking, her crying had turned to happy laughter. Meanwhile, her ma's heart ached for Timothy, the son who should be leaving with them. There had been no word about him or the crowd he'd left town with. She hadn't brought up Tim's name of late, for she knew Paddy was worried about him, although he would probably never admit it.

"Your turn, it is, me bonnie," her husband said to his wife. He took her hand as she gathered up her skirt with the other one, and helped her into the stagecoach, Paddy following her. Michael was the last of the family to get in. His mother moved to the far door, and helped Paddy settle Molly between them. Michael sat across the way, facing his ma.

A tall, stately, grey-haired man came out of the station, followed by Ted Spencer, the gambler. Kathleen took in a sharp breath. She had literally bumped into the gambler just after arriving in Santa Fe, and had again encountered him when he came to get the wagon and livestock he had won from Paddy in a poker game.

Her husband scowled and said, "Is it him, going with us now?"

The whole feeling within the coach changed as everyone in the McGinnis family recognized the gambler and remembered how much trouble he had caused them. The older man climbed in and sat beside Michael. The gambler, who Kathleen detested, followed. Before anything could be said, the stage leapt forward and left as it had arrived – in a cloud of dust. All their friends were left waiving good-bye.

Ted Spencer promptly pulled his hat down over his eyes, and as the stagecoach settled into a rocking, gentle speed, he fell asleep. He had stayed up late into the night playing poker, and had little sleep. Among his acquaintances as a professional gambler he seldom had close friends, he was known as Spencer. Most men stayed clear of him except while at the bar having a drink, or at the poker tables. He was a handsome man, and today he was dressed in an impeccable grey suit with a white shirt and black cravat. His hat matched his suit perfectly. The man was a smooth talker, but few trusted him, and there were rumors he could be brutal if crossed. He always wore a gun holstered under his coat out of sight. He rarely used it, but there had been times when he'd needed it. Many thought he cheated at cards, though no one in Santa Fe had caught him doing so.

When the gambler woke, he kept his hat down over his closed eyes. His thoughts were on Paddy's wife, he was sure he had never seen a lovelier woman. Though married and with children, there was an air of innocence about her. He had thought of her many times since seeing her in Santa Fe. He never thought he would see her again after winning their belongings, but while inside the stagecoach station he heard that she and her family were also heading to Silver City. He began to imagine her beside him, and a plan began to form in his mind. If she became his wife, her beauty and gracefulness would help him achieve a level of respectability in Silver City, which he yearned to have. He had visions of doing well there, and planned to build a large, impressive house. And she would be his. The fact she was already married did not pose a problem, he considered her husband stupid, and when the time came, he would take care of Patrick McGinnis. The children could always be sent east to school.

It was a warm April day, comfortably so, as they traveled south. A pleasant trip, but one marred for Kathleen and Paddy by the presence of the gambler. Kathleen hoped she would never have to see him again after he had taken away their belongings, and the loss of Mr. Grey, Paddy's horse, especially bothered her. While still on their farm, they had bought the beautiful stallion from a man traveling east. Her relationship with the horse had been so special; she remembered how he nuzzled her hand when she touched the side of his face. She missed him very much, and wondered what had become of him.

During the time the gambler slept, the older man introduced himself. "My name is Charles Stevens. Where are you folks going, and where have you come from?"

Paddy spoke about their farm in Ohio, and their plans to go to Silver City, then asked, "What about you, sir?"

"I've been east on a business trip," the man said, "And am on my home to El Paso and my family; it's been a long three months, and I'm really anxious to see them." He turned to Molly. I've a granddaughter just about your age young lady." It was very obvious the man loved children by the way he smiled at her.

"You say you are heading for Silver City, do you know anything about the area?"

Paddy had to admit he knew little, except for the fact silver was being mined there. "That's where I hope to get work," he said.

"Well, from what I've been hearing, that certainly is a possibility. There's a lot of silver being mined in the area." Mr. Stevens said. Then he went on to tell them about the town and the surrounding area.

"The town is growing rapidly, and is now the seat of Grant County. You can buy nearly everything you were finding in Santa Fe, though the town is not as large. The country surrounding the town is very diverse; to the south are hilly grasslands that quickly lead to the desert floor. Just over the mountain, west of town is 'chloride flats', where the Legal Tender mine is located; actually, there are two large mines in the area. Beyond that are hills and valleys that bring you to the Gila River and not far beyond the river is the Continental Divide. North and east of town, the elevation starts rising, and there are forested mountains with streams. That area is filled with an abundance of game, including bear, cougar, fox, deer, elk, and beaver; plus many fowl, one of which is the turkey; the whole area is very beautiful. There is one serious problem, though. Each spring the young Apache braves break out of the reservation in Arizona to make raids into these southwestern mountains, which are a part of the lower tip of the Rocky Mountains.

Kathleen had never given much thought to the Indian's plight; however, the idea of having to face Indians in Silver City frightened her, for her family's sake.

Mr. Stevens went on to say, "I have heard that Washington believes that the silver being mined in the area is good for the country, so they are sending more soldiers for protection. It remains to be seen if they will be of much help."

All Kathleen could think of was the whitened crosses they had seen along the trail so many months ago. She shuddered just thinking of them.

The morning grew warmer, as Molly slept across her ma's lap. Michael's thoughts went from Indians to bears, turkeys, and lizards. Ohio was so different from the arid land they were traveling through, there was little to see but flat land broken up by mountains along the river. It was uncomfortable being bounced around. Everyone had quieted down, either drowsing or staring out the windows as the land rolled by.

Around noon, the coach came to a sudden stop. Dust was everywhere! Some drifted through the open windows causing everyone to cough and struggle to breathe.

The driver stuck his head in and said, "Time to eat," to no one in particular. The travelers could see they had stopped beside a small, square adobe building, and they assumed it was the way station the driver had spoken of earlier. Quickly, before anyone else had a chance to move, Ted Spencer stepped out and went around to the side of the coach where Kathleen was sitting. He opened the door and offered her his hand to help her down. She was startled by his offer, but not knowing what else to do, she reluctantly gave him her hand and stepped out, Ted dropping his hand as soon as her feet touched the ground. As she turned her head toward her husband, she saw the anger on his face as he grabbed Molly, and stepped out the other side. Kathleen decided, for the rest of the trip, she would make sure she wasn't sitting next to a door, and that Paddy would get out ahead of her so he would be the one to help her down from the coach. She hurried around and gave one hand to Paddy, and one to Molly, looking toward several horses tied to a hitching rail some distance from where the stage had stopped.

"Oh look, Paddy," she said. "I can barely see it, but the horse tied on the far side reminds me of Mr. Grey!" As she was saying that, Molly twisted her hand out of her ma's and ran toward a large, mangy-looking brown dog, lying beside the door of the building. The dog rose to its feet, the hair on it's back standing up, and the dog began to growl, which quickly turned to a snarl. "No, no, me darlin'," Paddy said, as he snatched her up into his arms. "This dog is not our 'Old Tom' on the farm. We must be leaving him alone."

The dog had frightened Molly who started crying and clinging to her pa; both her mother and brother came running. All was confusion for a few minutes, with everyone distracted by the near disaster of the barking dog and the crying child. No one paid any attention when the distant horse began to whinny. Mr. Grey watched as his family turned away to join the rest of the travelers, and then disappeared into the small buildings.

Once inside, Kathleen saw there were two rooms. In the first one, there were two long tables, the first one occupied by several men. One of them was heavyset with jowls, and long dirty, straggly, blond hair. He looked to be a cruel man. After finishing his second cup of coffee, and a piece of pie, he flipped a coin onto the table, and then walked out the door. While the people from the stagecoach were eating, they could hear some sort of commotion outside. Apparently, the man who had just left, and his horse were having some sort of disagreement, with the horse fighting, and the man swearing. From the sounds coming through the open door, the people could tell the man finally had his animal under control, and was riding southwest toward the distant mountains.

Mr. Grey was gone, and his family didn't even know he had been there. So close.

Lunch was over, and the travelers were hurried out to the waiting stage. From then on, the days seemed endless. They traveled south following the Rio Grande River, sometimes on the east side, sometimes on the west. Each day they stopped at way stations or forts to eat. At Fort Craig, soldiers traveled south with the coach until they felt the danger of Indians was past.

The countryside was boring, even the mountains were barren. At one point, they traveled through a very long and dry valley with few signs of civilization, except for one lonely way station. The days seemed to blend one into another. As they drew close to Fort Seldon, there were large cottonwood trees growing along the river, which was teeming with beaver. Michael enjoyed seeing something different.

At Fort Seldon they were told they had been traveling on the part of the road called, 'Jornada del Muerto,' which meant 'Road of Death,' that part of the road was called that because many times the Apaches killed anyone traveling, either direction, on that part of the road.

Everyone was relieved to know they had passed that part of the trip safely, and the chances of being attacked from here on to Las Cruces, were slight. Fort Seldon was not far from the small western town, where the family would change to the stagecoach that would take them to Silver City. And when they left the fort, there would be soldiers traveling until they reached the western town of Las Cruces.

This part of the country had enjoyed an unusually wet spring, which filled the river valley, with wildflowers. Usually the rains did not arrive until July each year.

As they traveled from the fort, the passengers on the coach were refreshed, in spirit, by the moving water, flowers, and green grasses, trees, and fields showing the green of spring. Everyone traveling felt better, and was glad the dry, hot winds were behind them, or so they thought.

When they arrived at Las Cruces, the stagecoach pulled up in front of the Amador Hotel; the streets were busy with the usual saloons, mercantile shops, and other small businesses. The day was coming to a close, and as the sun dropped lower and lower, mountains to the east came alive with colors of pinkish red, that turned swiftly to a deep reddish-purple glow, and then it was gone.

After the family freshened up in their rooms, they went downstairs to a nice restaurant. The men ate hungrily as well as Molly, but Kathleen was very tired, and ate lightly. She wanted to get out of her clothes, the long skirt and sleeves had made the heat difficult for her.

The following morning, after eating a quick breakfast, they said good-bye to Charles Stevens, who would be heading on south to El Paso, Texas, and then they boarded the stagecoach that would take them to their new home. When it was time to leave, the gambler was nowhere in sight, Kathleen sighed with relief. But just as the stagecoach was about to leave, he came rushing out of the hotel, and the woman's sigh of relief turned into a frown of disappointment. Now they would have to deal with the gambler all the way to Silver City. Since a soldier had boarded just before the gambler, it was going to be a tight fit again inside the coach. Just as she had planned on that first day of their ride south, Kathleen had managed to make sure she never again was in a position where the man could assist her when she was getting out of the coach; Paddy had always helped her out after that first day.

After crossing the river; they traveled west, going up out of the valley that ran alongside the river as it wended its way south. The terrain changed, and they found themselves in true desert land. The day started warm, and soon turned hot. The spring's winds had begun to blow, leaving a trail of dust swirling behind the lonely stagecoach. The wind blew all day; and at noon, because the dust was so strong, the passengers ate a packed lunch inside the coach to avoid the hot sun and incessant wind. The stagecoach made few brief stops, and passengers needing to get out, hurried back quickly. By late afternoon, they arrived at Fort Cummings. The fort had been abandoned by the military, but was used as an overnight stop by travelers going to California, Silver City, or other destinations to the west.

Jane and Russell Murray had been the caretakers for several years; and provided good food, clean comfortable overnight accommodations, and cheerful hospitality. The couple greeted everyone, and set about seeing to their needs. Kathleen and Jane liked each other immediately, and spent the evening talking while they cooked the meal, and later when they cleaned up. Molly flitted between her pa and Michael; enjoying being out of the coach, and having the freedom to run off some of her energy.

Before it got dark, Russell took everyone on a tour of the fort. Michael was amazed at the fort's high outside walls, they were ten feet thick, and provided a great deal of protection from invaders. The entire fort was a tribute to the men who had built it.

The evening went fast, and the McGinnis family was sad to see it end. It had been some time since they had been able to sit and talk to such amiable people.

Early the next morning; after a good breakfast, the travelers climbed back into the stagecoach, and again headed toward Silver City. This could possibly be the most dangerous day of the trip. The road would take them through a narrow canyon, past Cook's Peak. At the top of the peak, a gold mine was in operation, and many of the men working in the mine were ex-prisoners. In addition, the miners often stole from travelers passing through the canyon; many people had been robbed, and often killed. Others were killed by Indians. Everyone was on edge as they entered the canyon, however, they encountered no trouble, and as they exited the canyon, everyone gave a sigh of relief, including the driver and the man riding shotgun. They, more than anyone else, knew the danger in the area.

The stagecoach crossed the Mimbres River, passed by a closed copper mine, and then turned west as they drew closer to their destination. The land changed at this higher elevation, and became hilly, covered with cottonwoods, pinon, and scrub oak trees. There were areas filled with wild sunflower bushes, and the yucca plants Mr. Stevens had mentioned. The yuccas reached high into the sky with ivory-white blossoms spiraling upward along the stems. The blossoms were striking against the backdrop of the higher mountains to the north.

The day was fading as they moved westward toward Silver City; everyone was fascinated by the beauty of the land, as well as the sky that was ablaze with vibrant colors that danced around lazy clouds.

Before they knew it, the stagecoach was in Silver City. It arrived on Main Street, and soon pulled up in front of the 'Newton Hotel'. It was late afternoon, and the stamp mills were pounding, pounding. The ruckus caused by the teamsters, eager to get the wagons and mules put away for the night, was unbelievable. It seemed like every mule was braying. All the saloons were going full tilt, and their honky-tonk music was rudely invading the evening air. The combination of the noises was overwhelming. While Kathleen wanted to cover her ears, the men and boy in the coach were enjoying the bedlam.

As the passengers alighted from the stagecoach, the driver recommended the hotel as the best in town. After getting all their belongings, the McGinnis family stepped into the establishment. Once the door closed behind them, the outside noise diminished substantially. The lobby was quaint and quiet, filled with gleaming oak furniture and overstuffed chairs. Behind the counter, a bald man with gold-framed glasses greeted the newly-arrived passengers. He agreed to keep the family's extra belongings in the back room, and gave them two rooms, one for Paddy and Michael, and the other for Kathleen and Molly. With the keys in hand, the family walked up a wide, oak staircase to their rooms on the second floor.

After cleaning up, they met, and went down to the hotel's restaurant. Everyone was famished. As they stepped into the dining room, Kathleen saw Ted Spencer sitting at the far table, when he saw her, he nodded his head. She feared this man as well as having a deep dislike for him, and quickly turned her head away. She sat down at the nearest available table that was the farthest away from him, and made sure she had her back turned in that direction. She began talking to Molly while thinking how shameless the man was. The fact she was married, had a family, and was a respectable woman who did not encourage, or appreciate his attentions, appeared to make no difference to him.

The trip that day had been exhausting, and after the meal, the family retired for the night. They fell asleep quickly, despite the muffled sounds coming from the saloons.

Chapter 5

The trail was dusty as the man, horse, and dog traveled through another canyon in the mountains east of the plains of San Augustine. There were no breezes in the deep divide, and even the pine trees were struggling with the dry heat.

Ezra Bowlin was riding to meet Chad and Cole Masters near the head of the Mimbres River. The man had met the brothers in Las Vegas, in the territory of New Mexico, east of Santa Fe. Chad had heard bars of silver were being shipped out of Silver City, taken by wagon to meet the railroad; from there the silver would be shipped east.

Chad knew the route the wagons would follow, and the three men agreed it would be a simple task to waylay one of the shipments, and get away with enough bars of silver to keep the three of them in money for a very long time.

On his way west, Ezra stopped in Santa Fe, and found a hostler, he also needed a better horse; one with speed and endurance. He found just the horse he wanted, and he was a beauty; the steal-dust stallion suited his needs perfectly. After a bit of wrangling to get the horse for the price he wanted to pay, the horse was his. He rode away satisfied; the horse was fast and sure footed, and had endurance that would be needed to make his getaway.

The day was waning, and after the hot, dusty day, Ezra was ready to stop for the night. He rode into a side canyon, where a small stream was burbling down over rocks.

He looked around and saw plenty of dead fallen branches under the trees for a fire; there was a small patch of grass where the horse could graze. There were no signs of other fires, and he felt it would be a relatively safe place to spend the night.

After getting off the horse, he uncinched the saddle and removed it along with the blanket. He checked the horse's mouth, and as he suspected it was full of dust. He removed the bridle and replaced it with a loosely tied rope around the horse's neck, then led the horse over to the fresh, cool water where it, gratefully drank deeply. The man was cruel, but never to his horse, as he knew his life might one day depend on the animal's loyalty.

While the grey horse drank, the man moved upstream to drink and splash his face in the cool, refreshing, mountain stream. After washing his face, he knelt to cup some water in his hand to drink. He heard the rattle too late, and a coiled mountain rattler struck him in the neck. The man grabbed at his neck, knowing full well what had happened, but it was too late. As the snake moved away, the man fell head first into the stream. He had no chance at all of coming out alive as the venom had gone straight to his heart. As his life drained away, his long, dirty blond hair floated in the water.

The horse, seeing what had happened, moved back from the water, watching the motionless man lying with his head in the stream. He was uncertain, not knowing what was expected of him, as this was not usual behavior, based on the people he had been around. He bobbed his head up and down, pounding his hoofs in the dirt, but the man did not move. The horse, with the dog following, turned away. It walked a short distance,

and then stopped to look back at the still-unmoving man. The dog wandered off looking for food, but the horse waited through the long night expecting the man to get up in the morning. When morning came, and the man still did not move, the horse left. A vague, long-ago memory of freedom came to the animal, and it sensed it was now free again. The horse moved along the trail he had taken with the man, and later came to a meadow that had a small river running through it. The morning was cool, the grass and fresh water looked inviting, and the stallion stopped to graze, drink and rest.

As the days moved on, the horse drifted southwest. When going through a stand of evergreen trees and tall, thick bushes, the rope, still around his neck, caught on a branch; it broke and fell away. As he lost this last connection with men, the horse realized he was free and on his own. But he had become used to having a man own him and take care of him; it would take time for him to adjust to this new situation.

The ranch lay in an area, sprinkled with meadows and rolling hills, with a stream flowing across the land. Pinon, Juniper, and Scrub Oak trees covered the surrounding landscape. Rich gamma grass grew in the fields, and the horses were flourishing on the rich nourishment the grass supplied. The ranch was located among the southwestern mountains of the New Mexico Territory; a good area for a horse ranch.

Many evenings during spring and summer, when the sun lowered in the western sky, the sunsets spun themselves out over the land and nearby mountains, surrounding the ranch. The clouds often intertwined with the rich colors, transforming the entire area with mystical beauty. This evenings' array of color was an extraordinary display, covering the sky from east to west.

Before going into the ranch house, the two men paused to watch the vivid scene. As the sun fell further toward the horizon, the colors changed from brilliant to muted velvet. Darkness crept over the hills, leaving the valley with a suggestion of light, which brought with it a chill in the air. Those sunsets were always a perfect way to end the day after long hours of work – seeing the beauty of Gods' creation, was their reward.

The partners were bone tired; it had been a busy day. After a hearty meal served by their cook, Maria, the two sat in front of a roaring blaze in the fireplace.; the warmth felt good, as had the opportunity to relax. What brought them to this time and place started years before when, fighting side by side in the War Between the States, they learned to respect and trust each other. The bond between them had grown strong. The horrors of the war were etched in both their lives; they understood each other, feeling more like brothers than friends. At the end of the carnage of war, they found work in Texas on the Bar-H horse ranch, owned by John Hazlet. There, the two men learned about the raising and handling of horses, where they came to a shared love of the remarkable animals.

After a number of years, they headed west and ended up in the mountains near Pinos Altos, where they spent several months placer mining. It was a tumultuous time, but successful. They found enough gold to start their ranch not too far from where they had done the mining. The summers in the high mountain areas were dangerous, for the Apaches had attacked several times. They had survived it all, and now they had their own place. Their ranch sat a little north of Silver City, a thriving community resulting from the large amount of silver found in the hills west of town.

The partners had proved their claim to the land by digging a well, putting up a building, and meeting the other requirements for homesteading. They gained title in Santa Fe, and now owned their own horse ranch – the result of years of hard work.

While relaxing, they discussed the day's work and what needed doing the next day. Aaron McGinnis, now called Mac because of his last name, suggested he should take time the following morning to go into town for supplies.

"We'll need to stock up on more ammunition; it won't be long before the Indians will be back in the area. Also, I ordered those young peach saplings, and we need seed for the vegetable garden. I'll check with Maria to see what she needs and pick them up for her."

So it was settled; both men fell silent, each deep in his own thoughts. Mac's thoughts went back to his youth. He had not thought of it for a long time, but there was always that nagging concern for Kathleen; he had never stopped loving her. So many years had passed since he had seen her, or any of the rest of his family.

His family, Irish immigrants had settled on rich farmland in Ohio. The McGinnis and O'Hare farms adjoined, and the families generally spent Christmas together, celebrating the birth of Christ as well as meeting on Easter, and usually Saturday nights, or whenever they had free time. There common love of their fatherland was shown through their times of singing and dancing; Mac cherished his memories of those evenings.

He recalled his older brother Paddy's splendid tenor voice, carrying over everyone else's singing. His brother was a true Irish lad and full of blarney. Being quiet, reflective, and shy, Mac had always been overshadowed by his outgoing brother. The differences in the two of them were especially evident when it came to Kathleen. She and Mac, then known as Aaron, were very much alike. During their growing up years, they had spent many hours talking abut life, books, and poetry; they had been the best of friends. Often, when they were deep in conversation, Paddy would make some silly remark, always wanting to be the center of attention. Although Mac never said anything, this had always irked him.

As the years moved on, Kathleen changed from a gangly, freckle-faced girl to a beautiful young woman. Her braids gave way to long, flowing chestnut brown hair that crouched comfortably down over her shoulders. Her large beautiful green eyes showed her gentle, loving nature. He had come to love her, but unfortunately, she had chosen his brother to marry; he had always wondered why she chose Paddy over him. His brother was unpredictable, one never knowing what he might do or say next. In contrast, Kathleen had been a gentle and kind girl.

He left shortly after their first son, Timothy was born. Finally he could no longer watch; so he left home to fight in the Civil War. When it was over, he'd written them from Texas, receiving back a letter written by Kathleen. No further letters were sent or received.

His partner, Pete Walker, was busy wrapped up in his own thoughts of the wild steel-dust grey stallion he had seen just two days ago when he was out hunting. It was alone, no mares nearby. He wasn't sure what that meant, but he had decided he would try to catch the horse. He had tried talking to it and it had hesitated before it galloped away. He realized it had been around people, but why it was alone was a mystery. He would make a search for it when he had time, and see if he could find any answers.

After a while, his thoughts turned to his mother. As a child, he had loved her dearly. As he grew older, his love deepened, and he began to see and appreciate what a kind, thoughtful person she was. She had lived her faith, and always thought of others first. Widowed early, she had worked hard to keep him in clothes and provide enough food. He had been her only child, and before he was sixteen, she died of consumption, leaving him alone. He had worked for a farmer who had been injured, and learned much there. When he joined the union army, he thought he was prepared for what lay ahead, but it was a very difficult time. The faith his mother had passed on to him had gotten him through the war.

Deciding to be Mac's partner had been a good decision. They were very much alike, and through their years together during the war, had built a strong friendship.

In the silence of the room a hard rapping on the door jarred both men out of their memories. Mac jumped up and opened the door. There stood Ben Stellar, their foreman, hat in hand.

"I was in town, and jus t as I was leaving I heard gunshots coming from Main Street. I'm thinking the Apaches could be back in the area because there was so much shooting. I hurried back here and told the men to get their guns and spread out around the buildings."

Both men buckled their gun belts around their waists, and grabbed their rifles as they ran out into the night, aware their horse ranch could well be the target of an Indian raid. They took positions where they could see anyone approaching, and waited. After several hours, they split the men into several watches just in case there was trouble later in the night, but all stayed quiet.

Love Comes in Many Colors

After breakfast the next morning, Mac hitched old Joey to the buckboard and headed to town. When he stepped into Hanson's General Store, he asked George, the proprietor, about all the shooting the night before.

"Well." The man answered, "A big argument started at the Silver Dollar Saloon, the fight moved outside, and before it was over, four men, including Tom Withers, was dead, and two more badly injured. Yesterday a group of strangers arrived in town, and I guess they're the ones that started the whole shebang. One of 'em accused Withers of cheatin' at cards, and before anyone knew what was happenin' it was all over with Tom dead, shot full of holes. The fella that shot him grabbed the money off the table and ran out to his horse. Then some of Tom's friends ran outside after the killer and was shot by the other strangers who jumped in their saddles and headed out toward the Burro Mountains. Sheriff Delaney 'n his deputy took off after them, ain't heard nothin' since. This town's really turnin' mean these days. I suppose that's what happens when mines start showin' rich ore. Used to be a nice town before that, except for the Injuns. Once the mines began overflowin' with silver, all the riffraff started coming to town, too bad."

The rancher was relieved in one way, that it wasn't Indians, but felt bad about Tom and the others who were shot by the strangers. He was also concerned about the many bad characters being drawn to town. These days, Silver City had dangers lurking in every saloon. With a loaded wagon, Mac headed back to the 'Pine Tree' ranch. It had been named for the tall pines north of their property.

Mac took Maria's supplies into the house and finished unloading the wagon. The ammunition was stashed away where it could be gotten to in a hurry. Then he put the small peach saplings and vegetable seeds in a large wooden wheelbarrow, and headed for the prepared garden area, and the spot he had selected for the orchard. He started by planting the young trees in several straight rows, then he put the vegetable seeds in rows in between the trees. The stream flowed nearby, and would be used for watering. He took time to fix the place alongside the stream that he could open up, allowing the water to flow into a channel that would water the whole area.

He had enjoyed working by himself, and it had been a good day. He felt a great deal of satisfaction from working with the earth. After all, farming was in his blood. By the time he was finished, muscles he hadn't used in a long time were complaining. He looked toward the snow apple trees he had planted a couple of years before, and saw they were coming into bloom. In his mind, he saw the orchard with all the trees fully grown and providing fruit for the ranch and others.

Mac was a tall, strong man; his skin was very tan, which enhanced the dark, red hair inherited from his ma. His face showed both strength of character and kindness. For the most part, he was quiet and gentle; but looking at him closely, one could also see a man of resolve, a man to be trusted. That night before sleep came; he laid thinking about Kathleen, wishing he could share all he had with her.

The next morning the partners were busy working with the horses when their neighbor, Fred Jackson, rode up. Staying on his horse he said, "Well, the Apaches are back. Several days ago they hit the Darcy's horse ranch this side of the Mogollon Rim. I know it's some distance west but you can bet it won't be long before they get here. They came from the reservation in Arizona and I heard they killed everyone but the youngest son, he was hidden in the large haystack, and the Indians left it unburned. Another family in the area took the boy to raise; at least he'll have a home. It's a dirty shame the things those braves do, looks like we're in for another hard year." The men talked awhile, and then Fred tipped his hat and headed for his place.

The Indians were back! Everyone in town and in the surrounding areas was worried and fearful as they all knew the danger they could be facing. There were no fortified places in town to go for protection. The outlying farms and ranches were on their own with each family preparing to protect themselves; sometimes they could, but sometimes they couldn't. The Indians killed without remorse: ranchers, travelers, anyone they came upon. Besides taking horses, they stole or killed cattle and other animals.

Although more soldiers had been sent to Silver City, there was not enough of them to cover the town as well as all the farms and ranches. And by the time they heard of attacks on the farms and ranches, it was too late.

Everyone began preparing for another difficult and dangerous spring.

Chapter 6

Golden fingers of sunlight stretched across the room, falling across Michael's face rousing him. When he turned to look at his pa, he saw that he had left, so the boy laid back into the warm covers, indulging himself in the quietness. It felt good to peacefully lie there, just to be alone; a rare occurrence these days.

After a few minutes with no sound coming from the next room where his ma and sister spent the night, he got out of bed quickly, fearing he would be the last one up. He went to the washbowl and cleaned up, then put on his pants, shoes, and socks. Before putting on his shirt, he went to the large mirror to comb his hair. What he saw surprised him; the face looking back at him showed few signs of childhood. His body, especially his chest, shoulders and arms were surprisingly covered with muscles, more like those of a young man than that of a boy. He had not realized he was growing up so quickly, although his shirts had gotten too small; so before they came south, his ma made him some new ones. Well, there was no time to think of that; he finished dressing, and then slipped quietly out the door, not wanting to wake his mother and sister, if they were still sleeping.

As Michael started down the stairs, he spotted his pa talking to a stranger. "I have a house a little north of town and it's empty. It's a nice house, but is in need of a lot of repairs; the last people pretty much wrecked it! If you're interested in renting it, and are willing to do the repairs, I'll lower the rent for you. I've been called out of town unexpectedly for at least two months, so I have no time to do the work myself. I'd rather have you take care of it and lower the rent, than leave it empty all that time.

Paddy was eager to see the house, especially since he and his family would have to stay at the hotel until they found something. A day or two more would take too much of their small supply of money.

At breakfast, Paddy McGinnis told his family about the house, and the generous terms the owner, Rupert Bascom, had offered. Everyone was excited, and wanted to see the house; so after breakfast, following the directions Mr. Bascom had provided, the family walked north of town until they spotted a house that matched the description Paddy had received. It sat quite a distance north of town.

The instant they saw the house, they knew it was the house for them. Although it was badly in need of a white-washing job, it was a nice size. But the best thing about the outside of the house was a yellow climbing rose that covered the roof of the porch that was just coming into bloom. Kathleen's face filled with wonder and delight as she reached out and picked a rose from a lower stem; to her, they were home.

Paddy unlocked the door, and they stepped inside. The house had been badly mistreated; the inside walls were as dismal as those outside. The house was filled with debris, doors hanging ajar, and many windows were cracked or broken. But none of that took away their excitement. In the parlor was a sad, old and tired looking divan, covered with dirt, and an overstuffed chair in the same condition. Kathleen knew she could clean the furniture, and make it look new with some new covers. In one corner of the room was a table and chairs; some of the chairs had broken rungs, something Paddy knew he could repair.

The kitchen, though dirty, was a joy to Kathleen. It had an inside pump in the sink, plenty of cupboards, a cooler open partly to the underside of the house, a screen to keep creatures away, which would keep fresh food from spoiling. There was also a wood heating and cooking stove, with a well for heating water, plus a working table with two chairs. It was a better kitchen than she'd had on the farm. The rest of the house consisted of two bedrooms and a sleeping porch. There was much work to be done, but that did not bother any of them. Paddy was really good working with wood, and making repairs. Kathleen knew how to clean, and loved sewing and fixing up things. It would be a good place to live.

They went out the back door and found an outhouse, plus a chicken coop. The yard had cottonwood trees along a small stream. Paddy found a nice spot in the sun where he would be able to have a vegetable garden. It was a perfect place; both Kathleen and Paddy could see in their minds how it was going to look when they finished cleaning, white-washing, repairing, and planting.

Early that afternoon, all the arrangements were made with Mr. Bascom; he lowered the rent, gave them two keys, and said he would set up accounts for them at both Hanson's General Store and Hollowell's Lumber Yard for the materials they would need for repairs.

The family picked up some supplies and started working on the house right away. While Kathleen scrubbed the kitchen, Paddy and Michael started in the bedrooms. They took the thin mattresses off the beds, hung them over the clothesline in the back yard, and beat the dust out of them, and left them to air in the sun until evening. The next step was to wash the floors and fix the windows.

That very night they slept in the house, and from then on they worked hard to get everything clean and repaired. Kathleen planned to put fresh covers on the divan and chair, but knew that could wait until later.

After Paddy and Michael dug up the dirt in the back and planted the seeds for their vegetable garden, Paddy was free to look for work. He found a job at the Legal Tender Mine on the first day he looked. So they began life in their new home.

After his first day at work, Paddy came home all excited. He told Kathleen that he heard some men who had worked at the mine went prospecting on their own, found silver, and staked claims. They now had their own mines, and the silver they found belonged to them; he wanted to do the same thing. Kathleen saw it as a pipe dream, but her husband was sure he could make his own claim someday.

Kathleen did not believe he was being realistic, and felt a great deal of apprehension; she was silent, although she decided then and there she had best use the letter of reference Mrs. Fern had written for her and go looking for work. She had started worrying the moment their family arrived in Silver City, and she heard the racket coming from the town's saloons. She was concerned Paddy might start drinking and gambling again, although there had been no signs he was interested. Time would tell.

The next day, Kathleen put on one of her best dresses, left Molly with Michael, and walked into town. She entered a seamstress and tailoring shop where she was greeted by a man with silver-rimmed glasses and thinning light red hair. "Hello ma'am, my name is Mr. Walsh." She explained she was looking for work as a seamstress. "I did sewing in Santa Fe, and have a letter of recommendation from the woman I worked for while we were there."

She handed the letter to the man who took it hesitantly saying, "I don't know, I already have two ladies working for me." After opening and reading the letter, he looked up at the woman. "My employees are good at basic sewing, but I see you are an accomplished seamstress and come highly recommended. I can definitely use someone with your professional qualifications. I'll tell you what, I have a lady coming to the shop at ten o'clock tomorrow; she is very particular about her gowns. I would like you to meet her, and help her decide on the style and material for a new dress. If you can arrive earlier, at nine, I can familiarize you with the shop, and explain what I will want you to do before she gets here."

After Jules Walsh agreed that Kathleen could do much of the work at home, and told her what she would be paid, if he liked her work, and hired her permanently, Kathleen walked home feeling relieved. She knew she could please the man, so now she had work.

Again, leaving Molly with Michael the following morning, she arrived at the shop on time. Kathleen was excited at the prospect of sewing; for it was something she really loved doing.

Mr. Walsh met her as she came in the door, and pushing up his glasses, immediately began showing her where things were, and went into detail regarding his expectations from all who worked for him.

When Mr. Walsh's customer, Mrs. Williamson arrived; she and Kathleen spent the rest of the morning selecting a pattern and material for the gown. Mr. Walsh was pleased to see that his new employee made several suggestions, modifying the pattern so it would be especially suited to Mrs. Williamson. He told Kathleen to take home whatever was needed to make the dress; he was looking forward to seeing the finished item.

When Paddy arrived home from work that evening, his wife explained about the shop, and that Mr. Walsh had no problem with her working at home. She would be able to watch over Molly, and the house, the same as she had done in Santa Fe.

Paddy knew how happy his wife was when she was sewing, and also saw Kathleen's wages as a way to rebuild the savings he had depleted with his drinking and gambling.

A week later, the dress was finished, and Mrs. Williamson was delighted, really liking the dress. Kathleen was relieved, and felt she had passed a major test. Mr. Walsh stood by, beaming at both the happy women.

A few days later, Kathleen met with Mrs. Firth, and her daughter, Penny. The girl seemed to be very outgoing and happy. She needed three new dresses for the summer.

Once the dresses were finished, Mrs. Williamson and Mrs. Firth spread the word throughout Silver City about Mr. Walsh's new seamstress, and her exceptional sewing skills and talents. The demand for the dresses she was to sew grew quickly.

Kathleen was busy, and time went fast. It was already June first, and it was Michael's birthday. Kathleen planned to bake a cake for her son, and fry chicken for supper. She just needed to figure out a way to do it so it would be a surprise.

She finally came up with an excuse to get Michael and his sister out of the house. "Michael, I need some things from Hanson's mercantile, do you think you could take Molly with you when you go to the store so I can have some time to work on the dress I'm sewing?"

"Sure ma, I don't mind. Do you think we could go exploring in town before we get the supplies?" She told him she thought that was a good idea. "I'm in no hurry for the supplies. Just stay away from the saloons." He agreed, and then took Molly by the hand, and they left.

After they left, she quickly got all the ingredients out for the cake, and hurried as she measured and mixed. When the cake was done and cooled, she wrapped it in a clean cloth and put it in the cooler; she would fry the chicken later. Then Kathleen got busy doing some work on the dress she was making for one of Mr. Walsh's customers. It was a pretty, light-green color, with a white collar and cuffs, and was going to make a nice dress for the woman.

While their mother was busy, Michael and his sister, wandered around town; heading down Main Street, and looking in store windows. They walked past a braying mule tied to a wagon; the owner was busy filling the wagon with supplies. Next, they saw a twelve-horse team and a very large wagon. Men were carrying out heavy long boxes and placing them in the bed. Michael did not know the boxes were filled with 300-pound bars of silver. There were horses tied to hitching rails, and men and women of all sorts were walking to and fro. The sounds of the mills crushing the ore were extremely loud; it was a busy town.

They started north on Bullard Street, and were about to cross over a side street when a man riding a handsome, grey-brown dun horse stopped near them. He was holding a wiggly puppy in front of him on the saddle with one hand.

The man spoke to Michael. "Young man, I found this little pup along the trail coming into town and haven't been able to find its mother or owner. We have several dogs at our ranch, and really don't need another. Would you like to have him?"

When Michael looked at the fluffy, golden-colored puppy, he wanted it more than anything else. "Oh, yes sir." Michael said. "Can I really have him?"

"You bet," the man answered. "Here he is; he's all yours; I hope your folks won't mind." "Oh, I don't think so," the boy replied. "We always had dogs until we lift the farm to move out here." "Good", the man said as he handed the wiggly puppy to Michael. "Take good care of him, boy." "Thank you sir", Michael said. "I will."

The man tipped his hat, and rode off down the street. Mac was pleased he'd found a home for the young dog. Little did he realize he had given it to Kathleen and Paddy's second son, though he did think there was something a bit familiar about the boy; he gave it no more thought.

Now that they had the puppy, they went straight to Hanson's, getting the supplies for their ma. Then Michael decided they should go home; it was hard to carry the supplies, and hold onto the puppy at the same time. He more than had his hands full! Soon they were out of town enough that he could put the fluff ball down. To his surprise, it followed right at his heels, and once in a while jumped up and down barking as if to say, "I'm so glad I'm yours." He was such a friendly fella that Michael named him 'Friendly', "That's a perfect name for you isn't it Friendly?"

By the time they arrived home, Kathleen had put away the dress, and was cleaning the house. The minute she saw what was following Michael, she started to chuckle. "What a cute puppy, Michael! Wherever did you get him?" Michael and Molly both started talking. "Whoa," she said. "One at a time, please?" Michael let Molly tell about the man on the horse. When she finished, he filled in a few of the details. "He's a great birthday gift, ma, isn't he?" She agreed, and laughed. "Maybe we should call him Mr. Birthday. I'm only teasing", she said to her son. Then Michael, just to make sure it was okay, asked his ma if he could keep the puppy.

"Why of course you can", she replied. "We need a dog around here", she said with a grin. So it was settled, Friendly was his.

Dinner was ready, and Paddy was expected any minute; however, it soon became evident he would be late. Kathleen put the food to the back of the stove, where it would stay warm. She felt a tad bit of fear, but refused to give in to it. She told herself he had probably been delayed, and would be home soon. But after waiting another hour, she became concerned. "Where is he," she wondered.

When she heard her husband coming up the path singing at the top of his lungs, she knew right away he had been drinking. Her stomach started to turn, and fear took over. She quickly turned to Michael. "Get some food, and take Molly and Friendly to your room. Try to keep Friendly as quiet as you can, and above all, don't come out until I tell you to."

He understood, and moved quickly. As they left the kitchen, Kathleen heard Paddy coming through the front door. "Katie, Katie," he hollered. She steadied herself, and slipped into the parlor to meet him. "I'm here Paddy." She was so afraid; she could hardly hear her own voice. Instantly, her husband became enraged! "Has the cat got your tongue now?" He bellowed.

She became so frightened, she did not know exactly what to say. Finally she croaked out, "How about some supper Paddy, you must be hungry. He sat down at the table, and thinking it might appease him, she filled a plate with food. She tried to put it in front of him so he could eat, but he simply pushed it away. Then he thrust a partly full bottle of whisky toward her. "Pour me a drink," he shouted at her. Trembling, she took the bottle, and poured a glass half full. She started to hand it to him. "Here, I'll do it meself?" he growled. He grabbed the bottle out of her hand, and filled the glass so full that the liquor spilled over the table and onto the floor. Paddy disregarded the spill and yelled, "Well, where's me supper, woman?" Kathleen kept praying, but all she could say was 'help'. As she pushed the plate back in front of him, she heard the puppy barking. "What's that?" Paddy asked.

She told him a lie, "I didn't hear anything." She had to say something, and was trying to keep everyone from getting hurt. Paddy seemed to accept what she said, and forgot about it. After finishing his drink, he pushed the uneaten food away and mumbled something incoherent. He went into the bedroom and fell across the bed, and was asleep immediately.

Kathleen was thankful, but unnerved. She sat down in her mother's chair with no idea what she was supposed to be doing. Finally, she gathered herself together, and fed her children, though she ate only a little. After they finished, she brought out the cake with a candle on top for Michael to blow out. She went through the motions for Michael's sake, but the joy was gone from the night. She had made Michael a shirt, and put some money in the pocket. He was really happy about all she had done, and hugged her in thanks. After having the cake, they did the dishes, cleaned up the kitchen, and went to bed. In order to have any room, Kathleen had to shove Paddy over to his own side. She left him on top of the covers and climbed in on her side.

The next morning, Paddy got up as if nothing had happened the night before. Kathleen was noticeably quiet, and looked tired; the night had been very difficult for her, and she had slept very little. Paddy paid no attention; he ate only a small amount of his breakfast, but downed two cups of coffee, then left for work with the lunch his wife had made for him. He threw the lunch away along the trail, and went straight to the saloon.

This was his pattern for the next two weeks. His wife learned to put aside a plate of supper for him; then she went to bed early to avoid more trouble. She had no idea if he was gambling, but he brought no money home. She finished the dress she had been making, and took it to Mr. Walsh at the seamstress shop. He was glad to see her as he had another dress to be sewn. She was thankful for the additional work, she needed to earn enough money to pay their rent at the first of the month.

Kathleen was busy sewing one day when Paddy arrived home shortly after one o'clock in the afternoon surprising her. He was very unsteady on his feet, and when he started through the doorway into the kitchen, he fell against the door frame. Without thinking, she rushed to catch him, but he turned with fire in his eyes. "Don't touch me!" He bellowed. He grabbed her by her beautiful hair, and threw her to the floor! When she tried to get up, he smashed her face over and over with his fist. She fell back to the floor, and tried to cover her face with her hands. "There," he thundered. "Leave me be!" He turned and left the kitchen.

Michael arrived just as his pa was hitting his mother, but it was over before he could do anything. As soon as his pa left the room, Michael ran to the bedroom where Molly was napping. He grabbed her, helped his ma up off the floor, and with Friendly following at his heels, got everyone out the front door. He had to keep his ma moving as she didn't act like she knew what was happening.

When they were on the path, just a little way from the house, his ma started to cry. He kept their little group moving as his pa was holding onto the front door frame and yelling at them at the top of his lungs. He was too drunk and angry to be able to follow them – for which Michael was grateful.

When they reached the end of the path, not knowing what else to do, Michael took the trail leading toward town. They soon came to a huge weeping willow near a small stream. Michael guided his sister, ma, and the puppy under its welcoming arms.

He was trying to wipe some of the blood off his ma's face when the man who had given him Friendly came riding by. Mac saw the boy tending the injured woman and pulled on the reins of his horse. He stopped and got down, tied the horse to the tree, and went to see if he could help. When he looked at the woman, her face and eyes gave him a shock! To him, she looked like an older version of his Kathleen. But no, he thought, she is in Ohio. Then he turned to the boy and asked what had happened. Embarrassed, Michael told him.

As Michael was talking, the man could see a large swelling beginning around the woman's lips, and here and there on her face. Again he thought how much she resembled Kathleen. On an impulse, he asked the boy their last name, and when Michael told him 'McGinnis', he could hardly believe it, Kathleen, here? Strong emotions flooded into him, and without thought he took her in his arms and quieted her sobs. Mac turned his head and asked the boy, "Has this happened before?"

"Yes sir," Michael said. "It happened last winter when we were in Santa Fe with the wagon train we took from Independence, Missouri. After we were in Santa Fe for awhile, my pa started drinking and gambling. One night he came home very drunk and was really mean; he hit ma pretty bad, but not like this! Then one night he gambled away our wagon, oxen, and his horse in a poker game. After that he felt bad about what he had done, so he stopped going to the saloons. Then my parents decided to come here to Silver City so pa could get a job. Now he's started drinking again. I think ma's been really scared, though she hasn't said so. I don't know what to do, sir."

Mac told Michael he was his father's brother, and explained that he had left home years before. "Don't worry, son. I'll take care of it."

When Kathleen's sobs had subsided, he gently lifted her head up, and wiped her tears away with his handkerchief. Then he said, "Kathleen, it will be alright. It's Aaron, I'm here and I'll help you." She gazed into his eyes, not fully understanding, because she didn't recognize him. Who was this man holding her?

"It's me, Kathleen, Aaron," he repeated. She was confused. "Aaron?" "Yes," he answered. "I will never let this happen to you again." She wasn't thinking clearly, but felt safe. He spoke to her, and asked if she thought she could ride his horse. "I want to take you out to my ranch. If you can sit on the horse and hold your daughter in front of you, your son and I can walk and I'll lead the horse." She shook her head yes, so Mac helped her get on the horse. He handed Molly up to her, and with the reins in his hand, they started for the ranch. As he walked, the man prayed for wisdom. She was his brother's wife, and he wanted to help her, her family, and his brother.

It was a long walk. When they arrived at the ranch, Mac carefully lifted Molly down, and then tenderly helped Kathleen. She wasn't very steady on her feet, so he kept his arm around her waist to steady her as they moved into the house. He helped her to a chair and had Molly and Michael sit down.

He quickly stepped into the kitchen and found Maria, and briefly explained what had happened and who he had brought with him. He asked Maria if she would help Kathleen. She said "Of course."

Going to Kathleen, Maria helped her up, and took the woman to her own room where she gently washed the woman's face, and put salve on the cuts. Then, seeing how shaky Kathleen was, Maria got her undressed, put one of her own nightdresses on her, and helped her into bed. Telling her to rest, she closed the curtains to block the light, and quietly left the room.

"I think she will be alright, but she's badly injured." Maria said to Mac. "I helped her into my bed so she could rest, maybe to sleep a while." "Thank you, Maria. I couldn't have done it alone," Mac said.

Now it was time for him to explain in more detail who he was to Michael and the little girl. "I am your father's younger brother. I've been gone from home for many years, but your ma, pa and I spent a lot of time together as we were growing up."

"My pa always called you Aaron, but that woman called you Mac," Michael said. His uncle explained, "I left home shortly after your parents got married and I fought in the Civil War. Somehow, through the years, people started calling me Mac for McGinnis, and the name stuck."

Then Michael went into more detail about leaving the farm and their time in the New Mexico Territory. Mac's heart broke for all of them – even Paddy.

After thinking it all over, he said, "I think I might be able to help your pa. We'll have to talk it over with your ma when she's rested. I need to be gone for a short time, and I want you to stay here for now. " He took them to Maria, and asked if she could give them some cookies to eat and milk to go with them. He also said the puppy looked thirsty, and asked if she would give him some water, then he told Maria he would be back in a couple of hours.

Mac rode swiftly, away to the house Michael had pointed out to him. He tied the horse to the porch railing, then quietly opened the door and searched for Paddy, but he was not there. Mac decided, as soon as Kathleen was rested he would bring them home. It was almost evening, so he would see they had supper first. He would spend the night outside so he could protect them if need be, and tomorrow, he would search out Paddy. His brother came in very late, but apparently went to bed as no one was awake. After another hour, Mac decided it would be safe to leave them. He had a hard time going to sleep that night. It wouldn't be long until daylight, and he knew he needed some rest, but there were a lot of mixed feelings to deal with. He still cared for Kathleen, but reminded himself she was his brothers' wife. He knew he had to try and help both of them.

The next day Mac went to town. As he stepped through the swinging doors of the saloon, the room was permeated with the smell of sweaty men, liquor, smoke, and cheap perfume. He saw a small, heavyset, bald-headed man, wearing glasses. He was playing the piano loudly, and a mixture of rough men and scantily-clad women were standing around singing to the bawdy music, all of them with drinks in their hands. Above it all, he heard Paddy's voice singing. In a way, it was good to hear him after all these years, but not in this place and under these circumstances. As Mac stepped closer to the group, he saw his brother standing at the piano with one hand holding a drink, and the other wrapped around a cheap-looking, fleshy, blond woman's waist. Mac rarely became angry, but as he saw the scene, he was filled with disgust and anger. Here Paddy was, with another woman, knowing that Paddy's wife was at home with cuts and bruises all over her face that he created. Mac had to take a minute to calm down before wending his way through the crowd toward his brother.

When he reached Paddy, he lightly touched him on the shoulder, and Paddy's response was immediate! He put his drink down on the top of the piano, let go of the woman, and turned with fire in his eyes, ready to fight! The two men looked at each other, and for a moment stood still. Paddy was confused as he saw a man who looked like his brother, but the thought that this man was Aaron was absurd. His brother, here in Silver City, in a saloon, didn't make sense.

When his mind was able to grasp the reality that this was really his brother, he stepped forward. "Is that you, me boy?" "Yes", Mac replied. "It's me, your brother. I heard the singing, and knew it had to be you. I could never forget your voice."

Paddy threw his arms around Mac, and the two embraced. Paddy's face was joyous. He patted Mac on the back as he led him to a table at the side of the room, away from the now-curious people. Mac thought his brother smelled like a brewery, most certainly not a good sign.

As they sat down, Paddy said, "This calls for a drink." And he yelled to the bartender to bring two double whiskeys. Mac tried to stop him, but as always, Paddy did what Paddy wanted. When the drinks were brought to the table, Mac shook his head. "No, I don't want a drink." Paddy shrugged his shoulders, lifted his glass and drank the contents down. When Paddy pulled the other glass in front of him, he asked his brother, "What are ye doing here lad?"

So Mac told him that after the war, he and his partner went to Texas where they worked at a horse ranch. "After a few years working there, we decided we wanted our own ranch and horses. Eventually, we ended up here in Silver City. Pete and I think a lot alike, and our work is beginning to pay off. People search us out when they are looking for a good horse. We're doing well."

Then he asked, "How in the world did you end up here Paddy?" Of course, he knew the answer, but he wasn't about to let Paddy know that. "I presume Kathleen and your family are also here. How old is Timothy now?"

"Let's see, I think he's seventeen. But we also have a younger boy, and wee Molly." Then Paddy talked about Kathleen. "She's a beauty, lad. Yes, me boy, our family, special they are, because of her."

What his brother was saying made Mac furious, but he kept his anger down. He didn't want to start any problems. Paddy then started talking about leaving Ohio, going to Santa Fe in a wagon train, and their decision to come to Silver City this spring. "I heard work there was, and I got meself a job right away. Mac lost it! He was so angry at Paddy that he couldn't stop himself and said, "If you have a job, why aren't you at work?"

By this time, Paddy, who had been drinking heavily before Mac came into the saloon, had finished both double whiskeys and the alcohol was taking over. Mac had hit a sore spot, and Paddy thundered, "I am me own boss, and I do as I please. Ye have no right to say anything about what I do or don't do." His anger grew and oblivious to the other people, he rose to his feet yelling at the top of his lungs. "It is me own business it is! I will answer to no man!"

Mac regretted that he had questioned Paddy, realizing his brother was irrational from the drinking. By now, every eye was turned their way. Paddy, dangerously angry, started toward his brother with his fists lifted. Mac knew he had to get away, and he didn't want to get into a saloon brawl with his brother, he jumped to his feet, and headed toward the saloon opening. Just as he was about to go through the swinging doors, a chair came flying through the air just missing him. Mac was outside in a second, and onto his horse. As he turned north to head out of town toward the ranch, Paddy stood in the open doors screaming after him.

Inside the saloon, Ted Spencer was sitting at a table playing poker. He had stopped to watch the two brothers. Thinking about what he had just witnessed, the gambler came up with a plan to get Kathleen's husband out of his way. He would somehow wait until the man had a few too many drinks, and he would talk him into a game of poker. By manipulating the cards, he could make it look like McGinnis was cheating. He knew that when he accused him of it, the man would react like he had this morning, and the gambler would use it as an excuse to shoot him. If questioned regarding his killing of an unarmed man, he would just say McGinnis was known to become violent, he thought he had a gun, and had shot first. There were plenty of witnesses who had seen what happened between the brothers, and they would testify saying how angry and dangerous McGinnis could get when he was drinking.

He was thinking that with the husband out of the way, he could have the woman for his own, and there would be no one to stop him. He didn't care about her young ones, as they could be sent away to school. Then, he could have Kathleen all to himself.

When Mac arrived at the ranch, he handed his horse over to one of the ranch hands. He asked him to take care of the animal, and then hitch 'Catch Me' to the buckboard. "I have business in town."

The man nodded yes, and Mac hurried to the house. When he got inside, he pulled Pete away from his lunch, and called to Maria to join them as soon as she could. Mac told Pete what had happened. "I guess I really blew it. I just couldn't keep silent thinking of

Kathleen and her children. Now I'm afraid he might take his anger at me out on them."

Maria overheard some of what Mac was saying as she was walking in to join the two men. Mac said, "I think I should bring my brother's family here. Paddy is very drunk, and extremely angry. Maria, while I'm gone to get them, please remove all my personal belongings from my room, and make up the bed for Kathleen and Molly. You can put my things in the bunkhouse, and make up two bunks, one for me, and one for the boy. I want to get my brother's family away from his house before he gets there."

When he arrived at Kathleen's, he explained to her what happened when he talked to Paddy. "I have never seen him so angry and unreasonable. I'm really sorry Kathleen, I thought I could help. I need to get the three of you out of here; there's no knowing what he might do when he comes home. Pack some things fast. I have the buckboard, and will take all of you to the ranch. You'd best hurry." "Alright," she agreed.

Michael and Molly had waited outside while their mother and uncle talked, but came in as soon as she called them. Michael and his mother moved quickly, gathering what they would need for a few days. Kathleen packed the dress she was working on as it needed to be finished, and she didn't know when she would be coming back to her home or what to expect.

Mac got them back to the ranch and settled in. Knowing Paddy might figure out where to find his family and arrive at any time, all the ranch hands had been alerted. They were told to have someone watching the road at all times, and if they saw Paddy, see if he was carrying a weapon. Then immediately come to let him and Pete know he was coming so they wouldn't be surprised.

On the third afternoon after Kathleen and her family started staying at the ranch, Paddy was seen walking up the road toward the ranch house. Everyone hoped there wouldn't be any trouble, and Mac had been told Paddy did not have a gun. He didn't appear to be angry, so he was allowed to come up to the house. Kathleen and the children had been kept out of sight, but she could see him through the curtains. Everyone was ready if Paddy started anything.

Mac stepped out onto the porch, and when his brother saw him, his lips started to quiver as he asked about his family. "Yes, Paddy," Mac said. "They are here and well." He could see his brother was very tired from the long walk; although it was still spring, the day was hot. When he started to talk, Paddy only got a few words out when emotion and weariness took over. His knees buckled, and he crumpled to the ground weeping.

Mac knew how emotional his brother had always been. He went down the steps and helped him up. Paddy kept saying through his tears, "Me bonnie lass, me bonnie lass, I can no be livin' without her."

Mac let him weep as he guided him into the house. He seated him, and got him a glass of water. Mac sat down, and Paddy kept saying, "I miss her, that I do, and ashamed I am for what I have done to her. I wish I had niver walked into that saloon in Santa Fe, that I do. Me life has become a nightmare, it has. I thought to stay away from it all, but stay away I could not do, and now . . . ." His words trailed off. Then after a minute he said, "I do not wish to hurt me bonnie one, I love her, that I do."

It was hard for Mac to see his brother so broken so he said, "Maybe we can do something together, you and I, to help you to stop drinking. You can stay with me, away from your family, with no drinking and gambling. If you are willing to do what I ask, you might get over the need for alcohol. It will not be easy for you to do without the drinking, but we can try. Some men have been able to get rid of the need to drink, but I can't guarantee it will work; the only way to find out is to try." Paddy agreed to stay at the ranch with Mac.

He did not see his loved ones as they had been quickly whisked away by Pete when he heard the man's decision. He or Ben would check on them often until the whole affair was resolved. He also knew Mac's plans might backfire, but hoped he would be successful.

The next couple of weeks were going to be very difficult for the brothers, and Pete prayed for his good friend, Paddy, Kathleen, and her children. He knew Mac was going to be involved in a big battle to save his brother, but also knew Mac was strong and a good man; if anyone would be able to help Paddy, Mac could. Mac was also praying, and his words were simple. "Help me, Father."

From then on, the days were long and difficult ones, especially the first week. Paddy surprised Mac. As hard as it was, he faced the days with courage.

Love Comes in Many Colors

His Irish heritage showed in the strength and stubbornness within him.

While the brothers were locked into tumultuous days, an astonishing thing happened to Kathleen. About a week after she returned home, a young boy came to the house with a message from Mr. Walsh asking if she would come to the shop right away. She quickly changed her clothes, and spoke to Michael and Molly who were in the vegetable garden pulling weeds. "I will be gone for a while to see Mr. Walsh at the shop. I've made some sandwiches for you, and they are in the cooler. I will be back as soon as possible."

As she drew near the shop, she wondered what in the world Mr. Walsh wanted her for, and in such a rush. Once inside, he came forward, his face covered by a huge smile. "Mrs. McGinnis, a remarkable thing has happened, Mrs. Simpson, whose husband owns one of the most successful silver mines in town, came in earlier today asking for you. She saw a dress you had sewn for a close friend, and she was very impressed with your work. She especially likes the fine, delicate detail. She asked to have you design and make a very special gown for her. This is a great honor for you, and my shop."

Kathleen was pleased, but a bit bewildered; she did not remember doing anything different on the dresses she had made for Mr. Walsh's customers. They had been made in her usual way. She was glad for more work, and it was enough that the man was very pleased. "This will undoubtedly bring other women in asking to have you do their gowns," he said to her.

The next morning, she met Mrs. Simpson at the shop. She had envisioned an older, mature woman, but found Mrs. Simpson was quite young, and very lovely. She told Kathleen that she and her husband had very recently been wed in Santa Fe. "We had a very beautiful and expensive wedding; my husband spared no expense to make it special, and it was wonderful! When we came here, I brought some bolts of very beautiful material to have my dresses made from. I have one of the fabrics with me. I want a dress for a very special occasion. My husband has planned a big party in a few weeks; there will be dancing, and I want my dress to be perfect!"

She showed Kathleen the soft blue silk material she wanted made into her gown; Kathleen was delighted at the prospect of sewing with this fine fabric; she had never seen anything like it before. Mr. Walsh's shop had a good selection of materials, but nothing of this high quality. "I think this will make a lovely dress for you. The blue material will show off your violet eyes perfectly," she told the woman.

They spent a long time deciding what style the gown would be. Mrs. Simpson knew little about fashion, or sewing, so Kathleen made some suggestions. "I think you will want a long, flowing skirt with large, puffed sleeves; tight at the wrists. The neckline should be low to show off your graceful neck, and a long sash will be perfect with your tiny waist. We want you to be especially beautiful at your first ball here in Silver City. Do you have a special necklace and earrings to wear?" "Oh yes, Mrs. McGinnis," the young woman said. "My husband gave me a beautiful diamond necklace with an amethyst in the center, and ordered earrings made to match."

Kathleen thought a minute and said, "Let's have an overskirt that falls part way, and lopes down at an angle. Everything must be perfect for our new young bride," she said with a smile. She took measurements, and after Mrs. Simpson left, Kathleen found a pattern in the shop to serve as a basic design for the dress that would lend itself to the modifications and additions she planned to make to it. She cut the dress out on one of the shop's very smooth worktables. She was concerned the table at her house might snag the delicate fabric. Looking through the shop, she found a piece of soft, extremely thin, violet-colored material to make a flower which would be placed on the outer skirt of the dress where it began its downward flow. After gathering the things she needed for the dress, she wrapped it all up and took it home.

Ten days later, as she was busy sewing, Pete stopped by to say Mac would be bringing Paddy home the next day in the late afternoon. She was nearly finished with Mrs. Simpson's dress, so she took time out to make an apple pie. When she and the children finished supper, she continued her sewing into the evening.

The next morning, she cleaned the house and went to the store to buy flour because she needed to make bread again, then she went to the garden and pulled some small potatoes. While the chicken was frying for supper, she cleaned the potatoes and got them ready to cook. By four o'clock, the chicken was ready, and kept hot in the pan that had been pushed to the back of the stove. She was ready for her husband!

When Mac brought him home, Paddy was rather subdued, but glad to be back. When he opened his arms, Kathleen moved into them, glad he was better. Over her husband's shoulder she mouthed the words "Thank you". Mac gave her a nod, put his hat back on, and turned away, filled with emotions for her he did not want to address.

As he rode away, holding the reins of the horse Paddy had ridden home, he realized how very tired he was. He was glad he had helped his brother, but it had been hard work with little sleep much of the time. He wanted to see Paddy whole and healthy and the family to be happy. He felt a great sadness come over him, knowing he had just left the only woman he would ever love in the arms of his brother.

It had been a very long time ago when he had left Ohio, because of his love for Kathleen; and now the hurt returned. With all the strength he had left, he thanked God for helping his brother overcome his weakness for alcohol and gambling. Then he asked Him to keep his heart toward Kathleen pure, and to watch over her and her children.

When he arrived home, he went to bed and slept nearly twenty-four hours. Pete would let no one near him, knowing he needed his much-earned rest.

Three days after Paddy returned home, the dress for Mrs. Simpson was finished. Kathleen had met with the lovely woman twice for fittings to make sure the dress would fit perfectly. When the final fitting was over, Mrs. Simpson was very pleased. "Thank you, Mrs. McGinnis. I love the dress! It is even more beautiful than I had imagined."

The woman was ravishing in the gown, and Kathleen imagined how she would look the night of the ball with her long, soft brown hair gently falling over her shoulders. Kathleen was pleased with the results of her many hours of work. She would have enjoyed seeing Mrs. Simpson wearing the graceful gown as she danced around the room in the arms of her husband.

Mrs. Simpson handed her ten dollars as a tip, something Kathleen had never received before, and the young woman went away, ready to hide the dress from her husband until the night of the ball.

Sometimes the seamstress wished she could have had such a life. At least with a husband that loved her like this man must love his wife. Often Kathleen felt lonesome for love; a love that was gentle and kind.

Chapter 7

Life was beginning to settle down, with Paddy back working and his wife busy sewing. One day after measuring a woman for a dress, Kathleen left the shop; she took what she needed to make the garment. On her way home, she stopped at Hanson's to pick up a few supplies. When she was paying for her purchases, Mr. Hanson handed her a letter – the first one they had received since moving to Silver City. Kathleen decided to slip the letter into her pocket, having no hands free between carrying her sewing, and what she had just bought. She wondered who it was from, hoping it was from Jeannie. She had written to her friend, but had not yet heard from her.

When she walked up the path to the house, she heard her son and daughter talking in the back yard. She put everything down, and went out to see what they were doing. She found them busy; Molly was raking the yard, and Michael was cleaning out the chicken coop. She saw how good Michael was at taking care of Molly, and knew she didn't have to worry when she had to be gone.

"Hi, ma", Michael said. "We decided to surprise pa and have the yard and chicken coop finished so he wouldn't have them to clean later." "I'm sure he will be pleased, and so am I", their ma said. "Are you hungry?" An immediate, "yes", from both of them, gave her the answer. "When you're finished, come in and we'll have lunch."

It didn't take long before they walked through the back door. While they were washing up, she got the food on the table. After they were sitting down and said grace, the two began eating, and she opened the letter Mr. Hansen had given her.

Dear Paddy and Kathleen,

We are finally coming to Silver City. The church conference has informed Richard he is being sent there to start a church. We are so glad we will be near you. Silver City is where Richard has felt all along God wanted us to be.

Thelma is well, and doing wonderfully. This trip will probably be hard on her, but she's excited about the move.

We are hoping you will get this letter in time, we should be arriving Saturday, June the twentieth if all goes well. It will be so good to see you again.

Until then, love,
Eve
(Both Richard and Thelma send their love.)

Kathleen could think of nothing she would like more than to have these wonderful friends living here in town. Knowing the dangers along the way, she would be praying they would have a safe journey.

That night, Paddy was a little late for supper. His wife felt a tad bit of fear, but she told herself he was just a little late, and would soon be home. Michael also noticed his father's lateness, but he did not mention it.

It wasn't long before Paddy was home; he was a bit excited, but all right, so Kathleen put her fear aside and fed her family. She had cooked a good supper, and Paddy gulped it down. After supper, he lay on the divan, and before long, he had fallen asleep. She looked at him, and thought about how hard he worked in the mine.

She went to her sewing, and left him to his rest. Before she put Molly to bed, Kathleen made her daughter take a tub bath; she was too grimy after working in the yard to get into bed. Kathleen pulled out the metal tub they kept behind the kitchen stove, and filled it with warm water. "Come on, young lady, let's get you clean, especially your neck and behind your ears."

Molly didn't want to take a bath, but her mother prevailed. In the meantime, Paddy woke up and went to bed. Michael was lost in a book he was reading while laying on the rug. After Molly was tucked in bed, Kathleen joined her son, and got back to her sewing.

The next morning, Michael and Molly went next door to spend time with their friends, Todd

Witherspoon and his sister. Their ma went back to sewing, trying to get some dresses done for Mrs. Firth's daughter, Penny. She was nearly finished with Penny's three dresses, only a bit more to do. All she had to do to get them finished was to have Penny try them on, so she could measure for the hems. Her boss had said another woman would be coming in the next day to see about having a dress made. She would be ready to meet both the woman, and daughter tomorrow afternoon.

The next day after lunch, she and Molly headed to the shop to meet Mrs. Firth and Penny. As they drew near, she saw a new sign above the door. In fancy lettering, it said 'Specialized Women's Designs', and beneath the first line it said 'Ladies Dresses, Men's Tailoring'. The old sign had only said 'Seamstress and Tailoring'; she wondered what the new sign meant for her.

As Kathleen and Molly walked through the door, Jules Walsh, who did all the tailoring work, came forward saying, "Mrs. McGinnis, so many women are coming in hoping you will create their gowns and dresses for them, and I felt you could do it; you are excellent in your work." Kathleen was pleased that he and the women she had worked for liked her sewing, but she knew more business meant more sewing for her, and she would need someone to help her. Otherwise, there was no way she could do it all, and she told Mr. Walsh that.

"I've already thought about it," he said, "and I planned to find someone to help you if you agreed to take on the additional responsibility. Do you know anyone that might be interested in the work?" She thought a minute, and remembered Eve. "You know, Mr. Walsh, I have some friends moving here, they should be arriving on Saturday. Eve Smith worked with me in Santa Fe. She and her husband are coming to Silver City to start a new church; some extra money might help them."

Mr. Walsh said, "A new minister in town? That sounds good! The only minister here right now usually spends Saturday nights in one of the saloons drinking. Most people are not very pleased with him. Some others, as well as my wife and I simply gave up on him, and we all meet Sundays at the 'Pine Tree Ranch' north of town. The two men who own it are fine Christians, and have been having meetings for a couple of years. It's mostly Bible studies, sharing and singing hymns. We often make a day of it in good weather. My wife always cooks something, and we have a potluck. There is usually way too much food, but it's a very restful, special time. That's been our church for a couple of years." She could not believe her ears, Pete and Aaron having church at the ranch? They had never mentioned it, even when Paddy was there over two Sundays.

Then Mr. Walsh said, "We have not had our get-togethers for the last couple of months, but I understand we will be going back to our old routine the week after the Fourth of July. I, for one, will be glad. Please do ask you're friend when she arrives if she is interested in helping you. Of course, all this extra time will mean more money for each dress, so I will certainly make it worth your time. I am glad you came to work for me, Mrs. McGinnis." "Thank you sir and I will talk to my friend about your offer. I do wish you would call me Kathleen." The man replied smiling. "Of course Kathleen, it's a nice name; I will be glad to call you Kathleen."

Just then Penny Firth walked in the door alone, the chimes welcoming her. Molly had settled down and was busy drawing pictures, leaving her mother free to help the girl. "Good morning, Penny. I'm all ready for you," the woman said.

"I hope I'm not late," said Penny, "My mother couldn't come today." "You're here right on time", the woman said. She showed the girl where she could change her clothes.

Penny went into the small room with all dresses in hand, and soon came out dressed in the first one, and she stood turning in front of the mirror. The printed dress had the same blue on it as her eyes. She looked at herself in the mirror, "I love it! It's really a pretty dress, I'll like wearing it to school." "I'm glad you like it, it's a good style for you."

The girl talked while Kathleen, pins in her pin cushion, measured and pinned the hem in place. When all three dresses were measured, the girl left, waving as she walked out the door. The woman thought she was a sweet girl, and beautiful with her blue eyes and lovely, long gently curling hair.

Soon after Penny left, the other customer arrived and ordered a dress. After she left, Kathleen folded the dresses that needed hemming, cut out a newly ordered dress, and picked out more thread, needles, and buttons. She was really getting busy these days.

As she and Molly walked toward home, she thought of the catalog pages Mr. Walsh had shown her advertising sewing machines, a new invention. There were several different makes, but the one that caught her eye was made by Isaac Singer. The ad said it would save a lot of time, and from the looks of things, even with Eve's help, she could use one. The ad also said it could be bought on time, so she decided to get more information to see if she could afford one.

The days sped by, Kathleen more than busy. She had a house to clean, a family to feed and lots of washing. Paddy's clothes were always filthy from the dust and dirt in the mine. She could hardly keep up with the sewing.

The Friday before the Smiths were to arrive, Kathleen went on a cleaning spree while Paddy was at work. There was a knock on the door, and under her breath she said, "Oh no, no company today!" But when she opened the door, it was Mac and Pete stopping by to ask how she and her family were doing. "We're fine, Paddy is busy at the mine, and has been coming home at the end of each day."

Then she remembered the Smiths, and she told the two men about the couple coming to start a new church. Mac and Pete looked at each other. "We were planning to tell you we will be starting up our meetings on Sundays in a few weeks, and wondered if you, Paddy, and your family would like to join us," Pete said. "Yes, I heard about those meetings from Mr. Walsh. I was hoping we could come."

"Of course, there were so many things going on, so we put it off for a while. We've heard the Indians are getting close to the area, and have to take that into consideration. Anyhow, do you think your minister might come to the meetings and teach us if he hasn't started his church by then?" Pete asked. "I'm sure he would, Pete. He, his wife, and her mother are wonderful people, and he is a fine man; I will certainly ask."

"Good," Mac said. "Well, we were just checking on you, see you soon." And they were off. As she closed the door, she was grateful that they and their ranch hands were keeping watch over her and her family. She went back to work with a song on her lips. Between Paddy not going to the saloons, her job, the Smiths, and Aaron and Pete, life was wonderful! She sang along as she cleaned the house, Molly helped hang up the clothes – at least where she could reach, while Michael swept and mopped the floors.

Saturday morning she did some baking; she made bread, and baked two blackberry pies. Michael and Molly had found the wild berries, picked them, and brought them home; something she hadn't seen in a long time. She wrapped everything up, and found room in the cooler.

"Ma, where's my blue shirt?" Michael called out. "It's hanging here in the kitchen ready to put on." She answered. When she saw him all clean and dressed, she realized he was not only growing tall, but was beginning to look quite handsome, time was certainly flying by. Then she thought of Timothy, wishing she knew where he was, and if he was alright.

Just then, Paddy walked through the door and, as he gave her a peck on the cheek she thought she smelled liquor on his breath. "Oh no," she thought. "Not now!"

After Paddy was ready, the family left. They walked into town to meet the Smith's who were to arrive that day. As they walked, Kathleen forgot her concern about Paddy, eager to see her friends.

The stagecoach turned the corner, and came to where Kathleen, Paddy, Michael, and Molly were standing. It stopped, and Richard Smith was the first one out, turning to help Eve and Thelma step down; the McGinnis family all there to greet them.

Kathleen rushed forward to hug the women, while Paddy and his son shook Richard's hand; Molly was floating in between everyone. They all began talking at once.

Paddy pointed out the hotel to Richard, and as they were talking, everyone drifted that way. The men and Michael carried the valises, and left the trunk at the station until they had a place to store it. Paddy told Richard he was sure the owner of the hotel would be glad to keep it until they found a place to live. Once the rooms were paid for, the men stood talking to the owner of the hotel, and the women were busy catching up on everything. A short time later, the three went to their upstairs room, all tired and hungry.

Once settled in their room, Richard told his wife, "I think it's a good thing we're here." Eve had been brushing her hair, but turned from the mirror. She asked her husband, "Why, Richard?" "I smelled liquor on Paddy's breath. I hope he's not up to his old tricks again", he told her.

"Poor Kathleen", Eve said. "I wonder how she deals with that. Yes, I think you're right, she needs to have people who love her around in case he gets like he was in Santa Fe. I was so in hopes Paddy had left that behind."

During supper, everyone visited. They talked about their lives since they had last been together, and what had happened with some of the people who had been on the wagon train with them. No one in the McGinnis family mentioned Paddy's drinking; how he had beaten Kathleen, or the time he had spent isolated with Mac on the ranch. The friends parted after supper, with plans for the newcomers to have dinner at the McGinnis' home the following day.

Kathleen spent Sunday morning cooking, and the house smelled enticing from the fragrant baked ham, and freshly baked bread. She thought, now we can worship with others again. Molly set the table, under close supervision, and her ma put a vase filled with yellow roses in the middle of the table. The soft green drapes, and the dark green velvet material that now covered the divan, chair, and rocking chair were a fitting background for the two additional vases of the sweet scented, yellow roses she placed in the room. She glanced around with pleasure, thinking that the house scarcely resembled the one they had moved into. To further compliment the greens in the room, she had added two yellow pillows on the divan.

Paddy had gone to bring their guests to the house. Being tired from all the rushing around, Kathleen was sitting on the divan, reading out of a book to her daughter, when she heard them walking up the path.

Love Comes in Many Colors

She set the book aside, straightened her dress, and went to meet them at the door.

The first thing Richard said was, "Ummmm, it smells good in here!" "Still always hungry?" Kathleen asked her favorite minister. He flashed a smile at her. "You know I am." Thelma and Eve laughed. "He's always hungry," Thelma said. "You'd think he's a growing boy." He grinned. "Come on, ladies. It's been a long time since breakfast."

Kathleen looked at him. He certainly didn't show any weight gain. Then she said, "Well, we're ready for a hungry man." She hugged the women, and Paddy took the ladies hats and gloves. He also took Richard's hat, and put them all on their bed.

"We're so glad you've finally come, we've missed you so much. Sit down and visit with Paddy, while I get the food on the table. Everything is ready, and we can talk while we eat", Kathleen told their guests. Eve offered to help Kathleen, and followed her into the kitchen. "I love your house, it's really lovely. I can see your hand in it all." "Thanks," her friend said. "It was fun to do. Paddy has done his share, the house needed lots of repairs, and he and Michael did it all."

The food was on the table, and after everyone sat down, Paddy asked the minister to say grace – which surprised his wife, but Kathleen was glad he had said it instead of her. After the prayer, the food was passed around. They enjoyed conversation and good food while continuing to catch up on the months they had been apart.

Richard complimented Kathleen, "This ham is delicious, and so is everything else!" She grinned and said, "I'm glad you like it." "Wait till you taste ma's pie. Molly and I picked the berries for her", Michael told them.

Everyone, except Paddy was having a good time. He was unusually quiet, but nobody noticed.

"I miss the Cobb's, especially Jeannie", Kathleen said. "Oh my goodness", Eve said. "I forgot to tell you. We received a letter from them just a week before we left Santa Fe. She said they found a piece of farmland just north of Fort Selden. I wish we could have stopped to see them, but the driver, of course, had no time. They filed a claim on the land, and planted corn on part of it. It took a lot of work, from what she said. They are close to the river, and have water to irrigate the land, and they've planted a vegetable garden, and put in a few saplings of fruit trees. They sound happy."

Kathleen and her family knew just about where the couple had settled. It was along the route they traveled when they came to Silver City earlier in the spring. Eve's voice broke into her thoughts. "The most exciting thing of all is that Jeannie is expecting a baby! She sounded so happy; I know they have been wanting to start a family for a long time." Kathleen was so happy for her friend. "Yes, Jeannie talked often about how much they wanted at least half a dozen children." "Yes", her friend said. "By the way, she asked me to give you their address if I saw you so you could write; you just send it to the fort. They get their supplies there as well as mail." Eve handed

Kathleen the piece of paper with the address written on it.

"I will take time tomorrow and write her. They sound happy, but I wish they were here instead, but there's little farm land here." "I miss her too, but we have each other", and Eve reached across the table, grasping her friend's hand.

Kathleen had been watching Thelma throughout the dinner. "Thelma, you look wonderful, even young I might venture to say! You look so happy." "I am, my dear. First of all, because you brought me to the Lord, what joy that has been in my life since then, but also because of these two wonderful people." She pointed to Eve and Richard smiling. "I can honestly say I have never been happier than I am right now. Eve and Richard are like my family." "We are your family, you're my mother, and we love you dearly", Eve told Thelma. "Yes," her husband agreed as he smiled at the older woman. "I don't know what we would do without you."

How remarkable, Kathleen thought as she remembered Thelma when she was a bitter and angry woman. She said, "I'm so happy for all three of you."

Meanwhile, Paddy said little, being with all of them made him feel really uncomfortable. He was especially uncomfortable around the minister, he didn't know if he could live up to everyone's expectations.

After lunch, the women did the dishes and cleaned up while Paddy and Michael took Richard for a short walk, and showed him around the area.

"This is beautiful country", Richard said. "I'm glad we weren't sent to the desert. We crossed some of it traveling here, and I've never been so hot!" Michael spoke up saying, "I hear they sometimes have snow here, but I guess it doesn't last long, I'm glad; I never really liked the cold that much."

Then Paddy showed Richard the vegetable garden where the tomatoes were turning light red. "It takes a while to get started, but everything seems to be growing fine," he said. As they were walking, the minister sensed that Paddy felt uncomfortable around him. On the other hand, Michael really seemed to be enjoying himself. Paddy excused himself and left. Michael took the opportunity to ask if he could come talk to Richard sometime.

"Of course, Michael, how about Thursday afternoon if we've found a place to live. I'll let you know where to come." "Thank you sir," the boy said. Just then Paddy returned, and the boy said no more.

In the meantime, Kathleen mentioned Mr. Walsh's need to hire someone to help her with her sewing. "I'm getting so busy I just can't do it all alone, would you be interested in the job Eve?" The young woman seemed really excited. "See Thelma, the Lord has gone before us." The older woman smiled and nodded.

Kathleen said, "You mean you were hoping to find work?" "Yes, either Richard or I, I most certainly would rather it be me so he can be free to get the church going. We could use some money; this move has taken much of our savings."

Love Comes in Many Colors

"I'm glad you can help me," her friend said. "When you're ready, let me know and you can start." So it was settled. The friends would be sewing together. Thelma was delighted. "I can handle most of the housework, leaving you free to work and help Richard with the church."

That night, Eve told Richard about the job offer and he said, "Are you sure sweetheart?" "Of course I am Richard. This will be a wonderful opportunity to spend time with Kathleen, and earn money at the same time! I'm happy that God has provided me a way of doing both."

Richard understood. Eve, Kathleen, and Jeannie had always been close. Now that Jeannie was living far away, it was good these two would have each other. "I'm glad this has worked out so well my sweet," he said.

He did not know why Michael had asked to see him, and wanted to pray about it before saying anything to his wife.

It was a busy week for the Smiths; they found a house in pretty good condition. They were glad it wasn't adobe, preferring houses made of wood. Many of the homes around were made from the mud. The view of the surrounding hills and mountains were very beautiful, and the sunsets were outstanding, with many colors. Although the house needed a cleaning and a few more pieces of furniture – they were happy with it. This would make a good home for the three of them.

Richard looked all over town for a building to use for holding church services. The only place he had found so far was a dance hall connected to a saloon! Dances were held there on Saturday nights, and when he went into the room, even though it had been several days since the last dance, and the door of the saloon was closed, the smell of liquor, cigars, and cigarettes was extremely strong! He had not yet made a decision regarding the room, hoping he could find a better place.

It was Thursday afternoon, and Michael would be arriving soon. Eve and Thelma walked down to the stores to do some shopping, that way Richard and Michael would have some time together. Shortly after they left, Michael was at the door. "Please come in, Michael," the young minister said. "We're here alone this afternoon, my ladies just walked to town. Please, have a seat." And he pointed to a chair. "It's a really hot day", he said. "Would you like a drink of water?" Michael nodded. "Yes sir, I would."

When Richard returned with two glasses of water, he handed one to Michael, who took a big, long drink – nearly emptying the whole glass! "Thank you. I was really hot and thirsty." "How can I help you, Michael?" The minister asked.

The boy hesitated a minute, and then reluctantly said, "My ma didn't tell you everything that's been happening, because pa was there. At least that's what I think. We've had a really hard time since we moved to Silver City. Pa was alright for a while, but then he started drinking again. The more he drank, the worse he got, and the last time he hit ma really bad; he threw her on the floor, and beat her on the face over and over! It was so bad, I grabbed her, Molly, and our pup, and we ran away from him. He was too drunk to follow, but as we left, he was hanging onto the front door yelling and screaming at us. We were all afraid of him. I took ma toward town, not knowing what to do, but she was crying so hard and stumbling, that I was afraid she would fall. When we got to a large tree with room to stand under the branches, we stopped. Her face was swelling, and her lips were bleeding. When I looked at her closely, I saw big, red spots on her face, they looked really bad! I didn't know where to go, or what to do."

"Just then a man came riding by on his horse, and when he saw ma crying so hard, he stopped to see if he could help. It was really strange, but we found out he was pa's brother, we didn't even know he lived here. He and ma hadn't seen each other since he left home in Ohio to fight in the Civil War. I guess he recognized her, but I'm not sure she knew who he was right away."

"When I told him what happened, he decided to take us to the horse ranch he and a friend own. He put ma and Molly on his horse, and he and I walked. When we got to his house, he had the woman that works for them take care of ma. She looked awful by the time we got there, because her face was so swollen! I don't think she even knew where we were. My uncle, Mac, and his partner were really kind to us, and took care of ma."

"Later on, my uncle took my pa to the ranch, trying to help him get over his drinking. At the end of two weeks, he brought him home. Well, I can tell it's not going to work, I can smell the liquor on his breath again, although it's only been once so far, but I know what it will lead to. I think ma knows too, but she hasn't said anything."

"Reverend Smith, I'm really afraid for my mother. I know if he keeps drinking, sooner or later he will beat her again! She's probably afraid when he comes home, and I don't know what to do!"

Michael was really upset, and Richard felt a sadness come over him. He had always respected Kathleen, and didn't like to think of her being so badly mistreated. He was also concerned abut Michael who was carrying a heavy load for a youngster.

"Michael, do you mind if I pray before we talk about this more?" "No sir. I was hoping you would." Ah, thought Richard. This boy believes in you, Lord. His mother has taught him well.

He got up, and went over to Michael. He didn't know why, but knew he was supposed to lay his hands on Michael while he prayed. His prayers were for Kathleen, Michael, and Molly as well as Paddy. "Lord, please help Paddy to turn away from drinking, especially for his family's sake. He's not a bad man, he just shouldn't drink. I ask, Lord, that you give Michael even greater faith that he might serve you well and loyally."

He continued praying for some time, and when he finished, before he took his hands away, he could feel God's presence upon the lad. The young minister wasn't sure what that meant, but he was sure Michael's life would take a different path from this time on.

Michael sat still for a moment, and then tears began to flow down his cheeks. Unashamedly he prayed, "I'm sorry Lord, I shouldn't hate pa. It's just that he can be so mean to ma. Please help us Lord."

Then Richard said, "I know it's hard, Michael. It's hard to forgive someone who's cruel, but remember it's not your pa we're dealing with here; it's the alcohol that makes him that way. Some people should never drink! Alcohol becomes more important to them than anything else, and they can't stop themselves from drinking."

Michael spoke up, "I vow to god I will never drink. Not ever!" "Good. Michael, you do know you must forgive your father, don't you? You need to stop the bitterness in you, as well as the way you think of your pa. No one can go forward in their spiritual life when bitterness and unforgiveness have control over their thoughts and mind."

Michael looked up, and Richard could see he understood.

Richard said, "That does not mean we forget, it means we understand what's happening in the person, and we start caring about them, and pray they will get over the need to drink. You can also pray for your mother Michael; in the end, it's only God who can solve this problem.

After sitting and thinking for a couple of minutes, Michael said, "I understand sir." Then he prayed, telling the Lord he forgave his pa. "Please Lord, help us all through this hard time, especially ma. Protect her from any more violence. In the name of Jesus, amen."

"Remember Michael, your father is in a very dangerous time in his life. No one can make the change but him." They talked a while longer, and when Michael left, Richard could see a change had taken place in the boy, and he thanked the Lord for that change.

After Thelma had gone to bed that night, Richard told his wife what had been happening to Kathleen and her children. "Oh Richard, how terrible it must have been for them. She didn't say a word to me about it, but knowing Kathleen, she has put her fear for herself and her family in the Lord's hands." That night, Eve asked the Father to protect her friend, Michael, and Molly. She remembered what Paddy had been like in Santa Fe after he started drinking.

The next day, Kathleen arrived at the shop, the small bells announcing her arrival. Mr. Walsh, apparently busy in the back room, poked his head through the long drapes. When he saw her, he smiled and nodded. He then closed the drapes and turned back into the back room where he was adjusting a suit he was making. She could hear them talking, catching a few words here and there. The customer he was helping said, "She's very beautiful. I want to give her all the things she should have, including lovely gowns and jewelry."

The voice sounded familiar, but Kathleen could not place it. She sat down to look through the buttons as she had miscounted how many she needed for the dress she was working on. The men continued talking, as Mr. Walsh asked the man to turn around, to make sure the suit fit correctly. Again, she heard the voice; she was trying to remember where she had heard it before. She had just found the buttons she was looking for when the two men came out of the back. "It will be ready for you by the middle of next week; the dark blue material you chose will make a very handsome suit," Mr. Walsh told the man.

When Kathleen glanced up, she saw the other man was Ted Spencer – of all people. She quickly turned away. Since he was looking at Mr. Walsh, she hoped he hadn't seen her. She wondered what woman he had been talking about. He was one man she didn't trust. She wasn't altogether sure why, but she was very uncomfortable when he was around. She hoped their paths never crossed again, but realized that living in the same town, they were bound to meet now and then, though her choice would be to never see him again.

After the gambler left, Kathleen put away the rest of the buttons and spoke to Mr. Walsh. "I've been thinking about those sewing machines I read about in the catalog. If I had one, I could use it to sew the long seams, and that would cut my sewing time, considerably; that would be a big help. I'm interested in the one Isaac Singer is offering to sell on an installment plan, and I was wondering if you could find out the particulars on it for me."

"You know Kathleen, I think you're right. I will be glad to check into it for you, although it may take time to get an answer back. I will write today to get the price, and payments. I'll let you know as soon as I find something out." "Thank you, Jules. I really appreciate your going to all that trouble."

As Kathleen hurried away, she was thinking about how busy she had become.

The big celebration planned to commemorate the Declaration of Independence was only a few days away, and the dress she was making had to be finished before then. She also had a lot of baking to do.

The next day, while she was sewing, there was a knock on the front door. When she opened it, there were her two faithful friends.

"Just checking in. How's everything going," Mac asked. She smiled. "Pretty good, I thought Paddy was starting to drink again, because I smelled alcohol on him, but it seemed to be a one-time thing. He's doing well, going to work; keeping up with the chores around the house, and yard. The rest of us are fine as well." "That's good news Kathleen," Mac said to her.

Pete spoke up saying, "We're going to be riding our two white horses in the parade; we just finished meeting with the committee in charge of the Fourth of July festivities. You and your family will be coming to the celebration, won't you?"

"We will; I'm baking to help the ladies who want to buy more books for the school. They figured a bake sale, along with contributions will bring in enough money to get them. Come see us, and maybe we can sell you something good to eat." Both men grinned. "You bet." Pete said. "We both have a sweet tooth; we'll be there as soon as the parade is over."

After the two left, Kathleen went back to work, she thought she should tell the Smith's about the celebration. Then she remembered she forgot to tell the two men that the Smith's had arrived in town, and forgot to talk to Richard about going to the ranch to teach at the first Sunday service. It seemed like there were just too many things going on to remember all of them. Well, she would go to the Smith's tomorrow after she was free, to tell them about the big July celebration.

The next morning she met with the woman at the shop, and gave her the finished garment. The customer was pleased with the dress, and Kathleen was glad it was finished. She left and walked over to see the Smith's.

"The house looks great!" she told Eve, who said, "Sit down dear, you look hot and tired. Thelma made lemonade early this morning, and it's been in the cooler, would you like some?"

"Would I, the weather has certainly turned warm, and that hill is really steep." She sat down, and after cooling down said, "I love your house, Eve, it's homey, and I'm sure you're pleased with it. I love the views, something we don't have."

As she looked north, she thought of the ranch, and remembered the visit from Aaron and Pete. Just then Richard came in; he went to the kitchen, and came into the parlor with a glass of the lemonade.

"Richard and Eve", the woman said. "I forgot I was supposed to ask you something. I'm not sure if I mentioned it, but Paddy's brother, Aaron, lives in the Silver City area. He and his partner, Pete, own a horse ranch north of town. For several years now, they have had a small gathering of people join them there on Sundays to worship God. I guess the only minister that's been in town is not liked too much, and that's why they started having the meetings at the ranch. When I told them you had moved here, they wondered if you might consider coming out there and teach until you establish your church. They stopped getting together for a while, I guess, but are getting ready to start up again. The only problem is they've heard the Indians have been nearby, and Aaron said what the young braves really want are horses. So they are concerned about people being at the ranch if the Indians attack, and want to wait a little longer until the danger passes. Right now, no one knows how close the Indians are."

"That would be great! I would count it a blessing to meet with people who worship and love the Lord. We're willing to wait. right now, I can't seem to find a decent place to have the church meetings anyway," Richard said.

"They are both good men," Kathleen told him, "and they have been very kind to me and my family." She didn't elaborate, and the Smith's didn't let on what Michael had told Richard.

Kathleen changed the subject, and talked about the Fourth of July celebration that would be held in two days. "I'm doing some baking to help the women buy new books for the coming school year."

Eve got excited. "Do you think Thelma and I could do some baking too? We would love to help." Thelma nodded, saying "That would be fun. It would give us a chance to meet other women in the town." "That would be great", Kathleen answered, "And I know the women would be really pleased for your help; the more they have to sell, the more money they can take in. I'll tell my friends you will be bringing something for the sale."

Eve and Thelma were ready to start baking; Thelma had starter sitting, and would make cinnamon rolls, always a favorite. Eve planned to make a cake, explaining that someday she and Richard hoped they might have a little one to send to the school. At this point, Thelma excitedly said, "I'm waiting for some grandchildren."

Kathleen smiled at Thelma's eagerness for children to love. What a change in the woman. Thelma was obviously happy.

The next day, Kathleen baked three pies and several dozen cookies. It took a good part of the day, and she was ready when it was time for bed that night. Tomorrow was a big day. She woke early the next morning to make donuts. In the midst of frying them, an extremely loud noise shook the valley. Later she found out, an amiable old black man was celebrating the Fourth of July in his own way, by hitting some anvils he worked with. He was hitting them with all his might, sending shock waves throughout the valley. Many of the children had heard him do this before and hopped out of bed, running to watch him without even stopping to put on their shoes.

Thus started the celebration – a bit early, but the noise made sure everyone knew the big day had arrived.

Chapter 8

The town was swarming with ranchers, miners, gamblers, cowhands, soldiers, and strangers. There were gentlemen with their fine ladies. Every kind of wagon could be seen from small to large. Horses, mules, and donkeys lined some of the streets, all either braying, neighing, or bawling.

One could see 'Ladies of the evening' and every bad man from the area and beyond, all mingling, either on the narrow dusty streets, or inside the saloons. The town was chaotic, with more noise than anyone wanted to hear. There was a feeling of excitement on the streets, and everyone was in a festive mood.

It was the Fourth of July, and everyone was celebrating the one hundredth year celebration of the independence of the states. Everyone from far and near was ready to celebrate.

Through the moving tide of humanity, the McGinnis family, including Friendly, wended its way to the booth where the newly made tables were filling with the women's culinary delicacies. Kathleen and Paddy, Michael, and even Molly, arrived with their hands full of Kathleen's contributions to the baked goods for sale, as Friendly trotted behind Michael.

The tables were filling up with cakes, pies, sweet breads, gingerbread, and cookies. There were plenty of tables, so there was plenty of room for more.

Kathleen's donuts were going fast. The Smith's arrived with the cinnamon rolls and Eve's cake, which was cut into pieces for those who only wanted something good to eat now.

Molly sat down on a log, joining other girls, all told not to move. Michael asked his mother if she minded if he took a walk to look around. "Of course, Michael, enjoy yourself, I'll be busy here at the booth until the parade starts. Why don't you come back so we can all watch the parade together?" "Thanks ma, I'll be back," and he wandered up the street, his dog at his heels.

In front of the 'Western Saloon, Michael saw five men he had never seen before. They tied their horses to the hitching rail, and then headed into the saloon; all with holstered guns tied around their thighs. Not a usual sight as there were orders that no man could carry a gun in town, but Michael knew plenty of men that did.

As Michael caught the strong smell of liquor, cigars, and cigarettes, he was reminded of the night in Santa Fe when he had drug his father out of a saloon; it was not a pleasant memory. Passing by the establishment, he heard the tin-pany music of the piano, with many people singing. That was a place he never wanted to be.

While walking, he met Todd, whose family lived close to their house. The two stood together talking as they watched all the activities going on around them. Close by there was a large pit, covered with hot coals where meat had been cooking through the night. The meat was covered with gunny sacks which were dampened off and on. Over that was a cover of pine branches – it smelled so good!

Not too far away was a cowboy dressed as a clown and doing tricks. Nearby, a man was selling apple cider, while other people were going past on their own quests. Michael saw it was nearly time for the parade to start so he turned to Todd and said, "Gotta go, see you later." He picked up Friendly and took off towards the booth. As he struggled to carry a growing Friendly, Michael wished he had left the dog at home. Heading to the Baked Goods booth to meet his parents, he bumped into a girl. Her hair was long and wavy, and it looked like the color of corn silk. She had the prettiest big blue eyes with long lashes he had ever seen!

"Oh, excuse me," he said, I'm sorry. I wasn't looking where I was going." She laughed, and her smile was radiant. "It's alright", she said. Spotting Friendly, she laughed again. "What a cute dog, he's all fluffy. What's his name?" When Michael told her, she laughed again, and reached out to pet Friendly who responded with a few wet kisses, his trademark. "No Friendly." Michael told the small dog. "That's alright," she told him, "he's so sweet!"

Just as Michael was about to say something more, he heard a voice calling, "Penny!" The girl looked toward the voice, then looked back at Michael with merriment in her eyes and said, "I'm sorry, I have to go."

As she walked away, Michael had the strangest feeling inside, and at the same time was thinking she was the prettiest girl he had ever seen. Little did he know that his life would change dramatically one day, because of this golden-haired girl.

Loud yelling coming from the area where he was going to meet his family interrupted his thoughts. He dropped Friendly, and ran toward the commotion, both he and Friendly dodging in and out of people as he headed toward the ruckus.

When he got there, he started to grin. There was Scotty, the toothless, bearded old man, trying to pull Cleo away from the tables of baked goods; she was munching on a pie, apparently enjoying every bite. "Cum out o'thar ya ole fleabag of a mule!" Scotty shouted, as he pulled at her halter. However, Cleo definitely had no intention of moving.

Michael joined in the laughter of the people watching. The women in the booth, including his ma, weren't enjoying the situation, and were scurrying around to move the baked goods from the reach of the mangy-looking old mule. The spectators continued to howl with laughter, tickled as they watched the mule and Scotty.

"Consarnit Cleo, git yourself outa thar," Scotty yelled as he pulled the rope; trying to get her to move. Michael quickly went over to help, and between the two of them, they managed to pull Cleo's head around so they could remove her head first. No one else came to help, as they were enjoying the entertainment too much to interfere. There stood the saggy-looking, lop-eared mule with berry pie all over her nose and face, berries dripping from her mouth! Finally, she was pulled away from the tables.

While the women, including Kathleen and Eve, were straightening up from the mule's raid, Michael and Scotty walked Cleo down the street, the old man scolding the mule all the way. Scotty's hat was awry, and his temper boiling; he was really angry with Cleo. He tied her tightly to a tree, and stomped off leaving her with the tell-tail signs of her escapade all over her face.

As they walked away, Michael asked, "Scotty, have you run into any Indians lately?" Smiling inside, waiting for the old man's answer.

Scotty pulled his beard and laughed. "Well, ya knowed I never chased no injuns ev'r, but I shoo nuff dun run into sum of them thar ugly lil lizards last week when I was down in thet thar desert. Yes siree, they are a still runnin' round with them thar stick in thar mouths!"

Michael just laughed. The old man was just too funny. The wild-haired man, holding his hat on his head said, "Well, I just guess I'll go into thet thar saloon an wet ma whistle." Michael replied, "Ok. See you later. We're having a parade, and my uncle and his partner are riding in it. I've got to go."

Taking pity on Friendly, who had followed him, he reached down and picked him up. "Hmmm, Friendly, you're getting heavier, you must be starting to grow up," his owner said. Then they ducked through the crowd, looking for his parents. By the time they got back to the booth, the sheriff was already telling people to move aside to make room for the parade. Everyone had stopped their various activities, and had come to line the street along the parade route. By the time Michael and his family got there, they could hear the music of the "Fife and Drum Corps," which was leading the rest of the entries.

When the Corps came into view people became excited, and were clapping with many of the men and boys yelling. Behind this group was a very big float that was pulled by four large horses, the sign on the front said, "Liberty" in large, bold print. On one side of the flat stood thirteen girls dressed in long white gowns with blue sashes at their waists, and golden-colored crowns on their heads. Along the other side were thirteen boys dressed as "Uncle Sam's"; all of this was to honor the original thirteen states. Now the clapping and whistling of the spectators became louder as some of the boys put two fingers in their mouths to make their whistles even shriller. The excitement moved to a higher pitch, and the noise level intensified. It was a special day, especially as most of the people lived on the surrounding ranches, and even a trip into town was a major event. They were all thoroughly enjoying this break in there daily routine of hard-working lives.

After the float moved on, people in the crowd started singing "Columbia, The Gem of the Ocean". Next came the Judge, the orator of the day; he was sitting in a decorated buggy, pulled by a high-stepping brown mare. The horse was much admired, and there was more clapping. The Judge was followed by more floats, decorated by miners who rode on them holding picks and shovels, as well as other implements used in their work; they made Kathleen think about her husband's hard and dirty job.

The noise level moved up yet another notch when two men riding beautiful horses appeared. The whistling and shouting was so loud, it drowned out the sound of the horse's hooves hitting the dirt and rock street. As the men passed by, Michael got so excited; he started waving and yelling, a difficult feat with a wiggly pup under one arm. The partners waved, and Kathleen and Paddy waved back.

Finally, a small unit of black soldiers from Fort Bayard marched by, one of them holding a pole from which the American flag fluttered. Everyone held their right hand over their heart, and the men removed their hats. The sheriff and his deputy brought up the end of the parade, they were well respected, and the people gave them a big hand, clapping until they had moved on. Then the tide of people filled the street, going toward the platform, or other areas of interest, where the festivities would continue.

Soon there was a huge crowd gathered in front of the platform. A small band located to one side began to play "The Star Spangled Banner", and a man stood up to direct the crowd in the singing. Then the band played "My Country 'Tis of Thee". The crowd sang with gusto, and by the time the second song was finished, Michael was filled with pride at being an American. He knew his grandparents had left Ireland to seek a better way of life, and he was glad he had been born in a country where people were free to choose their own path.

Then the Judge stood up, and came forward to speak. "My fellow Americans, we are assembled here today to celebrate the one-hundredth year of the signing of the Declaration of Independence of America. It's a great day to be gathered here - - - -.

The sound of shots rang out from the saloon across the street, and the crowd scattered in all directions, trying to get out of the line of fire. The young maidens, and Uncle Sam's from the float had been seated on the platform, but they wasted no time jumping down, fleeing to places of safety. The Judge stayed at the podium trying to coax the crowd to return. "It's all right folks. Don't panic. Come back, the shooting is all over."

Eventually, people cautiously returned; there had been no more shots. Later it was learned one of the strangers in town had shot another man in the shoulder over a card game, but that the injured man would recover. The man who had done the shooting was taken to jail.

After the crowd reassembled, the Judge continued his speech. After a while, Michael began to think the man would never stop talking. When he finally did, another man got up to remind everyone that there would be a dance at eight o'clock that evening on the platform, and he encouraged them all to come. With that, the crowd dispersed looking for food.

During the disruption of the speech, Michael was separated from the rest of the family, so he and Friendly wandered off on their own. As they drew near the pit where the meat had been cooking, he realized how hungry he was. He carefully counted out enough of the money his pa had given him to spend during the day to buy some of the meat for himself and Friendly. The meat was handed to him wrapped in a flour tortilla. Finding a place to sit out of the way, he shared his meal with Friendly. While he was still eating, the blond girl he had bumped into earlier walked over and sat down beside him; she had a tortilla filled with meat also.

For a minute, Michael didn't think he could breathe let alone swallow, but she started talking to Friendly who wagged his tail in response. She said, "So, you want some of this? Well, here you are." The dog quickly swallowed the piece she gave him. She rubbed his ears and told him, "You are a good little dog." Friendly cuddled up to her, thinking being fed and having his ears rubbed was very nice. Then the girl turned to Michael. "I haven't seen you here in Silver City before today. My name's Penelope Firth, but everyone calls me Penny."

Michael managed to swallow and say, "We haven't been here too long, about three months. My name is Michael McGinnis, and it's nice to meet you." "I think I know your mother," the girl said. "Does she work at the seamstress shop?" "Yes", he said. "She does." "Then I do know her, she made me some new dresses. She's really nice, I like her." It was Michael's turn to be pleased, because he thought his ma was "really nice", too.

Penny then said, "We've been in Silver City about two and a half years, we moved from Chicago.

I really like it here more than living in a big city. My father owns the bank in town." The two visited for a while, and Michael felt very comfortable around Penny. He liked her, and thought she didn't seem flirty like some of the other girls. She was just outgoing in a nice way.

Then Penny said, "The only thing I don't like is the Indians. They've been out east of town recently, and I'm hoping they don't get any closer to us. They really frighten me." Suddenly she stood up. "Well Michael, it was really nice meeting you. If I don't see you sooner, I will see you when school starts." He stood up and she reached out to shake his hand. When their hands met, he started tingling, and he felt breathless again. "Goodbye Penny," he squeaked.

She gave him another of her beautiful smiles as she turned away and left. Michael sat down again, thinking about her. Finally, he shook his head, telling himself not to be silly. Her folks were rich, and she wouldn't be interested in him. He moved across the street, and bought a glass of cider, then went looking for his family. They were at the booth again, and his pa and Reverend Smith had just gotten back with food for their ladies. People were buying the baked goods right and left. Michael had hoped for one of his ma's donuts, but they seemed to be all gone. His ma smiled at his expression of disappointment, as she reached under the table where she had put some aside, saving them for him. "Gee thanks, ma!" He took his first bite, thinking maybe he was in heaven. His ma made the best donuts he had ever eaten.

When Kathleen looked at Michael, he looked radiant, and she wondered about that; she knew her donuts weren't that good. He's eaten them all his life and his face had never looked like that before. "Are you having a good time, son?" He talked about the meat, the clown, and all the festivities – but he didn't mention Penny Firth.

Just about that time, his Uncle Mac and Pete came to the booth to see what was for sale, and Kathleen had saved some of the donuts for them too. They also bought two dozen cookies. She took the opportunity to introduce them to her close friends, the Smith's. "Ah, the new minister in town," Mac said. "We've been wanting to meet you."

Everyone but Paddy got to talking about the Smith's arrival, and about the minister coming to share with the small group that met at the ranch for worship. Of course, that means you and your family are invited to come, too," Pete said to Kathleen. "We couldn't get along without all of you there." They were all excited about their common interest in the Lord. Before the two men left, they gave a contribution to the women to help buy books.

That night when the dance began, the music could be heard all over town. Michael's family, Mac, Pete, and the Smith's – without Thelma, who had gotten tired and been walked home – got together again. His ma and pa were dancing, but stopped now and then to visit with people they knew. When they came over to where Pete and Mac were standing, Pete asked Kathleen if she would like to dance with him. She hesitated, looking at her husband, but he said, "Go on now, me girl."

So Pete whirled her out onto the dance floor; she was laughing, having a good time. Michael watched his ma, and thought she was the prettiest woman there, except maybe Penny, and after all, she wasn't a lady yet. He had danced all his life, so after getting up his nerve, he went over and asked Penny if she would like to dance. She looked at her mother who encouraged her to go ahead. Mrs. Firth knew Michael's mother, and felt her daughter would be safe with the boy. So the two danced several times, and were enjoying each other.

Mac stood back watching Kathleen, and yearning to dance with her, but his common sense told him it wasn't the thing to do. She was a lovely woman, maybe even more so than when she was a girl.

Richard Smith and Eve, holding hands, came over to Mac, and started talking to him. "This has been some day", Richard said. "I don't think Eve and I have ever had so much fun together before. I guess we haven't been married long enough yet for there to have been that many opportunities." Mac asked the obvious question, and was surprised to hear they had been married while traveling with the same wagon train that brought his brother and family west.

"We fell in love along the way, and were married at Fort Union. She's a wonderful woman." Grinning at his wife, Richard continued, "That's where we met your brother and his family; Eve and Kathleen have been close friends ever since."

When it was time for the family to leave for home, Michael and Penny stopped dancing; he had enjoyed his time with her and felt alone when she left. As he was thinking about Penny, he realized Pete was talking to him. "Michael, how would you like to ride out with me tomorrow? I plan to look for that horse I told you about. You ride Nell very well, and I'd enjoy having you go with me. I spoke to your parents, and they said you could come. What do you think?"

Those blue eyes of Penny's were suddenly gone from his mind. "Yes sir! I would really like that, Nell's a neat horse."

"I also asked your ma and pa if you could go back to the ranch with Mac and I tonight; you can ride my horse, and I'll ride one of the white horses, and lead the other one. With you already at the ranch, we can leave early in the morning."

Pete hadn't given any thought to the Indians. Yes, they had been nearby, but he had heard they were now over along the Rio Grande River.

Michael's parents and Molly took Friendly home, and Michael rode to the ranch with Pete and Mac. That night as Kathleen climbed in between the covers of the bed, she thought to herself that Michael was growing up. She had watched him and Penny dancing, and the thought came that she was a very pretty girl. "My my. Where have the years gone?"

The morning air was beginning to turn warm as Pete and Michael rode deep into the wooded area. They continued through a mixture of evergreen trees, some very tall with long needles that covered the ground. The whole area was beautiful, and the heavy scent from the pine trees was refreshing. Michael was enjoying the ride, and it felt good to be away from town. Pete was headed for a place where meadows crept along a cool stream that flowed through canyons in the mountains that were rising around them.

"I think this might be a likely spot for the horse; there is food and water close at hand", Pete said. He was prepared to take the horse to the ranch if they were able to capture him. Unfortunately, there were no signs of the animal, so they rode further. After searching several hours, Pete decided they might as well return to the ranch. Just as they were turning back, Michael spotted the stallion on a knoll some distance away. "There he is," Michael said quietly, pointing the horse out to Pete. "Gosh, it looks a lot like our Mr. Grey, that's the horse pa lost in a poker game in Santa Fe." They stopped their horses, and Pete said, "Are you sure?" "I think so. He has that really black spot on his face that comes down over one eye."

"Let's try walking toward him on foot," Pete said, and they both stepped down out of their saddles. After tying their horses to some branches, they moved slowly, walking toward the horse until it became agitated by their close presence. They stopped, and the horse calmed down. Pete, speaking softly, asked Michael, "Do you still think it's the same horse?" "Yes sir, now that we're closer, I'm very sure. What I don't understand, is how he got here? We're a long way from Santa Fe where I last saw him."

As Michael was talking, the horses' ears pricked up as if he was listening to Michael's voice. The horse took a few tentative steps forward, and then hesitated. Pete watched the horse closely, and then made his decision. "Michael, I think your right, the horse recognizes you. I'm going to stay here, and let you walk over to him. Go slowly, and talk softly to him; take your time. Take this rope with you; it already has a noose in it. When you've gotten close enough, and if he is standing still – and if you are sure it's your pa's horse, continue talking to him. If he balks at it keep talking softly, and let him calm down. He's more likely to accept the rope if he recognizes you. Be very gentle, and if he resists, wait until he quiets down. Just take your time."

Michael did exactly as Pete instructed. He took the rope, and began walking toward the horse, all the while speaking quietly. By the time he and the horse were face to face, it appeared the animal was comfortable having him so close. Somewhere in the past, the horse remembered flying like the wind across the fields with this person on his back. Michael, talking in a coaxing tone of voice, reached up and gently rubbed the side of Mr. Grey's face. The horse leaned toward Michael's hand as if to say, "I've missed you, and am glad to see you."

As the rope slipped gently over his neck, the horse was surprised. It snorted, and took a step back, but Michael continued speaking to him. "It's alright boy, everything will be okay. Do you remember me?" As he talked, the horse settled down.

Before long, the two were walking toward Pete. It was a slow process, but it was obvious that Michael knew instinctively how to handle the horse. He had followed Pete's instructions very well. Pete gained a great deal of respect for this son of Kathleen's.

When they arrived back at the ranch, leading Mr. Gray, the men gathered around to admire the steel-dust stallion; the horse had great lines, and was a handsome animal. As the other men stood around talking to Michael, Pete spoke to his partner. "Mac, I think this fall, after the Apaches are back on the reservation, it would be good to hire Michael, even though he will be in school; he could work on Saturdays. He's a natural working with horses; it would give him a chance to learn more, and he probably wouldn't be against making a little money. What do you think?"

Mac agreed with Pete and said, "I think it's a great idea, but before we mention this to Michael, I'll talk to his parents about it." As he said that, he realized the boy was growing into manhood – slowly, but surely. The Saturday job would help him learn about horses and life.

Later that afternoon when Mac rode back with Michael, he noticed how well his nephew rode. When they arrived at the house, Paddy was not home yet, so the man briefly explained to Kathleen, Pete's idea about having Michael work at the ranch on Saturdays come fall.

"But we wouldn't want it to interfere with his school work," Mac said. "Michael's a good student, and I think he can handle both the work and school, but I will have to let you know what Paddy says," Kathleen told him.

She was delighted, and surprised to hear Mr. Grey had been found. "However did you know it was him?" Mac explained that Michael had recognized the horse, and then talked the animal into giving up his freedom. "I guess they missed each other," she said. "Could we come to the ranch this weekend when Paddy's off work to see him?" "Sure, we'll make arrangements to get you out there," Mac assured her.

As he rode away, he thought to himself that Kathleen was even more beautiful than when she was young; she had grown into a lovely woman. Then, as other more-intimate thoughts about his feelings toward her came, he wiped them away knowing he could not allow himself to think about her this way. She was his brother's wife.

Michael's mother mentioned the job offer while the family was eating supper that evening. "They don't want him to start until the Indians are back on the reservation this fall." As Michael listened, he hoped they would let him work at the ranch.

Kathleen then filled Paddy in on all the details about Michael and Pete finding Mr. Grey that morning. "In the name of heaven, how could the horse have gotten down here?" Paddy asked. "This is a far piece from Santa Fe. Michael spoke up. "Pa, it's him alright and he looks good. Pete says we will probably never know how he got to this area." "They will come get us with the wagon on Saturday, so we can go to the ranch and see him, Paddy. You could probably ride him again. They will keep him at the ranch, but Mac said he's ours since Michael is the one who caught him", she told her husband. They made plans to go out to see Mr. Grey the following weekend.

Later in the evening, after the children had gone to bed, Paddy sat down and said to his wife, "It was all my fault. It was! It was me that lost him playing poker." Kathleen said to her husband, "All of that is behind us. You are back to the husband I married." He put his arms around her. "It's you that's made the difference. I love you, I do." As he kissed her, Kathleen thought how good it was to have her husband back.

The Indians struck the ranch that night while everyone was eating supper. The men were already wearing their gun belts, but grabbed the loaded rifles they had left by the door. They ran outside, and suddenly it was every man for himself. The Indians were concentrating on the corral where the horses were kept, and started circling. As Pete ran to the door of the barn, he began firing at them trying to stop as many as he could. Mac and the ranch hands were doing the same, all shooting as the Indians rode through the yard.

Quite a few Indians lay where they had fallen off their horses, shots were flying in every direction, and the men from the ranch were trying to find cover. Pete heard Harry yell out as a bullet hit him. Mac had gotten as far as the corral, and was down on one knee attempting to reload his rifle when he felt a jolt in his shoulder. As the pain took over, he began to feel really sick, and leaned back against one of the posts of the corral where he slid down, not moving.

Soon the Indians gave up and retreated. Some of the men checked the Indians who had been shot; they were all dead. The other men went to Harry and Mac, the only men from the ranch who had been injured. Mac had passed out and was bleeding heavily from a wound in his shoulder. Pete quickly called two of the men who came over, lifted Mac, and carried him inside the house to his bedroom, where they carefully laid him on the bed. Maria was at his side instantly; she took one look, and quickly went to the kitchen to get some leaves she had gathered earlier in the year. She made a tea of the leaves to help the healing process. While she was doing this, Pete was applying pressure to stop the bleeding. Maria returned to the bedroom with bandages, hot water, and the tea.

She took over cleaning the wound, while Ben was sent to town to get Doc Freeman. By the time the doctor reached the ranch, the bleeding had stopped, but it started again when he began prying out the bullet. It took the doctor a long time before he had it out.

"The bullet was lodged in the bone, which is badly shattered. It's going to take some time to see just how bad it is, and how the use of his arm and shoulder are affected. There is also, of course, a danger of infection, you will have to watch him carefully, and he should not be allowed to move. That bone in the shoulder is a pretty nasty wound. All I can say is keep the wound clean, and keep him still; even if you have to tie him to the bed. He's going to be in a lot of pain when the shock wears off. I'm leaving some Laudanum; it will help the pain as well as keep him sleeping most of the time."

Then Doc went out to check on Harry, who had been shot in the leg. The bullet had gone straight through the outer side of his thigh, just a flesh wound. One of the other hands had cleaned and bandaged the leg, and after looking at it, the doctor didn't think there was anything more that needed to be done. "It won't take long to heal, just keep it clean."

He turned to Pete and said, "I'm having to go out toward the Mimbres River. A woman there is due to have her baby, and while I was with Harry, they sent someone to fetch me. I won't be back for several days, but if Mac gets worse or starts to run a fever have someone come get me right away. If I'm not back, leave a note, just keep the wound clean."

After the doctor left, Maria opened up the bandages, applied the wet leaves from the tea to Mac's wound, and dipped the bandages in the tea before putting them back. As she was replacing them, she said a simple prayer that Mac would heal quickly.

While Ben was in town, he told Kathleen what had happened at the ranch. She was very concerned, and promptly went to pass the news along to Richard and Eve.

The next day, Richard rented a horse, and with the directions she had given him, went to the ranch to pray for Mac. Pete saw him coming, and was grateful for his visit.

"Is Mac able to have visitors?" the minister asked. "Yes, and I'm glad you've come", Pete said. "He's in a lot of pain when the medicine wears off. The doctor said he isn't to move around, so we have to hold him down so he doesn't reopen his wound or get an infection. Someone has to be with him at all times, he's really not too clear in his mind. The medicine only helps some, because of the high level of pain he's having, but he is sleeping a lot. We're all doing whatever we can to help him heal."

Richard moved over and laid hands on Mac and began praying. Mac was moving restlessly and kept saying, "Kathleen, Kathleen." The minister remembered her telling stories of her young years, and how close she, Paddy, and Mac had been.

After praying for Mac, the minister and Pete went into the parlor where Maria was waiting. Richard told them, "I'm glad I found out Mac was shot. We will keep him in our prayers, and I will be back to see him."

Then Pete said, "This will probably stop our meetings for a while, Mac's just not up to it." "I understand Pete, but please know we are looking forward to being part of your group. I can't seem to find a decent place to hold services, so perhaps we are meant to be here"

The men shook hands, Pete saying, "We will keep you informed. I'm not sure if I should mention this, but we've been watching over Kathleen. Paddy is inclined to drink, and was very brutal at times this year. Although he has not been drinking recently, and he and his family are doing well, Mac and I have been very concerned that he might start back with the alcohol again."

Richard replied, "Yes, I know. We've heard about the situation, and will keep watch over the family. I have already told Michael to let me know if there are any problems and that if Paddy starts drinking again, to bring Kathleen and Molly to our place." "Good",

Pete said. "We've really been anxious about their safety."

When Richard got back to town, he stopped to report Mac's condition to Kathleen and Paddy. She thanked him for letting them know, as they had been worried, Ben had stopped to tell them about the Indians, and Mac's wound.

That night, Kathleen prayed for Aaron. He had always been so special, and she remembered the years as they were growing up; so many years ago.

Chapter 9

The gambler kept waiting for the man, McGinnis to come back into the saloon, but Paddy was nowhere to be seen; so knowing Paddy worked at the mine, he began stalking him, and a plan began to form in Ted Spencer's mind.

Through the months since he and the McGinnis family arrived in Silver City, he had thought more and more about the beautiful woman. He was determined to have her as his own, and nothing would stop that from happening. Irrationality took over, and Ted Spencer chose the day he would kill Kathleen's husband. In his strange state of mind, he thought that when he killed the man, no one would blame him, nor would they see him when he shot the man.

One morning, Kathleen got up earlier than usual. Her husband always worked so hard, usually coming home exhausted after a long day at work, so today she would cook him a special breakfast, to show him how grateful she was. He had stopped drinking, and he no longer spent time in the saloons. He was more like the Paddy she knew when they lived on the farm.

Kathleen baked fresh biscuits. They had honey on hand, which he loved to spread on the biscuits. She fried bacon, and had eggs ready to fry when he came into the kitchen. There was a pot of coffee waiting. On the spur of the moment she fried a potato, cutting it in small pieces.

Kathleen had a hot cup of coffee on the table, when he walked in for breakfast. She cooked the eggs, and set the meal in front of him. She sat with him drinking a cup of coffee while he ate. The woman told her husband how proud she was of him as he ate hungrily. "I know it was hard on you to stop drinking, but you did it. You always work so hard, never complaining, and I am so happy. You are a good husband." They talked more intimately that morning than they had in a long time.

When he left with his lunch in his hands, he kissed her saying, "Me bonnie lass, you're the best wife ever, that you are." Kathleen followed him out onto the porch, and watched him walking away. He's a good man, she reminded herself.

After Michael and his sister were up and fed, they went out to the vegetable garden to pull out the weeds that were encroaching on the plants. Their father had given them the job; he had so little time to get everything done that needed doing.

Kathleen, feeling happy, hummed an Irish song as she washed the dishes and tidied up the kitchen. Then after making her and Paddy's bed, and did a small amount of washing, she began working on a lovely soft pink dress for Grace Simpson, trying to get it ready for the young woman to try on.

While sewing, she heard the front door open, and thinking it was her son, turned to see what he needed. What she saw was Ted Spencer, standing inside the closed door!

Suddenly she was frightened. "What are you doing here?" she demanded. "You can't just walk into my house. Get out!" she said to him, trembling. The man just laughed, which frightened her even more. "I'm here to get you, my pretty one. Your mine now! I have won!" Spencer said, as his face turned evil-looking.

"You're out of your mind. I'm married; you can't just walk into my house and say such a thing." "Oh no, lovely lady, you're mine now, the man repeated. She was so confused, and her voice grew louder. "Get out, I am *not* yours." She was terrified, and did not know what to do.

While looking at the man, Kathleen saw the door open quietly, and she saw Michael come into the room. Suddenly, her son flung himself at the gambler, knocking the man down. Both wrestled each other, rolling across the floor; first one on top, and then the other. Ted Spencer, being the heavier and larger, pinned Michael down in time, even though Michael kept trying to free himself, as he continued hitting at the man, with his one free arm.

His mother made a snap decision, and ran into the kitchen grabbing her large iron skillet. She ran back into the parlor; her son still pinned down. Kathleen raised the skillet high, and brought it down on the

Love Comes in Many Colors

back of the man's head. The man fell, sprawled across Michael, unconscious. Michael, squirming, tried to get out from under the man, but he was too heavy. Kathleen rushed to her son's side, and tried to pull Michael out from under the gambler. Once he was free, she told him, "Michael, go into the kitchen and get the rope your pa keeps beside the door. We need to tie him up before he wakes up!

The two tied the man's arms in back of himself. He then ran the rope down to his ankles, and tied them too. Just as they finished, there was a loud knock on the door, and Kathleen got up to run to the door.

Sheriff Delaney was standing there, and she said "Quick! Ted Spencer is unconscious and lying on my floor. We just finished tying him up; then she explained what happened. The law officer turned, and beckoned his deputy. As he walked through the door, the man had regained consciousness, and was struggling to get free. The two men lifted him up and roughly walked him out the door.

Once another man came to help the deputy, Sheriff Delaney turned back and spoke to Kathleen. "Ma'am, I'm really sorry, but I need to tell you that this man shot your husband on his way to work this morning. It took us some time to find out your husband's name, and who his family was. Men have been out searching for this man for several hours now. Mrs. McGinnis, I'm afraid your husband is not doing well. He was taken to Doc Freeman's place. I would suggest that you hurry, and go to him. I'm sorry ma'am."

Gasping, Kathleen said, "Oh no!" Michael, overhearing, said "Let's go ma. After I get you to the doctors', ill go get Reverend Smith." Grabbing Molly, he took his mother's hand, and headed them all to the doctors. His office was in his home, so Michael left Molly with the doctors' wife and hurried to get Reverend Smith.

The doctor explained Paddy's condition. "Mr. McGinnis was shot in the chest, injuring both his heart and lungs." The man shot him with a rifle; I'm afraid your husband will not live long," and then he took Kathleen in to see her husband. She softly told him, "The minister should be arriving soon, please ask him to come in when he arrives." Then she turned to Paddy. His eyes were closed, but when she knelt down beside him, and touched his arm, Paddy's eyes opened. "What happened, where am I?"

Her husband looked so pale. "It's alright, you're at the doctors, you're safe now." "Why", he asked. He started coughing, and blood spilled out through his lips. She gently wiped the blood away; trying not to frighten her husband. "There was an accident. The doctor will take care of you; don't worry dear, you're in good hands." She refrained from mentioning Ted Spencer. There was no reason to tell him what happened. "You need to stay calm and quiet", she told her husband. Then she bent over and kissed him gently on the cheek, and sat down in a chair the doctor brought over. Then Richard walked into the room after hearing what happened.

Kathleen touched her husband's hand, and prayed for him, not realizing Richard had come into the room. She told her husband, "We need to trust God, Paddy." The dying man murmured, "I don't know if He will be hearing me, I've never given him much time in me life." At that point, Richard moved forward, having heard Paddy's response.

"The Lord loves you Paddy, He always has. Just tell him how you feel about him, He will hear you." As Richard took his friends hand, Paddy softly talked to the Lord. "Sorry, I am, for all the wrong things I have done. I want to be right with ye Lord. You've always taken care of me family," the dying man told his Lord. "I thank you, I do. I want to belong to you." Then he spoke to his wife, "Sorry, I am for all I did to ye, me Katie. You're me bonnie lass. . . . . . .

The words ceased, his eyes closed, and Paddy slipped away. His wife started to cry. "Oh no, Paddy, don't go!"

Richard went to the grieving wife, and after letting her cry, he spoke gently, "Come, Kathleen. Paddy's alright now." And he walked her out of the room. She sat on a chair, quietly weeping as Richard made arrangements for a funeral at the cemetery the next morning.

Michael and his sister stood beside their mother, as she told them their father had gone to be with the Lord, Molly went into her mother's arms crying and confused. Her mind, hardly able to know what happened, but seeing tears in her mother's eyes, told her something terrible had happened. Michael felt like crying, but he would not. He was the man of the house now, and he would take care of his mother and sister.

Eve and Thelma came in the door, and seeing their friend crying, stood close at hand if she needed them.

After Richard had finished talking to the doctor, he gently took Kathleen's hand, suggesting it was time to go home. The woman rose, knowing there was nothing to do. She gathered her two youngsters, and walked home, one on each side; Richard and his ladies following behind. They would stay with Kathleen as long as she needed them.

Once they were home, Kathleen had no idea what to do, so she sat down in her chair with Molly sitting on the floor near her. She was weary and confused. Michael took his sister's hand and took her into his bedroom where he tried to help his sister, asking her if she wanted to play checkers. The girl said. "yes", but their hearts weren't in the game.

Finally, Thelma came in and took Molly with her, giving her a sandwich. It was early, but it distracted the girl. Michael did not want one, and disappeared out the back door.

Richard went to Kathleen, and told her they would be here with her. Then he prayed with Kathleen. Shortly after Richard prayed for Kathleen, Pete knocked on the door having heard Paddy had been killed when he was in a store. Eve opened the door, and Pete said he had heard about Paddy's death. "I came immediately to see what we could do; I know Mac would feel the same way."

After talking to Richard, Pete pulled up a chair and sat down beside Kathleen. "I'm so sorry about your loss, Kathleen." The words came tumbling out.

"Oh, Pete, that terrible man shot Paddy, and now we've lost him! I don't know what to do!" She looked so helpless and lost.

"Kathleen, I know this has been a huge shock. Just give it time, things will become more clear. Your friends are with you, and we will help in any way we can. Things will get better," he told his friend. Suddenly the tears began to flow, and she could not stop them. Pete handed her his handkerchief, and then put his arm around the weeping woman. He let her cry, knowing that was the best medicine for now. Eve came over and took his place, and he went looking for Michael. He found the boy outside, sitting on a large rock. He was throwing pebbles nowhere in particular.

"Are you alright son?" Pete asked Michael. "I guess so; it's really hard to watch ma. This whole year has been really hard on her, and now this! I can't believe that man shot pa." "I know," Pete agreed. "This is hard on all of you, Michael. I wish I could do something to make it all go away; but I can't. Your uncle and I will help as much as we can. For now, we will make sure you can stay here in the house.

"No," Michael said, "I can work. I've decided to stop going to school and try to find a job in one of the mines. That way, I can pay the rent." "Don't do it", Pete told the boy. "It would break your mother's heart. You need to finish your schooling. You are almost through with that part of your education. Now is the time to put your trust in God, your uncle, and me. Everything will work out in time, you'll see." Pete prayed with Michael, and the boy began to cry the tears so close to the surface, Pete put his arms around the boy, holding him gently. Then he told the boy, "I must go, but I will see you tomorrow at your father's funeral.

After Pete left, he stopped by and paid the owner of the house three months rent for Kathleen and her family, then he headed for the ranch. He was concerned about Mac, and how he would take Paddy's death. Certainly he was in no condition to be up and moving about, but Pete knew his partner well. Pete figured it would take some doing to keep Mac from attending his brother's funeral, Mac could be strong minded at times. How Mac would handle his brother's death, he did not know.

The following morning it was already hot and muggy. There were clouds, heavy with rain, skirting around the valley. Kathleen, her family, and the Smith's arrived at the grave site shortly before ten o'clock. Others were gathering, and she was surprised to see the Hansons, Mr. and Mrs. Firth, with their daughter, Penny. The Walsh's were there, and she saw Grace Simpson arriving with her husband, or so she assumed. Some of the men Paddy worked with were there, though Kathleen did not know their names. She was touched to see so many people.

She heard the buggy on the road before it came into view. When it did, she saw Pete, Aaron and Maria. Aaron's face was ashen, and drawn; his face, showing the pain he was enduring. Kathleen felt concern for her brother-in-law, thinking he should not be up and around yet. He shouldn't have come today, but she knew he would want to say goodbye to his brother. She understood, but feared the trip into town might cause him further injury.

As Pete and Maria got down from the buggy, they were holding tight to Mac. Kathleen, with Molly in her arms, went over to Aaron and spoke softly to him. "I am so sorry, Aaron. I wish this had not happened." She wasn't crying, but her emotions showed on her face. He, also knew what she was going through, and wished he could find words that would comfort her. "I'm sorry too, Kathleen. We've both lost someone we loved. Please, let Pete and I help."

By that time, Richard was ready to start, but waited until the two had spoken. Then Pete and Maria helped Mac to the grave.

Kathleen looked at the sky, and saw it was threatening to rain. She whispered to Pete, telling him to stop by the house before going back home. He nodded, saying they'd planned to.

Richard began reading Romans 8, verses 35 and 37 thru 39.

'Who shall separate us from the love of Christ? Shall tribulation or distress or persecution or famine or nakedness or peril or sword? Nay, in all things, we are more than conquerors, through Him who loves us!

For I am persuaded that neither death nor things present, or things to come, nor height nor death, nor any other creature shall be able to separate us from the love of God, which is in Christ Jesus our Lord.'

"Let us pray: Dear Heavenly Father, we place Patrick into your hands. He believed in your son, Jesus, and we know he is with you, in your kingdom.

Lord, comfort those who are left behind. Help them to keep their eyes on you during this most difficult time, now and ahead. Give the family hope and courage, as they face the future, knowing because of you, all will be well. In Christ's name, amen."

"We first met Paddy and his family while traveling west with others on a wagon train that was headed for Santa Fe. There were many hard and difficult days as we moved west. We faced drought, heat, and cold. We also went through Indian country, rain and long hard days. Often discouragement crept in as we faced what seemed insurmountable challenges. Patrick was always there with his quick wit, and his extra-ordinary tenor voice. He, above all others, either kept us laughing, or his singing washed away the trials of the day. He had a rare talent of encouragement, which kept us going day after day. We, who knew him then, and now, will miss him."

Richard finished with a short prayer: "Lord, be with Paddy's family in the days ahead, as they face the future. Help them with the knowledge that you are with them, and will take care of them. We ask in the name of Jesus, amen."

When Richard finished his prayer, Kathleen, her son, and daughter, placed the last of the yellow roses of the summer on the coffin where Paddy's body lay. Molly began to cry, so Kathleen knelt down beside her daughter, speaking softly to the small girl, and comforting her. Mac walked slowly to the grave site, and placed a handful of summer's wild flowers that Pete and Maria had picked on their way into town.

Friends went to Kathleen, expressing their sorrow for her and her children's loss. Those who knew Mac, long time friends, spoke to him. All could see, he was suffering from a great deal of pain as he stood, with Pete holding onto his friend. They could see his weariness, so they spoke softly and left, not wanting to add to his weakness.

Penny talked to Michael. "I'm so sorry about your father, Michael, God be with you." He was deeply touched by her. She still had those beautiful blue eyes, which he knew he would never forget.

Grace Simpson gave Kathleen a gentle hug. "We are so sorry for your loss", and her husband, graciously told the grieving widow, "Please, feel free to call on us if you need help."

As the couple walked away, Kathleen was touched by the man's offer. She thought, the man does not know me, nor Paddy, even though Paddy worked for him.

She would have been surprised to know James Simpson did know about Paddy.

Sometime back, Mr. Simpson had been told Paddy was one of the hardest workers at the mine. He was always joyful, often singing as he worked.

Several days later, a plain envelope was delivered to the McGinnis' home. Kathleen was surprised to find a rather large amount of money inside. She was grateful, but had no idea who to thank.

Kathleen, her family, Mac, and their friends, mourned the loss of husband, father, brother, and friend.

The woman, seeing the oncoming signs of a storm, spoke to Pete. "It looks like it might rain. Be sure to stop by the house, to avoid getting wet. Pete informed her they planned to do so.

Shortly after, Kathleen, and her family arrived at the house. Pete, Mac, Maria, and other friends arrived there also. Then the skies opened up with sheets of rain, falling onto the land. Everyone was glad to be safe inside, and it rained for some time before the storm moved east, over the mountains. It left everything clean and fresh and the air cooler.

Maria and Pete had gotten Mac out of the buggy and onto Kathleen's bed, covering him with a light blanket. The man was exhausted and hurting, and he was asleep before they left the room.

Kathleen faced the difficulty of having people around, though she was grateful for the love and caring, but she was very tired. Having had little sleep the night before, Kathleen fell asleep too, sitting in her chair.

Thelma, Eve and Maria gathered the food together. Some people had brought food, and Maria had baked a ham the night before. Eve and Thelma had baked several pies.

Everyone, including Michael and his sister, sat down to eat. All trying to be as quiet as possible, not wanting to wake the two sleeping. After eating, Michael and Molly went into the boy's room, which was the porch. He and his father had just finished closing it in two weeks ago, making it safe from the weather. For a while they played checkers, Michael wanting to be out of sight. Friendly had not joined them. He lay beside his mistress, sensing something was wrong, and no coaxing could convince the dog to move.

Kathleen woke with a start, wondering how long she had been sleeping. She heard her friends in the kitchen, speaking softly as they worked.

Pete and Richard were sitting on the porch talking. Pete's voice was soft, yet she heard him talking to Richard. "It's such a shame. She's had a difficult time here, especially before you folks arrived. Just as things were beginning to get better, that man had to shoot Paddy."

"I've been having a hard time with Mac. He wanted to come see Kathleen the minute he heard of Paddy's death, wanting to help her. He should not have come today. Mac has loved Kathleen since they were young, so, in a way, these last months since Paddy and his family moved here have been rough on him. He did all he could do to help Paddy, not wanting her to be hurt. Mac would never say anything to her about his feelings toward her. I guess he loved her way back when she married Paddy, and he knew he had to leave."

"I first heard about Kathleen when we fought in the Civil War together. As far as I know, he has never looked at another woman. Such loyalty, without reason."

"We are all worried about Mac. He doesn't realize it yet, but the doctor says he will never have free range of his shoulder or upper arm. That means he will no longer be able to work with the horses. Something we both have always loved. I feel sorry for Mac, and to tell you the truth, I'm not sure how I will be able to tell him about it."

Richard reminded Pete, "Mac's a good man, with a strong faith. He will work it out someway. Our prayers are even more important for them, they have both lost someone they loved, and both must face an uncertain future."

Neither man realized Kathleen had overheard their conversation; she was startled. Aaron loves me? Her heart said, "Oh Aaron. Why didn't you say something so long ago? Her mind said, No, and she changed her thinking, and said, "I must get up and do something."

Just as she stood, she heard the sheriff's voice outside on the porch asking for her. Kathleen stepped out the door, giving no indication she had heard anything, and spoke to the lawman. "I'm here sheriff, what is it", she asked. The man took off his broad brimmed hat, holding it in his hands.

"Mrs. McGinnis, I'm sure you would want to know that Judge Logan held a quick trial this morning. A number of men testified, saying they saw Ted Spencer shoot your husband yesterday as Mr. McGinnis was walking to work. It's strange, the man shot him in front of all those men; I can't understand why he wasn't more careful, though he hasn't been rational since we took him to jail yesterday. You'll not be seeing him again; the Judge quickly sentenced him to thirty years hard labor for murder. They have already left to take Spencer to the penitentiary in Yuma."

Kathleen felt relieved. He was a dangerous man, and she never wanted to see him again. "Thank you sheriff for telling me, I'm glad he's going to pay for killing my husband." The man shook his head and left, leaving the woman somewhat comforted.

Kathleen smiled at the two men, and touched Pete's arm as if to thank him for his goodness. She walked back into the house, and not knowing what to do, went into the kitchen to join her friends. The three were just finishing cleaning up from the meal that had been served.

Thelma, seeing Kathleen, suggested, "Sit down dear," pointing to the kitchen table where they had put a couple of chairs. "We saved some food for you and Mac," and she brought a plate of food to her friend.

Kathleen thanked the woman. She wasn't sure if she could eat, but she tried. The one cup of coffee she had this morning, hadn't helped much, yet she only picked at her food. The whole world was upside down! Her life completely changed. She asked where Michael and Molly were and Eve told her friend, "They played checkers after eating, but they grew tired, and Michael told us they were going to Todd's house for a while. They are fine, Kathleen. Michael has taken good care of his sister."

The mother was so grateful to have such a good, kind son. She told herself she must thank him later. She could not think of anything to say, and fell silent. Maria spoke up saying, "Mr. Mac, he is still sleeping, he should not have come. I only hope he hasn't hurt himself today, we tried to talk him out of coming.

Love Comes in Many Colors

The doctor told him to stay quiet, but he insisted. He had to come to his brother's funeral. I can tell you, he is not the best patient. He has always worked from dawn to dark, so he thinks he can do more than he should. Men are very strange." Maria speculated, "No common sense!"

Kathleen had to smile. She thought, probably more than one man thought that about women. She remembered Aaron in his early years. Gentle, yes. Kind, always, but hard work had been a big part of his life. Work on the farm was never ending, and Aaron, unlike Paddy, carried more than his share of the work, especially during growing and harvesting seasons. How would he be able to handle a life without heavy labor? She knew how much he enjoyed working with horses. That had been obvious, those few days when she and her family were staying at the ranch. She would continue to pray for him.

She wondered at the passing years. They had gone so swiftly, and who would have guessed they would all end up here, in Silver City, so very far from home. Pete came in interrupting her thoughts, "It looks like another storm is building up, Kathleen. I think we had better get Mac home before it starts raining again."

Maria insisted on feeding the man before they left, and she fed him while he was still lying down; he did not protest. Pete helped Mac out and onto the buggy, and the three headed home.

Kathleen watching realized how much pain the man was struggling with. There eyes met briefly, her seeing the man in a whole different way. The three made it back to the ranch before the skies opened up again. All three were tired, but the one suffering was Mac. He thought he had never hurt so much before, not even the day he was shot.

Once Pete helped his friend into bed, Maria came bringing some of the warm tea from the healing leaves. When Maria sat down and removed the bandages, she saw the wound had opened up and was bleeding. She gently cleaned the wound, put pressure on it to stop the bleeding, and then wet a small cloth with the tea. Then she added some leaves and covered the wound with a bandage, hoping the wound would heal quickly. Pete made up his mind, if the bleeding did not stop by morning, he would send for the doc.

Mac slept off and on for several days, needing to replenish his strength. Pete depended on Maria to watch over his friend, and he was grateful for her help. She was a good woman. A very pretty, good woman!

As summer marched toward fall, Mac began to heal. It did not happen over night, but the shoulder was improving slowly. He found out he would never have full motion with his shoulder again, and he was limited with his left arm, but nevertheless he was grateful the bullet had not hit his right shoulder. The doctor did tell him the arm would continue to improve with time.

Slowly, he began taking over the business of the ranch, the books, buying and selling. Every day he missed working with the horses, and he relinquished the work on the grove, though he kept a close eye on it. He made sure it was well taken care of. One of the men had worked on a grove before, and knew his business, so Mac let the man do his job.

In time, he began spending time with his mare. He would talk to her, and began rubbing her down every few days; Mac was determined to ride her again. It took time to learn how to saddle her, without using much strength from his left arm. It took weeks before he got the saddle on her back; she often side stepped his efforts. Slowly with patience, he managed to get the saddle in place, and buckled down. Then he had to figure some way to get into the saddle, but in time, he did. That first day he rode around the ranch.

By the end of summer, Mac became quite adept at mounting his horse. He had finally managed to accomplish his goal. The men had watched Mac as he struggled so he could ride the horse again. They all admired his tenacity, and all rejoiced with the man, though no one said anything about how they felt.

The Indians were gone from the area, and the long expected meeting with fellow Christians would be next Sunday. Mac was looking forward to the day. For him, it had been a long, hard and lonesome summer. He had not seen Kathleen or her family since the day his brother was buried. It would not be long until Michael would begin working on the ranch on Saturdays, and the man was looking forward to all the activity.

He had spent many hours through the summer, praying for Kathleen, and he wanted to see her, hoping she had been able to get over the loss of Paddy. He also hoped that life was full and happier for her.

Pete kept him informed about the family, but he missed seeing them.

Chapter 10

Golden colored leaves on the cottonwood trees beckoned fall to the valley, and to the surrounding hills. Everyone in Silver City, and those throughout the area were relieved the young braves had returned to their reservation in Arizona until spring. Michael was in school, and enjoyed being there with his friends. The boy liked his teacher immediately. Mr. Roe was somewhere in his fifties. The man was of middle height, and a bit broad around the waist. His pants were always rumpled; but his white starched shirts and smile were always evident as the students walked into the man's classroom each morning.

Michael really enjoyed his school time. He did well with history, reading, writing, and grammar, but maybe not arithmetic, which was a challenge every day. Todd Witherspoon was in his class. The two were becoming fast friends, and of course, there was Penny. The three gravitated toward each other during recess, and lunch time, often laughing, Todd, being the comedian. The three of them enjoyed many pleasant days.

Kathleen was constantly working these days, as was Eve, their work complimenting each other. Often Molly spent the day with Thelma if her mother needed to be at the shop, or spent hours upon hours sewing. The cooler weather was refreshing, and made her work much easier.

The ranch was running smoothly. Mac had adjusted better than anyone thought he would. He took sole responsibility of the finances, and the sale of horses. He and Pete planned the work schedule together each day, and then Pete spent his days working with the men and horses.

The time had come for the partners to start their Sunday morning meetings, which had always included a potluck luncheon after their time reading and studying scriptures together. This Sunday the two had invited Richard to come and head their time together.

During the summer, when it wasn't safe to be out, Richard and Eve had bible studies at their home. Nearly everyone that went to the ranch joined them, as did Kathleen, Michael and Molly. Now they all looked forward to going to the 'Pine Tree' ranch. The weather was good, and all the regulars always loved being out in the country, away from the noisy town.

Michael was now working Saturdays at the ranch, so he slept over. His family would be coming out with the Smith's the next day.

In preparation for the first meeting at the ranch, at least her first time, Kathleen baked three apple pies. The rest of the day was taken up with finishing one of the dresses she was working on.

The following morning, Ben arrived to pick up Kathleen, Molly, and the Smith family. As they rode to the ranch, everyone enjoyed seeing the many wildflowers that the summer rains had caused to grow and bloom. The ride was refreshing, the coolness now replacing the summer heat. Eve, Thelma, and Kathleen chattered as they fully enjoyed the ride to the ranch. Richard pondered the mornings' message he planned to give. He felt somewhat nervous, this being his first sermon he would give since coming to town. Yet, he did not want it to sound like a sermon. He finally decided to leave the message in the Lord's hands, and turned to the land as they traveled.

Once there, Pete and Mac were there to greet their good friends. Pete reached up and helped Molly down, and then he and Richard helped the ladies as he greeted each one.

Stepping inside the ranch house again, Kathleen felt so comfortable. There was a small fire burning in the large fireplace which warmed the room nicely. After taking off her and Molly's coats, Kathleen went to the large window facing town. The yellow leaved trees were scattered throughout the valley. All were dispersed among the many evergreen and scrub oak trees, making a lovely contrast on the land.

Others began arriving soon. Most of them, Kathleen knew, but the ones that were strangers were introduced by Mac. The last to arrive were the Firths, riding in a large fancy buggy. To Kathleen's surprise, the Simpson's were the owners of the buggy. She had not seen them since Paddy's death. She was delighted to see them all, and she gave the women a hug. She then was reminded of Paddy's funeral, and it caused her to wish her husband was here with her.

After everyone was seated and introduced, Pete turned to Richard, and gesturing to him he said, "I'm glad you're here with us today, please, the time is yours."

The man was sitting in his chair with his bible open on his lap. "First of all, I would really like you to call me Richard. We are extremely glad to be here with you this morning, to spend time in God's word. Then he suggested that those who had their bibles turn to Luke, chapter 10. He bowed his head, and asked the Lord to be with them as they read His word.

When that was done, he reminded them about the Good Samaritan. He read the verses that told the story of the man that was robbed and beaten, then left along the side of the road. He went on reading the parable of the Good Samaritan, which said that both a priest and Levite walked by, ignoring the injured man. Finally a Samaritan man saw the man and took him to an Inn. He both cleaned and bandaged the wounds. Then he gave money to the Inn Keeper to keep the man until he returned. "Now let's go to verse 25 and read thru verse 28", and he read:

> 25: *And, behold, a certain lawyer stood up, and tempted him, saying, master, what shall I do to inherit eternal life?*
> 26: *He said unto him, what is written in the law? How readest thou?*

*27: And he answering said thou shalt love the Lord thy God with all thy heart, and with all thy mind; and thy neighbor as thyself.
28: And he said unto him. Thou hast answered right: this do, and thou shalt live.*

After reading the scriptures, Richard said, "We have been here for nearly three months, and I am concerned about the lonely and hungry people who live here. There is no one to help them, and this is a very violent community. Many are here for money only, and of course, money is very important. It's a part of living, but there is one thing missing, or hidden in town; it is love. Love for the Lord is important, and it is what we have, but what about the many people who do not see our love?"

"It behooves us to let the love of Christ shine through us. Love comes in many colors. How often do we pray for, or with the lonely, hungry and lost people around us? We need to treat each person in the same way. Treat them with a smile on our face, and with a helping hand, never turning a deaf ear to one in need."

"Those who were not loved or cared for when they were young, will often find their needs taken care of in other places. We, as believers in Christ, need to love by our actions, as well as our words and prayers."

"How many times have many of us forgotten that? I've found myself being indifferent to people's needs, but that is wrong. Do we pass them by? Do we smile only, or do we help those in need? It's nice to be filled with food, and have fun, there's nothing wrong with that. We need to spend time together, but what about those who have been turned away from because of their speech or looks. Let's not ignore someone who is dirty or foul of mouth. Everyone deserves to be treated kindly and with understanding. I have seen hungry men on the streets of Silver City."

"I suggest it's time to care what happens to those people. I feel it's time to do something. For my part, I plan to open a small place where food and clothing can be given to the needy, God willing. I feel that's what my prayers have led me to do. We need to listen to people, to pray with anyone who needs help, and care for them the best way we can."

"All this will take time to happen. I would invite any of you that would like to help, to pray about it. Then if you feel God wants you to take part in this endeavor, let me know. Having a church is good and right, but caring for the hungry and lonely makes the church viable. First we must be children of God, co-workers with him, caring for those who don't know him or are in great need."

Richard continued on for a short time, and then ended the meeting with prayer. They sang a couple of hymns; each person pondering what they had heard.

Lunchtime was a happy time, but many were thoughtful. Most people there knew it was time to live Christ's words, not just speak them.

After the lunch, James and Grace talked, and they went to Richard. The man led them to a corner of the room where they could sit down, where James told the minister they had never given their lives to the Lord. "We've done very well, and we have all we need plus much more; however, inside of me there is an emptiness I've never been able to fill. Grace and I agree that we both want to give our lives to Christ, if we are acceptable." Richard smiled, and told them, "All are acceptable, and the Lord must be smiling, knowing you want to be in His family."

As they knelt with Richard, they both asked the Lord to forgive them for the life they had lived and their many sins. Richard took hold of each one's hand, praying for them, and then asked them if they wanted to accept Christ. They both spoke, saying yes. Grace had tears in her eyes, and James gulped, trying to control his feelings as God's love touched them both. The two men clasped each other with their arms and Grace' eyes sparkled as the love of God spilled out.

Kathleen and Lillie recognizing what happened, both congratulated the couple, and then each woman hugged their new sister in Christ. Many others congratulated the couple also.

While that was going on, Todd, Penny, and Michael walked to the meadow where the horses spent their days. The area had a fence to keep them in the area filled with gamma grass they could eat whenever they wanted to. Michael pointed out Mr. Grey, as they stood at the fence. The boy told his friends about how he and Pete found the horse so many months after the family lost him in Santa Fe.

Penny looked at the handsome horse; there was a wistful look in her eyes. "I've missed riding", she said. "You know, ride a horse; last year, sometimes if the weather permitted, Pete and Mac would let papa and me take two horses, and we would go for a ride. I learned how to ride in Chicago; there was a park where they rented horses. That was where I learned to ride. I hope papa and I can go for a ride before it gets cold."

Michael suggested, "Maybe you and I could go for a ride together." "Hey, what about me," Ted asked. "Gosh, I don't know Todd, Michael said, you probably would have the horses laughing by the time we got back." Penny giggled, saying, "Probably". Then all three of them laughed.

For Michael, it felt good to be with his friends, and away from town. Life had been so serious since they arrived in the territory. To Michael, this was a good day! Then they wandered on, laughing and talking.

After the Simpson's and Firth's left, Mac asked Richard and Eve if they would like to take a walk around the ranch. "I promised Kathleen I would take her to see their horse that Pete and Michael found nearby. I thought you might enjoy walking with us, maybe Thelma would like to go too." Eve said, "Let me ask her." She came back saying Thelma is enjoying talking to the Walsh's, she told us to go on and enjoy ourselves."

"This is such a beautiful area", Eve remarked as they walked. The day had warmed just enough to make it comfortable for walking. Kathleen stood talking to their horse; he recognized her, and nudged her gently with his head. "So you remember me, don't you boy?" Mac had two halves of an apple, so she gave the pieces, one by one, to the horse. She chuckled as she rubbed his neck, "You are so beautiful", his mistress said, wishing that Paddy was here with her. Mr. Grey belonged to him, but she always loved riding her friend.

After spending time with the horse, the four wandered through the apple grove that still had a few apples unpicked. As they were standing by the stream, Richard and Eve decided to explore, so they started walking toward the mountains as they followed the water. Kathleen could see Mac was tiring, so she suggested they sit and watch the stream. They chose to sit on a knoll overlooking the water; Kathleen sat with her hands clasped around her knees. This was the first time they had spent time alone, and they began reminiscing about their growing up years. Pretty soon they were laughing about some of the silly things they and Paddy had done. Mac said, "Do you remember the day Paddy started singing at the top of his lungs as we passed by old Mrs. Stokes place? She came out of the house with a shotgun in her hands yelling at him, "Stop that croaking you crazy kid!" Paddy got silly, and started hopping on his legs and hands, croaking like a frog. She got so mad; she raised her gun straight up in the air and shot it off; boy did we run!" They both laughed, and then Kathleen reminded him of the time the three of them were walking along the stream between their folk's farms. "For some reason, you turned and started walking backward, talking at the same time. Suddenly you disappeared, falling into the deepest part of the stream. It was so funny!" "I didn't think it was funny." "You would have if you'd seen yourself; you looked like the monster from the dark lagoon. There was watercress draped all over your head when you came up out of the water." Then they both laughed. It was fun remembering back to some of the crazy things they had done so long ago.

Soon the Smith's were back, and the four of them wandered back to the house. Mac introduced Nathaniel Green to Kathleen. Apparently he and her brother-in-law had been friends ever since Mac and Pete had come to the area. The woman thought he was a very pleasant man, she wondered why he wasn't married.

Soon it was time to leave. Everyone was tired, and were more quiet and reflective on their way home; it had been a good day.

That night after her youngsters were in bed, she thought about Richard's idea of helping others. She spent some time in prayer, wanting to know what the Lord wanted her to do, and somehow she felt she was to give time at the center when it became a reality.

It was halfway through November, and Richard's dream had come true. James Simpson, feeling he needed to help the minister, found a small two-room building on Texas Street, and after talking to Richard, he showed him the building, and rented it so the minister could start helping the needy people in town. It took time to gather clothing. the church group brought in used clothing that was wearable; Richard had insisted that any clothes brought in must be clean and in good shape.

Money was donated; it came to a sizable amount. This money could be used to buy food, including some root vegetables from the Chinese gardens in town. The rest, Richard bought from Hanson's General Store where he received a discount. Everyone was so willing to help; Richard was so grateful to all who did, soon the 'Samaritan House' opened. Eve slowed down the amount of sewing she did so she could help her husband. Thelma started picking up the slack sewing, and Kathleen was grateful for she had a number of dresses that must be finished soon.

Kathleen, hearing the 'Samaritan House' would start feeding people on Friday's at the lunch hour, rearranged her sewing schedule so she could help from ten in the morning until two. Todd's mother agreed to take care of Molly.

It was the first day of December. The air was crisp as she hurried to the shop; she needed to pin the hem of one of the holiday gowns she was working on. When that was done, she went straight to the Samaritan House carrying the dress with her. The winds had picked up, making the air colder.

When Kathleen arrived, she was shivering, but she warmed up quickly standing in front of the wood cooking stove. Mac was free, having paid the men early in the day, and he arrived at the house shortly after Kathleen. It wasn't long before a few men came in to eat, and both Kathleen and Mac helped where they could. People came straggling in, hearing about the free meal. It was obvious it would take time before people heard about the free meals.

While those working were busy, a very thin young woman and an equally thin small girl walked in, both poorly dressed and obviously very cold. Kathleen greeted them. My name is Kathleen, may I help you?" The young woman, almost like a child herself said "We're so hungry, could we have some food?" "Of course you can, come sit down over here, closer to the stove and I will get you some food." As the two were eating, Kathleen went into the back room where the clothing was. Looking for some warm clothing for the two, she found warmer clothes and coats, but she could not find shoes for the wee one.

Mac walked into the room, and she turned to him, "I've found some warm clothes I think will fit the two, but I can't find any shoes for the girl. They are so needy; I don't know what to do. I only found some socks, but that's not nearly enough in this cold weather." "Don't worry Mac told her. When they are through eating, I can take them to George's. I will buy them both some shoes, they both look like thy need them." "I wonder what happened to them, and why they are so thin and needy. Maybe Richard can find out where they live, and what's going on; they both look like they are starving. I hope we can help them somehow." Kathleen and Mac returned to wait for the two to finish eating.

Grace walked in, and after hearing about the young woman and child, she told Kathleen. "Keep them here until I get back, I think I know someone who might want to help them, and she hurried away. After Grace left, Kathleen went to Richard, and pointed out the two eating. When the two were finished eating, he and Eve took the two over to a corner where there were chairs. He let his wife do the talking, and she discovered that the blond young woman was only sixteen years old. "My mother died leaving me alone in the house. There was a man that lived next door, and he knew I was alone. One day he came over and raped me." She began crying, and Eve gently put her arms around the girl as she cried, the little girl clinging to her mother's leg. Finally Emily was able to go on. "He came back the next day and took me to his house. He used me whenever he wanted to, and then he locked me in the house when he went to work. I got pregnant, and he still wouldn't leave me alone."

"When my daughter was born, he beat me because she wasn't a boy. He began beating me whenever he was drinking, and he gave me very little to eat. I hardly had enough milk to feed Ida. The child still clung to her mother, and she began to weep again. Finally she calmed down and went on. When Ida was nearly two years old, he left the house one day and forgot to lock the door. I was so scared, but I grabbed Ida, and a blanket, and we fled hoping he wouldn't find us. A couple of days later, he was killed in the mine from an accident; at least that's what I heard.

I tried to go back to the house, but people had moved into it. Then I tried my mother's old house, but other people were living there also, so we have been sleeping in a shed ever since. The man from the Chinese Gardens gave us vegetables to eat, and once in awhile an apple."

By this time, Emily was crying so hard her body was shaking. Eve looked at Richard as she held the crying girl, "We have to do something to help her Richard."

Just then, Grace came back in with an older woman. She introduced Mary Johnson to the Smith's, and shook Richard's hand. She could see the girl crying, with her little one hanging on to her mother. As Eve stayed with the mother and her child, Richard walked Grace and Mary away from them.

He explained what had happened to the two, which distressed both women. Grace told Richard about Mary, "She's a widow, and lives alone. They had a girl, but she died when she was young." Mary spoke up, "I'm alone, and lonely. I have a fairly large home, and there is room for both of them; let me take them home to live with me."

Grace stepped in, "Mary is a lovely woman, and a good friend. She will take good care of the two. She's a very wise woman, and will know how to handle the situation." With Grace's recommendation, Richard agreed. "She's going to need a lot of love and patience. This girl has been through a terrible experience, and he filled Mary in with all the information.

"The poor thing," Mary said. "What a terrible thing for her to go through. I will use lots of patience. They can have a nice room of their own, and all the food they need to get physically well. I will love them so that they can get over this horrible life they've had; the little one will heal more quickly, but I will not take her mother's place, so they can both get well together."

Richard prayed with Mary, and then introduced her to Emily and her little one. Once the decision was made, Mac went with Mary and the mother and daughter. They went into George's and Mac bought them both warm shoes, and Mary bought them each a new warm dress. That night, the mother and child slept in a warm bed, covered by a feather comforter, but the little girl still clung to her mother.

The leaves had blown away by the cold winds that prevailed in the valley. The wildflowers had long since dried on their stems. Cold air settled over Silver City; winter was here, and soon it would be Christmas. It was Saturday and Michael was at work on the ranch, while Molly was with Thelma.

Most of Grace Simpson's gowns Kathleen worked with had higher necklines and straight, long skirts. The dress she was making for her this time had material that was difficult to work with. The dress was different, and very festive. Around the neckline were folds of the soft, deep red velvet material, causing the neck to be more easily seen. The sleeves were partially full to the wrists, the skirt flowing outward with a full petticoat. It was simple, but lovely.

Kathleen could see, in her mind's eye, the young woman dressed in this gown, with the exquisite diamond necklace around her neck. Grace had shown the necklace to the seamstress in the beginning, before a stitch was sewn.

Each Friday, Kathleen and Mac continued to work together at Richard's place.

They began to enjoy being together and helping people in need. The 'House' had people coming regularly to eat, and others were coming in and out all week, seeking clothing.

One Friday, just two weeks before Christmas, Mac walked over to where Kathleen was cleaning up after everyone had eaten. "Uh, Kathleen, do you think, just maybe . . . . ." His voice faltered.

She turned, "What, Aaron?" He swallowed, and started again. "Would you like to go out for dinner with me some night? We could go to the Franklin Hotel; they serve very good food there." She wiped her hands on her apron, and looked at him. He said, "Maybe?" Kathleen smiled at him, he sounded like an awkward boy. "I would love to Aaron." The man's face lit up like a kid finding a gold coin on the ground. It had taken all the courage he could muster to ask her, and here she had said yes, just like that. "How about the next Wednesday night?" Again she smiled. "That would be fine," she said. Mac felt like he was walking on air!

Pete had never seen his friend so happy. Finally he asked. "What's up, what's going on?" "She's going out to dinner with me next Wednesday." "She?" Then it dawned on Pete, Kathleen! He had to smile; his partner was acting like a young man, ready to go on his first date. Well, he wasn't young, but maybe, it was his first date.

"That's great! I'm sure you will enjoy yourselves." That sounded a bit lame, but he didn't really know what to say. Mac did not notice.

During the rest of the days before the big night, Pete often found Mac either whistling, or humming a tune. It was fun to watch.

Meanwhile, the very next day, Kathleen's soft green, wool dress was hanging on the line after she carefully washed it. The day was warmer, and it dried well. Paddy always loved it when she wore the dress. He always said, "It matches your eyes, it does."

"Paddy! My goodness, maybe I shouldn't have agreed to go with Aaron. She saw Eve later in the day, and mentioned her concerns. "Of course you should go, Kathleen. You need to start doing things that make you happy. You want to go don't you?" "Well, yes." "Good. Mac's a good man, and there's no reason you shouldn't go."

So the feeling of guilt drifted away.

By Wednesday, she was excited and nervous all at once. It had been a long time since she had felt this way; she had never gone anywhere except with her husband.

Kathleen heard a knock on the door, and when she opened it, Mac saw what a striking woman she was. Her beautiful hair was pinned up on top of her head, a pretty green comb, holding it in place. Her natural waves enhanced the hairdo, with curly strands around her face, and at the nape of her neck. Her eyes perfectly matched the dress she was wearing, and there were small gold earrings on her small ears. To him she was stunning, and for a moment, he was speechless. "Come in Aaron," she told him. He talked to both Michael and Molly, after saying quietly to Kathleen, "you're beautiful." Kathleen felt wonderful, but embarrassed. She said to her two children, "Enjoy your supper. It's on the side of the stove keeping warm."

Michael replied with a twinkle in his eyes, "I know ma, you've already told us."

She wondered what that was all about. Michael was really glad to see his ma and Uncle Mac going out together. He only said, "Have a good time, we'll be fine,"

Mac helped Kathleen with her coat, and then she pulled on her gloves. When they walked out, she saw the buggy. The horse was standing quietly. He helped her up with his right arm, and then joined her on the seat. She felt like a princess; sort of an old princess, she thought, but she did feel special.

As they rode into town, they began to talk. At first, it was a bit stiff, but by the time they reached the hotel, they were laughing about something, and they both began to relax.

Inside the restaurant, a woman took their coats, and hung them up, then a waiter walked them to a table Mac had requested; it was off to one side, rather private. The table was beautiful, with a white linen tablecloth, and napkins. In the center was a white candle surrounded by small pine boughs and a bright red bow nestled among the pine needles. Kathleen had never been in such a fancy restaurant before. Mac pulled out her chair, and helped her to sit down, then sat across from her. Kathleen slipped off her gloves.

The waiter told them what they were serving for the main course, and after they ordered, the waiter filled their glasses with water. When they were served their dinner, it was served on lovely china dishes. The roast beef was excellent.

The two found themselves lingering over the food, talking about old times; their lives, their work, the Samaritan House, and all the good Richard was doing. They laughed again about little things in their past; the evening was wonderful, both enjoying this time together. They were having coffee when the Simpson's walked in with friends. James spotted them, and the two couples stopped and talked to the two at the table. James introduced their friends to the couple, and then went to their own table.

After the party left, Mac said, "That reminds me, Richard told me yesterday, when I was in town, that James Simpson has decided he wants to build a church. They should probably start building in the next two or three months. He wants to do it so we will have a permanent place to worship. He and Richard have been talking about the building, and where to build it, that's all I know so far. "Wouldn't that be wonderful Aaron? He is such a generous and good man," she remarked.

As they talked, he told her he liked it when she called him Aaron. "I've been called Mac for so many years, but I like it when you say Aaron with that little Irish brogue of yours, it makes me feel young again. Well, sort of young." And he grinned. She in turn said, "I love talking to you as we did when we were young."

They sat looking at each other. He then reached across the table with his right hand, and took hold of hers; "Through the years, I thought of you often, and our early years. We spent a lot of time talking about all kinds of things; things then, including our future. I guess none of us dreamed we would all end up here, so far from home. You've changed little, a bit older, but still that beautiful person you always were."

She didn't know what to say, but she did not pull her hand away. It felt good, being with Aaron; when she was young, she always felt safe with him, and she did tonight.

Soon the waiter came, asking if they would like more coffee. They separated their hands, and Kathleen said, "thank you." The waiter filled her cup, and when Mac nodded, the waiter filled his cup also.

Somehow, Kathleen's feelings toward Aaron made an abrupt change, and she dare not speak, just listening to him as he went to another subject. He spent time talking about the Civil War, and some of the things he and Pete went through.

"It was the second worst thing I've gone through." She naturally asked, "What was the first? Aaron." The man wasn't sure how to answer her, wondering why he had said that. Then he told her, "That was when I left you behind." He thought to himself, why did I say that? Her eyes softened, and she said, "I think that's one of the sweetest things anyone has ever said to me." The lovely woman reached her hand across the table, and took his hand in hers, each remembering another time and another place.

The next day, as Kathleen still lay in bed, before getting up she remembered the wonderful night. She could almost feel his lips on hers, as he gently kissed her goodnight.

Chapter 11

The night before Christmas, the Samaritan House had dinner for the needy and poor people in town. Everything was going smoothly, with many of the church group either cooking, or serving the food to all who came in to take part in the dinner and festivities.

Several weeks earlier, James had supplied the place with another wood cooking stove, which helped a great deal; he also added on a small office, for Richard to use. It gave the minister a place to go when someone wanted to talk to him. Richard was so grateful to James for his help, without him, the Samaritan House would not have been possible.

After dinner was over, Richard gathered the children of the families at the dinner around him, and told the story of Christ's birth. Most of the parents, or other adults, stood around listening. Richard had a special knack with story telling, but there was one boy who continually kept talking, punching, and pestering the other children around him. Mac, seeing what was happening, went to the boy and softly spoke to him saying, "Hey, what about you and I try to find you a warm coat?" The boy's clothes were tattered, and he was without anything to keep him warm. This left the rest of the children free to listen to the story.

The boy followed Mac into the adjoining room, he was difficult, wanting everything he saw. Finally, Mac set the boy down and asked, "What's your name, boy?" "My name is Miles, but everybody calls me 'Scratch', what's it to you?" The boy was definitely on the defensive.

"Miles is a nice name, I used to know someone by that name; we were good friends. Do you have a good friend?" "Naw, the boy said. "Nobody likes me; they always tease me cause my clothes are dirty, and they say I stink." Mac could believe that! The boy went on talking, "Most of the time, by pa beats me; he's always drunk, and he's sure not going to wash my clothes, I can tell you that! I don't go to school much, so I don't care if my clothes are dirty, and mostly, my pa beats me. Nobody likes me, and I don't like them!" Mac felt sorry for the boy, "Tell you what Scratch; let's see if we can find you some clean clothes." The man kept praying he could find some answers to the boy's problems; it was a rough life for one so young.

They found clothes to fit the boy. As he undressed, Mac saw large black and blue marks all over the boy's body, some newer than others. "How often does your pa beat you Scratch?" "Everyday, if I'm at home, unless I can get away from him. I hate him! He didn't want me to come tonight, he says, "We don't need no charity, but he was too drunk to notice when I left. Mister, I'm kinda scared to go home with these clothes on, he might beat me again!" Then the boy said, "I don't care, he's nothin but a bum!" "Where's your ma boy?" "She's dead. I don't remember her; pa says she weren't no good no how."

After hearing all Scratch said, Mac thought, maybe if I go to the sheriff after Christmas is over, he might be able to get a warrant to remove the boy from his father, but then he would need a place to go. Mac would talk to Richard later.

"Do you go home every night Scratch?" Mac asked the boy. "Naw, he's always drunk, and if I don't show up he don't miss me much. Then I don't get hit. I mostly hang around one of the saloons 'til it closes. If nobody sees me, I can sleep in a corner someplace, and usually there's peanuts or somethin' I can eat."

The whole affair was a disgrace, and Mac was determined to help the boy. "What do you say, Scratch? Let's go back into the other room; they have some special gifts for all the kids. Let's go find out what they have for you."

By the time the two returned to the party, Richard and Pete were beginning to pass the gifts that had been donated by some merchants in town. Scratch stood there thinking, they won't have nothin' for me, and he was about to leave when Mac said, "Here boy, here's something for you," and the man handed him a cloth bag with a string cinching it at the top. When the boy opened the gift, he discovered it was full of marbles. He'd never owned any before, but he had watched other boys playing with them.

Scratch could not believe they were really his! This was the first gift the boy had ever received. He went over to the side of the room, away from the others, and started practicing hitting the marbles with the shooter; he was having such a good time, he forgot where he was.

Mac, on the other hand was telling Richard about the boy and his circumstances. Among those hearing was Nate Green. He listened for awhile, and then spoke up. "Why don't I take him home with me? I have an apartment attached to my mother's house, and I have plenty of room for him. I understand what the boy is going through, and so would my mother. When I was young, my father was a drinker, and beat both my mother and me until my mother left him. Later she remarried, after my father was killed one night stepping out in front of a wagon. The man couldn't stop the horses in time, and so he was gone. Let me help him, I think, between my mother and I, we can help him. My adopted father died a few years ago, and she gets pretty lonesome sometimes. I know the sheriff pretty well, and he might speak up for us to Judge Logan. I would like to give the boy a chance to grow up with people who care."

Richard, Eve, and Mac talked to Nate awhile, and decided that Scratch should have a chance to grow up with people who understood what the boy's life was like. They all agreed to pray Judge Logan would allow the arrangement. They all knew Nate was a hard working, good man.

Before the two left, Scratch was handed a gingerbread man cookie, all decorated with a face and buttons down the front with icing. "Do I eat it or what?" The boy asked. Nate said, "sure", so as they walked out of the building, and Scratch took his first bite of a gingerbread man cookie.

Just as everything was cleaned up, and everyone had left but Richard and Eve, a young couple came in, disappointed that they had stopped serving food. Their names were Joe and Ruth Jones. Richard sat down with the two, and when they finished eating, they began to tell him what their lives were like.

Richard found out the man had a job that paid little. "I work at the lumber yard; we hardly have enough money to pay rent on the shack we live in. There's no heat, and it's really cold. We have so little food", the young man said, "and Ruth is pregnant." Richard could easily see how thin the young woman was. "I tried to get a raise, but Mr. Turner doesn't like me, he calls me a dirty injun. My father was Indian, and my mother was not. I used my mother's maiden name, but I look Indian, I don't know what we're going to do. Before we moved here from Las Cruces, I worked in carpentry, but didn't earn much. When we got married, I thought if we moved here, I could work in one of the mines and make more money, but nobody will hire a 'dirty injun.' I look too much like one to fool anyone," We're both scared, and Ruth is getting thinner and thinner."

Richard found out they lived in the worst part of town, and knew it was a dangerous area for a woman to be alone in. He told them both, "Don't worry, first of all, we will send food home with you, and we have several blankets. Maybe some warm coats for you too, that should help to keep you warm. I'm pretty sure we can get you a better job. "Joe, come back at noontime, the day after Christmas. I will do the very best I can for the two of you."

He and Eve gathered together left over food. Ham, potatoes, and other leftovers they could find. In the bag were dried pears, apples, and a left over pie.

Richard took leave, and asked them when the baby was due. "When Ruth went to Doc Freeman, he thought it would be born early next June, but we don't have the money to take her back." "Don't worry Joe; I will see she's taken care of, trust me." He tried to encourage the two, and then prayed over them. Eve could see the young woman was afraid, and she told the couple, "There are good people here, and they are not prejudice, you will be alright." The two walked away with a touch of hope, and plenty of food to eat.

After closing up, Richard walked Eve home; Thelma had gone home much earlier. Then Richard headed for James' house, It was imperative he talk to the man. The two were very close friends by now.

The house was in an uproar! The Simpson's were having a big Christmas Eve party. Even though James had mentioned the party, he had forgotten. Richard waited where the butler suggested, and James came into the room, dressed for the party. He came over to Richard who shook his head. "I'm sorry my friend, I'd forgotten you were having a party tonight." James wasn't in the least concerned about Richard being there. The man respected the young minister more than anyone he knew. "How can I help you Richard?"

Love Comes in Many Colors

When he heard about the plight of the young couple, he asked, "You say this young man tried to get a job at my mine? There will be a few heads that will roll when I find out who turned the man away. They should have come to me before refusing him work, I will not tolerate prejudice. They will never treat men that way again."

"We need to get him work right away; I'm having a new office building built for the mine. One of the workers left town two days ago without notice, and I've been so busy; I haven't hired anyone to take the man's place. If the young man has done carpentry work as you say, we can give him a chance by letting him work on that building. If he does good work, then he can help build the church, I plan to start it as soon as the office is done."

"Now that we've decided to build it up on the hill close to where you live, we can get started as soon as the other job is done. You have the young man come by the day after Christmas at one o'clock, I'll be there. I will put him to work right away; we need to get them out of that miserable place, so I will give him an advance, plus help him find a better place to live right away."

Richard had never known anyone so generous before, and he tried to thank his friend, James just passed it off by saying, "Do unto others as you would have them do unto you," Right Richard?" So a grateful minister went home relieved knowing the young couple would be alright.

He told Eve, "James is such a good man, the best I have ever known; he is so generous, and his faith in Christ is already so strong, and it shows in all his kindnesses. I am so grateful, and humbled by this good man. Eve, I'm beginning to really believe the Samaritan House was the Lord's plan all the time! It is *His* place, and we are doing God's will." That night the husband and wife spent time in grateful prayer for the friends God had brought their way.

As Kathleen climbed into bed after arriving home, and settling down Molly, she fell asleep almost immediately. The day had been a busy one, between spending the morning baking for the Christmas Eve party, and then working the dinner at the Samaritan House, she was extremely tired. The pies she baked were not only for the dinner that night, but also to take to the ranch the next afternoon to share with the Smith's, Pete, and Aaron.

Just before sleep came to Kathleen, she thought of how much she was looking forward to seeing Aaron again, away from the Samaritan House. They had enjoyed going out together for dinner, and Aaron had been on her mind ever since.

The following morning, she fed Michael and Molly, and as they enjoyed their time together, she surprised Molly with a doll she had seen in Hanson's. Her mother had secretly bought the doll for Molly, and made a whole array of clothing for it. Molly kept dressing and undressing the doll all morning. For Michael, she had used Paddy's best coat, and changed it to fit him. Michael had grown so fast though, she didn't need to change it too much. Inside the pocket, she pinned a pocket watch for him; he was becoming a man, and it was time he had one of his own.

Love Comes in Many Colors

Michael was so pleased when he found the watch, after his ma suggested he look in the pocket. The first thing he did after dropping it in the pocket was to hug his mother, "Thanks so much, ma. How did you know I wanted one?" "I didn't, but you're old enough to have one. I am so pleased with you sweetheart, you're such a good person, and you make me proud. Your kindness shows in all you do." He flushed, but he loved his mother; he thought she was probably the best mother anyone could have.

Then he handed her a small box. She looked puzzled, wondering what was inside, "Open it ma." Inside the box was a lovely cameo pin. "Oh Michael," she said,

"I've always wanted one, its lovely! I think I will wear it today pinned to the neck of my blouse, I love it." She took his hand and squeezed it. Michael put his arm around his beautiful mother saying, "I love you ma."

The Smith's arrived at one o'clock, and they all went inside to visit awhile while they waited for Ben who was supposed to pick them all up at one thirty. The partners had insisted they all come out for the afternoon and for Christmas dinner. Kathleen was looking forward to seeing Aaron, away from the House. They had been so busy with the dinner the night before, and had no time to even talk. Their night out, and Aaron's kiss lingered in her mind.

As they rode to the ranch, they were all glad they were dressed warmly; it had turned into a very cold day. The sun was out of sight, clouds hanging in the sky. A few flakes fell on the trip, but they soon stopped.

Before Kathleen took Mac's waiting hand, she handed a package to Ben. "Merry Christmas Ben, and to the rest of the men, I baked some cookies for all of you, I hope you enjoy them." "Thank you ma'am, the man said. "No no, Ben, my name is Kathleen. We are friends, and I want you to call me by my name." "Yes ma'am, I mean Kathleen", and they both laughed.

The woman turned to Aaron and took his hand as he helped her down out of the wagon. Then he turned and lifted Molly out saying, "Merry Christmas wee Molly, at which her eyes lit up and a big smile was his reward.

He and her family walked inside together, Mac holding her hand. At first, she wondered what everyone would think, but his broad smile washed away her fears. Aaron took her and her family's coats, hat's, scarves, and gloves, and put them in his room on the bed. Maria had taken the others wraps and also put them on Aaron's bed.

The fireplace had a large fire going, and she moved over to it and held her hands out, trying to warm them, as did all the other guests. Everyone was admiring the Christmas tree that stood off to the left of the fireplace in the corner. It was a lovely full, tall tree, and it was decorated from things that grew in the area. It was a pinion tree, and the small cones were still hanging to it, sprinkled here and there.

There were bronzed colored yucca pods, the color changed by the cold in the area. There were also small gourds that were painted brightly with designs covering them, apparently the work of Maria. Scattered here and there were small bundles of dried summer flowers, and seeds all tied together with red ribbon making the tree very festive. Gently draped around the tree were strings of popped corn, again the work of Maria. On top of the tree was a copper star. Aaron told Kathleen the copper came from the closed copper mine in the area, and that he had made the star years ago. The tree was delightful. Kathleen noticed, beneath the tree, to one side was a large package wrapped in colored cloth.

Everything looked so beautiful! There were boughs of pine over the doors and windows, plus boughs of pine on the mantel. Kathleen noticed a beautifully crafted cross made of mountain mahogany. It was sitting among the pine boughs with two tall lit white candles, one on each side.

Pete came over, "Pretty isn't it?" "Very", Kathleen replied. "Mac made it several years ago." When she looked closely, she saw the words, 'He died on the cross for us' carved on the cross. Mac saw her looking at the cross, and joined her. "It's beautiful Aaron." "My father made one like it years ago when I was young. Don't you remember it?" he questioned. "You and your family were at our house more than once at either Christmas or Easter." His was a bit smaller; he always put it on the small shelves during holidays where my mother had other nick knacks." Then she remembered. "Yes, it was made of white pine, the color was different. Maybe that's why I didn't remember it. You made it to remember and honor your father, didn't you?" "Uh huh, I watched him making it. I was pretty young, but I never forgot."

Kathleen looked at him and said, "I think that's wonderful you did it to honor him. I always liked him; he was a kind and gentle man, and always lots of fun. I miss our parents, they were good people from the old country. Wouldn't it be wonderful to see Ireland someday to see the land our parents' came from?"

Before Mac could answer, Pete suggested everyone sit down. Mac took Kathleen by the hand, and led her to a seat beside him. Michael and Molly were sitting on the floor nearby. Maria came and sat on the floor beside Pete, which seemed perfectly normal to her.

After everyone quieted down, he read the verses from the Bible, starting at Luke, chapter 2:

Verse 1: And it came to pass in those days, that there went out a decree from Caesar Augustus that all the world should be taxed.
2: (and this taxing was first made when Cyrenius was governor of Syria).
3: And all went to be taxed, everyone into his own city.
4: And Joseph also went up from Galilee, out of Nazareth into Judaeia, unto the city of David, which is called Bethlehem; (because he was of the house and lineage of David:)
5: To be taxed with Mary his espoused wife, being great with child.
6: And so it was that, while they were there the days were accomplished that she should be delivered.

7: And she brought forth her firstborn son, and wrapped him in swaddling clothes, and laid him in a manger; because there was no room for them in the Inn.

Pete continued reading about the shepherds in the fields and the angel of the Lord, who came to proclaim the birth of the Savior. Kathleen was deeply moved hearing the story of the birth of the Lord and Savior of the world. He was her greatest joy, He and her Heavenly Father. When Pete finished, everyone felt like they were there at the Inn, even little Molly was quiet.

Outside, snow began falling softly upon the land as Aaron began to softly sing the carol, 'Silent Night, Holy Night'. Kathleen was amazed, she didn't remember his remarkable baritone voice; but of course Paddy's was always so powerful, no one could be heard over his singing. They all joined in singing with him. The candles flickered from some small draft, bringing a sense of holiness to the room.

When they finished singing, the room was quiet as they worshiped their Lord and Heavenly Father, each in their own way. Then there was a moment when their love flowed to Him who was their all in all.

Soon Mac started another carol, and they all joined in, it would be a memory long remembered. When the singing was over, Maria quietly slipped away, heading to the kitchen to finish the dinner.

One by one, each woman excused themselves, joining the young woman in the kitchen. After they were gone, though, the others began talking. Michael stayed quiet, feeling like he was in the Lord's presence, and the Lord was beckoning him onward into the walk He had planned for Michael's life.

The whole house smelled wonderful! Maria pulled out one turkey, replacing it with another for the ranch hands later. Pete shot them both very early that morning, and the two worked together cleaning, and then stuffing both turkeys with a dressing Pete's mother used to make, the man taught Maria the recipe several years before. Along with the turkey, Thelma had brought sweet potatoes she bought at the Chinese Gardens. The recipe called for unrefined sugar, or brown sugar. She was an accomplished cook, and the potatoes smelled marvelous.

Eve had made a salad of shredded carrots with raisins. Kathleen put her apple pies on the back of the stove to warm them some. Everything looked and smelled wonderful, and Pete's stomach began complaining, wanting to be fed.

Soon everyone was called to the table as the women finished bringing in the food. Pete would be cutting the turkey, everyone sat down where they were told to sit as Maria headed back to the kitchen. Pete and Mac brought another place setting and chair, and put it next to Pete's, who would be sitting at one end of the table while Mac sat at the other end. Pete then went into the kitchen. He soon came back holding Maria's hand and telling her he wanted her to join them. He brought her to the chair as he pulled it back for her to sit down; she not understanding. He whispered, "I want you here beside me Maria. She glanced around, feeling out of place, but she finally did as Pete asked. He put food on her plate as it was passed around. She felt out of place and uncomfortable, but what could she do? She didn't want to draw attention to herself; and of course she was not used to eating with others. She was only a hired hand.

As Pete helped her with the food, she kept her eyes down, and she ate lightly, trying not to be noticed. After the pie and coffee was served, she hoped she could disappear, but Pete insisted she join them. She didn't want to make a scene, so she sat quietly. Once dinner was finished, before anyone left the table, Pete went over to Maria, and kneeling down next to her,(she wanted to run and hide) Pete took her hand, everyone quietly watching; "Maria, I knew if I didn't have an audience, you would flee from me, and I want to ask you something. My dear, sweet Maria, I have fallen in love with you. You've captured my heart, and I think you know that already. I think you love me too, I've seen it in your eyes. Before everyone, I am asking you to marry me. You have become so dear to me, and I want you to be my wife."

Everyone held their breath. She hesitated, and small tears formed in her eyes. She had loved Pete for so long, but knew it would never turn into anything between them. People who were servants, didn't marry their boss! "Maria?" She looked at him; his eyes were so full of love. She finally said, hardly believing this was happening, "Yes Peter, I will marry you." He took a ring out of the pocket in his vest, took her hand, and slipped it onto her finger. He saw only her, and she saw only him. He pulled her up into his arms, and kissed her gently. She felt so loved, something she thought would never happen to her. When they separated, everyone clapped softly, all happy for Pete and Maria. Mac looked at Kathleen, she was so beautiful! He had been reticent to tell her of his love for her. He decided he must wait, but he felt like he had been waiting forever. Still, he would wait.

While the women were cleaning up after the meal, they all congratulated Maria one by one. Kathleen held her close, saying how very glad she was that her and Pete would be marrying, wistfully thinking about Aaron. She quickly turned the thought aside when Paddy came to mind, but she would not forget her yearning.

After dinner the friends all sat around the fire visiting. When Pete and Mac got up and, together, picked up the large package sitting by the tree and brought it over and sat it down in front of Kathleen she glanced up with a surprised look on her face, as if to say, it's for me?

As the men sat down, Mac said, "Kathleen, just pull the bow on top and the ribbon and cloth will fall away." She couldn't imagine what the large present could be, but she did as she was told. As the covering fell away, Kathleen let out a large gasp, "It's a sewing machine!", and a large smile covered her face.

Pete told her, "We knew how much you wanted one, so Mac went in to see Jules about ordering one for you. We both know how much time it takes to sew your dresses. We're lucky it arrived before Christmas." Her eyes were so big. She could scarcely believe it was really hers. A singer sewing machine!

Kathleen thanked them both with hugs, and then she dashed back to look at her wonderful gift.

Mac watched her, amused and happy; glad they had thought to buy her the machine. His affection for her was very evident. Kathleen felt his eyes on her, and looked up. Everyone could see the love between the two.

That night as she lay in bed, Kathleen thanked the Lord for the machine and her wonderful Aaron. Then Kathleen began to struggle with her feelings for Aaron. She felt she shouldn't have these feelings, and asked the Lord for help. Still, she fell asleep with him in her thoughts.

Nate tried to help Scratch, better known as Miles. He knew the boy was not used to living with people. Part of his life, the boy tried to stay away from his father, knowing his father might beat him. After the holiday, Nate took Miles to see Judge Logan, trying to get some kind of legality set up so Miles could stay with him and his mother.

The man explained what the boy's life was like. "I don't want him to have to live like that. According to the boy, the man is always drunk, and he probably doesn't even realize how hard he makes his life. There are black and blue marks all over Mile's body, some older and some newer. My mother is there to help me care for the boy."

Judge Logan told Nate, "I will give you six months to work with the boy, but that's only because your mother is there. I believe all children should have a mother's love." He signed the necessary papers saying, I will see you in July.

Love Comes in Many Colors

From then on life was difficult. Miles would supposedly go to school, sometimes he was there, but often he ended up on the streets, which was so familiar to the boy. Each day had its own troubles, but Nate would not give up.

Winter was over, and spring was in the air. Kathleen and Mac were on their way, going out for dinner. The two enjoyed being together, and tried to go out every week or so. Pete told Mac about a small Mexican restaurant where he and Maria had gone several times. "The food is good, and they have music while you're eating. We both have enjoyed going there," his partner told him.

The two chose to go to the same place; both had learned to enjoy Mexican food. They were having a wonderful time enjoying themselves. A man was playing a guitar, and singing during their meal. The music was delightful, making the couple feel light-hearted and happy, both in a festive mood. They did a lot of laughing; having a marvelous time being together. While eating desert, a young woman started dancing to the music. Under her colorful skirt were many petticoats, each a different color.

As the young Mexican woman danced she held onto her skirt with both hands, swinging her dress and petticoats back and forth, flashing the many colors. It was exciting to watch her feet move from side to side. She was enchanting as she moved across the floor; many people clapped to the music as she danced. The couple was having the time of their lives, enjoying each other's company.

After leaving, they walked toward Kathleen's house, she holding onto Mac's arm as they talked amiably. It was a warm evening, with the cotton from the cottonwood trees falling softly around them. The warmth felt good after the long cold winter. The night was quiet; a very unusual thing here in the area.

As they turned onto the walk going to Kathleen's house, the tall man stopped and looked down on his lovely companion. He reached down, cupped her chin with his hand, and gently kissed her. He wrapped his arms around her, and kissed her again, she returning his kiss. Then they stood, holding each other; simply lost in the moment.

"Kathleen," he said, "I have waited so long to tell you. I have loved you since we were young, and I have never stopped loving you, She looked up at him saying, "I love you too Aaron, and maybe some of it comes from when we were young. In those days I was young and a bit foolish, thinking more about being an old maid than love; now we are here together." He kissed her again, and then he asked her, "Kathleen, will you marry me? I so want you to be my wife." She smiled at him saying, "Yes Aaron, I would be honored to be your wife."

He reached into his pocket, and took out a ring. He took hold of her hand and slipped the ring on her finger, "I had it made especially for you." She looked at it; it was a gold ring with a rich garnet, surrounded with delicate gold filigree and small diamonds throughout. "It's lovely Aaron", she told him. Then he kissed her again. They were both so happy; they would be starting a brand new life, together; Mac's dream had finally come true.

Mac said to Kathleen, "Let's go tell that son of yours", and he grabbed her hand as they happily hurried into the house, both with big smiles on their faces. When they walked into the parlor, they saw Michael absorbed in a book he was reading. Molly was already in bed. "Look Michael", his mother said as she showed her son the ring on her finger. "Michael, your uncle has asked me to marry him, and I said yes." She looked up at her Aaron with a smile.

Her son put aside the book, and went to congratulate his two favorite people. He shook hands with Mac, and then kissed his ma on her cheek. "Gosh, that's wonderful! I've been waiting for this to happen." His mother was surprised, but he went on. "I've suspected you loved each other for some time now, I just had to wait until you knew it yourselves. Congratulations!"

Michael sat with them while they talked, and then he went to his ma and kissed her on her cheek. "Goodnight, I'm really happy for you both", and he left the room and headed for bed.

After talking a short time, Mac kissed his sweet Kathleen goodnight, and left; heading for the ranch.

Once Kathleen was in bed, she thought of Paddy. He'd been gone a long time now. She felt a tang of disloyalty to him, but then she said to herself, that part of my life is over now. Aaron is such a sweet and kind man, and I do love him. She thanked the Lord for this special man, and fell asleep. Her night was filled with happy dreams.

Love Comes in Many Colors

Mac came to the house nearly every night, the Indians were no where to be seen. He would spend the evenings with Kathleen, Michael and Molly. They all had fun together, playing games, or just talking. He even spent time playing dolls with Molly; she loved it when her uncle spent time with her.

Mac wanted Kathleen's family to feel comfortable having him around, he didn't want to marry Kathleen until the family felt like he was part of them. Kathleen knew it was hard on him, if he stayed too late; he always had to ride back to the ranch once their time together was over.

One evening, while it was still light outside, they all walked to the Smith's house. Neither Mac nor Kathleen had told anyone about their upcoming marriage, but it was time to say something; there was a wedding to plan.

Richard answered the door, and found to his surprise, that Mac was standing there with Kathleen, and her family. "Come in", he said, wondering what was going on. The minister invited them to sit down, and called Eve and Thelma to come. Both were just finishing up the dinner dishes. Eve told them, "It's good to see you. I don't think you have been here before, together." "What's going on?" Richard asked. Mac said, "We need to tell you that Kathleen has agreed to marry me." "How wonderful, we sort of thought this would happen, we've just been waiting for you to know it yourselves" Eve told them, and she gave them a big smile.

"What's going on here?" Mac asked. "Are we the last ones to know?" The Smith's just chuckled, "yes, I guess so. We all saw the handwriting on the wall", Richard said. "We just had to wait for you to realize it yourselves," and he gave them a big smile. "I guess we have another wedding to plan." "Well, not exactly," Mac said. Richard raised his eyebrows, but Mac went on, "Instead of two weddings, the four of us have decided we want to be married at the same time. We want to have it after the church is built." "Well now", the minister said, "I think that's a wonderful idea. James told me today it's only a few weeks away, and that would be a wonderful way to celebrate for us who love you."

"I talked to Pete, and he and Maria want to come and spend time talking with me, and to have prayer. If you two want the same, we can set some time to do that." They did make an appointment to talk with him, and they especially wanted prayer.

The evening was pleasant, and it was good to be together. Thelma and Eve made coffee, and put a plate of cookies out. It was a fun time, Kathleen loved being with these long-time friends. They had been through a lot together, and Aaron fit in perfectly she thought.

After Kathleen put her daughter to bed, Michael excused himself, leaving them alone. The two spent time talking about their future. Kathleen needed to spend some time with Maria about their wedding dresses. She was talking about the wedding when Mac interrupted her, "Kathleen, I need to talk to you about a change in my life." She looked at him, "Of course. I'm sorry I've been going on and on about the wedding, what is it Aaron?" "Well, you know I took over the books at the ranch, but I feel I'm not doing my part; the books really don't take that much time. I'm also concerned, I'm not sure if the ranch can take care of two couples. We've had to hire another man to take my place." She looked at him not fully understanding what he was trying to tell her.

"Well sweetheart, you need to know that Jacob Firth asked me if I would be interested in working at the bank. There was a man working there who took off with quite a large amount of money, and he needs someone he can trust to do the bookwork. I will have the title of vice-president, if that means anything. We talked about the problem of four people living off the money earned at the ranch, and that's when he offered me the job. I like doing books, and would have time to do the ranches books also.

My shoulder gives me problems every time I do other work on the ranch. I've talked to Pete about it, and it's agreed that I will earn money from the horses that are sold. This all means I will not spend much time at the ranch, which I will really miss. I love being out of town, and it's a joy to work with the horses, but I just can't do it anymore. Do you mind Kathleen? It's a good offer." She looked at him and smiled, "Of course I don't mind. I'm not marrying you because you own horses, or a horse ranch. What ever you do, I will love you exactly the same, I'm marrying you not the ranch."

He was so relieved, "You're sure", he asked. "Of course I am." He hugged her.

"You're a wonderful woman Kathleen McGinnis." Then they both laughed, both thinking the same thing, she would still be Kathleen McGinnis after they were married!

It was decided he would leave the ranch, which he loved dearly, and become a town dweller. His new job would be happening before they were married, but he would continue living at the ranch until the day of their marriage.

The church was getting closer and closer to being finished. Mac was working at the bank, and Kathleen was caught up with Maria; decisions about their wedding dresses and sewing that must be done. Right now, Kathleen was between sewing for women in the town so that left her free.

Both women wanted colored gowns instead of white. Kathleen's former marriage took white out of her decision, and Maria wanted a soft yellow dress, having seen some sheer yellow material she liked. Kathleen found a beautiful lavender material that was much like that of Maria's; that meant Kathleen must make two underskirts that matched their colors. Jules Walsh went to extra trouble to find enough material and ribbon for the two women, causing him to go to a competitive store to buy it, but he did. Both he and his wife liked both of the women, and he wanted to help. Each woman would use the matching colored ribbon that would be twined through their hair. Kathleen knew the yellow roses over the porch would be in bloom by then, so both women planned to carry a bouquet of the yellow roses.

It was Saturday morning, and Michael was working at the ranch. Mac came into town to see Kathleen, and spend the afternoon doing a few things.

Then they planned to stop by the church to see how it was coming along; Mac heard the stained glass window was in place and wanted to see it. This was to be the first large stained glass window in town, though several of the large homes in the area had some in their front doors.

As they walked into the sanctuary, Mac and Kathleen found Joe working. He was nearly finished building the mahogany pews; one could see he was an artisan working with wood. He had finished the pulpit which had carvings on it; Joe did excellent work, so precise. He stopped a minute to talk to the two. "Hello Joe, how are you and Helen doing?" Mac asked. "We're doing fine, thanks; we're both looking forward to the birth of our baby. Helen is feeling large, but very happy; she's looking healthy these days", the young man told them. "We're glad she's doing so much better. How much longer before the baby is supposed to be born?" Kathleen asked. "The doctor thinks it will be in about seven weeks." "That's great", Mac said. "Well we mustn't keep you; give our best wishes to Helen." "Thanks, I will", And Joe hurried back to his work.

The two looked up at the window behind the pulpit; James Simpson ordered it as soon as the decision to build the church was made. "Aaron, isn't it lovely?" Kathleen asked. The sun was in the right position, and light was spilling through the window, color spreading everywhere. They stood looking at the window. Christ was standing, holding a small child in his arms, it seemed so appropriate, considering the Samaritan House. They left the church very touched.

Love Comes in Many Colors

After leaving there, it was time to meet with Richard, so they went to the Smith's house. They sat talking with both Richard and Eve, "I just wish we would hear something from Jeannie. I've written several letters to her, and we've received no letter back, not one since that first letter", Eve said. "I've done the same thing", Kathleen said, "And I've heard nothing from her; I hope nothing has happened to them." Richard encouraged them to keep praying, "While were all together, why don't we take time to pray for them."

Richard and the rest all knelt down and prayed for their friend. Mac knew about the close friendship between the three women. He wasn't sure where the Cobb's had settled, he just hoped this had nothing to do with Indians.

Mac left for the ranch after they got back to the house. There were some things he needed to do. He kissed his dear Kathleen, saying "I'll see you tomorrow if all goes well", and left.

Chapter 12

George was about to close the store, when a young man, somewhere in his late teens walked in the door. He was followed by a woman who seemed older, and carrying a baby.

"Can I help you?" The owner of the general store asked? "I hope so". The young man replied. "We are trying to find Patrick and Kathleen McGinnis, do you happen to know them, and where they live?" "Why do you want to see them?" George asked, not wanting to send just anybody to Kathleen's house. "Well sir, they are my family. I understand they moved here last spring."

As the son of Kathleen talked, George noticed that the woman seemed to be unaware of her surroundings. "Yes, I do know your family", he replied, and gave Tim instructions on how to find the house. Timothy thanked the man, and turned guiding the woman out of the door. They turned, and went in the direction George told them to go, he heard the baby start to cry as they were walking away. Tim's hands were full, holding a pack over his back, and a satchel in the other hand.

Kathleen was in the kitchen, busy getting supper. Earlier, Mac stopped by checking on her, and then left for the ranch. She was trying to get the food ready for supper when she heard someone knocking on the door. Who in the world can that be, she thought. She wiped her hands on her apron, and went to see who was there.

When she opened the door, there stood her son Tim; she rushed forward. He dropped everything he was carrying, and his arms wrapped around his mother. She said, with tears of joy flowing down her cheeks, "My son, I didn't know if I would ever see you again!" Tim wanted to stay right there, in his mother's arms; he had missed her more than he ever dreamed he could. "Yes ma, it's me." Kathleen, while holding her son, saw Jeannie standing behind him, but there was no sign of recognition on her face, and there was a baby in her arms.

Tim moved away from his ma, and picked up the bags. Kathleen went to her friend, and spoke to her, but there was little acknowledgment. She asked Tim, with a puzzled look on her face, "What happened? How did you two end up together?" As he moved into the house he said, "Ma, she lost her husband last fall, and she hasn't talked since. Kathleen took her friend into the house, and sat her down; Jeannie looked so weary. Kathleen then turned to her son to get some answers. The baby began crying, and Tim told his mother "Abby's been fussing ever since we got here, I know she's really wet." He knelt down and got a diaper out of the satchel, and started to get the baby, when his mother said, "Here I'll change the baby." "No ma, I'd rather do it myself, where can I change her?" Kathleen, thoroughly confused said, "I'll get a towel", and led her son into her bedroom, the baby, crying hard before he could get her clean.

The baby began quieting down as he pinned on the clean diaper. "It's alright Abby, you're clean now", her son said as he picked up the baby girl, and walked back into the parlor. Jeannie was almost falling asleep in the chair, so Kathleen tenderly helped her friend up. She took Jeannie into her bedroom and helped her lie down. Then she knelt down beside Jeannie, saying, "What has happened to you, my dear, dear friend?" Jeannie looked at her, but not a word was spoken as tears trickled down onto her face. Kathleen wiped the tears away, but Jeannie was silent. After laying a quilt over her friend, Kathleen walked back into the parlor, ready for some answers.

Michael came into the room with Molly behind him; the two had been working outside when he heard voices, so they came in to find out what was going on. When he saw his brother holding a baby, he said, "Tim, is that you? We've all been anxious about you, and whose baby are you holding?" Then his mother asked more questions before Tim could answer. "What happened to Mrs. Cobb, and how did you two end up together?"

"What happened? Well, that's not easy to answer in just a few words", her son replied. "Could I first have a drink of water? I'm so thirsty."

After drinking the water, Tim began his story: "Johnnie and I chickened out, we decided we didn't want to take part in the bank robbery in Santa Fe. The night before, we took the two horses we were supposed to ride during and after the robbery, using the food and canteens of water we were supposed to use, and rode south, trying to get away."

"It wasn't too long before we would have to find work or starve, so we got a job working on a horse ranch. We didn't work with the horses though; we did the work no one else wanted to do, but it didn't matter. We worked there for a couple of months, but some kind of war between the ranchers was brewing, so we got our money, and headed east toward Las Vegas in the New Mexico Territory. Remember when we traveled through there on our way to Santa Fe? Anyway, summer was coming on; we both did odd jobs that barely kept us alive, and we had to feed our horses."

"Finally, when we had enough money to head back to Santa Fe, Johnnie went to his folks, and I went searching for you, but you were gone! Nobody seemed to know where you went. Then I remembered the lady you worked for, and I thought she might know where you were. She told me you left in the spring, and moved to Silver City. I had no idea where Silver city was, so I asked the sheriff, and he told me where it was located. He also said they caught the guys who robbed the bank. He said he was glad I wasn't among them. I didn't know he even knew I had been part of the group."

"I got a job in Santa Fe, and when I thought I had enough money to leave, I did. It took me awhile because I had to pay to have the horse fed and cared for. When I had enough money I headed south.

It was a long hot summer, sometimes working for food along the way. As it was turning fall, I was riding along the road just north of Fort Selden, when I spotted Mrs. Cobb. I would have missed her if I hadn't looked back; her bonnet had hidden her face. I stopped to talk with her, but before we said much, we heard lots of shooting, and Indians yelling back where her farm was. I tried to stop her, but she ran back to their farm. I kicked my horse and we practically flew up behind some rocks, my horse as frightened as I was. We stayed there for a long time and after all the shooting stopped, we made sure the Indians were gone. Then I rode back looking for her and Mr. Cobb."

"I finally found them; she was lying beside her dead husband. She had a large gash on her back, and it was bleeding badly, but she was alive. It took me a long time before I could get her away from him, she was hysterical, and did not want to leave him."

"Their house was burned to the ground, most people's houses were in the same condition, and many of them died fighting. There was one house still standing; it showed signs of being partially burned but somehow the owners had stopped the fire. They were still alive, and were friends of the Cobb's."

"The woman cleaned Mrs. Cobb's wound the best she could, but the only way to stop the bleeding was to cauterize it. The husband did that, it was awful to watch! You could smell the burnt flesh. She screamed, and then passed out. Ma, it was terrible to watch! The woman gave her some kind of drink, and she went to sleep."

"I stayed around a couple of days; I buried Mr. Cobb, and helped to bury others." By this time she was awake, but she was in a lot of pain. The couple suggested I take her to the doctor at Fort Seldon. I was able to catch a horse, and we put her into the saddle, tying her so she wouldn't fall off; then I took her to the fort."

"When the doctor looked at her wound, he recommended we stay there for a couple of weeks so her wound could heal. She stayed with an officer and his wife, while I slept in the stalls, and they let me eat with the soldiers. The doctor told me she was expecting a baby in about three or four months. I wasn't sure what to do, but we had to leave, so we went south to the town of Las Cruces. The doctor advised me to travel slowly because of the baby. She still wasn't talking."

"When we finally arrived in Las Cruces, it was turning cold at night, and the days were cool. I could tell by looking at her that she wasn't up to traveling anymore, so I sold the horses, and saved it for our trip by stagecoach to Silver City in the spring."

"After looking for a job, I found work in a shop that repaired wheels. I didn't dare use the money for a place to stay, and didn't make much anyway. I wasn't sure how I was going to take care of Mrs. Cobb, but the man that owned the shop took pity on us I guess, and told me we could stay in a backroom at the shop."

"He said he had lived there a couple of years until he married, and he would let us stay there as long as I worked for him. It was a dreary room, with only one small window. There was one cot, and a wood stove with lots of wood out back. I could cook a little, but I'm not much of a cook; I never paid much attention when you cooked, but I guess I learned. The man gave us several blankets to keep us warm, and I appreciated all he did for us. Without that place to stay in, I don't know what we would have done."

"I worked for the man the rest of the fall, and winter. It was hard to get Mrs. Cobb to eat anything, sometimes I had to feed her. I think she couldn't accept the loss of her husband; she still wouldn't talk. I think she wished she had died too. I felt so sorry for her, and did what I could. With only one cot, I slept on the floor. The only sound from her was crying in the night, and not much of that."

"The time for her baby to be born was getting close. I didn't know what to do, and there was no one to help. Finally, a woman who was leaving town told me what to do when the baby was born. She gave me some diapers and baby gowns left over from her last baby. She also gave me some clean cloths, and a large pan to boil them in when it was time for the baby to come. I bought some pins because I would need them."

"One night, after I had been asleep for a couple of hours, I heard her moaning and crying. When I got up to see what was happening, she said," "The baby's coming!" "She looked scared, and I was too. I had to help Mrs. Cobb when the baby came. I was glad

I had bought some scissors; I boiled everything, it was a long night. Finally, Abby was born just before dawn."

"After cleaning her and the baby, I was tired. She and the baby were sleeping, so I got some sleep myself. It wasn't too long before the man I worked for was at the door wondering why I wasn't at work. When I told him about the baby, he told me to stay with them, and get some rest. I was really grateful, I was so tired. I knew this wasn't easy on Mrs. Cobb, but there was no one else to help."

Abby's a little over two months old now. Mrs. Cobb somehow took care of her in the daytime, and I took over at night. She did nurse the baby, but she remained silent."

"As soon as the days were warm enough, I bought tickets for the stage, and we came to Silver City hoping the Indians were not out and about yet. Ma, she doesn't seem to care about Abby, I don't think she has ever been able to accept the death of her husband, and she's still not talking. My hope is she will come out of this terrible darkness now that she is here with you; it was such a long winter, I'm so glad to be here with you." There were tears in his eyes.

At first neither Kathleen, nor Michael said anything. His mother felt a great compassion well up inside her. "Tim, what a good man you have become. It must have been very hard on you, and I know Jeannie is grateful, somewhere down deep inside. I pray she will, indeed begin to get over this terrible tragedy."

His mother was so proud of Tim; she never dreamed he could be so caring. What a change had come over him since she last saw him. Kathleen knew she had to tell her son about his father, but how? She tried to be as gentle as she could when she told him about Paddy's death and all the circumstances leading up to that fateful day. She explained how his father was killed and who was responsible for his death. "Who?", he said. "It was the gambler, Ted Spencer, the man that won our wagon and livestock when we were in Santa Fe." "He came here?" her son asked. "Yes. He came on the same stagecoach that we came on. I never dreamed he would kill your father. I was afraid of him, but never dreamed he would do such a terrible thing!" She did not mention the man had come to the house. She felt it would be better to leave that unsaid.

"When we first came here, your father was doing well, and then he started drinking pretty heavily again; things weren't going very well." "I'll say they weren't", Michael said. "After pa started drinking again, he began to beat ma. He was awful when he got drunk. He was like another person; always angry, and he took that anger out on ma. The last time he did, he hit her all over her face, but I got us out of the house. She was crying so hard, we stopped under a big tree and I held her, letting her cry. That's when we found out Uncle Mac was here in Silver City. He was riding by where we were standing. He saw ma crying and stopped his horse, and got down to see if he could help in any way. When he got close to ma, he recognized her.

"Who's Uncle Mac", Tim asked. Kathleen explained, "He is your pa's brother, Aaron, he fought during the Civil War. I guess people started calling him Mac, and the name stuck. He lives here in the area; he and another man own a horse ranch together. Tim, he helped your father to stop drinking; I guess it wasn't easy on either one of them, but your father never drank again. For that I will forever be grateful."

"Your pa's death was a shock to us all, he died at the end of summer last year. I am so sorry honey. This is something we all had to handle in our own way."

Tim got angry at the news of his father's death. The anger quickly turned to sorrow. Kathleen went over, and took the baby out of her son's arms. She wanted her son to grieve the loss of his father in his own way. "Pa was always too good to me, I didn't deserve it; I was so selfish." He turned to his brother, "I'm sorry Michael. It never was fair to you. I wish I had been a better son and brother, and I wish I could have been here for you and ma when pa died. I think if I had been here, maybe pa wouldn't have been killed. I might have been able to stop that man from killing him." And he began to weep.

"No Tim", his brother said. "It's all over. I was here, and you were with Mrs. Cobb; she might have died too if you had not been there. I think that shows that God answers prayer, and was watching over all of us. The man was out of his mind; no one could have stopped him."

"I know ma and the Smith's were praying for you. I did too; everyone was praying for Mrs. Cobb; God does answer prayers." "But I've never given much thought about God", Tim said. "Well how do you explain it then? We've all been praying for you ever since you left Santa Fe. God knew where you were, and he always answers prayers; one way or another. That's the only explanation that makes any sense to me. You even helped Mrs. Cobb when she had her baby, and then you brought her here." Tim thought about what his brother had said. "Maybe you are right Michael, maybe God is real!"

Their mother was surprised with both her sons. Here was Michael with such a strong faith, close to convincing his brother that God was real. She realized something very special was beginning to happen to Michael, his faith seemed so mature; she wondered what kind of plans the Lord had for her youngest son. His faith seemed to be increasing constantly.

That night Michael shared his bed with his brother, it was the first time he felt no animosity toward Tim. It was as if the Lord had wiped it all away, however he had forgiven Tim a long time ago. Michael thanked the Lord that Tim was here and safe, and he also prayed for Mrs. Cobb.

During the night, Tim was up and down caring for the baby; how much his brother had changed! It was good to see him caring for someone so tiny.

Kathleen slept with Molly that night. Because the bed was narrow, she was restless during the night. She heard the baby crying and her son speaking softly to Abby. About four o'clock in the morning, she heard Jeannie crying. She got up quietly, so she wouldn't wake Molly, and went to her friend. Jeannie had thrown back the covers, and was rocking back and forth, with her arms around her knees – weeping. Kathleen sat beside her friend, and held her talking softly.

Words began to tumble out of Jeannie's mouth. "He's dead, he's dead, Larry is dead! I lost my sweet Larry!" Kathleen held her friend, letting her cry out all her sorrow. It was a long time before Jeannie stopped. Kathleen made eye contact with her friend, and began talking to her, the long silence was over. The two sat together, Kathleen listening until all the sorrow, pain, and fear was out. In time, the woman grew weary from all her emotions; she lay down, holding onto Kathleen's hand. It was a long time before Kathleen felt free to take her hand away. The following morning, Michael stopped by on his way to school to tell the Smith's that Tim had arrived the evening before with Mrs. Cobb and her baby.

"Mac stopped by early that morning on his way to work and found out the two had come in on the stagecoach yesterday evening. I'll tell you all about it later, but they are both alright. Tim has grown into a wonderful young man. I am amazed, and grateful Tim brought her here; she is such a close friend."

"I'm glad your friend and son are here, I'll see you this evening after work. I would like to meet this son of yours, and your friend." He gave her a quick kiss, telling her he loved her and hurried to work.

Later the Smith's came over, leaving the Samaritan House in someone else's hands. By the time they arrived, Jeannie was up; though Tim was still sleeping. It had been a long time since he had slept enough to catch up on lost sleep, and Kathleen didn't want to wake him yet.

Love Comes in Many Colors

When Eve saw Jeannie, she hurried to her friend, putting her arms around her. "We are so glad you're here. We are so sorry about Larry; I know this whole thing has been really hard on you, but you're here with your friends now. We are here to help in anyway we can." All the friends sat visiting, though Jeannie was still rather quiet, saying very little. She just wasn't ready yet, but they all understood.

When Tim came out of the bedroom, Kathleen set about getting her son some breakfast. As he stepped forward, shaking Richard's hand, the man told him, "We're so glad you are here, and safe. Your mother was worried about you; it seems her prayers were answered." The Smith's could hardly believe the change in Timothy. He was courteous and warm as he spoke to the couple. What a difference from the rebellious son he used to be.

While Tim was eating he heard Abby crying, and started to get up when Jeannie said, "Finish your breakfast, Tim, I will take care of Abby. You were up all night long, it's my turn." Then she turned and went to her daughter. Tim could hardly believe this was the same woman he had lived with all through the winter.

His mother saw the look on her son's face. "Jeannie and I were able to talk in the night Tim. She was able to cry and get a lot of the sorrow out, I think she will be much better now, though it will still take time. I think the first step to recovery will be taking care of Abby. Let her do it Tim, she needs you in a different way now. She needs your understanding, I know she has come to love you. Let her show that love by allowing her to take care of her baby now. She knows all you went through, and she's very grateful."

Tim agreed on the outside, but on the inside, he knew he loved Abby like she was his own.

The Smith's left, going back to the Samaritan House, telling their friends they would see them soon. Jeannie came back into the kitchen, carrying Abby after nursing her. Tim was finished with his breakfast, and was about to get up when the woman brought her baby and handed her over to Tim. His heart softened, with the love he felt for his sweet baby. Jeannie seemed happy to share her daughter with Tim; he had been so kind to both of them.

Life settled down in a sense. Kathleen's house was full of people, but Michael's schedule of school kept him out of the house a lot during the day. He, Penny, and Todd still spent their lunchtime together, but Todd now had a job after school, leaving Penny and Michael to spend more time together. Generally, Michael would walk his girl home after school. They talked of many things, even what they wanted to do with their lives after graduating from school.

Penny was the first one to find out Michael's dream. "I want to go to seminary, where I can learn how to be a minister. I want more than anything else to serve the Lord by teaching others about Him." "Really Michael, that sounds just like you, you are the nicest person our age that I know. I think you would be a wonderful minister!" "You, more than anyone else I know, reflect the love of God." Michael's face turned pink, "Well, I don't know about that, but that's what I want to do." The two spent some time talking. "Where do you think you would go? Where is there a school that teaches what you need to know?" "Gee Penny, I don't know, I guess Reverend Smith knows. I've been saving the money I earn on Saturdays working at the ranch, but I know school will cost a lot more. I may have to work a few years before I can pay for school."

The young man took Penny's hand. "I really like you Penny; you're such a nice girl. Actually, I like you a lot! Penny, would you be my girlfriend?" She laughed, saying, "I'm already your girlfriend, there's no one else I like; only you."

"No, I mean, if I go away to seminary, would you wait for me?" She looked up at him. He was so handsome; he had grown tall, and she loved his black wavy hair. What she loved most was his gentle and kind ways. "Of course I will wait; I'll wait as long as it takes Michael." He looked down at her, and those beautiful blue eyes. "You're so beautiful Penny", and he bent over and kissed her cheek. "There will never be anyone in my life, but you." She stood looking at him. I'm so glad Michael; I will be here waiting for as long as it takes." He wanted to fling his arms around her, but he simply said, "I'm so glad Penny." From then on, there was no one else in his life as important as Penny Firth.

In the meantime, Jeannie began getting better every day. Kathleen was trying to finish Maria's and her wedding gowns; she only had a short time with Mac these days. She missed their nights out, but her days were filled with people, and a baby. The sewing machine really helped, but there was too much going on, and little time to sew.

Earlier in the year, Judge Logan agreed to allow Nate Green temporary custody of Miles Hunter. The man was given six months, and at the end of that time, the Judge was to make a final decision on the boy's future. He was concerned that Nate was not married; the Judge simply felt a bachelor knew little about raising a boy.

For now, Miles was still a handful, and Nate's mother's health began going downhill. The man had hoped she could help with the boy, but she had little energy these days. The man wanted to help the boy, and he would not give up easily. Slowly, he began having Miles work on Saturdays, cleaning the pharmacy. Instead of money, Nate would allow him to take something from the store that cost what he owed the boy. Money would come later.

One Saturday, after closing the store, the two walked home. They walked into the part of the house where his mother lived. Nate walked over to his mother, who seemed to be sleeping in her chair; he noticed one of her china cups was on the floor, looking like she had dropped it, and he saw signs of tea on the floor. Nate spoke to his mother, "Are you alright mother?" She did not answer, so he touched her hand, hoping to wake her gently. Her hand was cold! His first reaction was saying, "Mother, don't go!" He knelt down beside her, and put his head on the arm of her chair crying. Then he remembered the boy, and hastily stood up, wiping away the tears with his hand. "What's wrong", the boy asked. Nate hesitated, and then said, "My mother was getting old, and sick. I guess she decided to go to heaven to be with the Lord." "Heaven! What's that", the boy asked. "Well, heaven is where God lives; it's a place where people will never be sad or hurt again." How does one tell a boy like Miles what heaven is like? Nate tried, but wasn't sure if the boy understood.

Several days later, after his mother's funeral, Nate and Miles were sitting on the veranda that spread across the front of the house. One door went into the man's apartment, the other into the house where Nate's mother had been living. The man was trying to explain life, death, God, and his son Jesus Christ, as well as heaven; a tall order.

The boy listened to all the man told him, and when he was finished, then he said, "Aw, I never heard about no heaven before, nor any God. My pa won't go to no such place, and neither will I! God's not real. Then the boy started to stand up looking disgusted. Nate took hold of the boys arm and said, "Who do you suppose made the birds we hear singing in the trees, or hopping on the ground pecking at seeds? How about the flowers that grow in the fields?" The boy answered saying, "How can I know where they cum from?" "A man cannot make them Miles", "I guess not", the boy replied. "Well son, lets talk awhile, and Nate continued talking about the things of nature. "Have you ever seen a butterfly going from flower to flower or a bee as it takes nectar out of flowers, and turns it into honey when he takes it back to his hive?"

"How about the moon, I'm sure you've been out on warm nights and looked up at a full moon. Have you wondered who made it, and the stars that fill the sky? Who could do all that?" The boy was quiet a minute and answered, "God?" "Yes boy, you're right; God is a God of love. It pleases him to make all the beautiful things around us for us to enjoy. He really loves us." "Yeah! Well how cum my pa gets mad and hits me, he never loved me." "Maybe your father was never loved himself, and doesn't know how to love anyone." The man told the boy.

"What's love got to do with anything? I ain't never been loved." "Are you sure boy?" "Yeah, I'm sure." "Then how do you explain that I brought you home so you could be safe, and so your father could not beat you anymore?" "That's love?" The boy asked. "Yes, it's one kind of love. I do not want you ever to be hurt again, and I want you to be happy. When we care about someone, we don't want them to be hurt, hungry, or alone."

The boy shuffled his feet, his hands in his pockets, and his eyes looking at his feet. He thought a minute, and then looked up; raising his eyebrows. "You love me?" "Yes boy, I do. I want you to grow up to be a good and happy man. I don't want you to spend your life begging so you can eat, or sleeping on saloon floors at night. I never want you to be hit or beaten again."

The boy's face blanched, realizing no one had ever loved him before, yet this man said, "I love you, boy." "Aw heck, I guess I'm glad I'm here with you, and maybe there is a God." Nate wanted to hug the boy he was so happy, but he knew he must wait. It would happen in time.

"Hey, how about you and me popping some popcorn?" Miles' face lit up, and he said, "Yeah, I'd like that." So the two went into Nate's apartment, and popped their popcorn; it was a beginning.

The man understood Miles a bit. When he was a boy, his father left his mother

And him with no place to go, and no place to live; they had little future. His mother worked for a number of years, doing menial work, and living in a small room. He was left alone a lot; he was able to go to school, but after school and in the summers he was alone. When Nate was twelve years old, his father was killed when he walked in front of a buggy that could not stop in time. Later that year, his mother married an older man who was a good man, and the man adopted him, the first year. He was then Nathaniel Green. For the first time, there was a good man in his life. Cedric Green was a kind man, and treated both his mother and him with kindness. After a couple of years, they came west; ending up in Silver City.

His step father used money he'd saved, and opened a pharmacy in town. The area was growing swiftly, and the business did well. In a few years, his father built a nice three bedroom home.

Nathaniel learned the business, starting at the bottom, and working up until he became a good pharmacist. When he was twenty-one years old, his father died, leaving the house to his mother, and the business to him with the stipulation he would take care of his mother. Last year he added a small apartment to the side of the house, and a large porch that went across the whole front. At the same time, he hired a woman to clean his mother's house to make life easier for her.

Now he and the boy were moving into the main part of the house so Miles could have a room of his own. The apartment would be empty. He also needed to figure out how to keep the boy.

Kathleen's house was full of turmoil. The days were different with a baby around. Her own baby would be starting school next year, and the days of crying babies were gone from her life. Each day was full of cooking, cleaning, and washing, washing, washing! There was little time for sewing. A whole week slipped by, and the two gowns for the double wedding were started, but there was much more to do. Yes, the sewing machine helped, but it was mostly silent. Kathleen was sleeping with Molly, giving her little rest. Michael was gone during school hours, but Timothy was under foot. He did help around the house but there were too many people around to get what needed to be done, done.

Jeannie was getting better everyday. Her breakthrough was the crying that first night, it had made a huge difference. Kathleen decided it was time to talk to her son. She sat him down and said, "You need to look for work, Tim. Abby's fine, now that her mother is doing so much better. Jeannie can take care of her now." The young man was so accustomed to watching over the baby, having never been far from her before coming to Silver City, and his mother could see his hesitation. Kathleen was concerned; she and Aaron weeks before made a decision to live here in this house for awhile. Her future husband wanted to build a larger house, but that would take time. She missed him, and their nights out. She did see him a short time every evening, but they were never alone. Kathleen tried to keep her commitment to the Samaritan House, but it wasn't easy. She finally went to see Richard about the problem. "Everything is a mess at my house these days. I can't seem to get anything done, and as far as our wedding gowns, I'm nowhere! There's so much happening at my house, I'm stopped before I get started. Jeannie is improving every day; it's good to watch her. She's more like her old self; it's all happening so quickly. I know she misses Larry, they were so much in love; a perfect couple. She has a lot to deal with, but the depression is slipping away.

I love her dearly, and Abby is a darling, but Aaron and I are getting married soon. It simply won't work with all of us living there. Jeannie's already talked about getting a job, but you and I know there aren't dozens of jobs out there for a woman with a baby. I am simply at my wits end! There's nothing I can do to change anything! Tim is going to look for work tomorrow; I certainly hope he can find a job. In the meantime, my house is full of people!" Her shoulders sagged in despair.

Richard tapped his fingers on his desk, trying to think of something that would help. Then Nate Green came to mind. Of course, he thought, that might be the perfect solution. "Give me a day or two Kathleen;

there might be an answer to this problem. It might take care of everything, and it could possibly help both Jeannie and Tim. I'll let you know, if what I'm thinking of might work."

"Thank you, Richard", the distraught woman said. "I'm always coming to you when I need help; you seem to be the problem solver these days." She felt some hope, as she walked home. Thank you Lord for Richard, he's so patient with us all."

Early the next morning, Tim headed to town, looking for work; not knowing about his mothers talk with the minister. After going to at least a dozen places, he found a shop south of Broadway where they built and fixed carriages, and also repaired broken wheels of all kinds. The place looked busy, and when Tim talked to the owner, he told the man, "I worked in a shop in Las Cruces where they repair all kinds of wheels. I've never worked on carriages, but I can learn. I'm a good worker, and I really need the work." The man rubbed his whiskers as he looked at the young man. He wondered if he really was a good worker.

"Are you willing to be here by seven every morning except Sundays, and work long hours?" "Yes sir, I am." "Well, I lost a really good worker a couple of weeks ago. He decided he did not like the west, and headed back to Indiana. I've tried a couple of different men, but they didn't work out. I really need a hard worker, there's lots of work coming in these days, everybody's wanting carriages. I'll give you a chance to prove yourself. It's up to you whether I keep you or not. Be here by seven o'clock in the morning. We'll see what you can do. I'll pay you a fair wage considering how much you have to learn. If you do well, I will increase your wages. I'll see you in the morning at seven sharp." "Yes sir, thank you sir, I'll be here before time." Tim was excited; this would give him a chance to learn a trade.

Two days later, Kathleen answered the door when she heard someone knock. Nate Green was standing there. "I'm sorry to bother you Mrs. McGinnis, but I wonder if I could speak to Mrs. Cobb?" "Of course you can, please come in Nate, and please call me Kathleen. You sit down, and I will get Jeannie", pointing to a chair. The minute the young woman came into the room, he jumped up. "I'm Jeannie Cobb, can I help you?" "Yes ma'am, I'm Nathaniel Green. Reverend Smith told me you might be looking for work." As he was talking, he judged her to be about his age. She was a pretty little thing, with long blond hair.

"I own the pharmacy in town, on Main Street. Several months ago I took a young boy in after being given temporary custody. The boy was being beaten by his father, and other than that, the man paid little attention to him. My mother was alive then, and was helping me with the boy, but she died over a week ago. I may lose the temporary custody because she's gone. He really needs a woman in his life, and if I don't find someone to help take care of him, I may loose the boy, and I don't want that to happen."

"I have a rather large house, with a one bedroom apartment attached to one side. I need a good woman to help take care of him in the daytime. You could stay in the apartment without cost, and I will pay you a weekly salary, so you would have enough to live on. I understand you have a small baby, and that would be no problem. I do need someone to watch over the boy, and help him with his homework, if I can get him to go to school."

"Reverend Smith recommended you highly, I'm in hopes you will be interested in the work. As far as privacy goes, there are two outside doors in the apartment, a front and a back door, which can be locked at night. We would not bother you after dark, except as the nights grow darker in the winter. I am so in hopes you will consider the job."

Jeannie liked the young man; he seemed to be a very respectable man, and Kathleen had mentioned his name as one of the church group. "Mr. Green, you do need to know, Kathleen's oldest son took care of me after my husband was killed, and was there when my baby was born. Those months were very difficult for me, and he was there to help. I'm very grateful for that care, and I'm not sure how he would handle being away from Abby; he's been with her since she was born. He does have a six day-a-week job." She didn't go into anymore details, but he knew the story thanks to Richard, who filled him in on Tim, and his involvement. Nate thought he must be an unusual young man to be so thoughtful and caring at his age.

"I'll tell you what, Mrs. Cobb, I have a three bedroom home, and one of the bedrooms is empty. I could let him sleep in the extra bedroom so he could be with you and the baby in the evenings. I would expect him to keep his room clean, and expect you to do his washing and do his linens as well as washing Miles clothes. I have little time at home to do the washing. If he would like to have the room under those conditions, it would be fine with me."

Jeannie looked at Kathleen, who had come into the parlor, and heard what the man said. "I don't know Kathleen; Tim's your son, and I don't want to take him away from you." Kathleen told her friend, "It's a good solution for Tim, he would be miserable without Abby. Talk to him Jeannie; he's a man now, and he needs to make his own decisions."

When Nate got back to work, he felt a glimmer of hope. The man was willing to do almost anything to keep Miles with him. He knew the young woman was a Christian, and that's what he wanted for Miles. The woman said she would let him know her decision tomorrow, but he knew she was going to accept his offer. To make sure, he asked the Lord for help.

The next morning, she agreed to his offer, and he was delighted. "When can you move in", he asked. She said she would be ready the next day. She told him that Tim agreed to his stipulations, and the man was pleased.

Saturday morning, Kathleen went with Jeannie; helping her to take her belongings. The two walked into the pharmacy, and Nate took the morning off, having someone take his place. The three walked to Nate's house; she liked it immediately! The rooms were very clean. It looked like a bachelor's apartment, the walls were pinewood; one wall was covered with bookshelves, with a few books left on the shelves. There was a rectangular carpet on the floor in the parlor, and the furniture was simple, but in good taste. The kitchen included a cooler to keep foods fresh, and there was a pump in the sink, with plenty of cupboards and a kitchen table. There was a wood cooking stove on one wall, and Nate showed her where the extra wood was stacked; it was just outside the back door, with a roof over the wood to protect it from the elements. The bedroom had a bed, and bureau with drawers, and a round mirror at the top. Over in one corner was a baby's bed beside a table with a lamp. Jeannie was pleasantly surprised. "How thoughtful of you Mr. Green, Abby's never had a bed before. Thank you very much." "You're welcome, we can't have a baby sleeping on the floor now can we?" The man joked, glad she approved. Nate took her back into the kitchen, and opened the cupboard doors. "You have plenty of dishes, and cooking pans. I also filled the cupboards with food, and he opened another cupboard. She also saw some vegetables. I bought a piece of meat to get you started, and the staples you will need."

Jeannie looked at the man, "This is all very kind of you. You are very thoughtful, and I really appreciate all your help." He smiled at her, "You haven't met Miles yet. Miles had just come home for lunch, as Nate had left him at the store so he wouldn't be under foot.

"Miles, I want to introduce you to Mrs. Cobb, she will be living here from now on. She will be here when you come home from school, and will help you with your homework." The boy spoke up, "My mane ain't Miles, it's Scratch." She simply said I'm

Love Comes in Many Colors

glad to meet you Scratch, this is my baby Abby." The boy looked at Abby, "That's a funny name", he told Jeannie. I named her Abigail, after my father's mother, but we call her Abby." The boy looked at the little baby, "Gosh, she makes funny noises", the baby had been cooing and wiggling in her arms. "Well Scratch, I think she's talking to you, in her own way. She's too young to talk yet." "Hmm", the boy murmured. "She's kinda cute, ain't she?" "I think so", Jeannie told the boy.

Thus began a long friendship between the boy and Abby. He thought she was pretty cute with her blue eyes, and curly blond hair. Nate got used to having a baby around. He often heard her crying in the night; it sounded far away, and it was comforting. He liked the young woman, and found her very mature and pleasant; she was also very attractive. Tim did all he was expected to do; he was so glad to be near the sweet baby girl, and his job was going well. He enjoyed learning about the wood, and how it was used to make all kinds of buggies.

Scratch was changing, right before the man's eyes. He was enthralled with Abby, and out of that came change. The boy went to school everyday; coming home pleased as punch with himself. Jeannie spoke to Nate, "Miles does his homework everyday, and I enjoy helping him." Miles generally spent time with Abby when his homework was finished, thinking she was an angel. He'd never been around someone so young before, and he loved being with her every day; always looking forward to his time with her. To Nate, the Lord was doing a wonderful thing. All the things the man had done, accomplished little in the boy, but the baby was causing the boy to change rapidly, and Nate was so pleased.

Although Jeannie was busy, she still had days when she still mourned her loss of Larry; scarcely an hour went by that her thoughts didn't turn to their days together. She missed his laughter, and his arms around her. Larry was always so positive, no matter what the circumstances were. His laughter, that she loved, was infectious; when he laughed, others laughed with him. She wished Larry could have seen his daughter. She knew he would love her as much as she did. Jeannie especially missed him in the night, lying beside him when he slept. At times she thought she could hear him say, "You will be fine Jeannie." She wasn't sure if it was him she heard, or if it was her own thoughts, but she did feel like he was near her more than once. She *was* doing fine, the Lord was strengthening her more and more; and she had Larry's baby girl, sweet Abby.

Tim would spend the evenings with her; sometimes Abby was awake, and other times she slept, but just seeing her made the day worth while. He was learning a trade that he enjoyed, especially working with the beautiful wood; some of the carriages were very fine. It gave Tim a good feeling to know he had done the best he could. Tim was happy, so different from the rebellious boy he was in the past.

God had taken him down a different path that turned his life around. Kathleen was so proud of Timothy; all her prayers were being answered.

Chapter 13

"Hurry up ma, Uncle Mac is here, and if we don't leave now, we're liable to be late for church!" It was very obvious to the adults that Michael was anxious to leave. Kathleen walked into the parlor with Molly at her side, the girl had on a new dress for the day. Friendly was at their side, probably in hopes he could go too. Anywhere, to him, would be exciting.

When Mac saw Kathleen, he went to her; hugging her, and whispering in her ear, "You're adorable this morning." Then he murmured softly, "I love you." She looked up at this man of hers; he is so special, she thought. "Thank you sir, you look pretty handsome yourself in your grey suit and hat. I love it when you wear that suit; it goes perfectly with your auburn hair."

She had on a grey dress, almost the same shade of grey as Mac's suit. On her head was a small purple velvet hat that softly hugged her head, and was tied around her neck. The man thought, she's even more beautiful now than when we were young. The dress showed off her tiny waist; she had kept trim all through the years.

Michael broke into his thoughts. "Come on you two, we don't want to be the last ones!" Both knew there was plenty of time, but they followed Michael and Molly. Mac was holding onto Kathleen's gloved hand. Once they closed the gate on the fence he had built to keep Friendly home, the dog started up a racket; complaining about being left behind.

When the four walked into the church those that were already there were gazing at the stained glass window with the image of Christ holding the child. The soft colors in the window spilled into the sanctuary, leaving the room serene.

Mac took hold of Kathleen's hand after sitting down, both in prayer. After she looked at Aaron, thinking he is so different than Paddy, and she felt deeply loved. While sitting, they saw a wooden cross; it was sitting on a small table in front of the pulpit, where Richard would be preaching. Carved on the cross were grapevines circling, and on the small platform were the words, "I am the vine, ye are the branches", John 15:5. Many people recognized Joe's artistic handwork.

The church was filled with the fragrance of fresh wood, which was delightful. There was a piano at the right side of the pulpit. Few churches in the west were blessed to have pianos, but there was one in most saloons. Mary Johnson sat down on the bench, and began playing softly, which was Mac's cue; Richard asked him if he would lead the singing of the hymns.

Kathleen loved hearing him sing, his voice was rich, yet touching.

After the singing, Richard; who was sitting on the first row, stepped up and stood beside the pulpit. He broke the silence by saying, "Isn't it incredible to be here this morning and be able to worship?" Then he prayed with all heads bowed. "We thank you Father for this beautiful church; where we can worship you, away from the noise and distractions in town. Guide us this morning with our thoughts, as we spend time reading your word. Teach us Lord to become more and more like you. This is our goal; to always reflect your love to the world around us as we live among those who do not know you. Give us your strength through all the good and bad times in our lives; and help us to never waiver from our love of you. We ask this in the name of our Lord and Savior, Jesus Christ. Amen."

Richard asked that all who had their Bibles with them turn to First Corinthians 13. Richard reached deep into their hearts as he talked of the many kinds of God's love, and their impact on everyone's lives; the people around, and those who did not know the Lord. He greatly challenged each one to become that love in action, and deed.

The sermon reached all who listened, not only because of the words spoken, but because of the man that spoke them; for they knew who and what he was. He was loved and respected; and all because he showed that very love in his life. When Richard knelt down, he prayed, "Father, we are here before you, and you know each one of us well. I humbly ask that you send your Holy Spirit to visit us this morning, and fill us with your great love. I ask this in the name of Christ our Lord. Amen."

Everyone was kneeling, and many felt the presence of God. Richard too, lost in that love, and it was some time before he stood, and gave a blessing saying, "May the blessings of the Lord be upon you all, my friends."

Later, everyone gathered together at the Samaritan House to break bread together, as they had always done at the ranch. A few newcomers joined them, having been blessed during the church service. Friends enjoyed each other's company, and made new friends. Penny was sitting by her mother and father, and everyone who knew the two were not surprised when Michael sat down beside his girl. They were spending more and more time together, and Penny noticed that he seemed quieter than usual.

Jeannie and Nate sat across the table from Richard and Eve; Timothy and Miles were close at hand. The woman was trying to keep her baby girl happy, which wasn't exactly easy; Abby got more and more tired, thus more and more fussy. Her mother was also growing tired, but did not want to stop others from enjoying themselves, especially Nate; he needed time to relax and enjoy his friends, so she dealt with her weariness.

After the meal was over, Pete stood up and got everyone's attention. "There are two people here today that we need to thank. We all know our beautiful church would not be if it weren't for James Simpson, and his vision of how the church should be built. His generosity and caring have given us so much; first the Samaritan House, which he made possible, and now our special church. Its beauty is unmatchable, as far as I am concerned. We all want to thank you James; you have done so much to allow us to care for others, and now a place to worship. It has been decided to show you our gratefulness by inscribing your name on a plaque to be placed beside the front door of the church; including the year the church was built. Again, James, accept our thanks for all you have done."

The man stood up, and with a tad of shyness, which rarely happened said, "My good friends, it has been Grace's and my pleasure to do this; we are so grateful that through you all; our friends, we came to know and love the Lord and his people. We pray the church will always be a blessing to all who come to worship the Lord, and for all those who will attend the church in the years to come. We did not do any of this for recognition, but out of love for our Lord; and you, our friends. God bless you all" and the humble man sat down and held his wife's hand. Everyone clapped; showing their affection and appreciation.

Pete then turned to their pastor, "There's one more we need to thank today. Richard, without your vision and unselfish efforts, the Samaritan House would not exist; so many lives would not have been touched by the love that comes from you. Those, whose lives have been so dramatically changed, have joined together with us; so we could give you something to remind you of our love and appreciation. If you will close your eyes, Richard; we have something to bring into the room." So Richard did as asked. While his eyes were closed, two men carried in two pieces of furniture. Pete said, "Richard, you may look now." When their friend and pastor turned, he saw before him a wonderfully carved, black walnut desk and chair. It must have been polished many times over, for it had a soft rich glow.

For once, the man of words had little to say, he was greatly touched by the wonderful gift, and he had a hard time quieting down his emotions. He saw the love of many friends before him; everyone watched their friend with great affection. Richard; a simple man who began the process that accomplished so much; a good man who loved God first, and then his fellow man. It was a touching experience, for everyone who knew him well. He gazed at the desk and chair, so beautifully made; as all his friends watched, he cleared his throat and then said, "What a wonderful gift. I will always treasure it, it will remind me of you, my special friends. May God bless you all." Richard touched the desk lovingly, fingering the carving around the edge of the desk. Everyone watched their gentle friend, who they had come to love; then everyone clapped.

Later, Richard thanked Joe; he recognized the young man's work, and knew how much time and effort Joe had put into making the desk. "Your work is superb Joe; I will always remember your gift of love." "Reverend, you will never know how much you did for Helen and me. You gave us faith in the Lord, but you also gave us hope; something we had none of. We will always remember your kindness to us." Richard smiled. "Thank you Joe, for your friendship. God has blessed me through you and Helen." As he spoke the words, there was a battle going on inside. He did not want people looking up at him, but rather to the Lord; He was the great giver.

After Joe and Helen left, Eve came over; looking up at her husband. What a thoughtful and wonderful gift Richard." "Yes it really is" and he smiled at his wife.

As people began leaving, Nathaniel and his newly formed group started for home. The man could see the day had taken its toll on Jeannie, he knew the long winter had been hard on her. She was carrying a wiggly and outraged Abby, who was getting more so every minute; she was definitely in need of a nap. It was a long day for mother and daughter, and before starting up the steps to the house, she finally relinquished Abby, letting Timothy take the baby girl. It was a good thing she did; when she lifted her skirt to start up the steps, she tripped and almost fell. Nate caught her, "Careful, we don't want you hurting yourself." The man was very tender, but held her arm firmly until he got her inside the apartment and sitting down. Timothy hurried away to change Abby; Miles right behind.

As Nate looked at Jeannie, he could see the weariness. She was still recovering from her difficult winter; along with the loss of her husband. "Are you alright", he asked. She smiled, "Yes, thank you Mr. Green, I'm getting better everyday. It was a very long day, and Abby would not settle down; too much going on." "Please, call me Nate; it's silly for you to call me mister. We are pretty much the same age, let's just be friends. I want to tell you Jeannie that your presence in Miles' life has made a huge difference in the boy." Jeannie smiled. "I think it's not me that's made the change, but Abby; he can't seem to see enough of her. Has he never had anyone to love before?" "No, I don't think so, I believe this is his first such experience. For me, it is a great thing to watch, as distrust and anger slips away", the man told Jeannie. "Its fun for me to watch too", she replied. "The boy is so devoted to Abby, I never dreamed she would have a suitor so early in life; it's good to see him change." Jeannie said as she smiled. "Yes", Nate agreed. "It's a good start."

Timothy came back with a hungry baby. The young man still had a tendency to watch over both of them, so he suggested, "After you feed her, you should lie down and rest awhile, I'll watch over Abby; she will probably sleep anyway." "Thank you Tim, I think I will." Nate stood up, "It's time to go", but Miles begged to stay. "Why don't you leave Miles here", Tim asked. We can play checkers for awhile." "Can I", the boy asked. "All right Miles, but only for an hour." The boy agreed, and Nate left. Soon after Nate went home, he felt lonely; not something he usually experienced, so he went out onto the porch where he could hear the two.

At the Smith's house, Eve was concerned; she knew her husband well. He'd scarcely said a word since they arrived home. Richard was quiet for sometime, and finally excused himself, saying he might rest for awhile. He had been quiet for such a long time that Eve tiptoed into their bedroom. She found him kneeling beside the bed, his head resting on his hands. "Are you alright Richard?" He raised his head, and looked at her. Though he didn't want her to know, she saw evidence of tears in his eyes. "What's wrong dear?" Finally he answered, "I don't want people to act like I'm someone special. I want them to see the Lord; that's who I want to reflect in my life." "I know Richard, that *is* who they see. They just don't realize it, but they do need to show their affection. Richard, they do see the Lord in you, they just don't understand, trust me dear. By your example, others will begin to change, and live like you. As a matter of fact, I do see that starting to happen. The Lord knows your heart, as I do." He turned and took her into his arms. "What would I do without you Eve, you understand me as no other would. I thank the Lord for you everyday; he held her tightly for some time.

Michael, encouraged by Penny, walked home with her and her parents. The Firth's invited him into the house; both liked Michael and his mother. Jacob and Lillie could see the closeness between the boy and their daughter. As the four of them were sitting in the parlor, Penny's father asked Michael if he liked working on the ranch. "Yes sir, very much. I only work on Saturdays, but I especially like being out in the country. I was raised on a farm, at least part of my life."

"The area where the ranch sits is so peaceful, and I certainly like the horses; they are beautiful animals." Jacob agreed. "I always loved horses myself, although I have little time to go riding these days. Are you thinking that's what you want to do with your life?" Penny's father asked. Michael hesitated. Penny was the only one who knew he wanted to go into the ministry. "Well sir, I do love horses, but I have made a different decision. I feel the Lord is pulling me in a different direction. I know he wants me to go into the ministry, and I have made the decision to follow his leading. I hope, after I graduate from school, I've earned enough money to go to seminary so I can become a minister. This is not a sudden decision; I've been thinking and praying about this for nearly a year now. It may take quite a while before I can earn enough money, but that's what I really want to do."

Penny's parents glanced at each other; surprised by the lad's answer. "Well", Jacob said. "I think that's an admirable goal, but it will take a great deal of studying to accomplish it." "I know sir, but that's what I want to do with my life, as I said; I have thought about this a long time, and I really feel that the Lord wants me to teach others about Him, and his great gift of love. I want to serve Him during my life." "Does your mother know about this?" "Well, no sir, but it's time to tell her, I am sure she will be glad to hear it. She loves Him very much herself."

That evening, as Penny's parents were getting ready for bed, Lillie said, "You know Jacob, our daughter and Michael love one another." "Yes, I realize that", her husband answered. "I guess that's why I wanted to know what plans he has made for his future. He seems to be very genuine about his desire to spend his life serving the Lord. We will have to wait and see what happens. He has one more year of school; a lot can change during that time. I feel he is a very trustworthy young man, but it would be best to keep our eyes open. It's a hard time of life, and none of us are perfect." Lillie said to her husband, "Perhaps, we might be able to help Michael pay for his schooling, when the time comes for him to go away to seminary." He nodded his head. "We'll have to pray about it, we do need to keep them both in our prayers; that the Lord's will be done, in both of their lives. He has a good Christian mother; I know she will be there for him when the time comes." Soon she and Mac McGinnis will be married; they are good people, and I'm really pleased with Mac's work. I'm glad I brought him into the bank, he doesn't really have to work, but I think he is doing his part in the community." "Mac is a good, honest, hard working man."

Jacob turned to his wife, and kissed her goodnight; then both turned to prayer, their daughter foremost in their minds.

Later, after his sister was in bed and asleep, Michael broached his mother about his future. "Ma, for a long time now, I've had the desire to become a minister. I haven't said anything to you before, because I wanted to be sure. It's just that month after month, the longing to become a man of God keeps getting stronger and stronger, and I can't ignore it any longer. I've talked to Reverend Smith about it; actually, we've talked several times, that's why he gave me all the books to read. He's never tried to influence me; he always says: If this is what the Lord wants of you, you will know, without a doubt. Well ma, I've come to that place. I do believe that it is His wish for my life. It may take a long time for me to earn enough money to go to school, but I don't mind. That's what I really want to do."

Kathleen was surprised in one way, yet, she knew her son had given himself to the Lord. The love of the Lord was very evident in him. "Michael dear, I'm so pleased and happy about your dedication, and your desire to serve the Lord. It shows in your kindness to others, and in your gentle and caring acts. So many people do not know what they are meant to do with their lives, I'm so happy for you Michael." Her son asked, "Ma, can I have your blessing? I won't do this unless you think I should; I really want to be sure." She answered her son, "Michael, this is not mine to decide, it's between you and the Lord, but I am so blessed to know how much you love him." "Thank you ma, I love you; you are the best mother anyone could ever want." "I love you too my son." Then she put her arms around him. Then he remembered, "Ma, there's something else", and he pulled back. "More?" "Yes, more. Penny Firth and I have promised ourselves to each other. She told me she would wait for me for as long as it takes. I do love her, and she loves me." "Well, well, she said to herself. What I've been thinking is true. God, give them wisdom", she prayed silently. "Son, she's a sweet and very positive girl. She always seems to be so happy with her life. I'm really pleased with your choice".

"Michael, someone your age requires a lot of strength with honor." He blushed. "Yes, I know ma.

I will always honor her, no matter how I feel. I've already asked God to keep me strong." "Michael, why don't we pray together", his mother asked. She took his hand, and they knelt together, asking God that his will be done. Then his mother asked the Lord to keep her son honorable, kind, and loving to all whose paths he might cross during his lifetime. Together Lord, we ask that you will watch over Penny, and if she's meant to be Michael's wife, let it be so." The young man felt so blessed to have such a loving and gentle mother; he loved her greatly.

The following day, Kathleen met Maria at the shop. This was the final fitting, and she wanting to make sure Maria's dress was perfect. Both women were thinking about their upcoming marriages, and both were feeling nervous; Kathleen was trying to forget it by keeping busy. Tomorrow Eve and Jeannie would be checking out her gown. She was so glad her friend was recovering from the loss of Larry. Kathleen loved Jeannie, and was glad she was here and safe. Her thoughts went back to Maria as the young woman spoke. "Senora, my dress is, how do you say it? Beautiful, I love it." "Good Maria, Pete will think his bride is the most beautiful of all. You are a striking woman, and the dress is perfect on you." Maria had never had such a lovely dress before, and when Kathleen spoke about her beauty, she became embarrassed and lowered her eyes. Rarely had anyone said she was even pretty. Yes, maybe Pete, but as a child she was the homeliest one in her family. Her four brothers were always considered handsome. Her sister's went from pretty to very pretty. She was the youngest in the family. Her large brown eyes always looked too big for her small face, and she was always way too thin. Only her father showed her any affection, but her mother was always mean to her, as if she was jealous. She would often hit her, although she never really knew why. She was the only one in the family her mother did not like. For someone to call her beautiful was something she hardly understood. Even when Pete called her that, it was hard for her to grasp what he meant, but she adored him.

When her family left Santa Fe and moved to Deming, south of Silver City, she lost the one person that ever really loved her as a child. That was her Abuelita (Grandmother). Maria still missed her, even though it had been many years since she had seen her grandmother. Pete suggested she write to the woman, and she remembered how excited she was when she got the first letter. Maria Continued to keep in touch, and they were becoming close again; though it was her grandmother's daughter-in-law that wrote down her sweet grandmother's words.

Kathleen saw the unbelief in Maria's face, so she told Maria, "Look in the mirror Maria." As the young woman saw her image, Kathleen said, "Now Maria, what do you see?" The young woman was quiet, and then said, "Si, I think it must be so!" "Of course", Kathleen agreed, "You're lovely."

The soft yellow material folded gently at the base of Maria's neck, and the sheer material flowed down over a full petticoat. The sleeves were partly full to the wrists, and a wide sash was tied in back with a large bow which showed off her small waist. Kathleen was very pleased; her own dress was much the same, though it was made of a sheer, soft lavender color. When Maria left with her dress in hand, the young woman seemed more self assured, and her friend was happy for her. Ben had been in town, and picked Maria up before going back to the ranch.

The following day, Eve and Kathleen went to their friends' apartment. Eve noticed the books on the bookshelves. "Nate does a lot of reading I guess, he left a few for me to read, but I have little time; Abby keeps me hopping, and Miles brings homework from school and needs help. I suspect he didn't spend nearly enough time in school before he came to live with Nate. You know, that man is a very kind person, what other bachelor would have taken on a boy like Miles. Nate seems to have the patience of Jobe, when it comes to the boy. I pray Judge Logan will allow him to keep the boy. I guess he will be making a final decision soon, about whether the boy can stay with him."

Eve changed the subject, but without rudeness. "I can hardly wait until Mac sees you in this dress Kathleen. The lavender color is beautiful, and your green eyes are a wonderful contrast. Jeannie, what do you think we should do with their hair?" They both thought about the problem. "I know", Jeannie said, "Let's pull their hair up on top of their head, and we can intertwine the matching ribbons in the hair, letting several strands of ribbon hang free." So it was decided. Then Abby began fussing, so the two women hurried away, each having things to do at home.

Aaron was having supper with her and her family. She was frying chicken, and while she was working in the kitchen, she was glad that the Smith's had insisted that Molly and Michael stay with them for a week after she and Aaron were married. Eve had said, "You need some time to be alone."

The day they had all been waiting for was here, and Mac wasn't sure if he would be able to breathe! Pete wasn't much better. One would think the two men were going into battle. Jacob laughed at them; "Don't worry fellas, you're both going to live, I can guarantee it"; neither man was encouraged by Jacob's words, so he suggested, "Breath deeply; do it several times, it will help!" Neither man wanted Jacob to know, but they did try. It was a desperate moment. Both men loved the women they were about to marry, it was just. . . . . Oh, they didn't know why they were acting the way they were! Mac thought, I've waited nearly twenty years to marry Kathleen, and here I am, afraid! What's wrong with me anyway? Both men were wearing new boots that made their feet hurt, but that couldn't be the problem, they'd both broken in new boots before. Who can explain the fear that hits a man before he gets married? Surely, it is a mystery.

Finally, with Jacob Firth talking about everyday things, the two men calmed down. Mac was wearing his grey suit; he'd had it cleaned at the Chinese Laundry in town. It was Kathleen's favorite, and he wanted to please her more than anything. Then he began fumbling through his pockets for the wedding band. "Where is the ring? He said out loud. Again

Jacob spoke, "Remember Mac? I have it in my pocket, no need to worry, I will hand it to you when you need it." Pete was watching Mac, and asked himself, is that the way I look? Then he smiled. "Don't worry my friend; I think we will get through this, together." He knew Ben had Maria's ring, but had to ask, "You do have the ring, don't you Ben?" "You two are something else", Jacob said laughing, and then the grooms began laughing. That lasted until Pete and Mac had to walk to the front of the church to wait for their brides.

In the meantime, Eve and Jeannie were hovering around their friends. A touch here, a touch there, they were satisfied with the women's hair. Both were lovely brides! Kathleen's hands were shaking, no matter what she did or thought. Maria was calmer, almost shy around Jeannie, and she kept seeing Pete in her mind; she adored him. She thanked the Lord, "You have blessed me so, I am no one, yet you love me."

Seeing Paddy in her mind, Kathleen talked to herself. No Kathleen, you were faithful to him all through the years, and now he is gone; you love Aaron, and he loves you. This is the right thing to do.

Eve and Jeannie walked down the aisle in front of the two brides. Kathleen and Maria followed, as they walked toward their men. This was the day they had waited for; each carrying a bouquet of yellow roses. Meanwhile they could hear the piano playing softly. When Mac looked at Kathleen, all his fears fled; she looked like an angel! At least she did to him. She looked perfect; the color of her dress and eyes went together so well. He couldn't turn his eyes away from her. To him, she was breathtaking, and she would soon be his wife. His dreams were coming true at last! Kathleen, in turn, saw the man she loved, and quietly; to herself, thanked God for Aaron.

Many thoughts tumbled through Maria's mind. All the bad things in her life were gone. She and Pete loved each other; that was all that mattered. The minute Maria came to stand beside Pete; she was so lovely; her beautiful dark eyes captured him. There was no one, nor anything more important right now than her.

Both men helped their ladies to kneel, and Richard spoke. "Lord, we are here today to unite these two couples in holy matrimony. They have chosen first to kneel before you to rededicate themselves; as well as dedicate their marriages to you, Lord." Their minister and friend knelt, as the couples said their vows to God, to live for Him always; and to carry his love into their marriages. After the prayer, they arose; each man helping his woman up.

Richard asked, "Who gives these women to be married?" Kathleen's son's and daughter stepped forward saying, "We do". Each woman smiled, seeing the young girl so serious, as they gave there mother away. Ben stepped forward for Maria saying, "I do, in place of Maria's grandmother." Richard then asked each man, "Will you love and honor her, forsaking all others", both men saying "We do". Then Richard repeated the question to the brides, both affirming their love and faithfulness. Then the young man spoke to Pete first: "You may now place the ring on Maria's finger." As he did, he said, "With this ring, I do thee wed." Aaron then saying the same thing, slipped the gold band onto Kathleen's finger, repeating, "With this ring, I do thee wed." When he said those words, there was the sweetest smile on Kathleen's face. Each woman repeated their vows to their husbands. Richard spoke, saying, "By the power vested in me, by the county of Grant, in the New Mexico Territory, and the Lord, who called me to this ministry; I now pronounce you husbands and wives. Gentlemen, you may now kiss your brides."

Aaron's kiss was gentle, as he reached down with his hand, and lifted Kathleen's chin to kiss her; a very special kiss at a very special time. Pete circled his arms around his wife, kissing her; both so much in love. Then Richard, with joy on his face, said to their many friends, "I am pleased to introduce you to Mr. and Mrs. Aaron McGinnis, and Mr. And Mrs. Peter Walker." Everyone in the room stood up, clapping as their friends walked up the aisle.

As the couples stepped out the door, rice showered down over their heads; some planting itself in the women's hair, and their husband's. It would be the next morning before the two couples found all the rice in their hair.

There were lots of good wishes, and laughter as everyone congratulated the couples. As soon as the four were free, Eve and Richard pulled them away, walking them to the Samaritan House with their friends following. When the newlyweds walked into the building, they saw a large white cake in the center of a table. The yellow roses that had graced the front of the church had their stems removed, and were placed around the cake. Someone had gone to the trouble of making yellow and lavender colored napkins, and there were pitchers of lemonade, and glasses at the ends of the table; with small saucers to hold the cake. When Kathleen looked at all the things that were done, Jeannie, Eve, and Thelma came to mind. She must thank them.

The brides stood at one side of the room, and were told to throw their bouquets; Emily, catching one, and Jeannie the other. The couples were told to feed a small piece of cake to their partners. Both women were dainty, as they fed their husbands, but Aaron managed to get frosting on Kathleen's nose, and around her mouth. Pete was even more awkward, with cake ending up on Maria's mouth, chin, and floor. This was something few had ever seen before, but it brought a lightness to the party, with the guests laughing; then everyone had a piece of cake and lemonade.

In time, Jeannie went looking for Kathleen, only to find she was gone; both men had coaxed their brides away. As Jeannie and Nate headed home with the 'family', Jeannie kept thinking about Larry. For her, the day seemed long, as she remembered the day she and Larry were married. Their marriage was very simple, with only a few family members and friends in attendance. Some days, she missed him greatly; their marriage only lasted a little over four years.

Nate noticed the young woman was more quiet than usual. "Are you alright Jeannie?" the man asked. She was slow to answer, "Well, I loved seeing my friends married, but I kept thinking of my husband. It's really hard to realize, I'll never see him on the earth again." "He will never know or get to love and hold Abby. You know, he was hoping we would have a girl, and now she will never know him. She looks a little like him; her hair is the same color as his, and sometimes I see a likeness of him in some of her movements."

As they drew near to the house, Jeannie said to Nate, "I'm so grateful you offered me this job, and allowed me to stay in the apartment. I had no place to go, nor any future. I really appreciate everything you've done Nate." The man told her, "I am so grateful that you've done so much to help Miles. He had a terrible life before he came home with me; he had a brutal father, but the boy is beginning to believe in humankind. The only problem is; I'm worried that Judge Logan won't let me keep the boy, he has a fixation that the boy needs to have *both* a mother and father. I'm in hopes that he will see the change in Miles since you came to take care of him. Would you consider going with us when we go to see the Judge?" "Of course Nate, I will be glad to go. I do hope the man will let you keep the boy, Miles really cares for you. Surely the Judge will take that into consideration." "I hope so Jeannie, we will just have to wait and see."

By this time they were home, Abby had fallen asleep in her mother's arms. Nate took Miles into the house, and they sat eating popcorn and playing checkers. He was free until Monday morning; he'd asked Mr. Temple to work in the store. The man was a retired pharmacist, which made it easier for Nate to take a day off here and there.

When Kathleen and Mac stepped up onto the porch, the new husband swept her up into his arms; regardless of his shoulder, and carried her across the threshold. He put her down, and put his arms around his wife. "You are so adorable Kathleen, and I love you. There were all those years when I would think of you; I never dreamed I would ever see you again, let alone have you as my wife. Kathleen, you are so precious to me", and he kissed her, her arms reaching up around his shoulders. "Aaron, I have never been happier." They were both, so much in love.

The next morning found them sitting on their bed, with Aaron brushing Kathleen's long, beautiful hair; finding a piece of rice here and there. They talked of many things from their childhood days, and then he held her as he softly sang an old Irish love song as she nestled in his arms; they had never been happier.

Before breakfast they thanked the Lord for the food, then Aaron prayed, "Father, we place our lives, and our marriage into your hands. We both love you, and know we can trust you to be with us as we spend the years you've given us together." Later that day, hand in hand, they took a walk over the lower hills in the area. They followed the stream; Kathleen picking a wild flower here and there.

Their days together went much too quickly; only Friendly knew of their happiness as he followed them wherever they went. On their third day, they went to say goodbye to Pete and Maria, as they boarded the stagecoach to go to Santa Fe where Maria's grandmother lived; the main reason for their trip. Pete never wanted to meet her immediate family, their cruelty to his wife was inexcusable, and he wanted nothing to do with them. However, Maria loved her grandmother, and Pete had promised to take his wife to see her; not having seen her for many years. Pete was carrying his pistol, just in case. One never knew where or when the Apaches might strike, and he wanted nothing to happen to his wife.

As the stagecoach pulled out, Mac called out, "God be with you." Kathleen did not envy them, she remembered well the long, hot, dusty days and nights; also the anxiousness she had felt, knowing the Indians might attack at any moment.

After saying goodbye, the McGinnis' walked into their favorite general store. "Hello George", Mac said. "How are you my friend?" "Good", was Georges reply, "And how are our newlyweds today? You both look happy enough." "Oh we are", Kathleen said. Her husband looked at her and said, "This is the sweetest woman ever." George grinned, remembering the day he and Jean were married. "So, that means you're really in love, I guess. Well, I'm happy for both of you, can I get you anything today?" "Yes George, we need a few supplies." As they were ordering what they needed, Richard walked in. "Well, look who's here! How are you two?" The man asked. "Great", was Mac's answer. "Good, I am glad the Lord brought you two together. Kathleen; Michael and Molly are doing fine, I think Thelma is really enjoying having Molly with us; I hope she doesn't spoil the girl too much. Your son is a blessing to have around; he told me his decision to go into the ministry, I'm really glad for him. Several months ago, I had the opportunity to pray over him, I knew then God planned something special for his life. It is rare for one so young to know his calling; what a blessing he must be to you Kathleen." "Yes, he is very special; he took over when Paddy and I were having problems, and he's always been a good, kind, and thoughtful son. I am blessed to have him."

Thursday rolled around, and Mac felt he needed to go back to work. The two didn't want to part, but life must go on. "I'll be back, sweetheart, the day will be over before we know it. After he kissed his wife goodbye, she asked; as an afterthought, "Aaron, why don't you come home for lunch?" "That sounds good, see you then." And he left. Around ten thirty, he showed up. Kathleen was surprised! "Jacob sent me home; he thinks I can catch up next week, so I took the liberty of renting a buggy. Kathleen, let's go to the ranch for the next couple of days." Kathleen was all for it, and packed enough clothes for a few days.

Ben saw the two when they arrived. "So, you have come home for awhile." He said to Mac. "Yes, and it feels good; how am I ever going to stay away? This ranch is so much a part of me." "Well, make yourselves at home; Cook is feeding us, and you can eat when we do. Just enjoy yourselves." And Ben went back to work. Mac took his wife into the house. He took their things to his old bedroom, where he had done so much praying and talking to the Lord about Kathleen.

They would not head back to town until Saturday afternoon, so while they were at the ranch, they picked some peaches; they were so sweet and juicy.

The couple also spent time with the horses, and took a short ride around the ranch; Mac not wanting to get too far away from the ranch, just in case. No one knew where the Indians were, so it was better to be careful. Mr. Grey had fathered a colt. He was only a few days old, and Kathleen couldn't stay away! She wanted to touch, and talk to him. "He's so beautiful, isn't he Aaron?" He had to agree; the young colt was almost like his father. Kathleen wanted to stand and talk to the baby colt, and Mac had to coax her away. "Come on sweetheart, let's go for a walk." So they wandered around the ranch, talking, talking, and talking some more. The days went so swiftly, and soon it was time to go home.

The day Pete and Maria left town, Nate took Miles to see the judge; he took Jeanie and Abby along also, both adults were hoping Jeannie's caring for, and watching over the boy would convince the Judge to give Nate full custody of the boy. Also, because Miles was no longer 'Scratch', in his own mind, nor was he the suspicious boy he was before would help Nate. As he made his case to the Judge, he explained the boy's improvements, and Jeannie's part in the boy's life. The Judge listened patiently, and then said, "If you don't mind Mr. Green, I would like to talk to you alone," So Jeannie took Abby and Miles out of the room. The boy was happy, being able to spend time with Abby, but Jeannie felt concern. "Now sir", the Judge said, "I do appreciate what you have done with the boy, but I still feel the boy needs a mother, one that will be with him during his growing years. Do you have anyone that might care enough to marry you under these circumstances?" The man was at a loss, not knowing what to say.

Finally Nate asked the Judge if he would consider giving him three days more. "Mrs. Cobb is a fairly new widow, with a baby not yet six months old. I am not sure. We have not talked about any kind of relationship, but if you would give me time to talk to her, maybe something can be worked out. She's very fond of the boy, but I'm not sure if she would agree to marry me. I would like some time to find out if we can come to some kind of agreement." The Judge was quiet for a moment, and then said, "I guess I could give you a few more days, let's see." He looked at his docket. "The earliest I could give you time, would be Monday morning. If you cannot come to some kind of agreement by then, I feel I must place the boy in a home, where there would be both a mother and father. Can you be here by nine o'clock? I have another case at ten." "Yes sir, I will be here." "Good luck young man. I do feel you are a good man." "Thank you sir, I will be here at nine o'clock sharp." The Judge nodded, and Nate walked out of the courtroom with dread in his heart. Thinking, do I want a wife?

As Nate joined Jeannie and the two young ones, he told her, "The Judge has given me until Monday." He chose to say no more at that time, especially in front of Miles. This was something he should not take lightly.

When they got back to the house, Abby was fussy, and needed a nap. Nate asked, "Can we talk while Abby is taking her nap?" She looked at the man, wondering what was on his mind. "Of course, are you going to be home until then?" "Yes, I've taken the day off. I will feed Miles and then take him to school, hopefully Abby will still be sleeping when I return." "I'm sure she will. I need to feed her before she goes down."

While Nate was walking the boy to school, his mind was in a whirl. Do I want a wife? Do I love Miles enough to make such a move? Jeannie's still missing her husband, would she be willing to marry me? Lord, I don't know what to do; I seem to be caught between a rock and a hard place. Jeannie is a pretty woman, and very kind, but I'm no beauty. Well, I'm not ugly, Lord; I guess I'm just a bit plain. Finally, in despair he said, "Lord tell me what to do?" Nate thought of every angle. Would Miles be happy with a mother? Then Abby came to mind, Miles would be broken hearted without her. What should I do? Then he decided, he wanted to keep the boy. He wanted to give him a happy life, so he made the decision to ask Jeannie if she would marry him. She is a sweet and honorable woman, he said to himself.

Around two o'clock, Jeannie came to his door. "Nate, she's asleep." He followed her into her apartment. Once they sat down, every thought flew away. Oh gosh, Lord, help! He blurted out, "Jeannie, do you like me at all?" "Of course I do, you are a very kind and considerate person, what's going on?" He steadied himself and said, "Judge Logan doesn't want to give Miles to me, unless I'm married. I have no girl friend, or anyone I'm in love with. I've thought and thought about what I am going to say, please bear with me," he begged. "All right, Nate."

Wondering what he would say. "I've been thinking", Nate said. "I really need a wife; the judge insists, or I will lose him. I would like someone who would love Miles, which I think you do already."

"You in turn, need someone to take care of you while Abby is growing up. If I lose Miles, there will be no job. I don't mean that as anything, but the truth." "Jeannie, would you consider marrying me? I would not ask much of you, you and Abby could have your own room in the house, and Timothy could stay in the apartment. There's no one else to ask, and I do not want to lose Miles; I am so fond of the boy. The Judge made it very clear, I will lose him, unless I'm married." Then Nate almost started to stutter, and his face turned scarlet red, but he struggled on. "I,- I know this is a big decision for you to make, I promise, I will always take good care of you and Abby. There's no one else to ask," Oh gosh, he thought. I'm repeating myself. Jeannie, I do well at the store, so you would never be in need. If you like, you can change the house anyway you want." Then he fell silent, afraid to hear her answer.

Many different thoughts raced through Jeannie's mind. "What about Larry? What would he think about this man becoming Abby's father? There was Timothy, how would she handle that? What about Miles, would he accept her as his mother? Would she ever fall in love again?" She sat quiet for some time; she wasn't sure how to handle this. She prayed silently, "Is this what you want Father?" "Oh dear, what should I do?" Finally rational thoughts began. Yes, Abby needs a father too, and she knew Nate would be there for her. After what seemed to be an eternity, Jeannie answered the man saying,

"Alright Nate, I will marry you. I realize you don't love me, but maybe that's the best thing." I'm not sure if I'm ready to love anyone again, but I need someone too. Maybe we can make a pact that we won't invade each other's life, unless we begin to care for one another. I know you like being a bachelor, so we would both have to give ourselves to this endeavor. I do think before we go any further, we should pray together, and then sit down with Miles and talk to him. We don't have to share everything, but he has a lot at stake in this marriage, he must be able to accept both Abby and me."

The man was so relieved. "Be assured, Jeannie", he told her, "I will never make any advances toward you, unless we both agree; that's what I want." She nodded her head. "Good Nate. Talk to the boy, and if he is happy with your decision, we will go ahead and marry, though I don't want anymore than a simple wedding. Would it be alright if Richard marries us? I know Eve and Thelma would be there, but I would like Kathleen and Mac there too." "Yes, of course. That would be my choice", Nate replied with relief in his voice.

Miles wanted to stay with Nate, and saw no problem with Jeannie moving into the house, because that would mean Abby would move in too.

The next morning, after he got someone to stay at the Pharmacy, Nate went looking for Richard. He found the man at the Samaritan House. "Can I talk to you Richard? It's really important." "Sure, come into my office so we can be alone." Once they were seated, Richard asked, "How can I help you?" How to start! Finally Nate got up enough courage and told Richard what was going on, and that Jeannie had agreed to marry him, so he could keep the boy. "We don't love one another, but we both do care about Miles, and Jeannie wants to help, so I can keep the boy."

Richard sat quiet for a minute. "You do realize you're obligation to her?" "Yes, I do. We don't love one another, but she understands I would lose Miles without being married, and being such a caring person, she doesn't want that. We both love the boy." "This is a big step Nate." "Yes I know; for both of us as well as Miles, but there's no other way I can keep him. Jeannie has no one but Abby, and if I can't keep Miles, then she would be out of work. She needs someone to take care of her and Abby, and I promised Jeannie, I would never make any advances toward her, unless she agreed."

Richard leaned back in his chair, holding a pencil in his hands. "That may be harder than you think, Nate. Women, somehow have a way of getting under our skins; in a good way of course. Jeannie is a fine Christian woman, and a very sweet one at that. We've known her a long time, and I know she misses her husband. I know that loss will begin to fade as time goes by; so you may have a struggle with that promise." "I will keep my promise to her; if our feelings change, we are adults and we will be able to work it out. I would never hurt her in any fashion", Nate told his pastor. "Alright; I will marry you. You say she wants Eve and Thelma, as well as Kathleen and Mac at your marriage?" "Yes, she specifically asked that they be there." "The two have gone out to the ranch for a couple of days, but Kathleen told Michael they would be back before evening on Saturday. She and Mac are to pick up the youngsters; they have been staying at our house this week. That means we only have Saturday night or Sunday afternoon, which day do you prefer?

Nate told his friend. "Saturday night would probably be better for their family, so they could spend Sunday all together." "That's fine", Richard answered, we will see you Saturday night. We will make sure the McGinnis' will be there. Don't forget. You and Jeannie must get a marriage license at the court house. Without that paper, I can't legally marry you!"

That evening, all four sat down, talking about the arrangement. "Are you sure this is going to be alright with you Miles?" The boy was quiet, thinking. "If you don't get married, would I have to go back and live with my pa?" "No Miles, but you would live with another family." Again the boy thought. "But I don't want to leave you. I kinda like being here, and besides, I can't leave Abby. What would she do without me?" Nate and Jeannie's eyes met, with a touch of humor in them. "Alright boy, if that's what you want, we will do this thing; we will become a family."

Tim spoke up, "Now that I'm earning money, I can pay rent if you will let me stay in the apartment, I would keep it clean and in order. I couldn't leave Abby; sometimes I almost feel like she's part mine", he said with concern in his voice. "I think that's a great plan. Now that we are getting married, it would be empty, and I would rather have you there than a stranger, you're already part of this family. Then the man smiled. "Let's see, I'm marrying Mrs. Cobb, and I get three more for free!' It was almost funny. Nate thought, I've been a bachelor all these years, and now suddenly I have a family. But somehow he felt good about the whole arrangement.

Jeannie laughed, speaking to her daughter, "Well little miss, you're doing pretty well; with two admirers around."

Saturday evening, Nate and his newly formed family arrived at the Smith's home on time. Within a few minutes, Kathleen and Mac arrived, with her two children crowding around her, both glad to see their ma. The four had time to visit, while the couple was closeted with Richard. Eve then explained to her friend, what was happening. Both women had concerns about Jeannie, each hoping the marriage would work out. Personally, the two were in love with there husbands, and hoped more for Jeannie, but each knew this was her business. They loved her too much to interfere, and they both liked Nate, he was a good young man.

After the two were married, Thelma and Eve brought out a cake and coffee, along with lemonade for the young ones. They wanted the two to have happy memories of their wedding. The time together was pleasant, as they were all good friends.

Later, when the couple said goodnight, Nate felt awkward, not sure what to do. He bent down and kissed his wife on the cheek, and said, "Sleep well Jeannie, I'll see you tomorrow," and they went to their own rooms.

As she was lying in bed, Jeannie thought of Larry, but knew life had to go on. She also knew Nate was a kind, and honorable man, and he would take care of Abby and her; and when she thought of it, it made her feel grateful. She turned to the Lord, "Thank you Father. You have provided for Abby and me, and Miles will be with Nate. I love you Father, and always will.

Jeannie fell asleep, feeling good about her decision, knowing her daughter would be taken care of.

Chapter 14

The trip to Las Cruces was uneventful, with no signs of either Indians or bandits; most likely, because a small unit of soldiers from Fort Bayard accompanied the travelers to Fort Cummings.

After a hearty breakfast the next morning, the coach left the fort, heading east across the desert floor. The day grew hot, and the winds picked up, blowing from the west. As they grew stronger, the dust billowed around the traveling vehicle, filling the stagecoach with gritty dust. This would not be the only day the Walkers would struggle to breathe; both using handkerchiefs to help from inhaling the dust.

When the stagecoach rolled into the dusty western town of Las Cruces that lay alongside the Rio Grande River, the passengers saw a very dusty town, full of all kinds of activity. There were many kinds of wagons that were used to carry goods to many towns in the area; Las Cruces was a busy town, full of commerce. Consequently, many people lived in the area; people also traveled both north and south from the area, as well as east and west. Las Cruces was truly a crossroad in the southern part of the territory, with El Paso, Texas to the south.

After alighting from the coach, Pete guided Maria to the Amador Hotel. This hotel was known for its beauty; unusual for most western towns. When the couple had cleaned up, they went down to find a place to eat. The man sent them down the street to a restaurant that could fill their needs.

Once they had ordered their meal, the Walker's sat talking; Pete overheard two men who had just arrived, traveling from Santa Fe. They were talking about how the areas Indians had struck along the road coming south. Their trip sounded dire, and Pete began to think it would be better to wait until fall to travel north, and he told Maria his thoughts. Maria disagreed with her husband. "Peter, we have to go, I wrote my grandmother we were coming to see her. I must keep my word. She's expecting us, besides the Indians have probably moved on by now. Please Peter, I have to go."

Her husband could see her side of it; however, he did not want anything to happen to his wife. He did not trust the Apaches, they were extremely fierce. They had lost their home, and were very angry, and often unreasonably cruel, especially to women.

The following morning while Maria was getting dressed, her husband went to a general store nearby. He bought a repeating rifle, and plenty of ammunition for both the rifle and his pistol. This trip north was against his better judgment. He had already fought more Indians than he wanted to, and he did not want anything to happen to Maria.

As the stagecoach headed north; the days were extremely hot. The winds continued blowing, hitting the stagecoach on the side, causing it to bounce around. The dust was almost unbearable, though the canvas flaps had been lowered and tied in place. Still, it did not stop the dust from filling the coach, which made breathing very difficult.

Most nights; the passengers slept in the coach as they headed northward, the driver, eager to get further north where they would be safer from the danger of the Apache braves. Once they got further north, the driver stopped in the small town of Albuquerque. It was time to change horses again, and the driver and his partner up front were pretty tired; they had traded places several times so one of them could rest, but it was not much help. For several days, Pete's long legs had been cramping; he was not a sitter, and his legs reminded him.

Once the couple was in their room in the small hotel where they were staying, Maria insisted on rubbing her husband's legs. She had come prepared, and pulled out a small jar of salve. Maria not only used the salve, but spent time rubbing his legs until his muscles relaxed. Pete almost fell asleep, and she would have let him, but he forced himself to keep his eyes open. First they needed to find someplace to eat, and then they could rest. After they ate, Maria fell asleep in his arms as he thanked the Lord, again for her, and her sweet ways.

After a quick breakfast the next morning, they began the last part of their trip to Santa Fe. Everyone climbed back into the stagecoach, each one eager to reach their destination which was still several days away.

When they rolled into Santa Fe, the weather was much better. Here the day was sunny, but the clouds of dust were left behind. Pete guided his wife while carrying their luggage to an elegant hotel. James Simpson had recommended it to Pete, knowing his friend wanted to take his wife to a special hotel. James had told him it was the best hotel in town, and it was very elegant. Once they were in their room, Maria's eyes took in the beauty. She had not seen real elegance before; there was a four postured bed with a feather comforter on top, and four fluffy pillows. Damask drapes hung at the windows; tied back by gold colored ropes. All the furniture was made from mahogany wood, including two overstuffed chairs, and a small round table covered with a lace tablecloth. A very large mirror, framed in gold; hung over a chest, where their clothes could be kept. A fancy folding screen stood in one corner of the room, where one could change their clothes.

Maria's eyes got so big, hardly believing there was such beauty. Pete smiled, "Pretty nice, huh?" She turned to her husband, "Oh Peter, it's so beautiful!" Her husband grinned at her. "Nothing is too good for my wife," and she went into his arms. "Somehow, I feel like a princess who has found her prince", she said. She looked at him, and he bent down to kiss her; her arms went up around his shoulders, and he whispered, "I love you Maria, I don't think I have ever been happier than I am right now." He kissed his wife again.

After resting, Peter said, "Maria, tonight wear the dress Kathleen made for you, I want to take you someplace very special." The dress was made of dark red velvet; it was far more lovely than any dress she had ever owned, except the gown she was married in. This dress clung closer to her body, showing off her lovely figure. As she was looking in the mirror at herself, Pete placed a very lovely gold and garnet necklace around her slender neck, then Maria put on her long earrings to match. When she had them on, he stood back, looking at his wife. To him, she was exquisite! He stepped over and hugged her. "Maria, you are so beautiful, and I love you so." Pete himself looked very handsome; he had a black suit on that Jules had made for him and the man had insisted he have a bow tie to wear while he was in Santa Fe.

As he held his wife, he remembered the first time he saw her. Maria had gone into George's mercantile shop, looking for work one day when he happened to be in the store. She was only in her late teens and rather thin, but with a look of determination on her face. When George said he had all the help he needed, she had replied, "I'm ver' hard worker, and will do anything", speaking with a strong Mexican accent. George only nodded no, saying "I'm sorry I have nothing to offer." Maria stood there a minute, and then asked, "Do you know anyone who needs help? I really need the work; I just arrived in town, and need work badly."

Pete remembered that he and Mac had already talked about hiring a woman to keep the ranch house clean, and they were tired of Mac's cooking, which was less than good. On impulse, he had spoken up and asked her, "Do you cook?" She turned and looked at him; that was the first time he had seen those lovely dark brown eyes. "Si senor, I cook ver' well. I'm ver' hard worker", she replied. He remembered her arms circling around his waist as he had ridden home on his horse; she sitting behind him. He had hoped he wasn't making a mistake. In those days she was only a slip of a girl, but he remembered wanting to help her.

Mac agreed they should hire her, so Pete gave up his bedroom until they built a small two room building just for her. It stood just outside the kitchen door, and it had a wooden bar she could slip across the door to lock it from the inside. Pete remembered how big her eyes had gotten when she looked inside, and realized this would be her home.

For a long time she only answered questions, or when they asked her to do something, she would answer by saying, "Si senor". Gradually, as she grew more self-assured, she began learning more English, and now look at her, he thought she was a beautiful woman, the one he loved.

Pete felt like it would be impossible to love her more than he did at this very moment. After the war, he struggled with many dark thoughts; sure he would never marry, but here he was, captured by her sweetness, and he loved Maria with all of his heart.

That night, Pete took his wife to see a play in a new theater in town. The man at the hotel suggested it to Pete when he asked if there was anything special going on in town; he did know theater groups came through town often.

This was something Maria had never experienced before. At one point the actors were in a moving scene, and she glanced at him with tears in her eyes. She took hold of his hand, and went back to watching. Pete watched her; he was so proud of his wife.

If he could have seen himself, he would have seen a handsome man dressed more like a fine gentleman than a man that usually wore a broad brimmed hat, jeans, and boots; he wasn't concerned about himself.

After the play was over, they went to a very special restaurant. More than one man glanced at Maria; she had not been seen in town before, and she was a strikingly beautiful woman. After eating, they danced a few dances; Maria followed her husband easily across the floor with grace in every step. Pete was so pleased to show her off; she was gorgeous, and he was so proud of her. Before long, the hour was growing late, and both were tired. Once they were in bed, he held his lovely wife in his arms; it wasn't long before she was asleep. He bent over and kissed her lightly on her cheek, and then fell asleep himself. It had been a long trip, and a long evening, but the evening had been so special.

The following morning, after lingering over breakfast, the couple wended their way to Maria's grandmother's house. Her family had been in Santa Fe for many generations; long before the white man came west. One of her ancestors had arrived with Juan de Onate when the explorer took possession of the area, claiming it as a part of Spain in 1598.

Amused, Pete watched his wife; she was so excited about seeing her grandmother again after so many years. "Slow down sweetheart, it's still early. You will have plenty of time to visit this grandmother of yours." "Oh Peter, I cannot, I'm so anxious to see her. It's been so many years." "Alright sweetheart", he answered, giving up. Maria smiled up at her good-looking husband thinking, I can hardly wait to introduce him to my Abuelita.

It wasn't long before they arrived at the house. It was like many other buildings in the area, all made of adobe bricks. A wall made of adobe bricks circled around the house and garden, with a gate at the front. When Pete opened it for his wife, a bell rang softly. The patio had many colored flowers circling around the bricked floor, and there was a large shade tree that stood in the center, shading part of the patio. It was very charming.

When Maria knocked, her Aunt Rosa; her Uncle Roberto's wife, answered the door. The two women had never met, but had written for several years. The two hugged each other, "Please come in", she said, and gestured them into the room with her hand; as the couple walked into the house, it felt cool from the adobe brick, and was pleasantly decorated in rich colors. "Please, follow me", she told the couple, and she took them into a side bedroom. The sunshine brightened the room with warmth that warmed the small woman.

"Abuelita," Maria said as she hurried to the small frail elderly woman; who was sitting in a chair with a knitted robe over her lap. Maria knelt down, gently hugging the small grandmother. "I've missed you so", and then she motioned for Peter to come. She said to him, "Esta es me Abuelita" (This is my dearest grandmother). Then the young woman turned to her grandmother saying, "Este es Peter, mi marvilloso esposo." (This is my wonderful husband, Peter).

The man knelt down; joining his wife, and gently shook the tiny, thin and wrinkled hand thinking, it's good, Lord, that I brought Maria now to see her grandmother. I'm glad Maria insisted we finish our journey. The small woman looked so frail and old.

Peter pulled up a long ago language he had not spoken in many years, "Estoy muy contento de concerna." (I'm so delighted to meet you). "Maria te amo mucho, y yo tambien." (Maria loves you so much and I do too). The tiny sweet woman smiled, looking so pleased. Peter continued speaking, "!Abuelita, yo amo a Maria mucho!" Y la amo, con todo me Corazon." (Grandmother, I love Maria with all my heart). Speaking soflty, Maria's grandmother answered Peter, "Gracias, yo se que amas a mi Nieta quiero que la cuidas pero mucho." (Thank you, I know how much you love my granddaughter, but I want you to take good care of her).

Peter nodded his head smiling. "Si, con mucho gusto." Then he turned to his wife, and kissed her on her cheek. "I must go sweetheart; when I've finished the business I have to do, I will be back. Enjoy your time with your grandmother. Maria's grandmother could see this mans love for Maria, and she was so pleased.

After he and Rosa were in the parlor, he asked her, "What time should I come back for Maria." I don't want her grandmother to tire." Rosa suggested, "Why don't you let Maria stay until two o'clock. They will have plenty of time to visit, and they can eat together. Maria's grandmother usually is tired about that time. Peter nodded saying, "I will be back at two", and he left, walking to the bank where he and Mac had investments.

When he finished his business, Pete wandered around town, hoping his wife was enjoying her grandmother. He stepped into a small restaurant and ate a light lunch. After his meal he left, walking through the busiest part of Santa Fe. As he grew tired, he sat on a bench under a large tree, and watched people going by. His thoughts went to Maria and her grandmother. He'd heard the story of her Abuelita; when she was young, and raising her family by herself; doing menial work to feed and clothe her children. Her husband was a drinker and in time disappeared.

While she was working, having to be away from the house, two of her three sons became uncontrollable, often getting into trouble. One of these sons was Maria's father. He, in time, married a disagreeable woman who bore him six children, Maria being the youngest. Her Abuelita only had one good son; that son was Roberto, Rosa's husband.

The woman was a woman of faith, like his own mother, even though their religions were different; both he and Maria had special women in their lives. Pete thought of his mother, and still missed her after all these years. She often came to mind.

Love Comes in Many Colors

When Pete decided it was time to go and join his wife, he wandered back to the house. As he walked, he saw a very special rosary made of turquoise stones; it was in a store window. He would take his wife to see the rosary and buy it so Maria could give it to her grandmother.

When Pete knocked on the door, Rosa opened it saying "Please come in Peter, Maria is just now saying goodbye. Her grandmother was growing tired, and Maria is helping her into bed to rest. She will be out shortly; please sit down Peter." The man sat down holding his hat in his hands. As she looked at the tanned strong looking man, Rosa thought to herself, he seems to be a good man. She could see the kindness in his face, and knew Maria had a special husband. She spoke up saying, "I'm so glad Maria is here now, my husband's mother has not been well; we've all been worried about her. When she found out you two were getting married and then coming to see her, she perked up a bit. I know Maria is a very special grandchild, and the two were close until Maria's family moved south to the small farming town of Deming. She worried that Maria would not be treated well, I guess those fears were warranted. Maria's grandmother is so glad Maria has a man who loves her, and treats her kindly; or so Maria has written."

"It's true", Pete told Rosa. "I do love her; she's an unusually sweet woman. I know she was treated badly by her family, especially by her mother, but that will never happen again. I will always treat her with love. She is so very special to me, and I will always take good care of her." Rosa, gratefully said,

"My mother-in-law will be so happy to hear about your love for Maria. There will be no more need for her to be concerned about her."

When the couple was walking away from the house, Maria remarked, "My sweet grandmother is growing old Peter. Time has hurried by so quickly, I wish we could take her with us, but I know that cannot be. She could never make that hard trip, and it would not be fair to my Uncle Roberto."

That evening, Maria wore her special dress again as they went to a very nice place to eat that the manager of the hotel recommended. As they sat down at a table with fine china and silverware, they saw a beautiful vase of flowers that sat in the middle of the table. A small stringed instrumental orchestra was playing softly; the atmosphere was peaceful and lovely. Pete thought his wife fit here perfectly. He reached across and held her hand, so grateful to the lord for this woman; who was beautiful both inside and out.

After eating they danced, joining others on the small dance floor. People stopped talking, watching the handsome couple as they glided around the dance floor. Later, the two sat talking about many things over coffee, enjoying the atmosphere, and being together. Maria had never seen such places, but she handled herself beautifully. The evening was special in every way, and they were so in love. When it was time to leave, Pete took hold of Maria's hand as she stood. Never in a million years would the young woman have ever thought she would be more than just a cook and housekeeper. Peter had romanced her both evenings since they arrived in town. Her whole self image began to change. She felt so loved, and responded to Peter with such love and gratitude, and he her.

The following morning, Maria was brushing her long dark hair, when her husband came over and took the brush out of her hand, then kissed her, holding her tight. Their love would be their strength throughout their years together.

After breakfast, Pete took his wife to see the rosary, suggesting that she could give it to her grandmother. "She needs something tangible to remember you by", her husband said. "I want to buy this for her, he told his wife. Maria said, "It's so expensive", but he paid no heed.

They arrived at Roberto's home with Maria carrying a box holding the rosary. When Roberto answered the door, they both sensed something was wrong because Roberto was not at work. The man graciously greeted them, shaking Peter's hand when Maria introduced him. "Is something wrong", asked Maria as they walked into the house; she was very confused. "I'm glad you're both here; my mother took a turn for the worse earlier, and we brought the doctor here. She has been going downhill for several months", her son told them. "When she heard you were getting married, and your husband was bringing you here Maria, she kept hanging onto life. She was so eager to see you Maria and the man you married. My mother has a strong will, that's kept her going until she could see you; it's like she's ready to go now."

"Oh no", Maria said plaintively. "Can I still see her?" The man spoke kindly, "Of course you can Maria. I know she would want to see you; she loves you very much."

The man opened the door to his mother's room. Seeing the two at the door, Rosa went to Maria and said, "She wants to see you dear." When Maria saw her Abuelita lying in bed, she knelt down, speaking softly, "Abuelita." Her grandmother opened her eyes; she first looked at her son standing beside Maria, and smiled at him; the woman's love for her son was very evident. Then she turned her head and looked at Maria, her very special granddaughter. Maria held up the rosary so the little grandmother could see it. "This is for you, Abuelita." The frail woman looked at the lovely rosary, her eyes softened, and when Maria gave it to her, the little woman pulled it up over her heart. Maria rose and gently kissed her grandmother on her cheek, both feeling their common love.

Maria tried to hold back her tears as Roberto went to his mother, kneeling beside her; putting his hand over hers and the rosary, telling her how very much he loved her. She smiled at her son, glanced at Maria, sighed, closed her eyes, and slipped away into the Lord's hands. Roberto cried softly, his wife going to him. Peter held Maria, tenderly; she with her head on his chest, softly crying. When Maria was able, Peter took her into the next room, leaving Roberto and Rosa alone while Roberto wept; his wife's arms around her husband. The doctor went into the bedroom, saying the tiny woman had passed on.

In time, Roberto and his wife came out into the parlor where Peter and Maria waited. Through tears, Roberto told Pete and Maria, "We thought my mother was going to die months ago, but when she heard you two were coming, she seemed to perk up. I just think she would not go until she could see you again. She wanted to know her granddaughter was safe and happy."

That night, Pete held his wife until she fell asleep, knowing what a difficult day it was for Maria.

The following day, they went to a mass dedicated to the little grandmother. The church was very beautiful, and extremely large, and old. Many people attended the mass for Roberto's mother. He and Rosa were well liked in the community, and many people attended because they had known Olivia Ramirez when they too were young and raising their families. Maria saw the turquoise rosary draped across the coffin, attached to a large, long-stemmed red rose, causing her to weep again.

After the mass was over, Rosa invited the couple to have lunch with them, and three of Maria's cousins, and their families. As they ate, they spent time talking about the woman they had lost, and visiting; getting to know one another. It was good for Maria, because it gave her some sense of family. It was a sad day, but also a good day in many ways. Pete also thought the meal was the best Mexican food he had ever eaten; Maria's cooking was close to Rosa's.

Many memories were mentioned, from the days when Maria and her cousins played at the house of their Abuelita. With the good memories, were sad ones for Maria; at her house, she always came last. Pretty regularly she was made to stay home and do house work; while her sisters and brothers went to all the parties at her grandmother's house. However, her grandmother had a way of making up for the lost time for this one special granddaughter, often asking Maria's mother to let the girl come and help her with cleaning. Instead of cleaning, they celebrated being together; certainly unknown to the girls' family.

Later, when Peter and his wife were in their hotel room, they talked. "Maria, I know this has been hard on you sweetheart, but your grandmother loved you very much. She only wanted you to be happy, and she needed to know you were. Your grandmother waited until she could see you and your happiness. I'm so glad you insisted on us coming onto Santa Fe. You must always remember how much she loved you, and the good times you had together." Being so weary, Maria eventually slept; Pete, holding her gently in his arms; his love for her continued to grow each day.

The following day was Saturday, and Pete did everything he could to lift up his wife's spirits; in time it did help some, but finally he knew he needed to take his wife home. He felt it would be too hard for her to handle her loss here in Santa Fe.

That afternoon, the couple stopped at Roberto's home, spending some time with the husband and wife. Pete told them they would be leaving Monday morning. "It's time to go home, there's too much here to remind Maria of her grandmother. We have appreciated your hospitality, and I enjoyed meeting you both. I'm glad we came when we did; Maria did get to see her grandmother, but it's time to leave. Maria's anxious to leave; the main purpose for our coming is now gone."

Roberto spoke up, "I understand Maria, but I am so glad my mother was able to see you and Peter." The man turned to Maria's husband, "It was good to meet you Peter, we will continue to write from time to time", Maria agreeing.

When the newly married couple left, the two men shook hands, while the women hugged; Rosa saying "I'm so glad you came. God bless you both, and may He watch over you, keeping you safe on your way home. Write and let us know you have arrived home safely." Maria promised she would.

The next morning was Sunday, and Pete talked the cook in the hotel restaurant to send up a light breakfast to the room, giving the man a generous amount of money to do so. After the couple had eaten, Pete took out a small Bible he had brought on the trip. First he prayed for God to bless their time in searching the scriptures, and reminded the Lord how much they both loved Him. Then he opened the Bible, and read from Matthew, chapter five; emphasizing verse four. "Blessed are they that mourn: for they shall be comforted." After reading the whole chapter, he talked about the kindness of the Lord. "Maria, something will happen in your life sweetheart, and you will be comforted. You will always love your grandmother and all she taught you in her words and deeds.

She will not only be special to your life, but you will be able to teach that love to our children, so that part of her will remain and live on. Our children will be blessed by her love, as you were."

"I still love my mother, and she often comes to mind. Her love continues in my life, even thought I lost her many years ago. Her love of the Lord is now a part of me as I love Him too. Nothing can rob us of all the things these two women gifted us with. Maria, we are so blessed because of these two special women. In one way they will never be gone from our lives; they were God's gift to us."

After thanking the Lord for his great gift of salvation, Pete thanked Him for Maria. "You have blessed me Lord, with this wonderful wife. I am so blessed to have her in my life. Bless her Lord, she loves you deeply, and I am also the recipient of her love."

That night, Maria looked at her sleeping husband. "He is so special Lord. You have taken such good care of me, and you have given me Peter." She knew how blessed she was.

When they stepped into the stagecoach, Rosa was there to say goodbye. She called out as they started moving, "Don't forget to write", and after the coach pulled away she asked the Lord for their protection. The couple settled back for the long trip home. Maria took with her a new white blouse and colorful skirt Pete had bought for her; the outfit brought out her Spanish beauty.

As the travelers headed south, they kept hearing warnings of the Indians. Almost every way station they stopped at, people were talking about the many raids along the river, and even when the road wandered away from the river at times. The man riding shotgun kept reassuring the passengers everything would be alright, but Pete knew better, there was no way to know what the Apache's would do. He was grateful that his two weapons were loaded, and he had plenty of ammunition if needed.

A pretty young woman, around eighteen years old, was traveling south to Fort Craig. Her name was Vera Stratton, and nobody knew the commander of the fort was her father; Commander Andrew Stratton. Vera grew up in a small township in Missouri. The house they lived in was a three room log cabin her father built. Her mother's father came to live with them when she was very young, and he and her father fought. In anger, her father left them and fought in the Civil War, and after the war, instead of going home, he stayed in the army; rising quickly in rank. Now he commanded Fort Craig, here in the New Mexico Territory.

Vera's grandfather died two years ago, and her mother died six months ago; leaving the young woman alone. Because her father had written a year ago from Fort Craig, Vera wrote him telling him her mother had died. Vera's father answered her letter with a short curt note in which he included enough money for her to join him. Vera was frightened, hearing about the Indians, and wished she could go home, but there was no home to go to; when she left, the Morrison's moved into their house.

She was a pretty, small, young woman with strawberry blond hair, which was swept up on her head.

She was wearing a blue bonnet on her head that was tied under her chin, with unruly curls that tenaciously fought for their freedom. Her eyes matched the blue of her bonnet and dress; her skin was a soft ivory color, and she had a few freckles, here and there, that were about to disappear. She was so hot, her long dress keeping in the heat, but she stayed quiet while everyone else took their turn at talking.

Vera was miserable and frightened; she'd never been more than four miles from her home before. She missed her mother, but she was gone. She did not know her father, only seeing a tintype photograph that was taken when her parents were married. His face looked stern, and she was scared. What if he doesn't like me, she thought; what will I do then?

They rode up onto the mesa where Fort Craig stood, overlooking the Rio Grande River. They were turning to enter through the open gates when Indians raced by; one turning his horse, and going inside of the fort beside the stagecoach. He killed two men before he was shot, and fell from his horse lying dead. When the people hurried out of the coach, Vera cringed, seeing the fallen Indian.

The women were herded into a small building, where two wives of officers stationed at the fort were staying during the fight. Once the women were inside; Pete ran, scrambling up on the rampart joining soldiers, and two men from the stagecoach. He lay flat, and aiming carefully at an Indian, he shot. The gun roared and the Indian fell from his horse, then another man joined him. Not having a gun, Pete handed the man his pistol with some ammunition.

The battle was hectic with bullets flying in every direction; one grazing Pete's head above his right ear, but he was unaware he had been grazed by a bullet. What seemed like hours lasted less than thirty minutes.

After an hour with no more signs of the Indians, Pete climbed down the ladder, holding his rifle in his left hand. The man gave him his pistol, which he stuck into the waist of his pants.

There was a soldier lying several feet away from the building where Maria was. He stopped and checked him, but the man was dead. He saw one of the windows broken in the building where he left Maria, and he felt fear rising in him. Grateful, she was alright; he put his arms around her. "Thank God, you're alright", he said to her. "I was so frightened for you Peter", and she sank into those familiar arms. When they parted she looked up and saw the bullet burn on his head, she cried, "You've been hit Peter!" Let me look at it; she had brought her satchel inside, and she quickly opened it. She took out a small jar with ointment in it, and a clean handkerchief she wet from a pitcher of water on a table.

"Sit down Peter", she told him. When he did, she proceeded to clean the burn and put salve on it. When she was finished, he stood up saying, "Stay here, I need to see if there's anything I can do to help." His wife understood. "I'll leave my rifle here for now", he said, and leaned it against the wall, and walked away to see if anyone was injured and needed help. Pete overheard two soldiers talking, "That's what I said, the commander was killed when that Indian slipped through the gates. Lieutenant Colonel Griggs has taken command of the fort now that Commander Stratton is gone. I'm sorry the commander was killed, but he was one mean man. Griggs will do a better job; I hope the army will leave things the way they are, this man is a much better man", then the two moved on, and Pete went to the fort's hospital to see if he could help. He spent several hours, helping as he could before he returned to his wife.

They sat in a corner, away from most of the women talking; only Vera was within earshot. "Maria, the commander of the fort was killed today by the Indian that came through the gates before it was closed." "Oh no! That cannot be true." The two turned, seeing the young woman that traveled south with them as she began crying. Maria stood up, put a restraining hand on her husband's shoulder, and went to the crying woman. "What's wrong dear, can I help?" Vera looked at her with tears streaming down over her face. "It can't be true. My father can't be dead. I've come all this way to come join him here at the fort. What will I do?" She sat down hard on a chair with her hands over her eyes crying uncontrollably, every once in a while, saying, "He can't be dead! He just can't be dead!"

Maria sat down beside Vera, taking the young woman's hand into her own, saying, "It's alright, you're here with us", not really understanding who was dead. The other women in the room were also concerned for the young woman, though they stayed away, wondering how this Mexican woman got into the room. Pete saw their prejudice, and knew they wanted nothing to do with his wife, which angered him. He walked over to Maria and the crying woman. "What's wrong", he asked, whispering to Maria. "I'm not sure Peter, she's crying about someone who was killed, but I don't know who."

Pete told his wife, "Let's take her outside, away from glaring eyes", and they walked Vera out onto the porch, and sat down on the steps. It was there they found out her father was the commander of the fort that had been shot and killed.

When Vera calmed down, Pete gently told her, "A young lieutenant has taken charge of the fort; I think it would be good to go and see him. He may know about your father's finances, or he could find out, there may be money you could use to go somewhere else. You stay here and I will find out if he has time to see you." Pete walked away leaving the two women sitting on the porch talking.

While waiting for Pete's return, Maria found out the details of Vera's coming here to Fort Craig, and she sympathized with her. She assured her everything would work out. "Don't worry Vera, Peter and I will see that you will be safe, and have a place to go."

When Pete returned, he told the young woman, the lieutenant would be free after lunch. "We will go with you when you meet with him." Maria told the young woman, "Don't worry, we will see you are taken care of." Again Vera burst into tears. "My mother died, and I was coming to stay with my father, there's no place for me to go."

Maria glanced at her husband, and he could read between the lines; she wants to take this girl home with us. His bride wanted to bring another woman into their house. Oh God, he prayed, I only want my wife. "Don't worry, everything will work out for you", he said lamely, hoping he was right.

After eating, the three walked into the Lieutenant's office. The minute he saw the Commander's daughter, Lieutenant Griffin knew something good had come from the tyrannical man, she was a pretty young woman, and he was very taken with the daughter of his former boss. Her face was stained from crying, yet she was enchanting. Her hair had fallen while crying, and the curly hair seemed to dance over her shoulders from the breezes that came through the door with the three people. He asked them to sit down, and then asked, "What can I do for you?" Knowing, of course, the commander was gone, leaving his daughter alone.

Vera began to speak, but couldn't do it; trying so hard not to cry. She had a terrible headache, and was so confused she didn't know what to say, for fear if she spoke she would start crying again. Pete took over explaining Vera's problem; saying "Vera has no money, all she had she spent coming here. She is hoping her father might have left some money that she could use to go someplace, though she is not sure where to go. Her mother is gone, and now her father also; he was the only one of her family left.

"I'm not sure about your father's finances", the young officer said, "But I will be glad to find out for you", he told Vera. "I have ordered your stagecoach to stay here for awhile, until we are sure the Indians are gone. Our experience is that they often hit on and off after the first attack trying to overtake the fort, and we want you to be protected. Then the blond haired man told Vera, "Your father's quarters are empty, and you may stay there for now if you like, that will give you some privacy." She started to protest, but he stopped her. "No, it was your father's quarters, so I will move in after you are gone." Then he gave Pete and Maria the room of the other soldier who died. He was a sergeant, and had his own room. Pete thanked the young commander, he remembered how the women had treated Maria, and was glad she would not have to deal with their prejudice, something he would not allow.

When Vera was alone in her father's quarters, she looked around the room. There was nothing attractive about the room, causing it to feel very cold. It showed that her father's first love was the army; perhaps his only love; he certainly never showed any love toward her mother or herself. Suddenly she wished she wasn't in his quarters, but she had no choice.

It would be nearly two weeks before the stagecoach could leave because sporadic raids continued. During that time, the new commander of the fort, Paul Griffin, began to like the young woman from Missouri, and she liked him, though he wasn't aware she was attracted to him. The time was slipping away, and the new commander did not want the young woman to leave. Paul began having her and the Walkers in to eat with him each night in his office. It was a fairly large room, Vera's father often slept in there reading late; he had always liked being in the room where the flag hung. He was a true military man, so Paul had the food served at the table where Vera's father always ate his meals.

After the ten days had slipped by, Paul knew he had to talk to Vera, so he had his aid bring her early one night, before supper. When the young woman walked into the office, he quickly got up and went to Vera. "Please Vera, sit down. I need to talk to you." She sat in a chair, he leaning against the front of his desk facing her. "Vera", he started, and then what he had planned to say slipped away. He tried again, "It won't be long before you decide where you want to go. Vera, I don't want you to leave; I'm afraid I have fallen in love with you, and I want you to stay and be my wife." Vera sat there, speechless. Yes, she knew she felt the same about him, but never dreamed he loved her! He went on, "Now don't say anything, please hear me out. I have never met anyone like you before; I can't get you out of my mind or my heart, and I don't want you to leave." He knelt down and said, "Please Vera, will you marry me?"

The young woman sat silent, with many thoughts whirling through her mind. At night she couldn't stop thinking about this young blond officer, never dreaming he cared for her. No words came, her mind in a whirl. He took her hand, "Please Vera." Finally, after what seemed like hours to him, she answered him. "Yes Paul, I would be honored to marry you." He stood up, and held the darling woman in his arms and kissed her, leaving both breathless. He whispered in her ear, "I adore you Vera." They both heard the Walkers talking outside the door, and parted.

Before this day, they had all talked about their lives. Paul knew the story of her father's abandonment of his wife and daughter, and Vera knew Paul was from New York and had gone to "West Point" in his earliest days; coming out of the academy as an officer. His father still lived in New York City, but his mother had died before he was twenty. When he was sent to Fort Craig, he thought he had come to the far side of the moon. This country was true desert, and he missed the greenness of the east, but he used the knowledge he'd learned. He was a good officer, using firmness, but also fairness; the men liked him. The commander, on the other hand, was a cold and uncaring man.

After their dinner, Paul cleared his throat, and looking at Pete said, "There is no one I can talk to about Vera, but we have come to love one another." In the midst of the man's sentence, Pete thought, he wants to ask us for our permission to marry Vera, which made Pete feel very uncomfortable as the young officer asked the question. Maria, seeing his face, whispered, "Calm down sweetheart, I can remember the night you acted much the same way." Paul was so scared, he scarcely noticed. He had stopped talking, but not sure why. He began again saying, "I find I have fallen in love with Vera, and I feel the need to tell someone how I feel. Her father is gone, and only you two know her. We want to marry; she's young, and I have to ask someone."

Pete cleared his thoughts, desperately trying to figure out what to say. "I think she's a sweet young woman, and she is in need of help right now"; he was going to continue on when Maria said, "I know what it is to be surprised by a man who loved me, but I also know my love for him has grown; he's a good, good man, and I see such a man standing here. If you two are in love, I think you should marry."

Pete sat there with his mouth open, so to speak, how wise his wife was. She was right; if they loved one another, they *should* marry. He spoke up, finally finding his voice. "Perhaps we should pray for God's wisdom". Paul was so relieved, and though he had already prayed, he asked Pete if he would pray for the two of them. As they put their heads down, their eyes closed; Pete prayed for the young couple. He knew what they were feeling; he and his wonderful wife felt the same way, loving one another.

"Lord, give these two the wisdom to make the right decision. There is nothing in life so sacred as a marriage between two people who love one another. These two have found each other far from there homes, and they feel they love one another. We know that nothing in life is without purpose, for you are our guide throughout our lives. Because of their love, I ask that you sanctify their marriage, giving them many years to enrich their time together. Keep them safe here on the frontier, for there are those who would destroy them without remorse. Enrich their lives together, making them truly one in spirit, and in love. In the name of our Lord and Savior, we ask these things. Amen."

Paul spoke asking, "Can I kiss you Vera", almost sounding like a small boy. The young woman stood up, nodding yes. Maria felt like crying; she was touched by this young couple's love for one another.

Paul looked into Vera's eyes. "I'm sure the chaplain would be glad to marry us tomorrow, unless you think that's too soon Vera, she shook her head saying, "If that's what you want Paul, but I don't have anything special to wear. The young man was so filled with joy, and he said, "You're lovely in anything you wear, your hair can be your crown of beauty", and he put his hand up and fingered her beautiful strawberry blond hair.

The following day the couple was married out in the courtyard within the fort. During the ceremony, one of the soldiers who played fiddle played a lovely song softly. It was beautiful, but a lonely sound here within the walls of the fort. When the couple were married, the men stationed at the fort all yelled happily, and as one. The men threw their caps into the air, even the men on duty at the walls called out; their affection for their leader was quite evident.

The rest of the day was one big party. The man who ran the bakery at the fort baked several cakes; enough for everyone to enjoy, and four men sang a love song in harmony. Pete could not believe the affection these men showed their leader. The couple danced while the violin played, accompanied by two harmonica's. It was a festive, long day, and come evening, after Paul thanked his men for the wonderful day, the two stepped into their quarters with all the men clapping, and a few men calling out their joy.

Later, when Pete and Maria retired, they lay talking about the whole day, and the apparent affection all the men had for their leader. "Peter, wasn't it a wonderful day? It was evident that the two truly love one another. What an unexpected and exciting day it was." Both knew love, for their love for one another grew every day.

Two days later, the stagecoach rode out of the compound, with Pete and Maria waving to the newlyweds. The rest of the trip went well, however they did see several small areas that were burned to the ground with people trying to rebuild. That was the way of the people who came west. They would not give up, nor would people stop coming west; just to have a piece of land that was their own.

The last day of the Walker's trip, clouds piled up, and the day darkened. Before long, rain fell heavily upon the land. The two men up front were hunkered down with their slickers on, and pulled up covering their broad brimmed hats. The horses struggled with the slippery muck as they traveled through the canyon below Cook's Peak.

As the stagecoach drew nearer to Silver City, the clouds moved to the east, leaving the air fresh and clean. After the long dusty days, it smelled so good. Once the two were home in Silver City, it was early enough for Pete to rent a carriage. He spoke to Tim saying it was good to be home. On their way out of town heading for the ranch, the couple stopped to tell Mac and Kathleen they were home, Maria staying in the carriage. Mac answered the door, and was surprised to see the two were home. "We left earlier than we expected", Pete told his friend. "Sadly, Maria's grandmother died shortly after we arrived; Maria did get to see her before she went though. We stayed a few more days after the funeral, and then left." Mac went out to Maria saying, "I'm so sorry Maria. I know this must be hard for you; I can remember all the times you talked about her. Pete said you got to see her, for that I am glad. I know how special she was to you."

Pete told him about the episode at Fort Craig. We were there two weeks before the driver and Commander of the fort thought it was safe for us to continue on the road coming south. He did not mention Lieutenant Commander Griffin, or his marriage to Vera, that would come later. Kathleen came to the door drying her hands on her apron, wondering who had knocked on the door. Mac, walking up to Kathleen, told her, "It was Pete and Maira; they came home sooner than expected. Maria's grandmother died the day after Maria got to see her. There was some trouble with Indians coming south, and they stayed at Fort Craig for nearly two weeks. They looked tired; Pete said they would see us at church on Sunday, and I invited them to lunch. I hope you don't mind." "Of course not Aaron, I am sorry to hear about Maria's grandmother. I hope she will be able to handle her loss. I'm sure the death of her grandmother was hard on her, she so looked forward to seeing her again, we must pray for her tonight." Her husband nodded.

After stopping at the McGinnis's house, the couple headed for home. Once they arrived, they were both relieved; the trip was over, and they were home. Ben told Pete, "So far we have not seen any Indians in the area, but we heard they were over along the Rio Grande, and there was more than one prayer said for your safety. I'm really glad to see you home and safe. Everything has been fine here, though we kept the men on shifts, just to make sure. We have four mares that have foaled, with more ready to do the same. The men have been busy branding the young stock, others breaking them. It's been a busy but fruitful time. Other than that, it has been peaceful here."

Pete was relieved to hear the good news. "Thanks Ben, I'm not sure what I would do without you." Ben helped his boss carry in their luggage. "I'll see the carriage is taken back tomorrow morning", Ben told his boss. "We just finished eating, but I'm sure cook has leftovers." After a light supper, the two went to bed. Both were very tired, and so glad to be home.

Chapter 15

Cooler breezes brought fall into the mountain valley. Michael, along with Penny and Todd were back in school; this was their last year, with Michael's future and time to leave in sight. The young man was struggling, when he was with his girl. It would be close to five years before the two could marry, and he did not want to wait that long. Penny was constantly in his thoughts, and he could not shake them away. Finally, Michael talked to his special girl. "Penny, I've been thinking, I don't want to wait to marry you, and I've decided to get a job after we graduate, so we can be married. I love you so, I do want to be a minister, but that would put off our marriage at least five years; I'm not sure I can wait that long."

At first, Penny wanted that too, but after thinking rationally, she answered him. "Michael, we can't do that, God has called you to the ministry. If you don't follow His plans for you, and go to the seminary, you will be turning away from Him and what he wants you to do in your life. We can't let that happen,

Michael. I love you as much as you love me, but we can't turn away from Him and what He has planned for you to do. Michael, I'm afraid our marriage could very well fall apart; we have to wait Michael."

Penny looked up at him, and he saw tears in her eyes. He knew she was right, still he did not want to wait, and he told her so. Suddenly; his sweet Penny became angry! "No Michael, No!" She stamped her foot saying, "You can't give up Michael", and she turned away, running home. Fear flooded through him, he suddenly felt he had lost his Penny. "What have I done?" he asked himself. He went home feeling lost, then the thought went through his mind; how dare she refuse to marry me! I've always honored her, and it was only love that caused me to mention my thoughts. He felt hurt and disgruntled, and it all came out in anger against Penny. What did he see in her anyway; if that's the way she's going to act, then maybe we shouldn't get married!

Those feelings only lasted about an hour, and he knew he had to apologize, both to the Lord, and to Penny. He prayed, "Please Lord, forgive me for even thinking I would not follow your plans for my life. You have given me so much love and guidance; I am so sorry, I do want to serve you Lord." Michael felt so ashamed; tears began to creep into his eyes, but he would not let them, even though that's the way he felt. He knew if Molly saw his tears she would tell their ma, and he no more wanted to hurt his mother than he wanted to hurt Penny.

After supper, he spoke to his mother; "I have to go someplace ma; I won't be long, but I have to go."

Kathleen surprised, looked at her son wondering what was happening. Michael never went out at night, and he looked so distressed. His mother had seen her son's sadness during dinner, and instinctively decided it was something she should leave alone. After Michael left, Mac asked his wife "Is something wrong with Michael? He wasn't himself tonight; I've never seen him so disturbed before." Kathleen answered, "I don't know Aaron, I saw a deep sadness in his eyes during supper. Mac said, "Do you suppose it could have anything to do with Penny? Maybe they had a fight, I've never seen him like this before; he was so quiet. Well", Mac told his wife, "Michael's a good person; whatever happened, he will do his best to straighten it out."

Penny answered the door when Michael knocked. The minute she saw Michael, she ran into his arms. "I'm so sorry Michael; I should not have spoken so." The soon to be man, looked at Penny, his special girl. "No Penny, I'm the one who should apologize. You were right, I cannot turn away from the Lord's plan for my life, nor do I want to. I don't know what happened, but suddenly I wanted you to be my wife, and felt I could not; nor did I want to wait so many years. I was very wrong; I must do what the Lord has planned for my life. I really do want to be a man of God." Then he held his Penny, unashamed. He loved her so. That short episode strengthened them both for the years ahead; for once he became a minister, he was always grateful to the Lord for Penny's strength. Michael knew in his heart, that he and Penny were meant to serve together, and because of her strength, they would.

Across town, there was a different kind of battle going on inside of Nate. He found himself in love for the first time in his life. Every morning when he saw Jeannie, he wanted to tell her of his love, but he could not. Jeannie was so dear to him, but he had made a promise that he must keep. He saw her everlasting kindness with Miles, and her darling little girl; the little one was growing and getting cuter everyday. He found himself wanting to be with Abby. He especially loved hearing Jeannie; as she sang to her child at bedtime, the woman's voice was very sweet, and it only caused Nate to love Jeannie even more, she had become so dear to him. At night when Nate kissed his wife goodnight, it was always hard; he wanted much more. He wanted to tell her of his love, yet he could not.

The first year anniversary of Larry's death came, and she started to slide back into depression. Nate understood what was happening, knowing when Larry was killed. The man began to do small special things, trying to keep his wife's spirits up. Every day or so, he would bring some small gift to her. Perhaps it would be a bar of lavender soap, or a bottle of cologne from the drug store. Once in awhile, he would bring her something sweet from the new bakery. Anything to take her thought away from the loss of her first husband. Besides that, Nate was always there with his friendship.

His efforts did not go unnoticed, and Jeannie began to respond to her husband's kindness. The woman began cooking special meals, or extra special deserts. She wanted to please him, and he began to see what she was doing. Jeannie saw the man's kindness; he never said an unkind word, nor did he appear to get angry. He had Miles and Timothy around much of the time, and often a crying baby, yet through it all Nate was so kind and patient. As time continued, she began to feel something akin to love; but she could not yet admit it, even to herself.

He thought Abby was adorable; her blond curly hair and her big eyes had captured him. Often Nate would hold her if she was tired and cranky, and often she fell asleep in his arms. He loved watching her while she slept, he almost felt like she was his at times. One evening, after Jeannie was finished with the supper dishes; Miles was off reading a book, and Tim was nowhere in sight. She walked into the parlor, knowing Nate was watching over her daughter. What she saw was Abby sleeping in her husband's arms, he asleep himself. Jeannie was so touched by the scene, and she found herself loving this kind man. "Lord, what shall I do? He told me he would never take advantage of me; that he would wait for me to tell him if I wanted him to love me." At this moment, she was sure she did love Nate, and wanted to be his wife in every way.

That night after all were in bed but the husband and wife; as they talked, Nate instinctively knew something had happened, but not really sure what the change was. Jeannie was talking, and suddenly he realized what she was saying; "Nate, sweet Nate. I know when we married we made an agreement, and you have been faithful to keep it, but I must tell you Nate; I have watched you, and you are such a kind man. I need to tell you that somewhere along the way, I have fallen in love with you; the gentlest man I have ever known. I cannot stop thinking about you." She stopped talking, not sure what else to say. At first Nate could hardly believe his ears. "Did you say you love me", he asked. Then he rose from his chair, and went to his wife and gently pulled her up. He took her into his arms, "I have never heard sweeter words", he told his wife. "I have loved you for a long time now, but I was afraid you would never love me."

Jeannie reached up, and put both hands on the sides of Nate's face. "I do love you Nate", and then she kissed him; such a gentle and loving act. He then circled his arms around his wife, and kissed her again. What he had dreamed of had come true. The two stood together for some time in each other's arms; then Nate gently picked up his wife, and carried her into his bedroom, her head lying on his shoulder. His dearest wife was his.

Several days later, the two decided they wanted Richard's blessing on their marriage; things were so different now. Nate went to talk to their special minister, explaining how he and Jeannie had fallen in love. "We would like to have you bless our marriage; not only because we love one another, but because we want to put our union into the Lord's hands."

Richard reached out and shook the man's hand. "I'm happy for both of you. I sort of hoped you would come to love one another; you're both good people.

Love Comes in Many Colors

I would be honored to dedicate your marriage to the Lord, and give it into his hands."

A few days later, the couple arrived at the church; Nate had taken off the afternoon. Only Abby would see her parents rededicate their marriage. Eve was glad to hold the sweet, wiggly Abby, she wished she and Richard had a child of their own. She wanted to hold her own baby, someday.

Reverend Smith, their friend, prayed over the couple while they knelt before him, and the God they loved. It was a very special time, both feeling especially blessed. They both wanted the Lord to be first in their marriage, and in their lives. For Jeannie, Larry was gone, though not in anyway forgotten. Still she loved Nate with all her heart; how that happened she wasn't sure, but she was happy again.

Thanksgiving was tomorrow, and the Green's, along with others were cooking for the big dinner the Samaritan House would be hosting; each cooking part of the meal. Kathleen and Eve were roasting a turkey; Jeannie and Nate were bringing a large amount of cornbread dressing; a recipe Jeannie learned from her mother, and Joe and Helen were bringing sweet potatoes they bought at the Chinese Gardens.

It was Thanksgiving Day, and while they were all putting the dinner together for their guests, Kathleen heard Jules was sick. It was strange not having Susan and Jules there, so Kathleen decided she would check on her friends. Tim and Emily were in charge of the young ones; the crowd was bigger than usual, keeping everyone busy.

Throughout the night, the four men; Richard, Nate, Mac, and Pete circulated among the guests, listening to their stories, and finding out their needs; hoping to help where it was needed. Toward the end of the evening, a very thin and frail man walked in. He had a young boy at his side, and they both were looking for a place to sit. Nate found them a place, and because the man looked ill, he brought the two plates, brimming with food. "Is this really free", the man asked. "Absolutely, you are welcome Nate told the man. The boy couldn't eat fast enough. He must be starved, Nate thought to himself. However; unlike the boy, the man only picked at the food, scarcely eating. Nathaniel sat down beside the man, "My name is Nate Green, are you two new in town? I don't remember seeing the two of you before." The man faltered before answering. It was obvious to Nate the older man was very sick, and he appeared to be in pain.

"We've been living in Pinos Altos. Last year; he paused and then continued, my wife became ill, and several months later died. The boy's parents were both killed during an Indian raid a few weeks later. The boy and I sorta drifted together, and shortly after that, I began getting sick. I owned a small gold claim; some days I couldn't work it, though the boy helped some. Eventually, a man took over the claim, and I was unable to stop him. I did have some money from the gold I had mined, but pretty soon, the money began to dwindle away. Finally, a couple of weeks ago, we caught a ride on a wagon that was coming down to Silver City, and found a small room we could rent."

Johnnie was able to get a job at the brickyard, doing odds and ends, and running errands; the job doesn't pay much." The man's face turned whiter, and he stopped talking; Nate could see the pain on the man's face. At that point, the older man pushed back his plate; groaning, he put his head down on his arms. Nate asked the man, "Would you like to lie down? We have a cot in the back room." The man mumbled, "Yes", and started to pull himself up, holding onto the table. He crumpled and Nate caught him.

Pete came running, "What happened?" "I don't know exactly, but I think he is a very sick man. He seems to be in a great deal of pain." The horse rancher picked up the elderly man, and headed toward the back room. Richard, seeing what was happening, hurried and opened the door for Pete. The young boy started to rise looking worried, but Nate stopped him. "People are taking care of your friend, why don't you stay with me", Nate said to the boy. Nate saw Pete talking to Mac, who headed out the door. Nate assumed Mac was going for the doctor, and he told the boy, "Don't worry, your friend will have a doctor to see what is wrong; it seemed to calm the boy down when he heard about the doctor. "How about a piece of apple pie?" When the boy said he would like that, Nate searched for the biggest piece of pie he could find, and brought it back to the youngster. While the boy was eating, Nate asked what their names were. "My name is Johnnie Nelson, and his is Gus Pruett", the boy told

Nate. "Do you think Gus will be Okay?" "I hope so", he told the boy. "Not to worry, the doctor will be able to find out what's wrong. You will be taken care of, no matter; you will have a place to stay."

The doctor hurried into the back room with Mac; closing the door behind him. After Doc Freeman asked a few questions of the older man, he used his hands, gently probing the man's abdomen. After checking the man's pulse, which was hard to find, he then turned to the men and motioned them out of earshot.

"It doesn't look good; all his symptoms lead me to believe at the very least, that this man has a large growth in his abdomen. It could be cancerous; he is a very sick man." "He says he hasn't been able to eat for some time; I'm not even sure how he managed to come here tonight. He may have been calling out for help." As the doctor was talking, the man could be heard in the background quietly moaning. Doc Freeman spoke quietly, "He may not have much longer to live."

Pete went out to find out information from the boy. When he came back, he told Richard, "The boy has no one else to care for him", which added another problem to the whole picture. The doctor suggested, "Bring Gus to my house, I will take care of him; I can help with the pain, so he will rest more comfortably." Pete spoke up saying, "I'll carry him, and he gently picked up the man and carried him to the doctor's house.

The boy saw them leaving, and started to rise so he could follow, but Nate said, "Stay here boy, I'm sure the doctor wants to help your friend." As

Richard was leaving, he stopped and spoke to the boy, "Would you stay with Mr. Green? I will be back." He told Johnnie, "You will have a place to stay, don't worry", and he hurried away.

Once Gus was lying down, the doctor gave him the same medicine he had given to Mac many, many months before. The young minister waited a few minutes until the medicine began working, then he pulled a chair to the bed where Gus was lying and questioned the man about the young boy. He found out he was orphaned, and Gus explained how he and Johnnie had joined each other. "The boy needed someone, I hope someone will take care of Johnnie; he's a good boy." The man grew tired and silent.

"Do you believe in Jesus Christ, Gus?" The man nodded saying, "Most always, I guess." "Gus, may I pray for you", Richard asked, as he took hold of the man's hand. "Yes, please", was the man's reply. The minister remained in prayer for some time, asking God to be with Gus, and to give the man peace; then he spoke to the man saying, "The boy will be safe and taken good care of." The man looked relieved, and then closed his eyes. Richard felt sorry for Gus, thinking this is a hard way to end one's life. He took the man's hand and gently squeezed it. "God be with you, Gus."

When Richard arrived back at the dinner; he first went to the boy saying, "Stay here Johnnie, I will be right back, but I wanted you to know Gus is being well cared for", and then he went in search of his wife. He told Eve what was happening. "The man is not expected to live long Eve, and the boy needs someplace to live. If it's alright with you, we can take him home with us; at least for now." She agreed, "Let's go talk to him Richard", and with her husband agreeing, they wended their way to where the boy sat with Nate Green. Nate left, leaving the three alone.

As the two sat talking with Johnnie, they were both drawn to the boy. He seemed unassuming and rather shy, but there was also a gentleness about him. Richard asked him about Gus, and then about his parents. "I like Gus", he told the couple; "Gus always treated me good, much better than my parents did. Is Gus going to be okay?" Richard was careful not to frighten the boy. "He's a very sick man, but the doctor is taking good care of him; we will have to wait and see. My name is Richard Smith, and this is my wife, Eve. We would be very pleased if you would come and stay with us for now."

Johnnie was surprised, but grateful. He liked them both, but was especially drawn to the woman. Her face looked so kind, and there was something else, but he couldn't determine what it was; he simply liked her. Both the man and woman seemed to be special people, and he felt safe. Johnnie nodded yes, saying, "Thanks, I wasn't sure what I would do without Gus." "Good", Richard answered and he reached around the boy's shoulder, giving the boy a gentle hug, which made him feel like he was wanted; something he wasn't used to. "Everything will be alright; the minister told Johnnie, who was older in spirit, because of the life he had led up to now.

After everyone was gone, and the place was locked up; the three headed home, Richard carrying the cot so the boy would have something to sleep on. He figured they could get a better bed, later if needed.

Thelma, having been taken home earlier, was surprised to see the boy. Eve touched her lips with a finger, as if to say, we will tell you later. The two women fussed over Johnnie's bed until they had it comfortable for the boy. After Johnnie got into bed, wearing one of Richard's old shirts, Eve covered the boy with a warm fluffy comforter to keep him warm. It was then she said a small prayer for Gus, and then thanked the Lord for Johnnie. Somehow that prayer comforted the boy, more than anything else she could have done. "Sleep well", she told the boy, and gently closed the door after herself.

When Johnnie was asleep, the couple talked with Thelma; making sure the arrangement was alright with her. Actually, she was delighted. "It will be good to have a youngster around." Somewhere in her mind, she thought Johnnie was 'someone to love and spoil'.

After the couple was in bed, Eve talked to her husband. "Johnnie seems to be a nice boy. I'm glad he's here and safe with us; he has a gentleness about him, and he has nowhere else to go. Maybe if the man dies, Johnnie could come live with us." Richard suggested, "Let's wait and see Eve, we don't want to say anything until Gus is gone, then we can think about it. We mustn't get his hopes up, yet. I know you have always wanted a child, I do understand Eve; I've always wanted children myself. If or when Gus dies, then we can talk to him. You're right, he

Love Comes in Many Colors

is a nice youngster; let's put him and our desires in the Lord's hands. If we're meant to have the boy, it will happen."

The two prayed, and then Eve snuggled into her husband's arms. He bent down and kissed her, "I love you Eve; you are such a joy in my life. I don't know what I would do without you." Eve loved this gentle husband of hers. They both knew they were meant for each other.

The boy woke up, not really sure where he was, then he remembered, "Oh yes, I'm at the minister's house. It was early and quiet in the house; he usually woke early. Because there was no one stirring, he laid in bed, remembering other times. Ever since he could remember, his parents moved from one mining town to another. If his father mined or panned a bit of gold, he usually changed it into money to buy drinks, usually drinking it all away. His mother spent most of her time in saloons, making her money that way; always drinking with the men. Johnnie remembered more than once, sleeping in back rooms in whichever place his mother was on any given night. Sometimes his mother remembered him, and sometimes not. He grew up eating whatever people shared with him; many times he went to bed hungry.

One man, Lou Morgan stood out in his memory. Lou allowed him to sleep in his cabin on a bed the man built for him. Johnnie ate with the man, and Lou shared his many books; it was he that taught him to read. Johnnie remembered how patient the man was as he struggled to read, and learn he did. In his minds eye, he could see the man as he packed his things.

After everything was packed and put onto the back of a mule, Lou rode away and he never saw the man again. It was a lonely kind of life; mostly he wanted someone to love him.

Gus came the closest to doing that, but now he was sick. The boy didn't know if he would ever see the man again. Johnnie was glad he was here with these nice people, but somehow, he felt it wouldn't last. It never had before.

Richard came home that night saying to Eve, "Gus died in the early morning hours this morning. I made plans to have an early short graveside service; I did it to help Johnnie; the Green's and Mac and Kathleen will be there to support the boy.

The following morning, after the graveside service, Mac told his wife goodbye, hoping she would stay away from the Walsh's. Disregarding her husband's warning, Kathleen walked to the shop, hoping Jules was better. If not, she would check with Susan. As she walked into the shop, Tom Anderson was there filling in for Jules, as he often did. As Kathleen asked about Jules, she was disappointed. "I'm sorry Mrs. McGinnis, Mr. Walsh is still sick. His wife told me this morning she wasn't sure when he would be back. She seemed very worried about her husband." "I'm so sorry to hear that, thanks. I think I will stop by their house, and see if I can help."

When Kathleen knocked on the door, Susan answered. "Kathleen, what are you doing here?" "I've come to help Susan, are you getting any sleep? You look so tired." "Not much Kathleen. Jules is so sick, I'm afraid to leave him." The younger woman told her friend, "You tell me what to do, and I will watch over him, you need to rest Susan; you look exhausted." At first Susan hesitated, not wanting to leave Jules side, "It's alright Susan, I'm free, so let me do this for you." Susan was so tired, and she agreed; she couldn't remember the last time she had slept. Finally, after Kathleen's insistence, Susan laid down.

When the doctor stopped by later in the morning, he was surprised to find Kathleen there. "You be careful Mrs. McGinnis, you could catch this sickness yourself." "I'm a strong woman doctor, I will be alright. Susan needed to get some rest, and I sent her to bed." The doctor admired her thoughtfulness, but he was concerned nevertheless.

It was obvious however, she was going to stay. She followed the doctors' orders, but Jules was coughing up a great deal of phlegm; there was no way Kathleen could protect herself. When Susan woke up she was glad to see her friend was rested. "I'll be back tomorrow morning", Kathleen said as she hurried away, needing to pick up Molly and start supper.

Friendly met her at the door. She pat him, "Good boy Friendly", he wagged his tail. "You want to go outside? Yes? There you go", as she held the door open. She watched the dog and thought; he's getting to be more like a small pony. Then she turned to start supper.

Kathleen returned to the Walsh's on Tuesday, and again on Wednesday. She felt a little under the weather; but gave it little heed. Mac did not like the idea of his wife being there. "You could get sick yourself", he told her. He was concerned; but she would not listen, and his concerns increased. She had made up her mind, and that was the end of it!

Wednesday afternoon, Doctor Freeman came into the bank, asking to speak to Mac. The minute the man saw the doctor, he became alarmed; Mac had heard what a dangerous illness this was. "You want to see me Doc?" The man's reply was unsettling. "Yes Mac. I'm sorry to tell you, but I sent your wife home this afternoon. She had a very high fever. I was afraid that might happen; you'd best check on her. I will try to get there to check on her as soon as I can. There are others in town coming down with this illness. This is a pretty serious sickness."

Mac immediately spoke to Jacob, telling him what the doctor said. "The books are balanced for today. I have a few other things I need to get done, but I can do those later. Kathleen is sick, and the doctor thinks I need to be with her. Is it alright if I leave early? I'm worried about her." "Of course Mac; if she's too sick for you to leave her, I can always send the work to you." "Thanks Jacob." He put on his coat, hat, and gloves; he could feel the cold when anyone came into the bank. The cold wind went right through his coat as the wind whistled around the buildings in town. It was really cold, and Mac was glad to get home.

There was no fire in the stove, so he got one started. Then he took off his coat, and went looking for his wife. He found her lying on the bed with Friendly lying up against her, "Come on boy, get down." Then he went to her; she was sleeping, but when she heard his voice she opened her eyes, and started to get up. "No sweetheart, you stay where you are, you're very sick." She didn't argue with him, simply sinking back into the blankets. Then she began coughing; it didn't sound good to him. He felt her forehead, she's burning up, he thought. He sat down on the bed, and took hold of her hand; it was hot too! Mac wasn't sure what to do, but he could see she felt miserable. Shortly he heard a knock on the door, and then the doctor walked in, "Mac!" He called out. The man went out to meet him. "I'm so glad you're here, my wife is so feverish, and I don't know what to do."

The doctor felt her forehead and said, "She's way too hot; her fever is rising. Get out your tub, and get it full of tepid water. Not hot or cold, we need to get her temperature down right away. She began coughing, so the doctor pulled out a bottle of medicine. "Give her a teaspoon full every two or three hours, and try to keep her head up; it might help her cough. "Take good care of her, this is a bad sickness", and hurried away, saying he would be back as soon as he could.

Mac quickly got out the tub, and started heating up several pans of water. When he finally got the water to the right temperature, he went in and woke his wife up. He tenderly encouraged her to get out of bed as he helped her up. Once he got his wife into the kitchen, which was fairly warm, he helped take off her nightgown and helped her into the tub. As she lowered into the water, she gasped, "It's too cold Aaron!" "It's alright, we need to get your temperature down; lie still and let the water do its work." She did as he said, but she kept shivering. He would not let Kathleen get out of the water until her forehead felt cooler.

Once Mac had his wife back in bed, it was obvious she was worn out, and she closed her eyes. She felt sick, sick, sick, but she would be fine now; her Aaron was here, though he was more than worried. He pulled a light blanket up over her, and sat down holding her hand. Maybe, he thought, her knowing he was here would help.

Michael and Molly came in from school, both shivering from the icy cold gusts of air that followed them into the house. Their uncle met them in the kitchen; Michael was standing near the store trying to get his hands warm from the heat. It was extremely cold outside, and the winds made the cold seem even worse.

Their Uncle Mac told them how sick their mother was, "She must have caught it while taking care of Mr. Walsh; he is a very sick man. Apparently it's easily passed to others, and I don't want you two catching it. Michael, I want you and your sister to get enough clothes to last awhile, and I want you both to go to the Smith's, can you do that?" The boy was immediately worried about his mother; "Will she be okay?" he asked. "I hope so, I'll do the best I can to take care of her, but I want you away and safe." "Can we see her?" Molly asked. "Sure you can", but he only allowed them to see her from the doorway. After seeing their ma, Michael quickly gathered all they would need, and put it into a satchel.

The winds seemed to pick up after they left; it whistled through the cracks, and around the windows.

Mac hated that the two were out in the cold; he had made sure they were wrapped warmly before they left. The icy winds had hurried into the house when the door was opened, Mac put on his sweater before sitting down to watch over his wife. He pulled another blanket up over her; the house was really cold. She mustn't get cold either, he thought.

He worried about the two, wishing he knew they arrived safely at the Smith's. The weather outside sounded brutal, though he did know Michael was very capable. Then the thought went through his mind, he's my son. Somehow that pleased him; Michael was an extraordinary sixteen year old. He had a mother that raised him to become a strong, fine person. He prayed for both of them; that they would stay well during this sickness.

When the two arrived at the Smith's, they were welcomed in; the place was warm, the fireplace warming it up nicely. They being there, made young Johnnie feel better. Before they all ate supper that night, they each held hands, as Richard thanked God for all there many blessings, and the food. Then he prayed for Kathleen, and the others that were sick in town. Richard and Eve did not mention how very ill Jules was; Richard heard that day the man had developed pneumonia. During the meal the adults tried to talk about other things.

Later, when the two were getting ready for bed, he told his wife how serious this sickness was. "We need to watch over the young folks in the house; perhaps not letting them go to school. I understand many people are getting sick, you and Thelma stay home with the young ones; I will do all the shopping. I probably should stock up on necessities, and extra food."

His wife agreed, but she knew her husband would be out and about, praying for the sick ones. That frightened her, so she kept praying for him. That night, Molly slept with Thelma, who held the girl in her arms until she went to sleep. Michael slept on the divan, he'd grown taller in the last couple of years, and would find it hard to sleep. That left him free to pray for his mother, Uncle Mac, and Penny.

He thought about leaving this coming summer. Michael would miss them all, but Penny was foremost in his mind. The future minister wanted to go to seminary, but he did not want to leave Penny. What if she changed her mind after he was gone? He never wanted to lose her; he wanted her to be his wife someday. How he wished he could hurry up the time, but that would not happen, so he spent time praying.

Mac grabbed a bite to eat, while boiling some dried beef in water to make broth for Kathleen. The man tried to get his wife to take some of the broth from a spoon. She swallowed a few spoonfuls, and then turned away. "Come on sweetheart, the doctor wants you to have some of this to keep your strength up", but she would take no more. He finally gave up.

Kathleen began coughing again, though it sounded like the sickness had gone into her lungs. He put an extra pillow under her head, hoping that would help. He also made her swallow a spoonful of cough medicine. He had to fight with her to take it, but she finally did.

Again her temperature began to rise, so he got a pan of tepid water and a cloth trying to cool her down; it helped for awhile. Then he tried to get some water down her, but that didn't work either. Finally, he put on his pajamas, and lay beside her. He could not allow himself to sleep, so he kept a hand on her; hoping her fever wouldn't rise again like it had in the afternoon. Several times during the long night, she needed to be cooled down. Once the fever spiked; like that afternoon and he had to put her in the tub. This time she was so sick, he had to carry her to the tub.

By morning, her cough had gone deeper into her lungs; she was so ill, she scarcely was aware of her surroundings or her circumstances; Mac was frightened! I've done all I know to do, and she keeps getting sicker and sicker. "Lord Help!"

His emotions took over, tears dripping down over his cheeks, and he could not stop them. "I can't loose her Lord, I just can't. Lord, please help her to get over this illness, she's so very sick."

Several days went by, he wasn't sure how many. Richard came checking on the two of them. "The kids are doing fine Mac, don't worry; we have them at home. The school closed down, but they did not go those last days. This illness is spreading like a wildfire." He and Mac prayed for Kathleen; Mac could not stop the tears. He swallowed hard, but it did not help, and he finally broke down crying. Richard understood, he knew the depth of his friends love for his wife. He prayed, "Lord, give Mac the strength to care for Kathleen. Give him the courage and faith to know you will heal her of this sickness. Be merciful

Lord, Kathleen and Mac love you deeply." After he was gone, Mac began to feel a touch of hope.

The doctor came, and listened to her lungs, he just shook his head. "Stay with her Mac, and pray. I've done all there is to do."

After the doctor left, Mac laid his head on his wife's hand, wishing she would be healed. "My wonderful wife, please, I beg you Lord, heal Kathleen", he prayed. She was finally sleeping peacefully; the coughing seemed to stop. He lay down beside her, so very tired and anxious. He fell asleep for the first time in, how long? It seemed to him he hadn't slept in days.

Mac was unaware how much this sickness was affecting the town. Christmas had come and gone, Mac unaware. A dark shadow seemed to hover over the town; everything had come to a halt, the pall hung heavy over Silver City. Nearly all the business establishments in town were closed; even the saloons had few people in them; after several days they were also closed. Richard closed the Samaritan House, except to hand out food or warm clothing; which he did himself.

The weather was still brutally cold, which somehow added to the fear. Of course the church was closed; there was no need for it to be opened. Everyone was off the streets; the mines were quiet, which meant the stamps that broke up the ore were also silent. People were fearful, and stayed off the streets. Many were sick, and some had died.

Grace Simpson was recovering, but the doctor was down; not a child or adult was seen. About that time, across town; Miles began coughing, and his temperature rose. Timothy, being home, took Abby into his apartment to keep her safe. Nate said, "I'll watch over him, but Jeannie would not let him. I've already been around the boy, let me do it", so he gave in. It was a good thing, because within a day, Nate began getting sick. Jeannie had her hands full; Nate was nearly as sick as Kathleen, though Miles seemed to shake it off in a couple of days. That gave the woman time to properly care for her husband, but it was hard. She was very worried about him; Jeannie had come to love him deeply. She'd already lost one husband, and she didn't want anything to happen to Nate; he was such a good and kind man. Jeannie prevailed, and in time her husband began to recover slowly.

After nearly two weeks, Kathleen's cough lessened, and she began to slowly recover. Finally, Mac was able to give her broth, and she accepted water. It was nighttime, and she was sleeping quietly. Mac lay down beside his wife thinking, I'd rather fight Indians, at least one could see them. Mac fell into a deep sleep. As he slept, he dreamed he saw his wife standing out in a field of beautifully colored flowers. A soft light seemed to fall over her, her long chestnut colored hair was loose and flowing in the breeze. She was so lovely, with a smile on her face. His beautiful Kathleen.

He woke with a start not sure why, but he noticed he'd forgotten to lower the lamp. He started to rise to take care of the lamp, when he heard, "Aaron?" He looked at his wife, and her eyes were open. "You're awake! Thank God!" Kathleen looked confused. "Have I been sick for a long time?" she asked. "Way too long, he answered, I thought I was going to lose you." He sat down beside her, holding her in his arms saying, "You've come back to me." He felt so relieved, it had been a hard battle, but she was getting better.

Each day she improved, and within a week it was time to bring the family home. Richard dropped by, delighted to see Kathleen doing so well. Mac asked the man if he would send the two home. "I've missed those two; they are my family now he told his friend and pastor. As he walked Richard out the door, the man told him that Jules had died from pneumonia. "I did not want to tell you until Kathleen began to recover, I didn't want you worrying more than you already were. Others in town have died also, Grace Simpson was as ill as Kathleen, but she is recovering. Nate Green was very ill, but he's nearly recovered now. Joe and Helen were both sick, but not nearly as bad as either Grace or Kathleen."

"Fortunately, at our house everyone stayed well, and it looks like there have been no new cases in town for nearly ten days. The doctor is still ill, but his wife says he's getting better." I know Christmas is over, but not many people celebrated much this year. Those who have been sick and their families are thankful that more people did not die. I have decided to wait another couple of weeks before having church services. I'm afraid people may come out too soon, and cause the sickness to spread again."

"I will send Michael and Molly back as soon as I get home."

Mac thanked his friend for keeping the two, "I wanted them to be safe," you're more than welcome Mac, I think maybe Michael may be bent permanently; that divan is much to short for him, but he's never complained." Richard smiled, and then left for home.

When Michael and Molly arrived home, their ma was sitting in her chair, a lap robe over her knees, and her robe on. She was still weak, but she was so glad to see the two; they in turn, hovered around her. "I missed you ma", her daughter told her. I'm so glad you are better", Michael said as he hugged his mother. "You had me worried" and he hugged her again.

Mac stood looking at his family, he was so grateful to the Lord for them. Then he thought, why not; why don't I legally adopt them. That way, someday when I'm gone, they will be my heirs. I would like to do that; it will give me something to think about.

The day after Michael and Molly came home, Pete stopped by to check on them. "We pretty much stayed home, hearing about all the many people in town that either died, or were very ill. This morning I ventured into town, needing to get some supplies, and George told me Kathleen was sick. I guess this was his first day back at work, and Richard told him about Kathleen; how is she Mac?" "Thanks to the Lord, she is gaining back her strength, I thought I was going to lose her. I've been doing the bank's books at home, but it's time to go back to work. I'm dreading going back, Jacob is a good man, and I've appreciated working for him, but I miss the ranch and all it means to me."

"Look Mac, you don't have to work. Like me, you have assets here and in Santa Fe. I know you haven't used all your money from the gold. Why don't you build that house you were wanting, out on the ranch? We are still partners, we worked hard to build up our stock, and there's no reason why you can't get out of town. Maybe you could enlarge your grove, and add some pears; they would grow great in the area. Think about it Mac."

"I miss our being together; we spent so many years working together." "Well, it's something to consider anyway. I've gotta run, Maria hasn't been feeling too well lately. Mac's eyebrows went up. "No, she doesn't have the sickness that's been going around, she has been sick every morning for a month now. I hate to leave her alone; she's really felt miserable, so I guess I had better go. Talk to Kathleen about the ranch, after all she was raised on a farm, just like you. Anyway, I've gotta go; see you soon." And Pete rode away. Mac's head was in a whirl; go back to the ranch?

Chapter 16

Joe was busy these days, constructing both business buildings and homes; working with the crew he'd worked with at the church. He was a quick learner, and efficient, everyone liked his work. The young man never shirked his obligations; always giving extra time if it was needed. He was also very responsible, and people began to forget he was of Indian ancestry.

It was this young man that Mac chose to build their home. "Joe, you know who the best builders are. If they are free, hire them; you will all be paid fair wages, and if extra work is done, there will be a bonus given."

The couple went to the land, and chose the spot where they wanted their home to be built. It was near the spot where they had sat along the stream so many months ago. There were several evergreen trees, and Mac insisted they be saved, if possible.

The husband and wife spent time drawing the plans; they wanted the house to be homey, yet with large rooms. Kathleen asked if they could have plenty of windows. The house they were now living in had few windows, and it was somewhat gloomy. Joe suggested positioning the house to use the summer and winter solstice, which would keep the house warmer in the winter and cooler in the summer. That suggestion came from somewhere back in his Indian ancestry.

The house was ahead of it's time, when it was built; one could walk into the kitchen or living room and see the land for long distances, truly a lovely sight. The barn was raised with its stalls for the horses, and Mac brought both his mare, and one of Mr. Grey's offspring. He also brought several more horses needed by the men who would work for them. During the months of building there were many pairs of curious eyes watching; three quail families were in the area with their unique sounding calls. Often the quail could be seen; with the father, as the head of a house, leading his family to food or water. He was at the front, scouting to make sure nothing would harm his brood; the mother at the back of the line, making sure none ventured out alone.

The large and homely looking roadrunners passed by almost everyday, running like they were being chased across the land. Wild turkeys could be heard gobbling, further back in the forest. Nearby, one could usually see the small pointed faces of the fox with their penetrating eyes, peeking from behind a bush or rock; ready to dash away at a moments notice. Deer would graze mornings and evenings, just outside the fenced area where the horses spent time out in the fields. At times a cougar or bear could be heard, roaring back in the deeper part of the timberland; a place where nature and man met, living side by side. Friendly had to be retrained, so he would leave the wildlife alone. He learned to lie quietly, watching it all unfold before his eyes. He was a good dog, and was told so often.

Spring was nearly gone; the house was finished, and soon it would be time for Michael to leave. After the boy graduated, Jacob Firth called him into the bank. Michael was surprised when Penny's father handed him a substantial check. "It all comes from different people who want to help you pay for your schooling." Michael knew his father and Mr. Firth were helping him, but he planned to pay them back. However, Jacob told him, "This is money, given by people who know you have a calling on your life, and they do not expect you to pay any of it back. We all know you will do your best, and they trust you. As for me, I believe you are meant to be a man of God; I wish you well Michael." He shook the boy's hand, and then turned to answer a question a clerk asked him. Michael would never know, for sure, where all the money came from.

On Wednesday, the week before he was to leave, he went to see Penny. Since they'd graduated, they'd seen little of each other, except at church. He told his mother he was going to see Penny, "We've had little time together, and I want to spend some time with her." His mother understood, but as usual, she was worried about the Indians. "It's alright ma, uncle Pete told me he heard they are way west of here, near the Mogollon Rim. "I'll be fine, and I promise I will be home before supper. He caught Nell, and led her to the barn. After cinching the saddle to make sure it was on tight, he rode away toward town.

Kathleen understood, he loved the girl, and his time away at school would be hard on both of them. She also knew her son would never live at home again, and probably not in Silver City. She dreaded the day when he would leave, yet this was something her son must do.

Lillie heard the knock on the door, but her hands were busy kneading bread, so she asked her daughter to see who was at the door. When Penny opened it, she saw Michael standing there, hat in hand. "Penny", he said, "I just had to come see you. Her dancing eyes showed him how glad she was to see him; Michael loved those dancing blue eyes. "You know I will be leaving within the week. We've been so busy moving, I've had little time to come see you. Could we go for a walk? I miss you Penny and I don't know how I will live without you. I've hardly seen you since we got out of school."

The girl took a quick look back into the house, and not seeing her mother, she stepped outside, closing the door carefully so her mother would not see them. Penny whispered, "Let's go." So he grabbed her hand, and they hurried away, heading up north, past the old house the McGinnis's had been living in. They walked up along the stream holding hands, glad to be together. The couple stopped under a large cottonwood, and stood looking at one another, feeling such love rise from within. Michael stood looking down on his Penny. "I'm going to miss you terribly, Michael. I don't want you to go, but I do; I don't know what I will do when you're gone." He put his hat down on a limb, and took Penny in his arms. In a weak moment he said, "Just ask me Penny, and I won't go", but she just shook her head. He bent down and kissed her; they both felt both desire and love rise up within them.

They were in such a dilemma, they loved each other, and he was leaving. It would be a long time before he would be back. He kissed her again, her arms circling around him. "You promise Penny; you will wait for me?" She nodded, afraid if she spoke she would cry. "When I get back we will be married", he promised her, and again he kissed her. At that time there was nothing more she wanted than to be his wife.

The young man knew they had to go back, but he did not want to let go of her, but he realized they had to leave. He gently said, "Let's go Penny; I'd best get you home." She nodded yes, knowing he was right, but she did not want to. Her good sense took over, and she said "Alright Michael, but I shall miss you terribly when you're gone. You will write to me, won't you?" He nodded, "Of course I will. If it weren't for God beckoning me on, I would never leave, but that will not happen."

"I know what he wants me to do, and I've dedicated my life to him, but Penny, I will be back; I promise you. This dream of being a partner with the Lord is something I really want to do, and I feel you are meant to be a part of my serving Him. Somehow, God let us meet, and fall in love for His purposes, so we will be together, and share our lives serving Him." She nodded. "I know Michael, I feel the same way, so we have to be strong and trust Him."

Michael took his girl by the hand, and they walked back to Penny's house. Before he left his girl, he kissed her, and then said, "I'll see you Sunday."

She watched him as he turned away, and went to his horse. He looked back at her, then climbed into the saddle, waved goodbye, and left. After he was out of sight, Penny began crying again. She went into the house, quietly opening her bedroom door, and lay on her bed weeping.

That's where her mother found her. "What's wrong Penny?" How could she tell her mother how she felt about Michael, she thought; but her mother knew. Mother's have a way of knowing. She saw Michael and her daughter walking away when she glanced out of the kitchen window. She understood, she was young and in love once too. She gathered her daughter into her arms; "It's alright dear, I understand. You're in love, just as I was once, and he's leaving. "Michael is a wonderful young man, I'm sure he told you he would be back, and he will keep that promise; God willing", her mother said, trying to encourage her sweet daughter.

"Mother, he asked me to marry him once he's through at the seminary. I said I would; I love him so much mother. Then her lips started to quiver with a new set of tears forming in her eyes. "Honey, you couldn't marry a better young man than Michael. Time will go faster than you think, and she held her daughter, soothing her with words of a mother's love.

Love Comes in Many Colors

The day Michael left by stagecoach, she was there to say goodbye, along with his family; which included his brother. "I'll write to you Penny", and then in front of everyone he kissed her goodbye; she tried not to cry, but she did.

Michael liked the school, everything was so green. He had forgotten how beautiful it was further east, though he missed the southwestern mountains. There was a small chapel on campus; he got into the habit of going into the small sanctuary early in the mornings before other students came in. Within those walls, he felt the closest to his Savior and Heavenly Father. It was a quiet place where he could tell them of His love. That small chapel helped him through the lonely times; there his love was strengthened, and there his goal was attainable.

Back home, the Smith's took Johnnie to see Judge Logan, having given him time to get to know them and decide if he wanted to be a part of their family,. They all signed the adoption papers, and *John* became their son, legally. The judge was more than pleased that the Smith's would be the boy's parents, and they would be raising him; he felt very good about the arrangements. He reached his hand across his desk, and shook both John's and the minister's hands, "I wish you a good life young man, you could not have better, nor kinder parents than these good people. I wish you and them my very best wishes for a happy life." John's new parents never pushed him into their faith, though he did go to church and school.

After they left, he sat thinking, I've never liked the shouting and condemnation many preacher's spew out, but I think I will try Reverend Smith's church. He felt the man was a different kind of minister.

Several months later, after Richard's sermon, which was more like a friend talking; John's heart was touched. While the members were singing the last hymn, he left the side of his mother; stepped out of the pew, and went forward. The boy knelt down, wanting to give his life to Jesus, his Heavenly Father. Richard went to the boy, and knelt beside him; he listened as the boy proclaimed his faith. Then a father's arms held his son as he prayed for the boy. From that time on, there was a real peace in the boy; all the ugliness of the past was gone.

As the weather grew warmer, Richard baptized John in the stream; his mother and grandmother watching. The boy grew to be a man who loved God greatly.

Judge Logan was in church the day John accepted Christ; after a few months, he followed the boy's example, appreciating the gentle message of love for God he heard each Sunday.

In the beginning, Richard had helped Michael find the right school, and through the years, he had mentored the boy. Michael felt a closeness with Richard, and often wrote him about his life, and asked him questions; he always received the answer he needed most. The young man found some of the subjects to be very challenging, but he would stick with it until he got the grade he wanted. When most of the students left for summer break, Michael stayed; picking up classes he was unable to take during the winter.

Those winters were challenging for Michael, even though he had lived thru the harsh winters on the farm. It was different here at the seminary, though he had warm clothing. He had to deal with slippery sidewalks and streets during the ice storms, those were always a challenge, especially because he worked in a large restaurant on the weekends. Coming home late after work was the most difficult. He liked the work, which broadened his understanding of people; he enjoyed working around all the different people. The weeks, months, and then the years went by quickly because his life was very busy.

Michael wrote to Penny every week, telling her all about his life, and the things he was learning. He mentioned his job, classes, or maybe he would write about his favorite professor. She, in turn answered every letter; as they shared their thoughts and feelings. Sometimes his father wrote to Michael; all those letters helped, especially when he was lonesome for home. Michael stayed in school year 'round, and he finished his schooling in three years; he would soon be on his way home.

He did well in his classes, and more and more, he felt the call on his life. Michael's professors felt he was a very promising student. Toward the end of his time at the seminary, Kathleen wrote asking him to go to a tailor and be measured for a suit. He was to send the measurements to her; and in turn, she would use them to make him a suit for him to be married in, and to use once he became a minister.

As soon as she received them, she began sewing the suit. When his suit was finished, she started sewing

Penny's wedding dress. She went to extra trouble to make a lovely gown for Michael's intended. Kathleen bought some delicate white material for the dress, she used a sheer white material to make very small white roses, which she sewed on the dress randomly; the thin white veil also had roses on it. The gown was one of the prettiest she had ever made; the sleeves were long, closing at the wrist. There was a very full petticoat, causing the skirt to flow outward.

When Lillie Firth saw her daughter in her wedding gown, she thought it was the loveliest gown she had ever seen. "It's beautiful Kathleen. Penny will be lovely in it on her wedding day!"

The evening Michael arrived home, Penny and his whole family were there to greet him. He went to Penny first and kissed her. "I told you I would be back!" He whispered into her ear, "You are so beautiful Penny", and he squeezed her hand.

"I've missed you so." Then he took her by the hand, and went to hug his special mother and father. "Michael!" He heard, and he turned, "How about a sister, don't I get a hug?" He was astonished! "Where is my little sister?" He asked, and then he scooped Molly up in his arms. "Here now, you've gotten pretty on me young lady!" He kissed her cheek, and put her down.

Richard, Eve, and Thelma were there to welcome him home; along with their son, John. Michael went to them, Penny in hand, "It's so good to see you both, I've missed you all. "I want you to know", he said to Richard; "Your letters helped me so much. You got me through some really difficult times, and I want to thank you." The minister and friend reached out and shook his hand. "Some where along the way, you've become a man, it's good to see you Michael; we're all so proud of you." "Yes, I guess I have, with a few bumps along the way." The young man replied.

Then he turned to Penny, "I bet I can beat you to that tree Penny!" She picked up her skirt, and said, "Just try", and she let go of his hand, and took off like the wind, with Michael right behind her. He yelled to his mother, "I'll meet you at the Smith's. I've got a girl to catch." And off the two went with Michael lagging behind a bit, but he would catch up!

Everyone laughed to see the two running away. "Well Richard", Mac said, "It looks like you'll have company for awhile." He picked up Michael's two bags. "It's good to see the young folks, they need some time together."

The Firth's stopped by the Smith's for awhile, and then Jacob said, "I expect Penny will be coming home soon." "Why don't you all come over to our house after church tomorrow for lunch?" It was agreed they all would go, and then Penny's parents left for home.

Within the hour Michael and Penny were at the Smith's door. "Come in, we're waiting for you, however your parents went home Penny." Richard said. They all stayed awhile listening to Michael telling them about the years he'd been gone. He would not let go of Penny's hand. After awhile, Michael walked his girl home. "I'll see you tomorrow Penny", "I'm so glad your home Michael, I have missed you terribly", and she went into his arms, feeling so safe and happy. Her Michael was home at last. "In time", he said, "I guess I had better go, or I might have to walk home. I love you Penny, meet you at church tomorrow." He hugged her, blew her a kiss as he left, and hurried to the Smith's.

The following Saturday was the day of their wedding. Michael was surrounded by his father, his Uncle Pete; which is the way he thought of him, and Penny's father. Unlike the other men, Michael was not uneasy, he had waited much too long for this day; when Penny would become his wife.

Everything was under control; his father had the ring, he had on his new suit, and he was ready. But, in where Penny was waiting, it was a different story. Penny couldn't get her hair to stay in place. It was up on top of her head, and somehow the comb that was holding it in place kept slipping. Finally Kathleen took the one holding her own hair back, and put Penny's hair up, and it worked! So Kathleen's hair was down that day, but she didn't mind; Penny was lovely. Kathleen pinned the veil on, and all the women sighed. The young woman was exquisite.

As Mary played the piano, Penny walked down the isle on her father's arm to her Michael; his eyes never left hers, he had never seen her so lovely. During the ceremony, as they knelt to pray, he held her hand. When he placed the ring on her finger, and they were pronounced husband and wife, he gently took her into his arms and kissed her. This was the most wonderful day of his life; up to this point. His Penny was his, finally.

The new husband and wife stayed in the same hotel where Michael and his family spent their first night in Silver City. It was in new hands, and even nicer than before. The families left them alone; they needed this time to be together.

After six days, Penny's folks had them to dinner. The Firth's were very happy, Penny had married Michael. He was an extraordinary person, though he did not seem to know it; that's what made him special. Michael was a very humble young man, who was very much in love.

The couple spent time visiting with the Smith's, and then the two went out to the ranch, staying a few days with Kathleen and Mac. Michael talked to his father. "I'm a bit nervous, it's my first church." "You'll do fine Michael, just be yourself", Mac told him. "You have a special way with people that one rarely sees." "Actually, you make me think of a.... younger Richard, but again you are your own man. Trust God, this is his idea; it will work out fine." That encouraged Michael. While they were on the ranch, they rode a couple of the horses, though they rode closer to town; no one had heard anything about the Indians yet.

Michael and Penny spent time; sitting by the stream where his mother and father had sat years before. "I wish we could live here someday Michael, his wife said. "It's so peaceful and beautiful here." He had the same dream, but didn't think it would ever happen; he just soaked in the sunshine, and the beauty to hold in his memories when they were far away.

The young couple seemed so happy; Kathleen was rejoicing for them, it's their time, she thought.

She and Aaron were as much in love as when they were married, and she hoped that it would be the same for Michael and Penny.

The day before Michael and Penny had to return to Silver City to catch the train heading for Santa Fe, where Michael's first church assignment was, Michael and Mac sat, talking while the women were cleaning up after supper. "It's difficult to leave, knowing we might never be back again."

The next day, while Michael and Penny boarded the train, Mac and Kathleen were sad, but they knew Michael would be a wonderful minister.

After Michael and Penny were in Santa Fe, Michael would remember the encouraging words of his father. He sat down and wrote to him.

"You are a wonderful father. My pa just couldn't give me what you have given me, I love you very much father."

That letter meant so much to Mac; he kept it tucked away in a small box with a dried yellow rose. Someday Michael would find that box with other mementoes tucked inside, and remember his kind and gentle father, and the mother he always loved.

Later that summer, there was a big scare. Indians were threatening everyone in the area, and the people all fled into town. Minute men stood on all the peaks and hills around the small town, trying to protect everyone. Pete's men brought in their horses, and made an emergency corral for them. Mac and their two men that worked for the couple brought in their few horses, putting them in with Pete's. The Walker's stayed with the Green's, they had room, and Kathleen, Mac, and Molly stayed with the Firth's.

The families worried about their homes on the ranch, and all the other buildings including their barns. It was a frightening time for everyone; there were people from the western valleys, as well as people from Pinos Altos and beyond that ended up in town. After several weeks, the Indians were heard to be in the mountains in Arizona, so people began going home. Many lost everything they had; others lost nothing. Out at the ranch the only problems were some sleeping quarters for their men, and a partially burned house; only two rooms were affected, and by winter it was repaired, along with all the outbuildings.

Mac and Kathleen lost the barn, and the corral; the fire had also burned right to the front door of the house. All they could figure was one of the summer showers had put the fire out. Again, a new barn had to be built, plus the corrals. Mac did as much as his shoulder would allow. For the rest, the two men who worked for them and two others Mac hired finished the rebuilding pretty quickly. Part of the barn, where the men slept was enlarged to make the men more comfortable.

Mac's grove was fine. The apples and pears were small, but the Indians had not touched the area. The peach trees were laden with large, ripe peaches, so both Kathleen and Maria canned the fruit; they also made pies, and served the peaches fresh with just a touch of sugar.

Mac's vegetable garden was untouched also, and both families enjoyed the fresh food. Kathleen added to her canned foods; tomatoes, peas, green beans, and carrots for the winter. Mac built a root cellar into the side of a hill, with a strong heavy door to keep not only some of the carrots, but other root vegetables fresh, including onions, sweet and Irish potatoes, and apples; which kept both families supplied.

Maria became pregnant in the fall, and spent three miserable months until the morning sickness subsided. Pete was elated; always talking about the baby to come. Finally, Mac reached a point where he'd heard enough about the baby, but out of respect for his long time friend and partner, he kept his thoughts to himself.

One night as he and Kathleen were getting ready for bed, he told his wife that he was glad, for her sake that she no longer had to have children. She looked at him and said, "Sweetheart, I can still have a child. It might be hard to go through it at my age, but I would like to give you a son." "Kathleen, I already have two sons and a daughter. They mean a great deal to me, so whether you have another child or not, I do love my family." Then he said, "Come here, you", and he held her, kissing his wife. He was a happy and contented man, for what he'd wanted most was in his arms, and he told her so.

The days seemed to go so quickly, and then soon, the years. Molly was ready to graduate from school. Michael and Penny were in Santa Fe, where Michael's church was. Maria and Pete's son was nearly five years old, and he had a small sister.

Love Comes in Many Colors

One warm spring day, Mac came home from town, having gone for supplies. After putting down the packages, he handed Kathleen a letter from her son; he had another one Michael had written to him. He was surprised, but pleased. Mac went out to the barn, and sat down on a bale of hay, the sun shining in through the barn doors. The man opened the envelope and pulled out the letter from his son.

August 23, 1888
Wednesday morning

Dear Father,

I have a few free minutes this morning. Penny is out doing a bit of shopping, and I am using this time to write to you.

Last night, as I was reading the scriptures, I read Luke 15, where the Lord told his disciples, this is my commandment, that you love one another as I have loved you, and you came to mind.

All through the years, you've always shone that kind of love. I never once saw you treat anyone with anything but kindness, thoughtfulness, and God's love; his love always evident, wherever you are, or who you are with.

During the years, I've watched you care for my mother with kindness, gentleness, and love. I will always be grateful you married her, and I thank the Lord everyday for you.

Part of what I love most, is your wonderful sense of humor.

When I get too lofty in my thinking, I remember you, and that remembrance brings me back down to reality.

You will always be very special to me.

> With great affection,
> Your son,
> Michael

Mac never forgot what his son wrote to him, and always prayed for the two, that God would bless them as they both served Him. That letter also, went into the box of memories.

Chapter 17

Six years after Michael and Penny were married, and working at the church in Santa Fe, Richard developed a heart problem. He was forced to slow down, which he hated, and he didn't always do; Eve watched over him like a hawk. The doctor gave him a small pill he was supposed to take everyday, which he often forgot, so Eve started handing it to him at breakfast.

The doctor also prescribed a nap every day after lunch, but even though Eve would remind Richard to come home for lunch and his nap, Richard would get busy and forget both. She suspected he could not acknowledge he had a health problem, but by nighttime he was exhausted, and could not eat; only falling into bed. His wife did not know what to do with him; it was like having a sweet, loving, naughty child! Eve didn't want to nag him, but she felt she had no choice.

At the same time, Thelma had become frail; time was taking its tole on her. She needed help to do the simplest of things. Eve loved them both, but it took lots of care giving; her husband being the biggest challenge. She struggled to get Richard to take care of himself, but the more she fussed at him, the more things he did that he shouldn't. One day he was quiet; he came home, and took his nap.

They enjoyed eating together that evening, and then they went to bed; just like old times, Richard held Eve in his arms. "I love you sweetheart. I'm sorry I've been misbehaving, it's just so many people are in need; either physical or materially. I do love you though Eve, always. You've been there beside me all through the years, helping me." He kissed her, and she almost cried. "I love you too Richard. I can't remember a day when you weren't a caring and loving husband." He was almost like he used to be.

When they went to sleep, she was in his arms, she knowing how much she loved him, and he loved her. In the morning she woke up, sleeping on her side away from her husband. She turned over, and was surprised that Richard was still in bed; he was always an early riser, often spending time in prayer before she woke up. "Richard, are you alright?" He didn't answer, so she reached over and touched him. The minute she felt him, she knew he was gone.

"Oh Richard, no, no, you can't leave me", but she knew he had, and she wept and wept. She put her arms around him, she didn't want to let him go; her wonderful husband had died during the night. Her heart was broken, and no matter how much she prayed and cried, she could not find comfort. Finally she got up, and with tears streaming down her face, went to her son. She stood, looking at him. He was nineteen years old already; he had been a joy to Richard and her.

"Richard." Again the tears would not stop. "John, wake up, John." When he opened his eyes, he saw the dismay on his mothers' face. "What's happened?" He was very alarmed; he had never seen her so upset before. She tried to tell him about his father, but she could not. She began crying again, and as he started to get out of bed, she began to crumple. He caught her, holding her as she sobbed; in time she quieted down.

"Your father", she couldn't seem to get the words out. "What is it mother? Is he hurt? Where is he?" "No John, he's not hurt, then she took a deep breath, and calmed herself down. "John, your father died in his sleep last night. I… I don't know what to do!" The boy threw a robe on, and they walked together into where his father lay.

There was such a peaceful look on his father's face. The young man knelt down beside his father with tears in his eyes, what will we do without him, he thought. In time he stood up and said to his mother, "He would want us to be joyful, because he is with the God he loves." He then guided his mother into the kitchen, made a pot of coffee, and gave a cup to his mother. "You will be alright mother; I will take care of you." With those words, he comforted her.

Later, when the doctor pronounced his father deceased, Doc Freeman spoke to Eve, "We've lost someone very special, but God has gained one who loved him. I'm so sorry for your loss, Eve; please, if I can help in anyway, do call on me. We've all come to love you both, and we will be there for you and your family." Eve was touched by his words of kindness. He put his arm around the bereaved woman, "We shall all miss him."

The doctor pulled John aside. "Do you think your mother would want him left here a few days, or should we have him buried soon?" John took a man's role, and replied, "I think it would be easier on my mother if he was taken away." Alright son, I'll see to it."

The church was filled to overflowing with the many friends wanting to say goodbye to their friend, and pastor; many there to support Eve and her son as well. It was a sad day for his family and friends. It was hard to believe Richard was gone; many shed tears at their loss. Both Mac and Pete spoke about their friend, and the huge impact he'd had on so many people in the town; he had been a friend to all. The Simpson's, especially James, was devastated, he felt he had lost his best friend. Mac sang 'Amazing Grace', a fitting song for one who always spoke of the amazing gift Christ gave to all. Kathleen could not stop the tears, as her husband; with his rich voice, sang a tribute to Richard and his wonderful savior.

Kathleen and Jeannie came by to see Eve often, they loved their friend, and they were there for her through the roughest days. John was a great comfort to his mother; he missed and mourned for his father as much as Eve did.

In a few months, Thelma passed away; she'd simply grown too old and tired. Those were hard times for the mother and son; John was much like his father, though they were not of the same bloodline, Richard's life had a tremendous influence on his son.

Love Comes in Many Colors

Later, when George Hanson wanted to retire because he was not as strong as he used to be; he sold the store to John. He asked only for a set amount to be paid each month by the new owner. The business did well as the town grew; eventually, he would marry and build an addition onto the house for his mother, so she would be near. Eve and John's wife really liked each other, and John wanted them to be close, but more importantly, he wanted his mother to have her own privacy; he was always a good son to her.

For several months after Richard passed away, the church did not have a minister. Mac and Pete took turns keeping the church going until a man was sent to take the minister's place. The new preacher was inclined to shout during his sermons, speaking mostly about hell and damnation, and the attendance began to dwindle as less and less people were coming to church. Many simply stayed home, reading the scriptures to their families or themselves if they were alone; even the staunchest attending stopped.

Several men wrote to the church conference, complaining; including Mac. It was nearly eight months before a letter was received by the minister, saying he was being replaced, and was given a date to leave. Most of the congregation missed worshiping together, they were friends. They all tried to stay close, keeping their friendships going. During that time, Mac also received a letter saying a new minister would be arriving in six weeks. He was told the day the man would be arriving; the new minister would be coming to town on the Deming Express train.

Three couples from the church were there to meet the train the new minister and his wife were to arrive on. Mac and Kathleen, Pete and Maria; both with their families, along with Nate and Jeannie with a growing Abby, and family were there to great the new minister. Jacob had planned for he and Lillie to be there, but some bank business interfered.

They were all on the platform when the train came huffing and puffing up the track. Once the train stopped, several men stepped off the train; no one waiting knew the name of the new minister. Then Mac spotted Michael and Penny getting off the train.

"Kathleen, its Michael and Penny!" His wife took a sharp intake of air, "Michael?" She asked her husband. Then she saw them.

Michael was carrying their luggage, and when they got close enough, he dropped the bags and hurried to his mother; Penny right behind. When he reached his ma, he hugged her, and then Penny hugged her also. "Ma, it's so good to be here!" "It's you Michael, I can't believe you and Penny are here; why didn't you tell us you were coming?" "We wanted to surprise everyone. I've been sent here to take over the church." Everyone was delighted to have the young couple here, only Pete saw the discharged minister as he got onto the train before it left.

After everyone greeted the couple, it was decided they would all go to the bank, and let Jacob know Michael and Penny were here. The man was so glad to see his daughter; she ran into his welcoming arms. It was a touching sight as father and daughter greeted each other, then when Jacob found out his little girl would be living here, he was so very happy. "We must tell your mother", and the man left the bank in Emil's hands, and they all went to the Firth's house. The man was beside himself with happiness; his girl had come home.

Lillie could not believe her eyes! "Penny, Michael, what are you doing here?" When she found out they were here to stay, she was beside herself with a mother's joy. Everyone felt such a relief they would be able to go to church, and knew they would hear a positive message again.

After visiting for awhile, Michael asked if they would all excuse him, "I won't be long; I need to go see Mrs. Smith." He gave Penny a kiss, "I'll be back soon Penny." She nodded; she knew how he felt about Richard being gone, and how concerned he was for Richard's family. When Eve answered the door to the young man's knock and saw Michael, she began to fight the tears. Michael went in and held her in his arms, letting her cry until she clamed down. "I'm sorry Michael; I can't seem to get over losing Richard." "I understand", he said.

"Please sit down." He sat on the familiar divan, remembering another time. "I was so sad when I heard my very good friend died", he told Eve. Even though Michael had written those words to her months before, she needed to hear it from his own lips. "I wanted you to know that I have been sent here to pastor the church. I know I will never be able to fill his shoes, but I will try. I loved him you know; he helped me so much through the years. When I was around fifteen years old, he counseled and prayed for me. That day, I knew I would be following in his footstep; I wanted you to know that."

She smiled at the young minister, "I know Michael, I remember him telling me he knew someday you would be a minister. He felt much like you were like a son to him; he loved you very, very much, and was so proud of you. I wish he could be here to see you, Michael." The two spent time together talking, "If you ever need anything, please let me know; I will be here for you", he told Eve. "You're very sweet, Michael, but I have John, and he is a good son. I have to tell you", she said. "I am so glad you're here to carry on Richard's dreams, and I think he would feel the same way."

After a few minutes, Michael told her, "Well I must go, the families, and Penny are waiting for me. Please pray for me, that I can accomplish the things he started, and that I can teach about our lord as well as he did." He kissed her on her check and left, going straight to Penny, and everyone waiting at the Firth's house. After he was gone, she spoke softly to her beloved husband; as she often did. "Well Richard, Michael is here; everything at the church and the needy in town will be alright. Michael has turned out just the way you thought he would." How she missed her husband.

Michael and Penny stayed at her parent's home; sleeping in Penny's old room. After they found a place to live, with Penny at his side, he reopened the Samaritan House. Michael knew he had to do that, not only for the people who needed help, but for Richard also. It took much of his time, getting everything going. There was a younger group of people who helped; including his brother, Timothy, Joe and Helen, and Emily. Most all that helped had received, and now they were ready to give.

Mac spent time working, helping his son, and many of the women who had worked with Richard; they gathered clothing, had bake sales, and cooked for the meals given to those in need.

James Simpson came to see Michael, and to honor his friend by helping financially whenever it was needed. The new minister was hesitant to accept the help, but James insisted. "I have much, and I want to give to those who have little and are struggling to make ends meet. I've watched you young man, and I see much of Reverend Smith in you. My wife and I are so glad you have been able to come home, and minister to all of us." He stood up and shook Michael's hand. "Please let me know if there are special needs" and he left. Michael mused about the man; this was the man pa worked for, he's the one that helped ma when we were trying to make pennies meet, and many other things. He knew so much about James' generosity. It was good to know there were such people in the world.

The two brothers became very close; Timothy remembering Michael's words of encouragement so many years ago, which made him become stronger and stronger in his faith. Such a difference as the brothers began to really love one another. Timothy really liked Emily; he had for some time, and they spent time together at the Samaritan House, as well as other times. Their relationship grew as they worked together at the house; Tim's feelings grew into love.

One Sunday afternoon, he walked to Mary Johnson's house, and asked Emily if she would like to go for a walk. Mary encouraged her to go saying, "Enjoy yourself Emily, go and have a good time." The two wandered to the hills behind her house, and then downtown; talking all the while, Tim had taken her hand in his. She was thrilled. She thought about him all the time, and knew she loved him, but didn't think he was that interested in her.

When they got in front of the church, Tim suggested they sit and rest awhile, he still holding her hand. After they talked about many things, Timothy got up enough nerve to say what he had been wanting to say all afternoon. "Emily, I've come to really care for you; I've liked you a long time now, do you like me?" That put Emily on the spot, and she thought, should I say yes? Finally, Emily said "Sure I do, you've always been a good friend to me." "No Emily, that's not what I mean"; now *he* was on the spot. Finally he just blurted out his feelings. "I think about you all the time, It's like you live in my head; you're in my mind from morning till night, you are so special to me." Again he thought, I'm bumbling this, oh just tell her you love her. "I love you Emily, I don't know why I haven't said anything; maybe I was afraid you would turn away. I really do love you so much."

She looked at him in unbelief, "You love me?" He nodded his head. "Timothy, I love you too, I thought you didn't like me very much, because you never said anything; I sort of gave up." He was overjoyed, and he took her in his arms; kissing her for everyone to see.

Every bell in the world went off in his head, she didn't move away; so he kissed her again, her hands up around his cheeks. Suddenly he said, "Let's walk." They walked up the street, hand in hand. He stopped and looked at her, "Emily, will you marry me? I don't think I can live without you", and he did not wait for her answer; kissing her again.

Emily's concern was for Ida, who was in her early teens, and she mentioned that to him. She also explained who the father of her daughter was; though he was gone. "He was very cruel to me, and used me many, many times. By this time, she was afraid he would turn away, and she dropped her eyes, crying.

Tim lifted up her head, and said, "That was not you're fault, I actually only think of him in disgust. He must have been an evil man; besides that was a long time ago, there's nothing in my feelings that include him. "It's you I love. You are so sweet, and I think I have loved you for a very long time now. You haven't answered my question; will you marry me Emily?" She looked straight in his eyes, and said, "Yes, I will." He kissed her again, overjoyed. He kissed her again with his arms wrapped around her; she had never been happier than she was right now. She had begun to think no one would ever love her. Then he said, "Come, let's go tell the world we're in love!"

He headed for the Green's house. They were really happy for the couple; he hugged a teenage Abby, and said, "Guess what? We're going to have a new person in our family." She looked up at him,

"Who? She asked. Emily sat down, and Tim said, "Emily and I are going to get married, will you come to our wedding?" The girl knew Emily well, and she hugged the young woman. "I'm glad; I think my Uncle Tim is lonesome sometimes.

When Tim took his sweet Emily home, he said, "I'll talk to Michael and find out how one gets married." Actually my little brother will be marrying us, and they laughed, and then kissed goodbye. "I'll see you tomorrow my love", and he left. Emily never dreamed anyone would love her because of her past, but Tim did; she felt such happiness.

Tim talked to his brother. "Congratulations Tim! I think that's wonderful, she is a lovely young woman. She's had years to get over her sorrows, and she deserves some happiness, and so do you."

When their mother found out Tim and Emily were going to be married, she got very excited. She talked to Emily at church the next Sunday. "Would you let me sew your wedding gown? I would love to do that for you." She smiled inside, thinking, I'm becoming an expert at wedding gowns. "I've had my share of experience during the years making them. This would really please me, Emily, to do this for you. Emily's answer was, "I don't have any money to pay for a dress." "That's no problem; I can do this for you and Tim. Please let me, I want yours and Tim's wedding day to be as special as mine was. I made Penny's dress, and I want to make yours." After a moment of thought, which included, Tim's mother is so nice, she answered, "Yes, I would love for you to sew my dress." Now she felt like one of the family.

Kathleen worked many hours sewing Emily's gown. Working on it brought back the day she and Aaron became husband and wife. She remembered how much in love they were on there wedding day, and what a special day it was. Well, they were still in love, she adored her sweet Aaron; what a special man he is, she thought. Each day he reminded her of his love, he never seemed to get tired of telling her how much she meant to him. "Lord, you have blessed me; I have two wonderful sons, and a daughter.

Molly would be the next one in the family to marry. She hoped her daughter would not hurry into marriage; the girl was now out of the house, and working in town. Her family had grown up so fast. Where has the time gone?

Emily's dress was more tailored; made of white taffeta. When the young woman tried it on, she was stunning. The pretty woman began to feel even more a part of the family; they were all so gracious to her.

Mac took Tim to be fitted for a new suit. The young man looked at his father and thought, I'm so happy for ma; she has a great man for a husband. Before they walked out of the shop he said, "Thank you father. I'm so glad I can say that", and he gently put his arm around the man. Mac was touched, he thought; I am blessed to have two special sons and a sweet daughter. He clasped his arm around Tim, "My pleasure son." It was a moment both would always remember. "Well now", Mac said. "Don't forget Friday night, we're taking the whole family out for dinner to celebrate your upcoming marriage."

"It's a celebration, a time for the family to remember our love for each other, and for Emily. She's a lovely person, Tim, and I know you two will be happy together. She needs someone special to love her, and I think you're the man to do it."

Later, Tim remembered his father's words; he realized he'd come to love this man who loved his mother so much. The love was always there when one saw them together. "Lord, help me to be the kind of husband and father that he is", and that's exactly what he became. Kathleen's husband was a special man, and all the family knew it.

The night before the wedding, the whole family gathered at Kathleen and Mac's favorite and special restaurant. The one they themselves had gone to many years before. The whole evening was pleasant, with lots of companionability and laughter. Emily felt their love, and was so blessed to be marrying Tim, and to belong to this extraordinary family.

The bride was lovely, as all brides are, but Emily, as far as Tim was concerned, was gorgeous. Kathleen had outdone herself; because the simple lines graced Emily's Lovely body and fair skin. Tim could not take his eyes off his bride, Emily felt like a princess marrying her prince.

Kathleen watched her two sons, Michael who was marrying his brother, and Tim. Both of them were kind, gentle men; so unlike their father. She was so proud of her family, how God had blessed her. When the bride and groom were pronounced man and wife, everyone clapped. She hadn't heard that since the day she was married, now so many years ago.

There was a small reception at Eve's house, she loved doing this for Tim and his new wife. What a change he had gone through, she thought as she remembered his rebellious ways from long ago. She hugged them both, and wished them great happiness. Then Tim took his bride home.

Molly was fortunate to get a job working at the newspaper in town; she did whatever was needed. The paper was started several years before, and though it was small, it did keep the residents informed about the happenings in Silver City. Her job was to do whatever the owner asked of her. Sometimes she sorted type, or cleaned the small press, which was always a dirty job.

She was learning to put the small type together to make words, which was difficult at first, but she'd learned to read upside down, backwards. So when the type was put together and printed, it could be read. Often she worked in the front, working on the books, ads, or helping people who came in for numerous reasons. She liked her job because of the variant work; the smell of ink was something she especially loved.

The job was special, but it meant she must move to town. Luckily she was able to get a room in a boarding house. A number of people had a room there, and they were served two meals a day; breakfast was at seven each morning, and supper was at six o'clock sharp in the evenings. The young woman missed her mother, father, and the ranch, but she liked being on her own; she felt safe because her two brothers and their wives lived in town also.

One day Molly was alone, working on some bookwork, when a very tall, blond and good looking man came into the shop; trying to get some information. He spoke with a strong southern accent. "Good morning, I was wondering if you might be able to help me. I have been all over this part of the west for the last year, trying to find an uncle of mine. We heard he had been killed, and I came to find out where and perhaps why. I've had conflicting stories told to me, and because I have not found anyone who saw him killed or heard about his death, I'm still looking."

"It's urgent I find him, if he's still alive. The last town I was in, my uncle had worked there for three years in a newspaper office. I'm afraid that if I can't find him here, I must return home; my mother is ill."

"I thought perhaps he might be working here, his name is Randolph Bascom. Does he, indeed, work here?" "I'm sorry sir, there's no one here by that name, nor have I ever heard the name before." Molly answered. The young man looked discouraged. "Because of my mother's illness, I cannot look much further."

Molly suggested he go to the county courthouse. At first he didn't hear her; he was thinking what a beauty she was with that red hair piled on top of her head, and those green eyes. He'd never seen more beautiful eyes. He said, "I'm sorry what did you say?" She repeated, suggesting he might look at the county courthouse. "If he has ever owned land here, or a claim, they could tell you." She stepped out the door, pointing to a building down the street.

"Thank you", he said, and he walked away toward the building she had directed him to, hoping he might get some information.

Molly forgot all about him, and when lunchtime came, she gathered the papers she was working on, picked up her bag, and went to a lunchroom, down the street. After getting her coffee and sandwich, she got lost in her work; only taking a bite of her lunch now and then. "Well hello", she heard, and looked up to see the young man who had been in the paper earlier in the day. "I hate to disturb you, but this chair, at your table seems to be the only one that's not filled. May I join you? I will be quiet so you can work uninterrupted." "Of course, please sit down Mr. Bascom, this isn't that important, I can do it later."

"My name is Christopher, but everyone calls me Chris." Then, after he ordered, she asked him, "Did you find out anything about your uncle?" "No, I'm afraid not, nothing at all. I guess I will have to go home without knowing what happened to him." She was silent a minute; not sure what to say. "I'm sorry your accent makes me think you're from the south, you've come a long way for nothing; that's a shame." "Yes, well I guess I've done all I can do, my coming west had something to do with a will my father left when he died. I will have to go home and say my uncle must have died, because there has been no recent sign of him; nor can I find any information about him."

"Where in the south do you come from?" Molly asked. "I live in South Carolina, not too far from the Atlantic Ocean." "I've never been near an ocean, or even a big lake; what's it like? The ocean I mean." Molly asked. Before he could answer, his lunch arrived. Once the waitress poured his coffee and left, he tried to explain what an ocean was like.

"Well, the thing I remember most is the sound of the waves as they break, and then the water runs up onto the sand. There's nothing like it, on calm days, it is so peaceful; when you hear the waves." "They break?" She asked. "Well the water rises up before it gets to the shore, and the momentum causes it to tumble over, sending the wave up onto the sand where it plays out, and then runs back to meet the next wave.

The sounds of the ocean are very peaceful on clear days, between the water, sand, and sea gulls. Sea gulls are a rather large bird, which continuously hover over the water, seeking small fish or crabs to eat. Their calls are part of the beauty of the ocean, along with the smell of salt in the air. There is nothing as beautiful or peaceful as watching the waves in motion all of the time. On winter, or stormy days, the water becomes almost fierce, and the waves are often much higher and swifter."

"The south is full of a myriad of different smells from the swamps to the many fragrant flowering trees, vines and bushes. We have a tree called the Magnolia tree that is covered with large fragrant blossoms in the spring and summer. The Honeysuckle grows wild, and then there is the Jasmine flower, probably the sweetest of all. It's also very green in the south, totally different from the west. I miss my home, its lovely; like you." Molly didn't catch what he said at first, when she did she blushed. "Oh, I'm sorry, I didn't mean to embarrass you, but you are very beautiful."

Just then the waitress came and refilled Molly's cup, Molly was at a loss for words; no one had ever said anything like that to her before. "Thank you, that's very nice of you to say that." What else could she say? She picked up her cup of coffee and took a sip. Chris was totally entranced with the young woman. After putting down her cup she said, "The south sounds quite charming; so different from here. My parents live north of town, and it's a very pretty area, but nothing like the south. I love living here; the air is fresh from all the different evergreen trees in the area. I've spent most of my life here in Silver City; we came here from Ohio when I was a child. Molly got the conversation away from herself; they talked, eating, and drinking their coffee.

Molly looked at her watch, "Oh my, I'm late getting back to work; I'm sorry I have to go, but it was good talking with you." She grabbed her papers and bag, and thrust out her hand, "It was good listening to you talk about the south. Goodbye." Then she hurried to pay for her lunch, and dashed up the street to the newspaper office.

It was Wednesday, and her day was filled with work, when the publisher owner came into the front to lock the door, and he saw Molly still working. "You're still here Molly? Its six-thirty, time to go home; tomorrow is another day!" She grabbed her bag, "Goodnight Mr. Pepperdine." After she was out the door, she heard the door being locked. Molly knew she had missed dinner; it was always served at six p.m. sharp. The young woman thought, maybe John hasn't closed the store yet, perhaps I could get a piece of cheese and an apple to eat; she felt hungry. When Molly got to the store, it was closed; "Oh pooh", she said out loud.

She turned to go to her room, when she heard a familiar voice. "Is something wrong, can I help?" She looked up to see the young man, Chris Bascom, standing there. "Time got away from me, I didn't realize how late it was, and I guess I missed my dinner, again!" The young man told her, "That's easy, let me take you to dinner. I get lonesome being by myself so far from home. It would be a great pleasure for me to take you out to eat." She started to say, "That's alright, I think - but his wonderful smile and courteousness captured her. "Thank you, Mr. Bascom; I would be pleased to have dinner with you." "Please, call me Chris", he said.

He took her to her parent's favorite restaurant; the one they had taken her to many times. When they walked in, the waiter she knew said, "Hi Molly, can I get you a table?" "Hello Harry, this is Mr. Bascom. I'm sorry", and she looked at the young gentleman; "This is my friend Chris." "Nice to meet you", the young man said as he shook Chris' hand, "This way please."

After they ordered their meal, they sat talking; it wasn't long before people heard laughter coming from their table. They both felt like they had known each other forever. Chris had become lonesome on his long search for his uncle; for him, the time spent with Molly was especially wonderful. The two took their time eating, enjoying each others company. They had little in common, but that seemed unimportant. Inside, they were much the same, that's all that mattered. The two enjoyed eating their pie, and drinking their coffee as they visited; neither one wanting the evening to end.

When Molly went to bed that night, she could not sleep. She tossed and turned, trying not to think about Chris; she tried thinking of other things, but the soft spoken southern gentleman stayed in her thoughts. She'd never enjoyed herself more than the time spent with Chris.

The next day the young man stopped in the shop, asking if she would like to go out for dinner again that evening. Thinking that he probably would be leaving before long, made her feel sad; she thought that it would be better if she didn't get to know him too well. The trouble was she already liked him too much. Molly agreed to go, against her better judgment.

A week went by, and they spent all her free time together; though she did go to church without him. By that time, she knew she loved him, not really sure how that happened. Then, to think he would be leaving, turned her stomach into knots. What will I do when he goes, she asked herself; and found no answer.

He came as usual, asking if she would like to go to a different restaurant, "I'll be leaving in a few more days, and I really would like to spend those evenings with you." Even though she knew it would be better not to continue this friendship, she knew she already had strong feelings toward him, and agreed to go anyway.

The following evening, she told him, "Chris, I don't think we should see each other again. You're leaving soon, and it will already be hard to see you go." His face paled. "Molly, please, it's already too late; I can't get you out of my mind, nor my heart. I'm afraid I've fallen in love with you; I simply can't go and leave you behind. Darling Molly, I want to marry you, and take you home with me."

Not caring if anyone saw them, he came around her desk, pulled her up and kissed her. She just, sort of melted into his arms, "Please, my beautiful Molly, tell me you love me too. I know you do; I've seen it in your eyes." The young woman knew she loved him. She shouldn't have let this happen she thought, but she knew she loved him too much to turn away.

Molly tried to think calmly, but he kissed her again; she put her arms around his shoulders, and kissed him back. "Chris, I love you too. Oh, how could I have allowed this to happen, your home is so far away from my family. How can I leave them?" She thought, how can I let him go without me?

He stayed two more weeks, though he knew he shouldn't have, she still didn't take him to church, not wanting to face her family; she was in a quandary. What to do?

After dinner one night as they were walking home, he stopped and took her into his arms and kissed her. Then he asked her, "Molly, I know how fast this has gone, but I have fallen in love with you. Will you marry me darling?" She started to protest, but he gently put his hand over her mouth. "Molly, I have to go, I cannot stay any longer, and I can not leave you behind, either. Please darling, hear me out. I love you, and I know you love me too, there's nothing we can do to stop our love. Please Molly, I beg of you, marry me. I will always take good care of you, I promise. I've told you a little about what my home is like, I must now tell you the rest."

"I grew up on a very large plantation. My father died two years ago, and now my mother is very ill. My uncle is gone, so she needs me to handle the men that work in the cotton fields, as well as all the other people that work for us. Now I must go home, and tell her my uncle seems to be gone. I cannot find him, so I must leave. Telling my mother her brother is, indeed gone will hurt her a great deal, they were very close. He was a wanderer at heart, and I'm afraid this will really undo her; I'm afraid for her. I will hate to tell her; she had such hopes he might be alive. He was to inherit the plantation, but if he was not alive, it would go to me, so you see Molly, I must go home."

She listened and then said, "Alright Chris, I will marry you; I will never be able to marry anyone else, it's you I love." He held her tightly in his arms. "Darling, I'm so happy, then they kissed; she knew she would go anywhere with him.

"Molly, I need to get permission from your parents to marry you," She nodded, "Yes, I know Chris, I only hope they will agree, and let us marry." "We will have to make them agree!" She had to laugh at that, "I don't think you can make any Irishman say yes, unless he wants to, but we can try." "Sweetheart, I have legal papers with me, proving that I have come from the south, and I live on a plantation; where it is, and how big it is. At least, that might help to convince your family. I've always been a Christian, maybe we should pray about this, asking God to help us when we speak to them", and so they did pray, asking for His help.

When he left Molly, she was both excited and fearful to leave her home, and loved ones; to move so far away from all she knew, but there was no doubt in her mind this was what she wanted. She loved this gentle, soft spoken southern gentleman.

The next day was Saturday, and Molly did not have to work, so Chris rented a buggy, and they went out to the ranch; Molly praying all the way. Chris was entranced with the western beauty he saw in the area; he could fully understand her hesitance about leaving home.

Kathleen was caught unawares, "You want to do what!" Chris knew he was facing a formidable woman, "Lord, help me"; he breathed as he said again, "I love your daughter, and I want to marry her, we love one another." Molly nodded, chickening out after seeing her mother's reaction, but Chris persevered. "We need to get your consent; we wouldn't want to marry without your approval." Her mother said, "You two sit down, and don't move. We need your father here Molly", and she hurried out to find Aaron. She was distraught, to say the least.

"Aaron, he wants to marry Molly, and take her to South Carolina. I don't even know who he is!"

"Calm down sweetheart, let's go in and get all of this straightened out."

"You say you want to marry our daughter? How long have you known each other?" Mac asked. "Almost four weeks sir, but we love each other; time doesn't count, what matters is we love each other. Molly is a wonderful young woman, and I have never met anyone like her before. She's the one I've always dreamed of."

"I know this is sudden, but we don't have time to court each other, like most do.

My mother is ill, and I have to go home; I simply cannot go without her, I love her too much."

Mac was at a loss for words. Finally he spoke to Chris saying, "We know nothing about you, nothing at all. How can we let our daughter go off with you? You are a stranger to us." Chris pulled out a few papers from a leather packet, as he told them about his uncle; the plantation, his ill mother, and his role in this strange story. He handed the papers, one by one to Mac. "The plantation hires over two hundred people to work, they are freed slaves, and we pay them an honest wage; enough for them to live comfortably. My father fought in the Civil War for the north, he did not believe in slavery. We treat all our workers with respect. Our family has a great deal of money, but we no not spend it unwisely."

"Now, because I could find no trace of my uncle after a year of searching here in the southwestern part of New Mexico; and because my mother has become ill, and cannot run the place anymore, I must go home, and take over the responsibilities of our land. I must leave, but I cannot leave without Molly, I love her; she's a wonderful young woman. The most important thing is she's a Christian, and so am I. We love one another. I promise I will always love her, and take good care of her." Chris said all of this while holding Molly's hand.

Mac read the papers, and then looked at his wife. "What he says is true Kathleen." She was stunned! She never dreamed her daughter would live apart from them. "Oh please ma, it's true; I do love him, and I can't let him go without me." Then Molly began to tear up.

What could she do? Kathleen did not want to lose her daughter, but Molly had the right to leave and be loved like she did. She looked at Aaron, and knew he was thinking the same thing. After a couple of minutes, she said, "Molly, I understand, truly I do. I know what it's like to love someone", and she took Aarons hand, she needed his strength. "I wish you didn't have to go away, but how can I say no; you two love each other, it's obvious."

"Molly dear would you two allow your brother to marry you? We don't want you leaving without getting married." Molly nodded, and Chris said, "Yes ma'am, I understand he is a minister; it would be an honor to be married by him."

Molly rushed into her mother's arms, "Thank you mother, I love you so much. I don't want to leave you, but I must go with Christopher. I love him with all my heart."

The two held each other, and then Kathleen straightened up, "Well, we have things to do; first come with me, Molly. She turned to the two men, "We will be right back", and she walked Molly into her bedroom. She opened up her hope chest that Aaron had made for her years before.

The mother reached in, and gently took out her lavender wedding gown. "Molly, let's see if this will fit you, it should; we're pretty much the same size. I have kept it clean all these years; this should work." "Oh mother, I had forgotten how beautiful it is, you mean I can get married in your dress?" "Yes dear, it's yours now." The dress fit perfectly, so they folded it carefully, and went out to join their men. "Well gentlemen, let's go search for our son, and brother. We need to have a marriage."

Kathleen refused to cry for her daughter's sake. That might come later, but for now, the time must be joyous for her one and only daughter, as she marries. Mac and Kathleen followed Molly and Christopher into town, she holding on to the dress, and her mother's wedding ring tucked away to give to Chris when they got to Michael and Penny's house.

"I hope Michael's home Aaron." "Don't worry sweetheart, we can find him if he isn't." Her Aaron was always so encouraging.

Fortunately, their son was home; he'd just come in. When he heard what was happening, he hugged Molly, introduced himself, and shook hands with Chris. "Could the three of us talk awhile?" He asked. I would like a chance to know this man of yours, Molly." The two agreed, so he took them into the small study.

Michael asked Chris about his background, and about his faith. After talking awhile, he suggested they pray. He talked to his loving savior and father, asking for His love and protection over his sister, and his soon to be brother-in-law. Chris was deeply touched by Molly's brother; a gentle man of God. He would always remember him, and try to emulate this gentle man.

Penny had sent their oldest son to get his Uncle Tim, and Emily; so they all could be at the wedding. Kathleen gave her mother's wedding ring to Chris, explaining the significance of the ring. "With this comes an Irish blessing upon your marriage", she said. For the first time, he saw into the heart of his sweet Molly's mother.

Molly was lovely; her beautiful red hair intensified the color of the dress. Penny had a rose bush outside, and there was one white rose left on it, that Molly held, her fingers protected from the thorns by a white ribbon that Penny wrapped around the stem.

After the simple wedding, Mac took the whole family out to eat, giving them all a chance to get to learn a little about Molly's new husband. Their time together went by way too quickly. Chris couldn't take his eyes off his new bride. It wasn't long after they had finished dinner, when he shook all the men's hands, and gave a bow to the women before they left.

The family was quiet for a few minutes, feeling their loss, then Michael assured his mother, "He's a good man, I could tell he loves God and Molly. You will have to trust the Lord, ma; Molly will be fine."

Love Comes in Many Colors

But they all knew how much she would be missed, especially by her mother.

The following day, the newlyweds went to church. Chris was so impressed with Molly's family, everyone was so kind; even people he didn't know who were friends. He especially loved Molly's mother, and he really liked her father, and brother Michael. Chris made up his mind they would always keep in touch.

When they stepped onto the train on Monday, the whole family was there to say goodbye, except those who were working, but their wives were on hand. After the train pulled away, Kathleen began quietly weeping; her baby was gone. How could this have happened? But, she knew, she would have gone with Aaron anywhere he asked, but that thought did not take away the lonesome feeling as Molly left. She would always miss her only daughter.

That night, the parents prayed for Molly and Christopher; that they would be safe and happy. What else could they do?

Chapter 18

Timothy and Emily had twins, making their house full because Ida, their big sister was still there. The twins were not identical; the boy looking much like Tim's father, Paddy; with many of his grandfather's mannerisms. He definitely liked to be noticed. His parents named him Timothy Patrick, and he showed his Irish heritage. Julia Mary, his sister, was more demur; resembling her mother, and the mother's quiet ways. Their big sister was growing up, and the time of fear in her life was over. It was good to see both the mother and daughter doing well.

The parents took great care in raising the twins; Julia gave them few problems, but Tim spent time trying to direct his son in a different way; encouraging him when he was good, and teaching him he was one of many, rather than allowing the boy to become self-centered. Tim remembered how spoiled he was as a child, and suspected his father was too. The parents never putting one child above another, worked hard to raise them right.

Michael and Penny had three children, starting their family after they moved to Silver City. The oldest, young Michael, who eventually was called Mike, grew up to be much like his father, and grandfather Mac. Aaron was the second son, who was called Ron; he was more introspective. He was much quieter than his older brother, and became a lover of books and writing. He expressed himself well, with words both in writing and speech. Later in life, people would enjoy his books, for they would be filled with the ways of man; thoughtful and rich.

Their daughter, Kathleen; who wanted to be called Kate, was a free spirited child. She was difficult to raise, no matter what her mother or father said or did. She had a rebellious streak from her earliest years, making it hard for her parents. Many prayers were said, night after night, and year after year on her behalf. Michael always tried to teach her the ways of love, God's love, as did her mother; but she always turned away from their efforts. Nothing they said or did made much difference; Kate was Kate. As she grew older, into her middle teens, she had a lovely singing voice, taking after both of her grandfathers. She sang in school programs, and around the house, but never to God.

Kate grew up in the church, but when she reached sixteen, she stopped going; never giving God much thought. When she turned eighteen, she met a handsome man who was passing through town; a roaming man. She was singing in one of the saloons, though her parents did not know she was there. Her mother could smell cigar smoke on her clothes, and mentioned it, but Kate yelled at her mother, telling her it was none of her business. Penny told Michael, but it only worried him, for their daughter was uncontrollable.

The man's name was Ross Kilkenny, and he had a strong Irish brogue. He knew how to flatter a young woman, and he told Kate she had a beautiful voice, and she could make a great deal of money singing in New York City. Because he was so good looking, she fell for his flattery. It filled her mind with all kinds of unreal dreams that had to do with her looks and voice. She did not share these thoughts with her parents, and one day she took her things, put them in a bag, and climbed out her window. No note to tell them she was leaving.

It happened that one of Michael's friends saw Kate and the man boarding the train. She was gone. There was nothing they could do about it but put her into God's hands. Their daughter was young and vulnerable; her parent's hearts were full of sorrow.

The Green's watched Abby as she grew into a young woman. They had two other children, a boy and a girl. Growing up, Abby was always popular with her peers, and by the time she was eighteen, she stood four foot, eleven inches high in her bare feet.

A darling young woman, who was quick in thought, and humor, plus always fun to be with; she had many friends, but she was never interested in boys. Her love was saved for Miles. Their relationship had always been close, and she'd always loved him from the time she was small. That's just the way it was, she did not seem to know the extent of her love for him, nor did he.

The realization of that love did not come full circle until he was hurt at work one day. Miles worked for one of the stores in town, and that day, when he was standing high up on a rickety ladder, the step broke, and he went hurtling down onto a wooden box. The doctor said he had broken the bone in the calf of his leg; with the bone piercing through the skin. It was a severe injury, and very painful. A splint was put on the leg, and he would have to stay off the leg for at least six seeks, if not more.

When Abby heard about the injury, she was there to help him. Even though her mother took care of him, Abby was there, undaunted by the fact she really wasn't needed. She felt she could at least help, her Miles. Their relationship grew and changed for Abby. For Miles, he'd always loved her, from babyhood; with Abby being there, Miles love for her increased and changed. For her, it was a surprise when she realized how much she loved him; far more than a friend.

One day, when she went into his room, he held out his hand, and she took it, and all the love for him from childhood came full circle. She knew he was the only man she would ever love. She began spending more and more time with him, and one day he told her how much she meant to him. "I think I have loved you, Abby, since you were that darling little baby, and to me you are still a darling. Will you marry me Abby? I will never find anyone else to love; I know I'm older than you, but that doesn't stop my love for you."

Her eyes teared up, yet a smile crossed her face and she said, "Oh yes, Miles; I want to be yours always." As soon as he could walk, they stood in front of Michael as he pronounced them man and wife. The young man, a few years older than his new wife, could finally hold her in his arms. She was so short, that he picked her up in his arms, and kissed her.

It would be a lifetime of love for both of them, though they would have their disagreements at times, they never stopped loving one another. What strange turn's life takes.

Kathleen's birthday was coming up, and Mac came home after doing some necessary shopping. He put everything down he had, and that old familiar look showed on his face. It told his wife, he'd been into some kind of mischief. She knew from experience, asking would not work. She thought; I might have to wait until he reveals his secret, but she couldn't resist asking anyway. "So now, Mr. McGinnis, what kind of trouble have you been up to today?" He grinned, and held up two small pieces of paper. You'll have to guess, me beauty!" "How can I guess? Well, let's see now, you needed paper, so you brought two pieces home! No? Well, your fingers got caught in a candy jar, and two pieces of paper stuck to them."

He shook his head again, with that same look, "You're going to whip me with those two small pieces of paper." He shook his head with that look in his eyes. "Oh Aaron! Stop teasing me, you rascal", she said. So he came over and handed the papers to his wife. She looked at them, startled. "Train tickets? What ever for? And don't you dare say guess!"

He put his finger under the destination on the ticket. "Charleston, South Carolina?" Her eyes got big, and she looked at her husband. "Molly! We're going to see Molly!" "Yes Ma'am, we leave next Wednesday. You have one week to get ready."

"Aaron, we're going to see Molly!" She got so excited; she hugged him, and kissed, and kissed, and kissed him. He finally came up for air, "Hey, I gotta breathe!" And they both started to laugh.

Kathleen loved watching the green countryside they rode by. "It's so beautiful Aaron, sort of graceful like; what a lovely place for Molly to live. I can hardly wait to see her, Chris and the children. It seems so long since she left home; almost ten years now."

He watched his wife with such affection. I'm so glad I thought of this, he thought. "Happy birthday Kathleen" and she turned and squeezed his hand. "Thank you Aaron, this is the best birthday present I could ever have!" He bent over and kissed her forehead, and then her eyes showed him how much she loved him.

When they stepped down from the train, Molly came rushing up to them, with Chris right behind. She was beautifully dressed, a lovely southern lady. "Ma, you're here! You're still so beautiful, I'm so glad you've come." Molly put her arms around her mother, not wanting to let go. "I've missed you so much." Kathleen hugged her daughter, so glad to finally get to see her. Chris took hold of Mac's hand.

"We're very glad you've come to visit, Molly's been so excited. Welcome to the south."

Then Molly turned to the father she knew best. She gave him a hug, saying "Thank you for coming, and bringing ma to see us. I missed you both so much." To Mac it felt good to see Molly. "We've missed you too honey, you look wonderful."

"Come", she said, grabbing both of their hands; Stan and Chris will bring your luggage, and she took them to a very fancy carriage. The black man put the luggage in the back of the carriage, and then climbed onto the front seat. With a slight flick of the reigns, they were on their way.

The countryside was lovely; along the road were large Magnolia trees in bloom. The fields were very green, with many flowers, and vines growing everywhere. Kathleen mentioned how lovely the countryside was and the large blooms on the trees. Molly told her ma, "Those trees are called Magnolia trees; we have a lot of them on our property. Wail until you see where we live, the land is so beautiful; with flowers everywhere."

Kathleen said, "You are more beautiful than ever Molly, this place is good for you." When Kathleen and Mac saw the very large southern mansion, they were truly astonished. They'd had no idea the luxury Molly lived in! "Your house is beautiful", Kathleen said. "I don't think I've ever seen a lovelier place. Her eyes were busy looking everywhere; the grounds were as lovely as the house.

Chris pointed out the smaller houses off a ways from the house. "That's where all our workers and their families live. Each house was painted white, with white fences; all covered with flowering vines. "There's a wonderful fragrance in the air", Kathleen mentioned. Molly informed her mother, "Part of the odors you smell is from the Jasmine plant. They grow all through the area, and there's Honeysuckle vines that grow wild, everywhere.

As they stepped down from the carriage, there were several black women standing, waiting to greet the guests. Molly introduced them all to her parents, the last woman, Pearl, she told her mother was her right hand, and very sweet. "Pearl, this is my mother, and father; Kathleen and Aaron McGinnis." The woman said, "Yes Ma'am, I'm glad to meet y'all. This here girl, is someone special, she is. We all love her."

Kathleen knew about Pearl from Molly's letters. "Thank you Pearl, for taking such good care of our daughter, and grandchildren, it's a real pleasure to meet you," Pearl smiled, "Thank you ma'am." "They all help to keep this large home going", Molly said, and she smiled at all of them.

Once they were in the house, Chris asked Missy to see their guests bags were taken to their rooms. "Yes'suh" And she took the man that was carrying the bags up the stairs. As they went into a very large and beautiful Parlor, Chris said, "Please sit down, you must be tired and thirsty." Molly asked one of the women to please bring some cool lemonade. The young woman was very pretty, and she curtsied before she left. It was no time before she was back with a tray of drinks, and small cakes.

Both Kathleen and Mac looked around the room. It was very grand, with high ceilings, large draped windows, and extremely beautiful furniture. They visited for awhile, all feeling how good it was to see each other. Then Molly said, "Would you like to go to your rooms and rest awhile? I know how tired one can get traveling by train. When the children get home from school, we will let you know; they are very anxious to meet you."

Kathleen admitted she was tired, and it was so warm, she felt sticky from the humidity. Mac wanted to stretch his legs out, clean up, and put clean clothes on. When they were taken upstairs, they found a sitting room and bedroom. Kathleen and Mac had never seen such luxury before, everything was beautiful! After cleaning up, they both laid down awhile, each tired from sitting for so many days.

By the time the children were home from school, they felt refreshed. Christopher was a perfect host, seeing to their every need. When Kathleen saw the children, she was astounded to see her granddaughter looked very much like her own mother. "I'm so glad to meet you, how old are you Janet?" The girl smiled, and said, "I'm seven years old." "My, you're a very grown up young lady." Then Molly introduced young Christopher Jr., who was nine, to her parents.

Mac remarked to the young Chris, "You're quite the young man, and he shook hands with the boy. Their father said, "Let's sit down, why don't you two play a duet on the piano for your grandparents?" The boy didn't appear that he wanted to play, but his sister did, so he gave in and sat down beside her. They played a lovely piece by Mozart, they were quite accomplished. "My, you two play beautifully", their grandmother said. I've never watched anyone your age play before, thank you for playing; that was very kind of you." Somehow, the boy felt good, after all.

After a light supper, everyone went outside, and walked around. The sun was down, and the twilight was much cooler and much more comfortable. A large white long haired dog followed the children, often chasing after a stick one of the children tossed. They all spent time looking out across the cotton fields, they seemed to reach into the far distance.

They walked to the edge of a forested area; the trees were huge, with moss draping from the branches. The first time either Kathleen or Mac had seen such sights. While Mac was fighting in the War Between the States, he had heard of these . . . . forests.

After wandering around smelling all the different smells; from swamps in the distance, to the fragrant flowers everywhere, they went and sat on the large veranda. While they were sipping cool tea, Chris said, "Tomorrow we will go see the horses, I know you both ride, so if you would like to, we will go for a ride around the place. We want you to really enjoy yourselves.

As they were riding, it was obvious what a busy place the plantation was. There were many men working in the fields; keeping the weeds down, everything was well cared for. Kathleen loved riding through the countryside, she thought; what a lovely place for Molly and our grandchildren to live. Once they got back, and were relaxing with the usual cool drink Mac said, "I don't think I've ever seen such a large piece of ground planted before. How many people does it take to keep a place like this going?" Chris's reply was, "We have close to two hundred and fifty men, women, and children living here."

"It's a pretty big endeavor, getting everything done; it keeps me busy though. I do have a foreman, John Taylor, who works with the men; there is a lot more to growing cotton than meets the eye. We have had some really good years, for sometime now, though there's been years when drought took most of the crop; it balances out somehow."

"There are those who are in charge of the vegetable gardens; it takes a lot of food to feed this many people. We also have those who raise cattle and sheep for food. We have a teacher on the premises, teaching the children, which is rare in this part of the county."

"During the growing and harvesting seasons, the men have to work long hours, but after the fall plowing, things pretty much settle down, and that's when they do all the repairing, painting, and cleaning up. Well, that's enough about business, how is Silver City doing these days? It was a nice town; a bit noisy, but I loved the area. That's where I found Molly, who is so special to me."

Mac told him, "The mines have slowed down, with less and less silver ore being brought out of them, that's helped to eliminate a lot of gamblers and thieves; many men have moved on. The Indians are long gone too; all of this has quieted the town. We love the area, though I must admit, it's nothing like here."

The men continued talking, so the women excused themselves, and went into Molly's sitting room. There the two could spend precious time together. "Molly, are you happy dear?" Her mother asked. "As happy as you thought you would be? I know you've written so, but I have to ask." "Oh yes ma, maybe even more so. Chris is so good to me and the children, he is a very gentle, and kind man; a true southern gentleman. I still love him as I did when we were married; we get along wonderfully."

"He had a difficult time when his mother died, she was a good woman, and they were close. It was hard for him to accept she was gone, but he never turned away from me; rather he drew closer. I'm truly happy ma. I was pretty shy when I first got here, but everyone was so kind to me; I quickly got over it. Chris's mother and Pearl welcomed me with open arms."

"I am so glad you let us marry ma, I do miss you, father, and the family, but this is where I'm meant to be." Her mother felt relieved. She'd always gotten letters saying things were well, but still it was good to see them together, and know the happiness she could see on her daughters face."

They talked about Michael, Penny, and their family; they also talked about Tim's marriage to Emily and their two children and Ida. "That's the thing I miss most, all of you", her daughter said.

One Sunday, they all road into Charleston to go to church; it was a small white church. The minister was an older man, and he was a very different kind of speaker than the ministers in Silver City; getting a bit more excited as he talked, but Kathleen was glad Molly and Chris took their children to church.

After church, Chris took them to a very fancy restaurant. They had a Southern Fried Chicken dinner; the meal was excellent. After their meal, they rode around the city, in their fancy carriage. "Much of the city was destroyed during the Civil War; most of the plantations were also burned, but we were fortunate that our place was not touched. My grandfather was an Abolitionist, and of course, he fought with the Union Army." Chris informed his guests, "Because of my grandfather, our home was saved."

Mac told the young man that he and his friend also fought for the Union Army. "That was a terrible war, so many lost their lives. "I really have put my time fighting out of my mind; at least most of the time. Chris, I hope you never have to fight, and kill men; it's something one never gets over."

After they were back at the house, Chris went to check on something that had happened during the afternoon, and Kathleen and Molly were off looking through the house. Mac lay down, resting; remembering the war, not something he did these days. The nightmares were gone, but he did still remember the sight of a field full of bodies after a battle. The man turned to prayer, not wanting to remember those days anymore.

Several days before Kathleen and Mac were to leave; Chris and Molly took them to the ocean. They let the two explore the ocean alone, sitting on a sand dune, watching the two walk the area.

The westerners stood, watching the water as it swept up onto the shore, and then rushed back to meet another wave. Neither one had felt such peace before; well, maybe during a special sunset at home, but that was always gone too soon. The smells of the sea captivated the couple. They walked on the sand with their shoes off; a wave would encroach upon their feet, often bringing with it shells or small creatures; perhaps a crab or two. It was the most exhilarating thing they had ever experienced.

Their daughter and son-in-law enjoyed watching the two; Molly wanted them to feel the peace that comes when one first explores the ocean. That day, the sea gulls were very active, seeking food from both the water and sand.

Kathleen and Mac were having a great time, often laughing when the water would hurry after them. It wasn't long before Mac became playful, splashing the water towards his wife; she squealing and lifting up her long dress so it wouldn't get wet. Soon they were laughing, something that was always a part of their life. Neither one wanted to leave; they listened to the roar of the waves, and watched as other birds ran across the sand. They gathered sea shells, having such fun. The afternoon was a wonderful experience; they would never forget the sound of the waves as they rushed onto the shore.

Once back in Silver City, Mac was so glad he had decided they should go to see Molly. He was happy Kathleen was able to see her daughter Molly, Chris, and the grandchildren. He'd loved every minute of their time there. Although Kathleen would always miss her daughter, she would know she was happy, living with her husband and children in that lovely land.

One year Molly, Chris and their children came to visit, the children were older, but seemed happy. Molly was a handsome woman. The whole family spent time with the Bascom's; all making them feel welcome.

Three years after Michael's parents came back from the south, he and Penny received a letter from their daughter, Kate. The letter was so sad, all the dreams she had when she left Silver City, had not come true. Yes, she did sing in New Your City, but she only sang in bars. Ross stayed with her for awhile, but when she didn't make much money, he got tired of her, and moved on. She had a daughter within a few months after he was gone, who is now eight years old.

"Susan is a pretty girl, and there are a lot of bad men here. She's so pretty, and men look at her in the wrong way, I'm really afraid to raise her here", Kate wrote. Then she asked, "Papa, can we come home? I know I'm not worthy of your love, but I have nowhere else to turn. I don't even have the money to come home, and I hate to ask for help, but I'm so worried about my daughter. Papa, please forgive me from turning away from you and mama, I should have listened to you; you were right, God is the only one we can really trust. I miss you so much, please, may we come home?"

Both Michael and Penny had tears in their eyes; they both loved her, and wanted her and their granddaughter home and safe.

Michael wrote to Kate, he took some money out of the bank, and put it in the envelope with the note:

"Dearest Kate, We have prayed for you every night since you left. There's nothing to forgive, we did that years ago. It was so painful when you left, because we were very worried about you. We love you sweetheart; you must know that in your heart. Your mama and I have missed you terribly, as have your brothers. I'm enclosing enough money for your trip, and any expenses for food or whatever else you need. Come home sweetheart.

Send us a telegram, telling us when to meet you, the train no longer comes to Silver City since the mines have nearly played out, but it does go through Deming. We will be there to meet you. Know we have always loved you, and now our granddaughter. Papa.

It was a long trip traveling on the bumpy dirt road to Deming. They had one extra tire with them, a good thing too, because one of the tires went flat after going over a sharp rock. They owned a model T-Ford, but this was the first time they'd traveled far.

Funny thing, on the way down to Deming, Michael had to smile to himself about those lizards climbing up on their sticks to keep their feet from frying. He hadn't thought of Scotty for years.

The reunion was touching to those who saw the woman and her child step off the train, and see the woman rush into her parent's arms. When Michael let go of his daughter, he took off his glasses, and wiped them, and his eyes. Then he turned to Suzie with a grandfather's love. She was a bit shy, but that did not stop him from bowing and kissing the princess's hand as he called her. Suzie liked him right away, he looked so kind. He looked much like she imagined he would, but there were silver hairs mixed among the dark ones. While her mama was in her mother's arms, Michael and Suzie became friends.

Kate went back into her father's arms, "Oh papa, I've missed you and mama so much; I love both of you." "Me too, sweetheart, always", her father replied. He noticed the lines on her face, Molly had lost some of her beauty, but he would never mention it to his daughter. When he turned and looked for Penny, she was kneeling down, holding her granddaughter in her arms.

That night, after their two loved ones were in bed, they talked, "Michael, she looks so much older than she should. She's had a terrible life I think; she's changed, and lost much of her beauty", her mother said. "I know she's had so much sorrow; we mustn't bring it up unless she does. We can just be grateful she's home", Michael said.

It took Kate a few years working before a good man fell in love with her, and they were married; the hard years were gone.

Pete and Maria's son, Peter Jr., grew to be a handsome young man; he had his father's good looks, and his mother's darker skin, all the girls chased after him. Peter sewed a few wild oats, but in time, after his parent's were gone, he accepted his parent's faith. He then came back to the ranch, bringing with him a sweet young bride. He grew in his faith, and loved his family. His two sisters both married; one moving to California, and the other staying in Silver City.

Kathleen and Mac grew older, always loving one another, and their family. The years took its toll on Kathleen, with the lines in her face, growing deeper, and she began to weaken. Mac was always by her side, helping her and loving her. The day she died, Mac seemed to loose his fire for life, and within a year, he was gone.

The family mourned their loss; they were both so deeply loved. Michael was the hardest hit, his mother was his strength thru his growing years, and his father was much more than a parent; he was his friend.

As the years fled by, Michael and Penny moved to the ranch. He would retire in another five years, but they had a car, and he could travel back and forth to town. Just after they moved, Ron came out one evening. "Papa, mama, I have prayed about it, and have decided to move to California. They have a good collage in Los Angeles, where I can learn more about writing, and the world we live in. Please pray for me papa, I need the Lord's guidance. I'm sure I will have to work some to help get me through school, but I have been saving as much as I could, so I could attend college. I will miss you both, but we have the telephone now, so I can probably call once in awhile, but I will always write." His father prayed for his son, and then they talked for a long time.

After Ron's arrival in California, he began writing prolifically about the area, and culture to his parents. "It's so different from Silver City", he wrote. "Los Angeles is a fairly large city, with many diverse cultures; I have learned much about the state." He sent volumes of words about its history, going back to when the first Spaniards came from Spain; they were the first to arrive in the area.

"Many priests came also, and built missions up and down the coast, using the local Indians to build them. They built magnificent buildings out of adobe where they all worshipped. Many Spanish men came to the area, and were given grants for land. As the area was finally won over by the many people coming west, the area grew fast."

"Gold was found many years ago; north of here, and in time, the people from Spain lost much of their land."

"The Pacific Ocean is fascinating to watch, the salt air is both invigorating, and compelling. Once you see it, you want to sit, or walk along the beach, or swim in its waters. Many fish are caught and sold for food."

"To the east are very high mountains, and they continue pretty much from one end of the state to the other, with extremely hot deserts to the east of them. It's a fascinating state, and I have much yet to learn."

"The temperatures run from one hundred or more degrees in the deserts, to around the seventies along the coast in the summer. Here, the rains are mostly in the winter time, unlike there in Silver City."

"I wish you were here to see and experience it all, but because you are not able to, I will write often; telling you all that I see and learn."

"I love you, and miss you both, and the family. Give them all my love, as well as feel my hugs for you both.

Your son, Ron."

Michael and Penny loved living out in the country. Both had lost their parents one by one, which would always leave empty places in their lives. Their later years, after Michael retired, were contented ones, for their faith was strong, giving them a great peace and a real joy as they grew older.

They saw there children and grandchildren nearly every Sunday after church, either at the ranch, or their families homes. Michael had a vegetable garden to tend, as when he was young. There were several apple trees, a couple of peach trees, and one pear tree, much of the orchard that Mac had planted so many years ago, was gone.

The two would sit on the porch in the evenings, if the weather allowed, and they would watch the sunsets. The quail were still in the area, and once in a while a roadrunner or rabbit could be seen.

Houses were encroaching upon there half of the ranch. Penny remembered the first day her husband had stood in front of the members of the church, he was tall then. A kind, gentle and understanding man; with a touch of humor, he'd gained from his mother.

His wife always loved him, and his special ways. Michael's memories often went back to his beautiful mother, who taught him the ways of God's love, and the kind and gentle father, who loved, and cared for his mother until her death. He was the man who raised his apples, pears, and peaches for the people living in Silver City; a place where many kinds of love existed through the years, in these southwestern mountains of New Mexico.

CPSIA information can be obtained at www.ICGtesting.com
Printed in the USA
LVOW06s1525310314

379675LV00001B/126/P